The Art of Second Ch

By Georgina Heffernan

Chapter One: A Marvellous Mistake

Maggie's eyes fluttered open, and they were met with the gentle embrace of morning light, casting a soft, welcoming glow upon her room. In the distance, a neighbouring apartment's radio hummed, its melodies wrapping around her like a comforting shawl. As she extended her arms above her head, the fatigue from her journey the previous night melted away. At last, she had arrived in Rethymno, a vibrant city nestled on the island of Crete, Greece. Excitement pulsed through her, and she wriggled her toes in anticipation, thankful for the serendipitous turn of events that had brought her here.

Her memories of the night's journey were a blurry haze. The winding roads leading to the "Aegean Breeze" apartment complex were cloaked in darkness, and her conversation with the cab driver was a distant echo. The gentle whirr of the air conditioning had filled her ears, accompanied by the distant sounds of music and laughter emanating from nearby clubs, all while the city's luminous lights streaked by her window. But now, bathed in the shimmering daylight, she could fully appreciate the beauty of her new surroundings.

Maggie's gaze swept over her ground-floor apartment, and she let out a deep, contented sigh. Pristine whitewashed walls exuded tranquillity, magnified by the azure blue shutters that basked in the sun's warmth. With every step, the polished marble floor offered a refreshing, revitalising sensation. Eager to explore the awaiting vistas, she made her way to the living room.

Stepping onto the balcony, she was greeted by an awe-inspiring sight. The expansive Aegean Sea stretched before her, its crystal-clear waters shimmering under the radiant sunlight. For a moment, she shielded her eyes, then opened them again to behold a mesmerising tapestry of blues and greens that merged effortlessly into the horizon. A wide smile graced her lips as she took in the salty air, filling her lungs with invigorating freshness. This was exactly where she needed to be.

Below, she watches people strolling along the beach, each person seemingly immersed in their own world. Some leisurely walked their dogs, others jogged or cycled, while a few contentedly soaked up the sun.

To her right, an upmarket hotel dominated the landscape, its sleek architecture and glass walls reflecting the brilliant sun. Its pristine wooden decking was adorned with well-heeled holiday-makers sipping on fresh orange juice, attended to by waitstaff in crisp navy and white uniforms, who catered to their every desire. The guests luxuriated under elegant black and cream awnings, on canvas daybeds swathed in chiffon curtains that danced to the rhythm of the breeze.

Turning her gaze to the left, a vibrant tableau unfolded. The public side of the beach was a lively mix of multicoloured sun umbrellas, neon inflatable unicorns, and pink flamingos, creating a stark contrast to the hotel's exclusive and sophisticated atmosphere. A diverse array of people, of all shapes and sizes, dotted the sand. Some lounged under the warm sun, while others frolicked in the playful waves. Next to a group of bronzed and toned Germans, a tattooed and sun-kissed couple dozed on a sunbed.

Overhead, the sound of jet skis revving their engines filled the air, leaving trails of white foam, while parasailers floated like vivid kites against the boundless blue sky. It was a symphony of colour and activity, and Maggie's heart swelled with exhilaration and anticipation. She revelled in her new surroundings, absorbing the sights and sounds of this idyllic resort.

Her eagerness to explore every corner of her quaint apartment led her swiftly indoors. She swung open the white Formica cupboard, her curiosity instantly ignited by its contents. Her eyes widened with excitement upon discovering the holy trinity of sachets: coffee, sugar, and powdered milk.

As a self-proclaimed caffeine aficionado, she knew precisely what needed to be done. Without delay, she reached for the petite plastic kettle stationed beside the sink, its vintage mustard and brown hues suggesting it had graced this very spot since 1975. With unwavering determination, she filled it with tap water and flicked the switch to "on."

The scent of the budget-friendly chicory coffee enveloped her senses, and as she took a sip, a comforting warmth flowed through her veins. Though it wasn't her usual brew, it did the job, and she found contentment in its simplicity.

After placing her cup on the table, she settled into one of the white plastic chairs on her balcony, savouring the breathtaking vista that lay before her. Her heart swelled with joy as she contemplated the next three months on this idyllic island, a rare gift bestowed upon her by Artists Connect. It all seemed almost too good to be true, a testament to the wonders of remote work enabling her to immerse herself in a new country, culture, and community.

Excitement coursed through her thoughts as she envisioned the artists and creatives she would soon collaborate with. She hoped to soak in knowledge and inspiration from their unique perspectives and experiences. This job posting abroad marked a significant milestone for her, igniting a sense of purpose that surged through her veins. She couldn't help but chuckle heartily as she ruminated on the series of serendipitous events that had brought her to this point. A simple mistake on the Artists Connect grant application, one that suggested the organisation would be physically present in Greece to assist artists, had transformed into a golden opportunity, courtesy of her boss, William.

William was a charismatic character, to put it mildly. His ruddy complexion and unruly sandy hair seemed to bear the marks of a lifetime spent chasing the sun, and his infectious energy radiated from the moment he entered a room. Despite his occasionally eccentric behaviour, there was a magnetic quality to William that had a soothing effect on those in his presence. And soothe he did when he deftly spun that mistake into a brilliant and daring initiative. Through a combination of charm, persuasion, and audacious imagination, he had convinced everyone that it was all part of a hands-on, boots-on-the-ground approach to the project. The result? Maggie's thrilling three-month work contract.

Everything seemed to fall perfectly into place for her. Her lease had just expired on her apartment in Dublin, her gym membership had lapsed, and her night-time photography class had wrapped up. Even her best friend Alison had moved to London, leaving her with a blank slate for new possibilities. She saw this as an opportunity to immerse herself in a new culture, to expand her horizons and to do something meaningful. As she sat on her balcony, sipping her subpar coffee and staring out at the turquoise sea, she couldn't help but feel grateful for the unexpected turn her life had taken.

For years, Maggie had been stuck in a never-ending cycle of monotony, working at Artists Connect with endless projects that lacked excitement or adventure. But that was all about to change. The promise of exploration and discovery filled the air, and she felt a thrilling sense of anticipation that she hadn't experienced in years. This was her chance to break free from her routine and immerse herself in the beauty and mysteries of a foreign land.

As she searched through the welcome pack on her kitchen table, her stomach growled with hunger. But when she found a buttery croissant nestled inside the plastic wrapper, she eagerly tore it open. The flaky layers melted in her mouth, creating a symphony of textures and flavours that transported her to a Parisian café. It was a moment of pure bliss, a fleeting taste of France in the heart of Greece.

Her mind drifted from the beauty of the turquoise sea to thoughts of her charming and enigmatic boyfriend, Alex. He had a wild mop of curly hair and a bright smile that could light up a room. Maggie had first seen him play with his band, Ramshackle, at a small pub in Dublin, and he had captured her heart with his raw talent, magnetic personality and beautiful heartfelt songs.

Their relationship had been a whirlwind of adventure and passion, but it had also been marked by uncertainty. Alex was a free spirit who had been hurt deeply in the past, leaving him wary of taking the next step in their relationship. Despite this, she knew that Alex was the one she wanted to share all of her adventures with, including this one in Greece.

She longed for him to join her on this journey, to experience the beauty and magic of this ancient land together.

As she took another bite of her croissant, her mind drifted to the future she longed for with Alex. She dreamed of a life filled with love and adventure, a family, a house, and a dog. Maggie knew there were obstacles to overcome, but she was determined to make it work. She was patient, understanding, and supportive, even when frustration set in. But for now, she focused on the present, the excitement of what lay ahead, and the hope that Alex would soon be by her side.

In a week or two, he would join her in Greece, and she felt hopeful about finally moving their relationship to the next level. After five years together, she knew that marriage was the next step. Maggie envisioned exploring the winding streets of Athens, dancing in the moonlight on the beaches of Mykonos, and marvelling at the ancient wonders of Crete. She couldn't wait to share all of this with Alex, to create memories that would last a lifetime and possibly prompt a proposal.

Her anticipation was palpable as she thought about the breathtaking beauty of Crete, the warm embrace of the sun, and the unhurried pace of life. She hoped that the magic of the island would help him realise how much they were meant to be together. But even as she smiled at the thought of their reunion, she tried not to get her hopes up. Alex's fear of commitment was real, and she had learned to accept it as a part of him. Despite his flaws, she loved him deeply for his passion, creativity, and unwavering sense of self.

As the morning sun spilled over her balcony, she sipped her coffee, lost in thought. The potential turning point in their relationship was just around the corner, and she couldn't help but feel nervous. What if things didn't go as planned? What if Alex couldn't commit, even in such a beautiful place? These thoughts plagued her mind, but she tried to stay positive. They had been together for five years, and their love had endured many challenges.

Just then, there was a faint knocking at the door. Maggie felt apprehension, wondering who could be calling on her so early in the morning. She cautiously made her way towards the door, opened it slowly, and found a man standing on the other side. He was dressed in a plain white shirt and khaki shorts, with a warm, inviting smile on his face. She couldn't help but notice his rugged, weathered features, which spoke of a life spent outdoors. His eyes twinkled with a friendly gleam as he greeted her in Greek, but when she apologised for not speaking the language, he switched to English.

"Good morning," he said cheerfully. "My name is Panagiotis. I work at the hotel. I just wanted to make sure you settled in okay." Maggie felt a wave of relief wash over her as she realised he was a hotel employee. She introduced herself and thanked him for his concern . As they talked, she couldn't help but notice the genuine warmth and authenticity that radiated from him. He was a man who had lived a simple, honest life, with a deep connection to the land and the sea.

He flashed a kind smile at her . "If you need any help, just let me know," he said in a relaxed tone. "Remember that you can use all the amenities and services of The Aegean Breeze. We offer our guests everything they need, from the restaurant, gym, and spa to the beach, which is just a few steps away." She felt drawn to his friendly and open manner.

"Thanks, Panagiotis," she said, feeling genuinely grateful. "Your help means a lot. And I might take you up on that tour offer." His eyes crinkled with warmth as he smiled at her. "Anytime, my dear. Just ask for me at reception if you need anything. The official opening of the hotel for the tourist season is only a week away."

Maggie shut the door behind her with a contented nod, relieved to know that she had someone to turn to if needed. As she strolled towards the balcony, she inhaled a deep breath of the salty air and savoured the stunning view that greeted her. The hotel's warm and welcoming terracotta facade appeared more magnificent in the bright morning sun, perched on the edge of the sea. A grand entrance adorned with two stunning fountains on either side greeted her, surrounded by lush greenery and vibrant flowers that added a burst of colour to the already breathtaking scenery. Her gaze drifted towards the heart of the hotel, where the crystal-clear water of the central swimming pool awaited her.

Already being prepared for the season, comfortable loungers and palm trees were arranged to provide a shady spot to escape from the hot Greek sun. The sunlight reflected off its surface, causing it to shimmer and sparkle, an enchanting sight to behold. With the hotel's opening just around the corner, the staff were working tirelessly to ensure that everything was perfect, polishing and cleaning at a furious pace . She couldn't wait to indulge in the serene atmosphere by the pool, engrossed in a good book while sipping on a cold drink, as the gentle breeze caressed her skin. It was evident that the Aegean Breeze hotel was committed to making this season one to remember.

As she entered her modest, traditional Greek-style apartment, she was struck by its contrast to the hotel's opulence. Reserved for hotel workers and university teachers, the whitewashed walls were peeling and in need of a facelift, but exuded a sense of simplicity and authenticity typical of Greek architecture. The vibrant bougainvillaea vines snaking up the walls breathed life into the facade, while the geraniums in baskets and pots on windowsills added a touch of charm, making it feel like home. It was clear that William, her boss, secured the apartment at a bargain price.

As Maggie retraced her steps toward her bedroom, a surge of anticipation coursed through her veins, electrifying her senses with an irresistible excitement. The very thought of unzipping her suitcase and unveiling its hidden contents ignited a palpable eagerness within her. With a delicate balance of care and whimsy, she embarked on the task at hand, each item of clothing drawn from the depths of her bag with a touch of familiarity and a hint of playful indulgence.

An eclectic assortment spilled forth, revealing glimpses of Maggie's distinctive style—a testament to her innate ability to weave together vintage treasures and thrift store finds into a tapestry of self-expression. Despite the modest salary she earned at Artists Connect, her unwavering eye for fashion ensured that she always radiated an air of effortless sophistication and individuality. Amidst the carefully curated selection of garments, a worn pack of tarot cards emerged as a cherished relic, symbolising Maggie's fascination with the mystical and the enigmatic. These cards, bearing the marks of countless shufflings and whispered fortunes, echoed her inquisitive nature and occasional flirtation with the unknown.

Yet, it was the weathered framed photograph of George Michael that commanded the spotlight, evoking a wave of nostalgia from her teenage years when she idolised the pop icon with an unwavering devotion. Oblivious to his true identity as a gay icon, Maggie had treasured this memento throughout the years, unaware of the profound impact he would have on the LGBTQ+ community. Residing atop her bedside locker, the photograph exuded a talismanic energy, its enduring presence instilling a sense of comfort and summoning a smile with the infectious warmth of George's gorgeous smile. She knew it seemed silly, but once she had George looking over she felt that everything in Crete would work out just fine.

With a discerning eye, Maggie meticulously sorted her clothes, creating neat piles upon her bed. The fusion of patterns and textures told tales of her vibrant personality and eclectic tastes. Beautiful Asian prints adorned dresses, depicting ethereal birds and delicate roses, while blouses boasted a wild leopard print that exuded an untamed allure. Skirts danced separately from pants, each with its own narrative to unravel through fabric and form. And in the realm of footwear, an assembly of shoes stood as silent testaments to Maggie's versatile spirit—funky sneakers mingling with elegant heels—a diverse array reflecting her insatiable appetite for adventure and self-expression.

Amidst the fashion commotion, another gem emerged—a vintage necklace featuring two lovebirds from her boyfriend, Alex. With the lovebirds perched gracefully together, it felt like a tangible embodiment of Alex's devotion, a talisman to carry with her wherever she roamed. Completing her collection, oversized sun hats and large sunglasses added both practicality and a touch of glamorous charm. These accessories, poised to shield her from the Mediterranean sun while exuding an aura of effortless elegance, were the final strokes on the canvas of her ensemble.

Maggie took her time with each item, carefully placing them in the dresser or hanging them in the closet, making sure everything was in its proper place. She wanted to look her best for her first day at the resort, so she was very particular about how she arranged her clothes. She then pulled on a navy polka dot dress, smoothing out any wrinkles and admiring how the polka dots accentuated her slim legs while minimizing her stomach. With a sense of satisfaction, she moved on to her hair and makeup, applying each product with precision and care. She styled her long, dark locks in beachy waves and finished off her look with a straw boater-style hat, dark sunglasses, and a pair of wedge heels. Fully prepared, she felt like a true movie star, ready to embark on her adventure at the resort.

As she strode out into the street, the warm sun on her face, she was immediately struck by the bustling activity around her. She let out a soft sigh - it felt like utter bliss, like she had landed in heaven. The Aegean Breeze, once a sleepy resort, was now a hive of activity as it emerged from two years of COVID restrictions and a decimated tourist economy that had forced many businesses to close. Even though it was late March and the official opening was a week away, the hotel was in the final stages of preparation for the upcoming tourist season. A team of about eight men worked hard to ensure that the hotel looked as up-to-date and fresh as possible. She saw the walls being painted shades of cream and terracotta, colorful flowers being planted, and a large statue of a peaceful-looking Buddha being carried to the entrance by three builders. Meanwhile, new glass windows hovered precariously overhead on a crane.

Despite the feeling of weariness and desperation among the business owners, there was also a palpable feeling of optimism and earnestness in the air. George, the hotel owner, greeted Maggie with a warm hello. He wore a simple white shirt and blue jeans that were stained with paint and dirt from the day's work, and his face was lined with deep wrinkles that spoke of a lifetime of hard work and experience. His eyes shone with a sense of pride and determination despite the challenges they had all faced in the past two years.

As she continued down the street, the sound of construction filled the air, punctuated by the occasional shout or clang of metal against metal. Workers scurried about, painting, hammering, and sawing. A cloud of dust rose from the ground, mingling with the salty sea breeze that blew in from the nearby beach. Through the open windows, she caught glimpses of the hotel's newly renovated rooms and facilities. The vibrant colors and modern décor looked like they belonged in a glossy travel magazine. She couldn't wait to see the finished product when the hotel officially opened in just one week. As she looked around, she couldn't help but feel a sense of hope and renewal that buoyed her spirit. The Aegean Breeze was being reborn, an ode to the resilience of the human spirit and a testament to the power of community. And Maggie, just a small part of it all, was grateful to witness it.

Turning the corner, her eyes were immediately drawn to the bright and bustling storefront of Olympos Market. The sign above the entrance was adorned with vibrant colors and a bold, cursive font that seemed to dance in the sun. As she approached the door, a group of skinny cats caught her attention. They huddled together, their eyes fixed on her, as if pleading for a scrap of food. Once inside, she was transported into a world of sensory overload.

The store was alive with the sounds of Greek music and the chatter of tourists browsing through the aisles. Giant inflatables of all shapes and sizes hung from the ceiling, swaying gently in the breeze. She couldn't help but feel like a child in a candy store as she took in the neon bikinis and beach gear that lined the shelves. The air was filled with the aroma of coconut-scented sunscreen, and Maggie couldn't resist grabbing an essential bag of coffee as she made her way deeper into the store. She was drawn to the intricate pieces of Greek pottery that were on display, imagining how they would look on her mantle back home.

As she continued to explore, her eyes scanned the shelves for necessities such as bread, spotting it next to the long-life milk and hard liquor. And it was here that she realized the one glaring omission from the store's wares - fresh fruit and vegetables. Instead, every type of alcohol imaginable was on offer, from whiskey to tequila, and vodka to gin. It was as if the store had been curated specifically to cater to the indulgences of the holidaymakers that frequented the resort. As she left the minimart, she couldn't help but feel a sense of irony. The store, a mecca for those seeking pleasure and relaxation, was devoid of any real nutrition. And yet, she couldn't deny the allure of its vibrant colors and bustling atmosphere - a true testament to the power of indulgence.

As she made her way down the narrow pathway, she couldn't help but notice the buzz of activity emanating from the hotel construction site nearby. It was as if a colony of worker bees had descended upon the area, each one tirelessly working to build the towering structure at breakneck speed. She turned a corner, and suddenly found herself on the main road leading from the Aegean Breeze hotel to the centre of Rethymnon. The four-mile stretch was bursting with energy and possibility, and she was eager to explore everything the town had to offer.

The warm, balmy breeze was a welcome respite from the rain-soaked climate of Ireland, and she savoured the opportunity to relax and soak in the vibrant atmosphere of her new surroundings. On one side of the road, an array of traditional Greek restaurants and seafood joints jostled for attention, each one featuring laminated menus and faded photographs of mouth-watering delicacies Moussaka, Tzatziki:, Greek Salad and a Long dead Octopus . Bars and eateries displayed a range of themes, from the classic blue and white Grecian style with pretty blue shutters and baskets of flowers to modern minimalism with glass, marble, and sculptural-looking plants.

On the other side of the road, the beach was divided into sections, each corresponding to the bar or restaurant on the opposite side. The sections were colour-coded like a football team, with some areas luxurious enough to make even the most jaded traveller swoon. Four-poster day beds, and giant white bean bags were arranged among beautiful plants, with attentive waiters at the ready. In other sections, however, plastic and outdated sun loungers sat under faded and torn sun umbrellas, a stark reminder that not every corner of paradise is created equal. As Maggie walked along the beach, she couldn't help but feel as though she was a player in a grand game, each section representing a different strategy in the quest for ultimate relaxation and indulgence.

She felt a sense of liberation as she began her leisurely walk down the picturesque coast road towards the centre of Rethymno that Saturday. The salty sea breeze caressed her face, reminding her of the vastness of the ocean and the endless possibilities that lay ahead. The sun blazed down on her skin, enveloping her in its warm embrace, as she meandered past vibrant souvenir shops that beckoned her with colourful trinkets and treasures. She couldn't resist the temptation of picking up some famous Greek soap, the scent of which transported her to a world of exotic spices and herbs. She also grabbed a pair of fake designer sunglasses, admiring her reflection in the mirrored lenses. The lemon ice cream she bought from a corner shop was a welcome treat, its sharp tang cutting through the sweltering summer heat and offering a refreshing respite.

She took her time, stopping at any shop that caught her fancy, relishing the freedom of exploring at her own pace. As she crossed the road and walked down to the beach, the refreshing sea water lapped at her bare feet, beckoning her towards its cool embrace. She watched holidaymakers revel in the ocean and engage in water sports, the sound of their laughter and joy filling her heart with a sense of happiness.

The adverts for sunset cruises on one side of the beach appealed to her sense of romance, while the small fishing port on the other side, where local fishermen came in with their daily catch, sold it to the locals, capturing her imagination with its authenticity. She knew Alex would love this place, and she couldn't help but daydream about his arrival. Would he propose on the beach, or whisk her away to Santorini and ask for her hand as the sun set? The idea filled her with a sense of certainty, like a powerful metaphor that transported her into a world of endless possibilities. As she confidently proclaimed to her sister Catherine on the phone earlier that week, "A woman knows."

Finally, she arrived at the heart of Rethymno, a city steeped in cultural and historical significance. Its beautiful beaches, archaeological sites, Byzantine churches, quaint villages, and cosmopolitan resorts were a testament to its rich and diverse history. Maggie was thrilled to be experiencing it all for herself, her camera at the ready to capture the beauty of the old town.

She discovered a labyrinth of cobbled alleyways and narrow streets, dappled with shade from overhanging vines and bougainvillaea, lined with charming cafes, shops selling local crafts, and restaurants serving up the best Cretan food and Greek dishes. The old buildings from Venetian times, with their doorways and arches set in mellow stone walls leading to enticing courtyards, were a reminder of the city's rich cultural heritage. The town was filled with historical sites, 16th-century buildings, churches, and olive trees lining the pretty plazas. It was like stepping back in time, as though the buildings themselves were powerful metaphors, transporting her to another era.

She was in awe of the contrast of old and new in Rethymno, a city that exuded a blend of tradition and modernity. As she explored further, she discovered the stylish side of town with contemporary restaurants, cafes, bars, and some of the best hotels - that was Alex's style, and generally the kind of thing she avoided. But she could appreciate the beauty of the newly developed part of the city. As she walked through the streets, she could hear the distant sound of traditional Cretan music and the smell of freshly cooked seafood wafted through the air.

She stopped at a small taverna and ordered a plate of grilled octopus, tzatziki, and a glass of local wine. The flavours exploded in her mouth, and she closed her eyes, savouring every bite. After finishing her meal, she continued her exploration of Rethymno. She stumbled upon a street artist who was painting a beautiful mural of a mermaid on the side of a building. Maggie watched in awe as the artist expertly applied layer upon layer of paint to the wall, creating a stunning work of art. She realised that the mural was more than just a beautiful painting; it was a reflection of the city's deep connection to the sea and the mythology that surrounds it.

As the sun began to set, she made her way back to the beach to catch a glimpse of the famous Rethymno sunset. The sky was a brilliant shade of orange and pink, and the sun appeared to be melting into the sea. She sat on the sand and watched as couples strolled by hand in hand, families played in the water, and the occasional fisherman cast his line into the sea.

Maggie couldn't help but feel a deep sense of peace and contentment as she sat there, surrounded by the beauty of Rethymno. She knew that this trip would be one that she would never forget. The city had captivated her with its blend of history, culture, and natural beauty. As she made her way back to her humble apartment, she couldn't help but feel grateful for the opportunity to experience such a special place and soon, very soon, she would not be experiencing it alone.

As the next morning arrived, a calm Sunday unfolded, free from the usual cacophony of construction work. Soft sunlight seeped through the curtains, gently illuminating the room with a warm glow. Sheslowly opened her eyes, adjusting to the morning light, and directed her gaze straight ahead. She observed the play of shadows created by the leaves, as they danced and mingled with the gentle rays of light, casting a subtle pattern on the whitewashed wall. A momentary sense of tranquillity washed over her, and a small, contented smile curved her lips as she stretched her body, relishing the pleasant feeling of being fully rested and at peace.

Without a second thought, she reached for her kimono, a lovely silk robe in shades of cream and lemon with subtle patterns of orange and peach flowers and green leaves. As she slipped it on, she appreciated the feel of the smooth, cool fabric against her skin. Throwing on an old pair of plastic blue flip flops, she made her way to the kitchen, eager to make her morning coffee, a ritual she took very seriously. She had the proper ground coffee she had bought at the Olympus mini mart the day before, and she savoured the aroma of the fresh brew as it filled the silent apartment. She poured herself a cup of coffee and took a sip, feeling content and grateful for the simple pleasures in life.

With her brew in hand, she grabbed a notebook and pen and headed to her balcony. She opened the glass doors, stepping outside to be greeted by the golden beach stretching out endlessly before her. The turquoise water sparkled in the sunlight, while the palm trees swayed gently in the breeze. Her gaze lingered on a flock of seagulls, gliding gracefully in the sky, their white feathers a striking contrast against the blue expanse.

As she watched the seagulls glide through the sky, she couldn't help but think of Alex and his bohemian view of life. He always used to say that life was like a bird in flight, moving and changing direction with each flap of its wings. The seagulls in front of her were a perfect representation of this idea, gracefully riding the wind currents and adapting to their surroundings. She felt a pang of sadness as she thought of Alex. She missed him terribly and wished he could be there with her to witness the beauty of the moment. She made a mental note to call him , to share with him the beauty she was experiencing and to remind him of his own wise words.

Maggie was fully engrossed in her thoughts when she heard a faint meowing sound, as if someone was pleading for help. She looked down from her notebook and saw a small, scrawny kitten with matted fur staring up at her with big, pleading eyes. Her heart broke at the sight of the helpless creature, and she couldn't bear to ignore its cries.Without a moment's hesitation,she stood up and went to the kitchen to get a saucer of milk. She opened the fridge and found a carton of milk, pouring a small amount into the saucer. She carefully carried the saucer back to the balcony and set it down on the cream tiles, hoping the kitten would drink the milk.As soon as the kitten saw the saucer of milk, it eagerly ran over and began to lap at it with its tiny pink tongue.

She smiled as she watched the little creature drink, happy to have helped it in some way. She reached down and stroked its soft fur, feeling a sense of warmth spread through her body.As the kitten finished drinking, it climbed up onto her feet and rubbed its head against her leg. Maggie couldn't help but laugh at the adorable display of affection. She had made her first friend on the island of Crete. As the cat scampered away, satisfied and happy, she couldn't wait to see it again and make sure it was well taken care of.

A few moments later she opened her laptop and began scrolling through Pinterest. She was captivated by the breathtaking wedding dresses that adorned the screen, the intricate lace and delicate embroidery that seemed to come to life before her eyes. As she gazed upon the bohemian beach wedding dresses, she was transported to a world of flowing, ethereal beauty.

In her mind's eye, she could envision herself walking down the sandy aisle, the gentle breeze blowing her hair as the sun set in the distance. The brides in the photos looked effortless and carefree, with glowing skin and tousled hair, exuding a sense of joy and happiness that seemed unattainable to her. She couldn't help but notice that all the brides seemed to be tiny, with slim waists and toned arms. A pang of realisation hit her that if she was ever going to fit into one of those dresses, she needed to shed the extra weight she had gained from comfort eating while her significant other was on tour. And what better time and place than now?

With newfound determination, she spent an hour scouring the internet for the perfect fitness plan. She wanted a program that would help her achieve her goals without sacrificing her love of good food and wine - if such a plan even existed.. Finally, she stumbled upon Go-fit, an online platform that allowed her to book virtual training sessions with certified fitness and diet coaches. And there she found Kateryna, a Ukrainian fitness instructor who specialised in helping women achieve their fitness goals in a safe and sustainable way.

Maggie was immediately drawn to Kateryna's warm and encouraging demeanour, as well as her unwavering commitment to making fitness accessible to everyone, regardless of their experience level. With a sense of excitement and hope, Maggie booked 10 sessions with Kateryna as her fitness and diet coach, ready to take the first step towards her new life. Satisfied with her purchase, she then logged onto her email and opened a message from William. He had selected four talented artists for her to work with during her time in Crete, and each one had a unique style and perspective. As she read through the descriptions of each, Maggie couldn't help but smile at the range of personalities she would be working with.

Thomas barely met the criteria for the project, but with few applicants, they had taken a chance on him. Atticus, the eccentric painter who used only recycled materials in his works, a Syrian refugee called Nader who used his camera to tell his and other refugees stories, Eleni, a performance artist who was known for her boundary-pushing and often controversial pieces.Her heart swelled with a mix of emotions - excitement, curiosity, and a touch of apprehension. Each artist was a unique and powerful force, and she longed to delve into their world and understand their craft.

As a program manager at Artists Connect, her job in Crete working with the Minoan Art Alliance was crucial in providing assistance to disadvantaged artists. She pored over countless applications and carefully distributed grants to fund extraordinary artistic projects. Her passion for creating opportunities for overlooked artists never faltered, and she took great pride in her role.Closing her laptop, she couldn't help but feel both exhilarated and anxious. Working with this diverse and eclectic group of artists would be a challenging journey, but she was up for it. She yearned for this opportunity to collaborate and learn from them, knowing that it would not only benefit them but also broaden her own personal and professional horizons.

From a young age, she had been completely enthralled by the world of art, captivated by its originality, innovative style, and cultural significance. The dream to become an artist had been burning inside her since childhood, and she chased it with an unwavering determination. Her love for art was evident from a young age, as she would spend countless hours lost in her own world, drawing and painting on every surface she could find.

One particular incident stood out in her memory, where she had covered the walls of her room with a mural of vibrant colours and shapes. Though her mother had been furious at the time, scolding her for making a mess and ruining the walls, she couldn't help but notice the beauty of her creation. The colours blended together in a way that was both chaotic and beautiful, and the shapes seemed to dance across the wall. It was a sign of the incredible talent that lay within her, and Maggie knew that she had to nurture it further.

She was accepted into the prestigious Carlisle College of Art in Dublin, where she spent four years honing her craft. But the end of year three proved to be a crushing disappointment when she failed half of her classes. Her dream of painting huge, colourful canvases that made bold statements about life, the world, and the human condition had been shattered. She had never seen it coming, and the harsh reality that she just wasn't good enough hit her hard. Her role now was to always be the supporting cast member, cheering from the sidelines and watching as others achieved their dreams. It was a bitter pill to swallow, and even years later, she was still haunted by the what-ifs and the possibilities of what could have been.

Maggie's world crumbled the day she failed out of art college. The shattered fragments of her dream lay before her like broken glass, reflecting only despair and confusion. For five long years, she battled a suffocating depression that left her adrift, uncertain of where her life was headed. Her once-bright aspirations were now just distant memories, and the daily struggle of existence seemed to mock her, daring her to find a purpose in life. Yet through the darkness, she clung to one unwavering belief: art had the power to transform lives. Though her own artistic journey had been cut short, she was determined to promote and empower other artists, to champion their work and help them find success. She threw herself into her work at Artists Connect, a not-for-profit that would give other artists the recognition they deserved, and watched as it slowly gained traction.

Still, the disappointment of her own professional failure lingered, a constant reminder of what could have been. Her former classmates went on to success and fame, while she laboured through one dead-end job after another, each one a dreary performance devoid of passion or purpose. Yet even as she lost herself in these jobs, she never lost sight of her ultimate goal: to create something meaningful, something that would make a difference. And so she persevered, building Artists Connect into a thriving community of artists and enthusiasts. She poured her heart and soul into the project, and it breathed new life into her, rekindling a sense of purpose and direction. For Maggie, promoting the work of other artists became a new source of fulfilment and meaning, a way to find her place in the world and make a difference.

Now, at 36, she had found a sense of peace with her life, yet the lingering regret of what might have been still haunted her. The spectre of her own failed dreams loomed in the shadows of her mind, a constant reminder of what could have been. But even in the midst of that regret, she knew she had found something worth fighting for. And as she looked back on her journey, she knew that every step had led her to this place, this moment, this purpose.

Chapter 2: Daydreams and Fantasies

Maggie spotted her phone lying on the table, she reached out without hesitation, her fingers deftly dialling the all-too-familiar number. Her heart raced with anticipation as the phone rang. She couldn't wait to hear Alex's voice and tell him about the wonders of Rethymno. However, as the ringing persisted, her excitement turned to anxiety. Why wasn't he answering? Had something happened? Finally, Alex's voice broke through the silence. "Hey, you," he said, his voice groggy with sleep. Maggie felt her heart swell at the sound of his voice. "Hey, yourself," she replied, feeling a rush of warmth flood her chest. "How was the tour?"

Alex's tone shifted, laced with excitement. "It was incredible," he said. "We played to sold-out crowds every night. I've never felt so alive." Maggie could almost see the glimmer in his eyes, the spark of passion that fuelled his music. She felt a pang of envy, wishing she could be there by his side, sharing in his success. But she didn't want to bring down the mood. "I'm so proud of you," she said, her voice sincere.

There was a pause, and then Alex spoke again, his tone softening. "How's Crete treating you?" he asked. She hesitated, unsure how much to reveal. But she knew she had to be honest with him. "I miss you," she confessed. "It's exciting but it's been tough without you here." There was a beat of silence before Alex responded. "I miss you too," he said, his voice heavy with emotion. Her heart ached at the sound of his voice, and then he dropped the bombshell. "I hate to say this, but I've been delayed. The band got invited to play at Counterflows, a festival in the UK. I can't pass up the opportunity."

Maggie's breath caught in her throat. "For how long?" she asked, fearing the worst. "Three weeks," Alex replied, the regret in his voice palpable. "I know it's a long time, but it's crucial for the band's exposure." Maggie felt tears prick her eyes, the thought of three weeks without Alex almost unbearable. "I understand," she said, trying to steady her voice. "But I'll miss you so much." "I'll miss you too," Alex replied. "But I promise I'll make it up to you. I'll bring you something special from the UK." She managed a smile, grateful for his attempt to lift her spirits. "I'll hold you to that," she said. "Just promise me that you'll get someone to water the plants." "I will," Alex assured her. "I love you, Maggie." "I love you too," she replied, the words a bittersweet reminder of what she'd be missing.

As she hung up the phone, she felt a pang of emptiness gnaw at her. Three weeks without Alex felt like an eternity. But she wouldn't let it break her. She'd been through long-distance before and she'd survive this too. She walked back to her apartment, lost in thought. She had a sudden urge to be outside, to feel the sun on her skin and the wind in her hair. She changed quickly into a pair of shorts and a t-shirt and grabbed her keys, determined to shake off her gloomy mood and to explore more of Crete.As she walked along the beach, she let the salty breeze wash over her. She felt a sense of clarity wash over her as she realised that she couldn't just sit around waiting for Alex. She needed to make the most of her time in Crete, to explore and discover new things. Maggie smiled to herself as she realised that this was just the beginning of her adventure in Crete. Who knew what other surprises were waiting in store.

She strolled into the grand lobby of the Aegean Breeze, the crisp air conditioning sending shivers down her spine. The scent of fresh lilies wafted through the air, and she paused to take it all in. As she scanned the array of brochures before her, she felt a thrill of excitement. Each one promised a different adventure, each one offered a chance to explore the beauty of the island. She browsed through the glossy brochures, her eyes scanning over the breathtaking photographs of Crete's rugged terrain and ancient ruins. She couldn't decide which tour to take, as each one seemed more captivating than the last.

The promise of a visit to an olive farm and hiking the island's tallest peak seemed thrilling, but it was the prospect of delving into Crete's cultural treasures that truly enticed her. As she was lost in thought, a voice interrupted her reverie. "I'd recommend the trip to the Palace of Knossos," a deep voice said, and she spun around to see Panagiotis standing before her. His passion for culture and history shone in his sparkling brown eyes, and Maggie felt an immediate connection with him.

As he spoke of the local museums and churches, she found herself nodding along in agreement. She could sense his enthusiasm for the island's cultural offerings, and it was contagious. As he pointed out the various cultural tours available, she knew she had found the one for her. "Tell me more about the Palace," she asked, intrigued. "I've always been fascinated by Greek art and I want to learn more about its roots and heritage."Panagiotis smiled warmly, his eyes locked on hers. "The Palace of Knossos is an archaeological wonder that dates back to the Minoan civilization," he explained. "Its ancient artefacts and frescoes tell the story of a lost world, and it's a place where you can truly immerse yourself in the beauty and history of Greece."

She felt a thrill of excitement at his words, and she knew that this tour would be more than just a cultural excursion. It would be a chance to explore the mysteries of the past and the present, to uncover the secrets of a lost world. And with Panagiotis by her side as a knowledgeable guide, she knew that this journey would be one to remember. She wandered back to her apartment with a handful of glossy brochures in her hand and a feeling of excitement. She was glad to have a few days off to settle in before she started her job and she was determined to make the most of them.

That night, alone in her bed, her sleep was restless, the sheets twisted around her limbs like shackles. Her dreams were filled with ancient ruins and lost artefacts, but they soon took a dark turn. In her nightmare, she was walking through the halls of the Palace of Knossos, but she was different. She was much larger than she remembered, her clothes straining against her body. She was eating a giant croissant and people around her were whispering and pointing at her, their eyes full of judgement. Maggie tried to ignore them, but she couldn't shake the feeling of shame that engulfed her.

As she made her way through the halls, the walls started to close in on her, suffocating her. She tried to run, but her legs felt heavy, as if she were wading through thick mud. She was trapped, unable to escape the torment of her own mind. She woke up in a cold sweat, gasping for air. Her heart was pounding so hard, she thought it would burst from her chest.She sat up in bed, her breath coming in ragged gasps. She wrapped her arms around herself, feeling exposed and vulnerable. The nightmare had awakened a deep-seated fear in her, one she thought she had buried long ago. The fear of being judged and rejected for her appearance.

She got out of bed and walked to the window, staring out at the moonlit sea. The cool night air caressed her face, calming her nerves. She took a deep breath and tried to shake off the nightmare, telling herself that it was just a dream. But the fear lingered, a dark cloud hovering over her.Maggie knew she couldn't let the nightmare control her thoughts. She needed to focus on the adventure that awaited her in the morning, the chance to explore the wonders of Crete. She lay back down, pulling the covers up to her chin, and tried to calm her racing heart. She closed her eyes, focusing on the sound of her own breathing, and eventually, the soothing rhythm of it lulled her back to sleep.

This time, her dreams were filled with bright colours and vibrant scenes, as she imagined herself exploring the Palace of Knossos. She saw herself walking through ancient halls and admiring the intricate frescoes and sculptures that adorned the walls. She imagined the smell of incense and the sound of distant music, as she delved deeper into the heart of the palace. She felt a sense of wonder and awe, as she marvelled at the sculptures and frescos that had survived the test of time.Finally, at about 3am she drifted off to sleep, the rhythmic sound of the waves lulling her into a peaceful slumber.

The next morning when she woke, she dragged herself to the kitchen, she was tired from the sleepless night before and her mouth was parched. She opened the fridge and reached out for the bottle of orange juice, her fingers wrapping around the cool plastic.With a quick twist of her wrist, the cap gave a satisfying pop, breaking the seal and allowing the contents to flow freely. She set the cap aside and poured the juice into a tall glass, the liquid splashing gently against the sides. As the juice settled, she noticed that it was a less vivid shade of orange than she was used to, almost as if the sun had been drained of its warmth before it could ripen the fruit.

Ignoring the thought, she brought the glass to her lips, letting the sweet and tangy flavour wash over her tongue. She closed her eyes, savouring the taste as memories of lazy summer afternoons flooded her mind. The cool, refreshing sensation was a welcome distraction from the heat of the morning and the weight of her thoughts. As she took another sip, she couldn't help but feel a pang of nostalgia. The sweet tangy orange juice was a reminder of simpler times, before the complexities of adulthood had taken hold. But for now, she was content to enjoy the simple pleasure of a cold glass of juice.

She couldn't help but feel a sense of anticipation growing within her. Today was the day she would explore the ancient wonders of Crete, a land steeped in history and mythology. She took a deep breath, feeling the rush of excitement course through her veins. She knew she couldn't let the nightmare of the previous night control her thoughts any longer. Today was a new day, filled with endless possibilities. As she made her way out of the apartment and into the bright sunlight, she couldn't help but notice the vibrant colours of the city that surrounded her. The buildings were painted in shades of pink and blue, with brightly coloured shutters and ornate balconies adorned with flowers. The streets were bustling with people, the air filled with the sounds of chatter and laughter.

She made her way to the bus stop, her heart beating faster with each passing moment. She was eager to explore the Palace of Knossos, to immerse herself in the rich history of the island. As the bus pulled up, she took a deep breath, feeling the rush of excitement coursing through her veins. She stepped on to the bus, her skin damp with sweat, the temperature sweltering. She wiped her forehead with the back of her hand and took a long swig of water from the bottle in her hand. As she looked around, she spotted Panagiotis, their guide, waiting for her along with a group of other tourists. ""Yassas Maggie," he greeted her with a smile."Are you ready for the adventure that awaits us?" she nodded eagerly, excitement bubbling up inside her.

She had dreamed of this moment for months, and now, she was finally here. Grateful for the photography class she had taken at the local college, she raised her camera, ready to capture the beauty of the world around her. Exploring the wonders of Crete was her passion, and she couldn't wait to begin.

With the group assembled, they boarded the local bus, and she settled into a seat by the window, camera at the ready. The bus jolted into motion, and they began their journey through the winding roads of Crete. Each twist and turn revealed a new vista of breathtaking beauty, and her senses came alive with wonder and excitement. As they passed quaint villages nestled amongst the hills, their white-washed houses gleaming in the sun, Maggie felt her heart swell with awe. Small churches with bright blue domes stood out against the green hillsides, and the occasional herd of goats could be seen grazing contentedly in the fields.

As they climbed higher into the mountains, the air grew cooler, and they passed through small mountain villages, their narrow streets lined with charming shops and cafes. She watched the locals go about their daily lives, smiling and waving at the tourists passing through. Approaching the coastline, the bus wound its way along the coast, passing by small fishing villages and bustling beachside resorts. Colourful fishing boats bobbed in the water, their bright paint gleaming in the sun, and her camera shutter clicked continuously, capturing every breathtaking moment of their journey.

As they approached the palace, the bus turned onto a narrow road that wound its way up the hillside. The palace loomed into view, an imposing structure of stone and marble that seemed to rise up out of the landscape itself. The building was surrounded by lush gardens filled with vibrant flowers and exotic plants, and herheart throbbed with excitement as the bus approached the entrance to the ancient ruin..Stepping off the bus, she felt the warm sun on her face, complemented by a cool sea breeze. Panagiotis led her and the other tourists through the gates of the Palace, and Maggie was already transported back in time. The halls were filled with relics of a long-gone era, intricate carvings, and vibrant murals that spoke of its rich history. She trailed her fingers over the cool stone walls, marvelling at the craftsmanship that had gone into creating this masterpiece. Walking in the footsteps of royalty and gods, she felt her soul stir with wonder.

As she followed Panagiotis through the labyrinthine corridors of the temple, her camera dangled around her neck. She was spellbound by the frescoes that adorned the walls, each image more mesmerising than the last. With every step, she felt as though she was venturing deeper into the annals of history, and her heart swelled with a sense of awe.The museum's halls were lined with ancient artefacts that spoke of a bygone era, and Maggie couldn't help but feel a sense of wonder and reverence as she beheld the treasures of the past. But one statue, in particular, caught her eye. It was a portrayal of the Greek goddess of love and beauty, Aphrodite, crafted with the utmost skill and precision.

She approached the sculpture, her gaze fixed on the delicate curves of the goddess's body. The statue was breathtaking, and yet, as she looked at her own reflection in the glass case, she couldn't help but feel a pang of disappointment. She would never be as beautiful as Aphrodite, not even with the aid of all the makeup and Photoshop in the world. Suddenly, a voice cut through her thoughts, as if reading her mind. It was Panagiotis, and his words hung in the air like a quiet revelation. "The beauty standards of ancient Greece were impossible for anyone to achieve, even a goddess," he said, his tone soft and contemplative.

Her curiosity was immediately piqued, and she turned to face him, eager to learn more. "What do you mean?" she asked, her voice barely above a whisper. Panagiotis smiled gently at her, his eyes shining with the wisdom of the ages. "The ideal proportions for female nudity were based on this sculpture," he explained, gesturing to the statue beside them. "But in reality, even Aphrodite herself would have had imperfections and vulnerabilities. No one is perfect, not even the goddess of beauty. And anyway, it's really our flaws that make us beautiful. Perfection is cold."

She looked at the statue again, and as she did, she began to see the flaws she had missed before. There were small cracks and chips that had been expertly smoothed over, but were still visible if you looked closely enough. And the curves of Aphrodite's body were not flawless either; there were slight variations in the symmetry that made her appear more human than divine.

For the first time in a long time, Maggie felt a glimmer of hope that maybe her own flaws and vulnerabilities weren't so bad after all. She looked back at the sculpture, this time seeing it in a new light. The faint smile on Aphrodite's lips suddenly seemed more relatable, as though the goddess herself was acknowledging the struggles that come with being a woman. It was a moment of revelation, and she felt as though she had been given a flash of insight that would stay with her for the rest of her life.

As she turned back to Panagiotis, Maggie couldn't help but feel grateful for the knowledge he had shared with her. She knew she still had a long way to go in accepting her own body, but for the first time, it didn't seem like such an impossible task and at least she had made the first step by booking the fitness session with Kateryna. "Thank you," she said softly, a small smile tugging at the corners of her lips. "I feel like I understand things a little better now."

Panagiotis nodded in understanding, his own smile warm and genuine. "That's the beauty of art," he said. "It has the power to help us see ourselves in a new light." As the sun sank below the horizon, casting the sky in hues of pink and orange, her legs carried her wearily to the bus stop. Her camera, a heavy weight around her neck, held the memories of the day's adventures. The excitement of exploring the ancient temples and artefacts had worn off, leaving behind only exhaustion and aching muscles. She sank onto the hard plastic seat of the bus, longing for the comfort of her hotel bed.

As she boarded the bus, she found an empty seat and slumped down, grateful for the respite. She tried to keep her eyes open, but the hum of the engine and the gentle swaying of the vehicle soon pulled her into a deep sleep. The images of the day played through her mind like a movie, each one more breathtaking than the last. When the bus arrived at the Aegean Breeze complex, she stumbled off, barely able to keep her eyes open. She made her way to her room, her body protesting with each step. She collapsed onto her bed, still clothed and still clutching her camera, and drifted into a peaceful slumber.

The following day marked the start of Maggie's job with Artists Connect in Crete. She would be working with the Minoan Art Alliance, an EU-funded project that aimed to support and promote local artists. She had a busy day ahead, with a visit to the office, meetings with the team, and an avalanche of paperwork to contend with. Despite her fatigue, she couldn't help but feel excited. She was embarking on a new adventure, and she was eager to see where it would take her.

Chapter Three: Doubts and Discoveries

The next morning, Maggie sprang out of bed, her heart brimming with anticipation for the day ahead. A surge of excitement coursed through her veins as she contemplated the fresh start and the thrilling new project that awaited her. With a cup of steaming coffee in hand, she delved into her closet, embarking on a half-hour quest to find the perfect outfit—one that would capture her playful and utterly unique personality.

Ultimately, her gaze landed on a graphic tee featuring none other than the Mona Lisa blowing an oversized pink bubble of bubblegum. The irreverent take on the conventional art world perfectly mirrored Maggie's own outlook. She completed the look with a delicate necklace, a cherished gift from Alex, featuring two lovebirds perched on a delicate branch, and a silk midi skirt in an understated shade of grey. Her signature cat's-eye black eyeliner and well-loved white trainers added the finishing touches.

Armed with her notes and laptop, she carefully organised them in a folder. Her inaugural meeting with the Minoan Art Alliance was just an hour away, and she was steadfast in her determination to make a lasting impression. With a deep breath, she faced herself in the mirror, her heart aflutter with anticipation. Her outfit was an audacious declaration of her creativity and individuality, yet a tinge of self-doubt crept in. Was the graphic tee too audacious for a business meeting? Was her dainty lovebird necklace too whimsical? But time was ticking, and Maggie knew that being late would be far worse than any daring fashion choice.

With a steadying breath, Maggie smoothed the fabric of her skirt and perfected her trademark cat's-eye black eyeliner. She aimed to let her attire convey a message of confidence and creativity, even though she harboured a bundle of uncertainties about the upcoming meeting. Stepping out of her apartment, she encountered a flutter of nerves dancing in her stomach. Nevertheless, she rallied herself and marched resolutely toward what she hoped was her promising future. The vast, open sky above seemed to mirror the boundless possibilities of the day.

Her ears caught the first sounds of construction workers nearby, infusing an extra layer of excitement into the already bustling street. As she navigated the sidewalk, her attention was drawn to the vibrant Olympus Mini Mart, its wire magazine stands proudly displaying the latest issues of renowned publications like National Geographic and Vogue. The glossy covers beckoned temptingly, but Maggie was resolute in her focus.

Amid her stroll through the lively streets of Crete, Maggie found herself immersed in a sensory whirlwind. An array of storefronts allured her gaze, showcasing a medley of handcrafted treasures and unique trinkets. Each item exuded artistry, from meticulously embroidered textiles to lovingly carved wooden figurines. While ambling along, she inhaled deeply, savouring the rich aromas of freshly baked bread, fragrant coffee, and exotic spices wafting from the charming cafes and restaurants that adorned the cobblestone streets.

Maggie strolled through the bustling streets of Rethymno, her senses inundated by the tantalising aromas wafting from every eatery she passed. Sizzling dishes and toothsome pastries beckoned to her taste buds, causing her mouth to water with each inviting aroma. But beneath her confident facade, her thoughts were a swirling maelstrom of emotions.She was excited about her new project and the possibilities it held, yet a twinge of sadness gnawed at her heart. Alex's absence left an ache that she couldn't quite shake. Doubts besieged her. Could she truly trust Alex heading off to that festival without her?

A heaviness settled in her chest as she pondered whether he'd ever propose, or if she'd spent her prime years waiting for a dream that might never materialise. Questions about her relationship and career path swirled, clouding the once-clear direction she'd envisioned for her life. Amidst the foreign sights, sounds, and scents of Rethymno, her confusion deepened, and she looked up to the sky, silently seeking guidance from her cherished late grandmother, Elizabeth."Please, Grannie," she whispered, her voice barely audible. "If he's meant to be my future, give me a sign. Any sign. I need to know."

In the distance, the soulful melodies of traditional Greek instruments serenaded the air. The warm breeze carried their harmonious notes, infusing the surroundings with an infectious joy. Maggie's heart swelled as the bouzouki, drums, and clarinet wove their enchanting music, soothing her troubled mind. Suddenly, a cluster of street vendors in a nearby park captured her attention, particularly a jewellery maker who stood out. His nimble fingers worked with a fluid grace, crafting intricate pieces with wires and beads, each bearing the mark of meticulous care. Her gaze was fixed on his craftsmanship, captivated by the delicacy of each silver chain and the shimmering gems that adorned them.

As the sunlight danced off the polished silver, the jewels sparkled and created a mesmerising spectacle. Maggie couldn't resist the urge to stop and admire these unique creations, each one more beautiful and enchanting than the last. The jeweller exuded a bohemian spirit with his loose-fitting attire and carefree demeanour, yet his eyes held a profound passion as he painstakingly shaped each piece. She found herself entranced by his artistry, fascinated by the intricate Greek symbols woven delicately into the silver wire, each piece a masterpiece in its own right.

In the vibrant park, the jeweller himself was the true revelation. His sun-kissed tawny skin, eyes that danced between shades of green and blue, and a cascade of dreadlocks tumbling down like a wild mane created a captivating sight. His smile, warm and unpretentious, felt strangely familiar, as if they'd been lifelong friends. Her heart sank when she realised she had no cash to purchase one of his exquisite creations. Apologetically, she explained her predicament, revealing only a card in her possession. His grin remained unwavering as he plucked a piece of silver wire and a small rose quartz gem from his tray.

In a matter of moments, he transformed these simple materials into a breathtaking ring that left Maggie breathless. "It's beautiful," she whispered, but before she could object, the man had already slipped it onto her finger. "It's yours," he said with a gentle smile, and she couldn't help but notice how perfectly it fit.

As she admired the ring, the jeweller elucidated the meaning of the Greek symbol adorning it, carefully crafted with strands of silver wire. It symbolised the interconnectedness of all things, emphasising that Maggie was part of a grander tapestry, holding the power to shape her destiny.

A shiver ran down her spine at his words. Staring at the ring in wonder, she felt as though she'd received a swift response to her earlier plea to her beloved late grandmother, Elizabeth. She was stunned, her very core shaken. Reality jolted her as she glanced at her watch and realised she had a mere ten minutes before the pivotal meeting. Panic surged as she comprehended how lost she'd become in the moment, utterly losing track of time.

Bursting out of the park, she darted through the bustling streets, navigating the throng of people and traffic in a frenzied sprint toward her destination. Her heart raced, and her palms grew slick with sweat. Every second mattered.Chaos swirled in her mind as she tried to make sense of the labyrinthine streets of Rethymno. She felt utterly lost, both physically and emotionally. Her entire future hinged on this meeting, yet she found herself wandering aimlessly, like a bewildered child. Panic clawed at her as she grappled with the realisation that she was drowning in unfamiliarity.

Stopping strangers for directions, her chest tightened, breaths grew shallow, and conversations with locals were lost in translation. It was as if she were trapped in a never-ending loop, circling the same block repeatedly, her world spinning in confusion.Glancing at her phone, dread washed over her as she saw the battery icon dangerously low. She had to locate the office quickly or risk missing the critical meeting altogether.

Doubts crept in, and she wondered if this was a cruel twist of fate, a sign that her destiny was meant to be one of failure and disappointment.

Just when she thought all was lost, a group of students appeared in the distance - and she could hear them speaking English. With a spark of hope, she jogged towards them, her heart pounding with anticipation. She approached them, her voice trembling as she asked for help. The group of students seemed to size her up for a moment, but one of them stepped forward with a friendly smile, offering her a glimmer of hope Maggie felt a sense of gratitude wash over her as one of the students gave her clear directions to the office. She raced towards the building, her heart pounding in her chest as she finally arrived at the door.

She took a deep breath, steadying herself for what lay ahead. This meeting was the most important thing in her life right now, and she knew that she had to give it her all. Her eyes filled with relief and gratitude as she thanked him and began to jog towards the yellow and blue sign with the initials MAA. Her heart pounded in her chest as she reached the door, knowing that whatever lay ahead was crucial for her future. She took a deep breath to steady herself, ready to face whatever lay beyond the glass door.

She approached the sleek front desk of the Minoan Art Alliance's office, her heart pounding with anticipation. The woman behind the desk glared at her through narrowed eyes, her severe short haircut and dark sculpted eyebrows adding to the sharpness of her features. Her piercing gaze seemed to bore into Maggie's soul as soon as she stepped through the door."Πώς μπορώ να σας βοηθήσω;" the woman spat in Greek, her tone laced with a sharpness that made her flinch.Maggie, feeling slightly confused, mustered up the courage to respond, "I'm sorry, I don't speak Greek. I'm here to meet with Demetris Papadopoulos about a project."

The woman let out an exasperated sigh, as if her lack of understanding was an inconvenience. Switching to English, her Greek accent colouring her words, she said, "You're fifteen minutes late?" Maggie's confidence waned further in the face of the woman's annoyance. She hurriedly apologised again, trying to explain her difficulties finding the office, but the woman cut her off with a dismissive wave of her hand.With a curt gesture, the woman instructed her to wait on a red plastic chair. As she waited, she couldn't help but feel a sense of unease settle in her stomach. The woman's harsh demeanour had left a sour taste in her mouth, and she couldn't shake the feeling that the Minoan Art Alliance was not the welcoming community she had hoped it would be.

She looked around the room, taking in the sterile decor and stark white walls, and wondered if she had made a mistake in coming here. As she sat in the uncomfortable chair, waiting for her appointment, her mind began to wander. She wondered what kind of people worked in this drab, lifeless place. Were they all as unpleasant as the woman at the front desk? She imagined a sea of disinterested faces, all staring blankly at their computer screens, their souls sucked dry by the monotony of their work. Perhaps they had once been artists themselves, full of passion and creativity, but had lost their spark somewhere along the way.

In the recesses of her mind, she empathised with their plight. She pictured a collective of souls who had surrendered their artistic aspirations for the security of a paycheck, their dreams buried beneath layers of bureaucratic red tape and stifling conformity. The sterile environment, devoid of any semblance of inspiration, seemed to mirror their inner struggles. It was a sombre notion, interrupted abruptly as the woman at the reception desk interjected. "Go down the hall to the right," she commanded, her focus promptly returning to the computer screen before her. "Knock on the third door on the left. Mr. Papadopoulos will determine if he can spare a moment for you."

With those curt instructions echoing in her mind, she rose from the chair, her determination propelling her down the polished marble corridor. Each step forward resonated with purpose, a steady rhythm guiding her towards the unknown. Nervously, she approached the door, her mind buzzing with anticipation and curiosity. After a moment, a deep voice called out from inside, drawing her closer. "Come in," it beckoned, and she obliged, crossing the threshold into a realm of possibilities.

Instantly, her gaze fell upon Demetris, a figure of authority and success. Clad in a tailored charcoal suit that exuded confidence, he stood as a beacon of professionalism. "You must be Maggie Millar?" he inquired, his tone businesslike yet cordial. Maggie extended her hand, shaking his with a mix of eagerness and apprehension. She tried to suppress any feelings of intimidation, determined to match his energy and embrace the opportunity that lay before her. And just as the air settled, Demetris turned his attention to the woman beside him.

Emily Winsor emerged, radiating an air of authority and control. Her pristine white shirt and sleek black trousers spoke of unwavering professionalism, accentuating her poised demeanour. Her blonde hair, restrained in a severe bun, added a touch of formality to her overall presence. With precision and confidence, she extended her hand, her grip firm and commanding. "Nice to meet you," she uttered in a clipped English accent, her words measured and distant. Maggie couldn't help but feel a flicker of self-doubt as Emily's sharp eyes meticulously assessed her Mona Lisa t-shirt and trendy trainers, silently scrutinising every aspect of her appearance.

As she embarked on her presentation, Maggie introduced "New Voices," a project with a noble aim: to offer a platform to underprivileged artists facing limited opportunities. The heart of the project was an art exhibition that would not only celebrate the budding talents of these artists but also provide them with the vital support needed to break into the fiercely competitive world of art. While Maggie's enthusiasm radiated, she couldn't ignore the subtle hints of doubt lingering in Emily's expressions—the raised eyebrow, the fleeting flicker of scepticism. Emily, finally, unveiled her own perspective on the exhibition, her response crisp and tinged with a touch of disdain. "Quite the ambitious endeavour," she remarked, her voice infused with scepticism. Maggie's heart sank, and an anxious nibble on her lower lip betrayed the inner turmoil brewing within her.

In the room, a palpable tension lingered as Demetris, the vivacious project lead, leaned back in his chair, exuding an infectious enthusiasm. His eyes blazed with passion as he fervently expounded on the goals and objectives of the project, his words painting a vivid picture of the Minoan Arts Alliance's mission. Yet, Emily's countenance remained marked by a scowl, a stark contrast to Demetris's contagious excitement. While he ardently outlined their mission to support budding artists and infuse the arts scene with renewed energy, Emily's disdain seemed to cast a shadow over the room, threatening to dampen the spirit of collaboration.

Undeterred by Emily's scepticism and the weight of her gestures, she remained resolute. She knew her ideas had value and her determination burned bright. This project meant too much to her to let doubts overshadow her drive. Standing in the presence of these formidable individuals, Maggie was determined to navigate the complex dynamics and prove the worth of her vision.As Demetris's words lingered in the air, she couldn't ignore the stark contrast between his vibrant enthusiasm and Emily's visible disdain. The tension crackled between them, hinting at an imminent clash of opposing forces.

The stark difference between Demetris's infectious passion and Emily's frosty demeanour revealed the challenges that lay ahead. She recognized the allure of the project's mission, but the apprehension of working alongside Emily was an undeniable reality. As Demetris spoke, she found herself nodding in understanding, captivated by the Alliance's commitment to nurturing young talent. Each artist he described came to life in her mind, their unique personalities and artistic styles vividly portrayed. His enthusiasm and passion for the project were contagious, drawing her deeper into the possibilities.

"You're in for a treat with Atticus," Demetris said, his eyes sparkling mischievously. "He's a vibrant soul with a flair for celebrating the LGBTQ+ community through his art. His paintings are a powerful celebration of love, diversity, and acceptance. With bold colours and striking imagery, he captures the essence of the human experience, advocating for equality and understanding." Oh, and he has a thing for hats, you'll see what I mean when you meet him."

Emily raised an eyebrow, her scepticism evident. "I'm not sure how that aligns with our project goals, but let's see what he can contribute."Demetris continued, shifting to a more serious tone. "Then there's Nader, a Syrian refugee who arrived in Lesvos a few years ago. He uses his camera to tell the powerful stories of himself and other refugees. His work deserves wider recognition, and we want to help him make an impact through his art."

She quickly jotted down her thoughts, feeling a strong sense of responsibility to amplify Nader's work and give it the platform it deserved. Emily nodded in agreement, her professional façade softening slightly. "That's an important cause. Let's explore how we can showcase Nader's work effectively." Demetris's eyes sparkled mischievously as he continued, "And then there's Eva. She's a fearless performance artist known for pushing boundaries and stirring up controversy. Her provocative pieces challenge societal norms and ignite conversations. I have a feeling you'll find her quite intriguing." Emily's expression remained sceptical. "We need to ensure that Eva's art goes beyond mere controversy and has a meaningful impact," she cautioned.

"Last but not least, there's Thomas," Demetris revealed, his voice tinged with a touch of nervousness. "He's quite the character, and his abstract works are challenging, to say the least. He didn't go to art school, but there's something raw and captivating about his talent. I must admit, he enjoys a drink or two, which adds an interesting twist to things." Demetris leaned in conspiratorially, his eyes darting around as if guarding their conversation.

She couldn't help but laugh at Demetris' description of Thomas, the enigmatic artist with a penchant for a drink. Her laughter echoed through the room, a genuine burst of amusement. She could already imagine the intriguing world Thomas would bring to their project. Demetris sighed with a hint of disappointment. "We didn't have many applicants for this project," he confessed, his shoulders slumping imperceptibly. "To be honest, Thomas is a bit of a wildcard. We'll see how it goes." His words carried a mixture of uncertainty and hope, leaving a sense of anticipation hanging in the air.

As the meeting drew to a close, Maggie couldn't help but be intrigued by the contrasting dynamics within the room. Demetris exuded boundless enthusiasm and unwavering support for the artists, while Emily remained cool and detached, her scepticism palpable. Gathering her thoughts, she summoned a surge of courage to address Emily directly, her voice cutting through the tension."Emily," she began, her tone steady and resolute, "I understand your concerns, but I truly believe that Nadir, Eva, and the other artists bring unique perspectives that can profoundly enrich our project." Maggie's gaze locked with Emily's, a hint of defiance lacing her words. She expressed her conviction in the artists' potential to challenge the status quo and ignite meaningful conversations, their fresh and unapologetic approach to their craft.

Emily's icy facade softened ever so slightly, curiosity mingling with her scepticism. She posed a genuine question, inviting her to share her confidence in the artists' abilities. Maggie met her gaze with unwavering determination, taking a brief moment to let the weight of the question settle."These artists embody a fresh, unapologetic approach to their craft," she explained, her words measured and deliberate. She painted a vivid picture, conveying the thought-provoking nature of their works that pushed the boundaries of conventional art and embraced new narratives. Her conviction grew stronger with each phrase, underscoring the profound impact their voices could have.

Emily maintained her guarded demeanour, yet a flicker of contemplation danced in her eyes. Undeterred, she pressed on, her voice resolute. "Our collaboration has the potential to bridge the gap between artistic vision and pragmatic considerations," she continued. Her words carried a sense of possibility, highlighting the transformative power that diverse perspectives held. She promised an exhibition that would challenge preconceived notions and inspire all who experienced it, emphasising the inherent value in embracing such a collaborative endeavour.

A brief silence settled over the room as Emily pondered her words. The atmosphere crackled with anticipation, the outcome of their exchange hanging in the balance. Finally, a subtle crack appeared in Emily's composed demeanour, and she offered a faint nod—an understated acknowledgment. "Alright," she conceded, her tone devoid of sarcasm, her guarded facade momentarily melting away. "Let's explore the potential these artists hold and push the boundaries of what we thought we knew."

She felt a wave of relief wash over her, mingling with a surge of excitement. It was a pivotal moment, a glimmer of shared understanding that promised growth and transformation. As the meeting drew to a close, Demetris expressed gratitude for her contribution, assuring her that he would carefully consider her proposal. Emily, still displaying a trace of scepticism, nodded silently in acknowledgment. Leaving the meeting room, she carried a mix of emotions—relief for having presented her ideas, yet disheartened by the lack of enthusiasm from Emily. She couldn't shake the nagging feeling that Emily had already made up her mind about the project, casting a shadow of doubt on its prospects even before hearing her pitch.

Walking down the hallway toward the exit, her thoughts wandered to the diverse personalities discussed during the meeting. Evangeline, the boundary-pushing performance artist unafraid of controversy. Nader, the storyteller capturing the power of his and other refugees' experiences through photography. And Thomas, the unpredictable wildcard with raw talent and a bit of a drinking problem from the sound of things. Yet, it was Emily who occupied her mind the most. She couldn't shake the sense that there was more to her than met the eye.

She wondered if Emily's composed exterior was a mere facade or if her disinterest ran deeper than it seemed. She made a firm mental note to press on with the project, undeterred by Emily's reservations. The cause was undeniably worthwhile, and the talented artists deserved the opportunity to showcase their abilities to a wider audience. Stepping into the embrace of the warm Greek sun, a surge of determination coursed through her veins. She was ready to stand up for her convictions, even if it meant challenging the formidable Emily Winsor.

Chapter Four: The Weight of Judgement

Weary from the weight of the meeting, Maggie embarked on the four-mile walk back to her apartment, feeling the exhaustion seep into her body. Her mind spun in a whirlwind of fragmented conversations, leaving her with a jumble of emotions—an undercurrent of foreboding, a spark of excitement, and the sensation of navigating uncharted territory. Slowly strolling along the winding coastal road that led to her apartment, the vibrant tapestry of city life unfolded before her like a living canvas.

Lost in her thoughts, her footsteps carried her farther along the way until she stumbled upon a bustling bar. Its facade was adorned with captivating women who exuded an irresistible allure reminiscent of the Kardashians. With practised grace, they enticed passersby with promises of affordable cocktails and the prospect of an exhilarating night out.

Mixed feelings of admiration and envy washed over Maggie as she caught glimpses of their carefree demeanour and unwavering confidence.

However, her attention was soon captivated by an enchanting establishment that called out to her with an irresistible allure—Kiki Beach. Nestled on the corner, its facade showcased a picturesque balcony overlooking Retheymon beach, seemingly beckoning weary souls to seek solace in its inviting wicker chairs while gazing out at the vast sea. With the sun gracefully descending, casting a warm golden glow, a deep longing awakened within her to unwind and savour the company of a chilled glass of pinot. The scene held such beauty that she couldn't resist capturing the moment with her camera, framing the sunset perfectly within the centre of her chilled wine glass. She shared this mesmerising image on Instagram with a heartfelt caption:"Savouring the magic of a Cretean sunset, where the world's worries fade into the horizon."

As the sunlight gradually waned, casting a gentle glow over the surroundings, she gazed drawn to the serene expanse of the sea and looked at her new rose quartz ring with a mix of admiration and wonder.Holding it between her fingertips, she studied its captivating hues and intricate patterns, her eyes tracing the intricate veins that seemed to breathe life into the stone.

The rhythmic ebb and flow of the waves against the shore offered a moment of calm in what had been a stressful day. However, the tranquillity of her surroundings was abruptly shattered by the shrill ring of her phone, signalling the arrival of her sister Catherine's voice crackling through the receiver, disrupting the peaceful moment.Catherine and Maggie had always had a complicated relationship, characterised by a mix of love, resentment, and unspoken expectations. Catherine, with her solid, wide hipped figure and fiery red curls, possessed a prominent nose that seemed to detect flaws in every aspect of her unconventional life. She had a sharp intellect and a sharp tongue to match, often using her biting wit to mask her own insecurities. While Catherine exuded confidence as the owner of a modest chain of three coffee shops in bustling Dublin, her success was often overshadowed by the nagging feeling that she was missing out on something greater.

Maggie longed for a deeper bond with her sister, yearning to bridge the gap that had always kept them apart. However, Catherine remained firmly entrenched in her disapproval of Maggie, maintaining an impenetrable fortress of judgement. Their interactions were tainted by veiled criticism, unsolicited advice, and the subtle sting of passive-aggressive remarks that had persisted since she failed art college. Despite their differences, they remained connected by the complex ties of family and a shared history that prevented them from drifting too far apart.

Catherine's voice crackled through the phone line, carrying the weight of her disbelief and disappointment. Each word sent a shiver down Maggie's spine as she braced herself, her shoulders tense and her posture instinctively straightening, preparing for the impending storm of disapproval."It's exactly what it sounds like," she replied, her voice fragile yet resolute amidst the rising tide of emotions. The strain in her tone was palpable, a silent tremor beneath her composed facade. "Alex has been invited to perform at the renowned Counterflows festival in the United Kingdom. It's an opportunity that has ignited a fire within him—an opportunity he can't afford to miss." Catherine's disbelief lingered, unspoken questions hanging in the air. Frustration blended with a touch of envy as she finally found her words, her tone simmering with restrained emotion. "What kind of opportunity is this?" she questioned, her words laced with a mix of exasperation and envy. "After aimlessly touring for three months? He has no excuse, Maggie."

Her gaze momentarily drifted away, catching sight of a seagull gracefully descending from the sky, skimming the surface of the sea with breathtaking elegance. The tranquillity of the scene stood in stark contrast to the brewing storm of their conversation. With a weary sigh, she replied, her voice now tinged with exhaustion. "I understand your concerns," she said, her words weighed down by empathy. Her gaze dropped, and her fingertips lightly brushed her temple, as if trying to ease the ache that had settled there."But I can't help but believe in him. This isn't about him getting out of his commitment to me. It's about his genuine passion," Maggie asserted, her voice tinged with defiance. Her hand instinctively rose to her chest, fingers curling inward as if protecting her heart.

Catherine's sharp retort sliced through the air, scepticism dripping from her words. Her body stiffened, her jaw tightening before she released a slow exhale. She crossed her arms, seeking solace and stability in her own embrace."Passion can often be used as a convenient excuse, Maggie. Don't let yourself be blinded by it. You deserve someone who truly prioritises you and your relationship, just like James does for me. I genuinely want that kind of happiness for you," Catherine softened her tone, revealing a hint of understanding beneath her usual criticism. Her eyes welled up with tears, her hand rising to brush a tear from her cheek with a sweeping motion of her fingertips.

Catherine's words had struck a nerve, but her response carried the brilliance of a well-crafted symphony. "It's about understanding that life is complex, where our expectations sometimes need to adapt and evolve." Catherine's tone softened, offering a glimpse of understanding beneath her customary scepticism. "I appreciate your concern, Catherine, truly. But I firmly believe in Alex, and I believe in us." Her gaze locked onto a seagull soaring through the vast expanse of the sky, its wings outstretched in a breathtaking display of freedom. It was as if nature itself affirmed the boundless possibilities that lay ahead.

Catherine's voice, dripping with scepticism, pierced the pregnant silence surrounding them. "I understand that you believe in him. But sometimes, it feels like you're compromising, sacrificing your own dreams for the sake of this... unconventional relationship." A surge of emotions coursed through her , a potent mix of frustration and defiance flowing like a tempestuous river in her veins. "I understand your concerns, Catherine," she replied, her voice filled with quiet determination. "Love isn't always a straightforward path. It's messy, complicated, and requires sacrifices. But it's also about finding someone who makes all those struggles worth it."

A tense pause settled between them, a fragile stillness reflecting Catherine's contemplation. When she spoke again, her words carried a begrudging acceptance. "I guess I just worry, Maggie. I want you to have a love that uplifts you, that doesn't ask you to compromise your own happiness." Her fingers traced the rim of her wine glass, seeking comfort in its cool surface. Her next words held a hint of that begrudging acceptance. "I hear your worries, Catherine. I truly do. But I've made my choice, and I believe in it. Alex and I are in love. It's not perfect, but it's real. And I hope that one day, you can see that too."

As their conversation came to an end, a whirlwind of emotions swirled within her . She placed her smartphone on the table, its screen reflecting the fading light of the setting sun. Turning her gaze back to the vast sea, she sat in contemplative silence, feeling as though someone had just slapped her across the face. The phone call left her reeling, the sting of disapproval etched deeply into her consciousness. Catherine, a constant presence of judgement and condescension in her life, had a way of slicing through her sister's every decision, leaving wounds that festered long after the conversation ended. No pleasantries could be found in their exchanges; they resembled a battlefield, where each word carried the weight of an unspoken battle cry.

In the aftermath, as the echoes of Catherine's criticisms reverberated in her mind, she found herself transported back to their childhood home, where the walls held the stories of their shared history. She recalled a quote that had adorned their mother's study, written in elegant calligraphy, now faded with time but etched deeply in her memory: "Sisters are like flowers in the same garden; each one unique, each one blooming in her own time." Yet, in the garden of their sisterhood, Catherine's bloom seemed perennially shrouded in thorns. The mere mention of Alex, her art college failure, or any of her life choices became fuel for Catherine's judgement, as if she held the authority to dissect and critique the very essence of her sister's being. It was a dance they had perfected over the years—a twisted waltz of veiled insults, cutting remarks, and unsolicited advice.

With every interaction, Catherine's words chipped away at her self-assurance, undermining the fragile petals of her confidence. The tender buds of hope, nurtured by dreams and aspirations, were swiftly crushed under the weight of her sister's disapproval. It seemed Catherine's purpose was to dim her light, to cast a pall of doubt over her endeavours.It had eroded Maggie's confidence, making her play small, in this world and in this life .And yet, as she sat in the aftermath of the phone call, a flicker of resilience burned. within her. She refused to surrender her dreams at the altar of Catherine's judgement. She longed for a sisterhood that embraced empathy and understanding, where the bonds of love would transcend the need for validation. But perhaps, she realised, the garden of their sisterhood was destined to bear thorns and blossoms in equal measure.

In the stillness of the moment, as the echoes of Catherine's voice faded, she clung to the memory of that faded quote, seeking solace in its wisdom. Sisters were indeed like flowers, each with their unique essence and journey. She vowed to water her own roots, to cultivate her own growth, even in the face of Catherine's relentless storm.With renewed determination, Maggie whispered a silent promise to herself: to rise above the thorns, to find her own path towards fulfilment. The weight of her sister's judgement would no longer hold her captive. She would navigate the garden of sisterhood, finding her own patch of sunlight, where she could bloom authentically and unapologetically.

Chapter 5: Fitness and Friendship

As the morning sun bathed Maggie's room in a soft glow, a mix of excitement and nerves pulsed through her veins. Today marked the beginning of a new chapter, her first online fitness class led by Kateryna, a Ukrainian trainer she had stumbled upon on the GO FIT platform. With her fingers poised over the keyboard, she hesitated for a moment, taking a deep breath to steady herself. With a determined click, she joined the virtual session, and her screen came alive, revealing the gateway to her fitness journey.And there she was, exuding an aura of strength and vitality that seemed to transcend the digital space. Clad in sleek workout attire, a harmonious blend of black and blue, Kateryna embodied the essence of dedication and expertise. Her tousled dark blonde hair framed a face that radiated health and vitality, accentuated by a genuine smile that reached her eyes.

Her living room provided a backdrop rich in captivating details, a tapestry of personal stories etched into its walls. Meticulously arranged shelves held cherished memories captured within ornate frames. Delicate embroidery and intricate carvings adorned these frames, showcasing Ukraine's rich artistic heritage. The unassuming furniture exuded understated elegance, with a robust wooden dining table at the room's centre, surrounding it were chairs that had embraced countless conversations and laughter, embodying the essence of kinship and connection. Above, a resplendent chandelier hung suspended, its delicate crystals refracting a warm and inviting glow, casting a mesmerising dance of light throughout the room.

As the digital connection stabilised, Maggie gathered her courage to delve deeper into the conversation with Kateryna. "Hey, Kateryna," she began, her voice infused with genuine concern. "Before we start, I just wanted to say that I've been following the news about the situation in Ukraine, and I just wanted to say that my thoughts are with you and your country. I can only imagine how incredibly tough it must be for all of you."

A mixture of gratitude and resilience flickered across Kateryna's face, a testament to the indomitable spirit of her people. She took a deep breath, her voice resonating with a touch of vulnerability as she responded.

"Thank you for your kind words," she replied, her voice carrying the echoes of countless stories of pain and endurance. "Indeed, it has been a challenging time. The war has brought immense suffering and loss to our nation. But we hold onto a saying: 'Be like the willow and bend with the wind.'"

Maggie leaned closer to the screen, captivated by the wisdom encapsulated within those words. She could sense the depth and power behind the sentiment. "Tell me more about this saying," she urged, her voice filled with a yearning for understanding. Kateryna's eyes sparkled with a mixture of pride and resilience. "The willow tree, known as 'Ukraine's willow,' has become a symbol of our spirit," she explained, her voice carrying the weight of history and the unwavering determination of her people. "Just as the willow gracefully sways and bends with the force of the wind, we too strive to adapt and endure, even in the face of the harshest storms. The willow teaches us the art of resilience, reminding us that strength can be found in embracing change and remaining steadfast in the face of adversity."

Maggie's breath caught in her throat as she absorbed the profound meaning behind the willow's analogy.. "That's incredibly inspiring," she whispered, her voice filled with awe and admiration. Kateryna nodded, a soft smile playing upon her lips. "For me, exercise and staying active have become my solace," Kateryna continued, her voice resonating with conviction. "It's where I find release, where I can channel my energy and let go of some of the anger that I have in my heart." Her gaze dropped to the carpet, a vulnerable admission of the emotions she carried. Maggie's eyes widened with understanding, sensing the depth of Kateryna's struggle.

"That's incredibly powerful," she responded, her voice filled with genuine respect. She allowed a few moments of silence to honour the weight of those words before Kateryna steered the conversation in a new direction.

"Ah, George Michael, a classic choice!" Kateryna's eyes sparkled with recognition as she noticed the picture of the iconic singer on Maggie's bedside table, nestled next to her yoga mat. A smile played on Maggie's lips as she nodded. "His music has always resonated with me," she shared, a hint of nostalgia in her voice. "Growing up, my mother played his songs all the time, and they've become a part of my life's soundtrack."

"You should see me when 'Faith' comes on," Maggie laughed, her cheeks flushing with embarrassment. "I can't resist dancing around the apartment like nobody's watching." Kateryna grinned in response, a knowing look passing between them. "Well, dancing is a fantastic way to get your body moving," Kateryna encouraged. "Whether it's dancing to George Michael or following a workout routine, movement is essential for our well-being."

Maggie nodded in agreement, her curiosity piqued. "Speaking of workouts, what should I expect from the classes?" she asked, eager to delve into the fitness journey ahead."Great question," she replied, her voice brimming with enthusiasm. "In today's class, our goal is to build strength and increase endurance. We'll be incorporating a variety of full-body exercises, as well as some high-intensity intervals to get your heart rate up. By the end of the session, I want you to feel empowered, accomplished, and ready to take on anything.What are your goals?"

In a moment of vulnerability, Maggie's words trembled with a mix of hope and uncertainty. "I need to lose weight," she confessed, her cheeks flushing with embarrassment. "Because, well, I'm planning on getting married, or what I really mean is I'm expecting a proposal."

Her admission hung in the air, leaving an unspoken question of whether she was seeking validation or assurance. Kateryna's response, however, was filled with genuine excitement and unwavering support. "How exciting!" she exclaimed, her eyes shining with enthusiasm. "But I want you to remember something, Maggie. This journey is not just about weight loss—it's about transforming your health, your mind, and your soul. Do this for yourself, not for anyone else."

In that instant, she felt an instant connection, as if Kateryna's energy and enthusiasm leaped through the screen and touched her soul. Maggie braced herself, feeling slightly self-conscious in her plain black leggings and oversized t-shirt. The session began with Kateryna's resolute voice guiding her through a series of flexibility exercises. Each attempt only emphasised her lack of flexibility, leaving her breathless and struggling to keep up. A pang of embarrassment washed over her as she realised how terribly unfit she had become. Kateryna chuckled, amused by Maggie's exaggerated expressions of struggle. "Well, we'll have to remind those muscles what they're here for! No slacking off on my watch."

Relief and determination mingled within Maggie as she replied, "I hope I can stretch my way out of this pretzel-like state. Your encouragement and patience will definitely help me keep going!"

Kateryna reassured her, "Just remember, Rome wasn't built in a day, and neither is flexibility! We'll take it one stretch at a time, and before you know it, you'll be surprising yourself with your new agility." As the session continued, Maggie's laughter mixed with determined grunts and occasional exclamations of surprise. With each stretch, Kateryna provided gentle guidance and motivating words, keeping her focused and motivated.

"Is it normal to feel like a rubber band that's about to snap?" Maggie blurted out mid-stretch.

Kateryna reassured her, "Absolutely! Your body is adjusting to new movements and ranges of motion. Just listen to your body and don't push too hard. We'll find the right balance together."

Maggie caught her breath and grinned at Kateryna, expressing her gratitude. "Thanks for being patient with me. Your guidance makes these stretches less intimidating."

"You're doing an incredible job, Maggie," Kateryna acknowledged with pride. "Remember, fitness is not about perfection; it's about progress and the willingness to step out of your comfort zone. You're already on your way to a healthier you!"

Their banter continued throughout the class, turning the challenging exercises into moments of entertainment. Maggie's exaggerated groans and Kateryna's playful encouragement filled the room. "Is there a medal for the world's most inflexible person? Because I think I deserve it!" Maggie exclaimed, mid-stretch. Kateryna wagged her finger playfully. "No negative self-talk, Maggie! We're on a mission to unlock your inner yogi. You'll be a contender for the limber champion in no time!" Their lighthearted exchange kept the atmosphere light and entertaining, transforming what could have been a gruelling workout into a shared experience of laughter and camaraderie.

Thirty minutes later, Maggie's exhaustion was offset by her contagious enthusiasm. She mockingly flexed her arms, a cheeky smile gracing her face. "Watch out, world! The next Cirque du Soleil star is in the making. Kateryna joined in the fun, applauding with exaggerated enthusiasm. "Bravo, Maggie! The big top awaits your incredible feats of flexibility!" As the class drew to a close, the sense of achievement lingered in the air. Maggie's exhaustion was tempered by a newfound confidence and a belief that she was capable of more than she had initially thought. The once-daunting experience had transformed into a journey of self-discovery and growth.

Kateryna beamed with pride, "You've done an amazing job today! "Maggie nodded, a sense of gratitude shining in her eyes. "Thank you.This class has been so much fun and I'm excited to learn from you."Kateryna's genuine smile radiated warmth and encouragement. "I'm thrilled to hear that, Maggie. Remember, fitness is not just about physical strength, but also about nourishing your mind and spirit. Together, we'll get there."

Closing her laptop, Maggie allowed herself a moment to gather her thoughts and think about the conversation she'd had with Kateryna It wasn't just about shedding a few pounds or getting in shape; it was about reclaiming her health and embracing a future that was no longer bound by limitations.Gratitude washed over her as she reflected on the connection she had forged with her; she felt fortunate to have crossed paths with someone who embodied such strength in the face of adversity.

Feeling the need to rejuvenate herself, she made her way to the bathroom, seeking solace in the coolness of running water. Splashing her face, the sensation awakened her senses, bringing a renewed clarity to her thoughts. As she stepped back outside onto the balcony, the serene expanse of the surrounding waters greeted her, a stark contrast to the turbulence that Kateryna's homeland faced. Leaning against the balcony railing, surveyed the peaceful waters ahead. The contrast between her own privileged life and Kateryna's hardships struck a chord deep within her. She couldn't ignore the vast divide between her beautiful surroundings in Crete and the war-torn reality that Kateryna faced in Ukraine. It was a stark reminder of the privileges she enjoyed and often took for granted.

A wave of shame washed over her as she contemplated the vast differences in their lives. While she basked in the beauty and tranquillity of Crete, Kateryna endured the turmoil and hardships of a war-torn country. The stark contrast made her realise the immense privilege she possessed and the injustices that others faced. As the sun dipped below the horizon, casting a warm glow over the landscape, she took a deep breath, feeling ready to embrace the challenges and rewards of her journey towards improved health. She knew that it wouldn't be easy, but she was motivated by the realisation that she had the opportunity to make a positive change in her life and honour the privileges she had been given.

Chapter 6: A Stroke of Delusion

Three days later Maggie stood in front of a worn-out door splattered with graffiti, nestled within the winding streets of Rethymno. The moment of meeting Thomas, the first artist she would collaborate with for the esteemed "New Voices" project organised by the Minoan Arts Collective, had finally arrived. Summoning her courage, she pressed the doorbell, its chime resonating through the quiet alley. In response, the door creaked open, revealing a tall figure standing in the doorway. It was Thomas Evans, the enigmatic "wildcard" applicant, as described by Demetris just a week prior.

There he stood, with tousled hair and clothes adorned in vibrant paint stains, amidst a lingering scent of beer and cigarettes in the air. Recognition flashed across his face as he commented, "Ah, you must be the woman from Artists Connect. Come on in, I guess." She stepped inside cautiously, her eyes taking in the cluttered studio. Empty beer bottles littered the floor, mingling with unfinished artworks, cigarette stubs and discarded brushes.

'Sorry about the mess,' he exclaimed, punctuating his words with a hearty laughter before collapsing onto a worn black leather armchair, adorned with colourful splatters of paint. She nodded, her concern concealed behind a polite smile. As Thomas settled into the armchair, he embarked on a self-indulgent monologue about his art, his gestures animated and exaggerated, revealing a man who seemed to have indulged in more than a few cans of beer, Maggie suspected.

Amidst his passionate explanation, her gaze wandered to the countless silver trinkets adorning his wrists, hands, and neck, gleaming in the light. His fingers idly traced the intricate patterns of his tattoos, a web of lines and shapes cascading across his arms and peeking from beneath his sleeves. Unkempt waves of dark hair framed a face adorned with a defiant stubble that defied the confines of grooming. A silver hoop graced his left ear, glimmering as he leaned forward, emanating an aura of rebellious nonconformity. His appearance, much like his art, sought to convey a sense of edgy rebellion and non-conformity.

With a theatrical flourish, Thomas leaned back in his chair, a mischievous glint in his eyes. "Maggie, my dear, let me share with you my motto as an artist," he declared, his voice brimming with confidence. "I live by a simple creed: 'Art should challenge, provoke, and disturb. It should tear down the walls of convention and shake the very foundations of the establishment.'" She couldn't help but raise an eyebrow at his grandiose statement. She nodded politely, masking her scepticism, as she wondered how his artistic vision would translate into something meaningful or if that was even possible.

Her gaze wandered towards a nearby canvas, and her worry deepened as she beheld the abomination before her—a grotesque depiction of a nude woman. The painting resembled a chaotic explosion of primary colours and shapes, as if a paint factory had vomited its contents onto the canvas. Clumps of dried spaghetti protruded from the surface, serving as an unconventional texture that defied any logical artistic purpose. The entire composition was further marred by what appeared to be globs of chewed bubblegum and crushed soda cans haphazardly glued onto the edges.

Suppressing a giggle, she struggled to find words that wouldn't crush Thomas's creative spirit. "Thomas, this is certainly... a bold exploration of artistic expression," she managed to say, her voice strained with the effort to withhold laughter. Thomas beamed, mistaking her response for admiration. "Yes, it's a revolutionary piece, pushing the boundaries of conventional art," he declared without any hint of self doubt or irony.

However, it was as her gaze landed on a specific corner of the canvas that her heart sank. In the midst of the chaotic swirl of colours, an alarming sight awaited her—a sizable patch of blue and green, unmistakable mould thriving on what had once held promise. To add to the distress, faint teeth marks marred the edges, hinting at the unwelcome presence of rodents. In that moment, as Maggie stood there, grappling with the weight of what she had witnessed, her worries grew more tangible. The mould-infested canvas seemed to mirror her mounting doubts about Thomas's capacity to produce anything of genuine value.The studio housed many other works of similar nature, each displaying various types of pasta, twisted and deformed, while others featured old beer cans affixed to the canvas. The cans had been ruthlessly cut open, and nailed to a canvas exposing their putrid silver interiors that emanated a foul stench.' Fucking hell, she muttered to herself in a barley audible whisper.' I'm screwed'.

'Did you say something? ' Thomas responded, with a quizzical look on his face.She leaned forward, meeting his gaze head-on. "Thomas, I understand that you have a unique artistic perspective, and that must be why you were, ahem, selected for this project in the first place. But collaborating with me on this project isn't about diluting your vision; it's about enhancing it, pushing boundaries, and exploring new possibilities. Do you understand?."

Thomas took another drag of his cigarette, exhaling a cloud of smoke that seemed to hang in the air between them. He leaned back in his chair, a smirk playing at the corner of his lips: "Collaboration? Look, I appreciate your enthusiasm, but I don't need anyone meddling with my artistic vision. It's raw, it's authentic, and it's beyond what most people can understand." With that, he dipped an old piece of wood into a can of neon paint and , with a dramatic gesture, splashed the remnants across the dirty white studio walls.

Her concern deepened as she surveyed the aftermath, her eyes fixed on the streaks of pink paint descending down the wall, mirroring her growing unease.Her eyes scanned the cluttered studio, each bizarre creation begging for a semblance of coherence. "Thomas, I get that art can be subjective, but we also want to create an exhibition that resonates with the audience. We need to find ways to engage them and invite them into our artistic journey, invite them inside that unique mind of yours, " she said carefully choosing her words.

Thomas paused for a moment, his gaze fixed proudly on the tangled mess of spaghetti on the canvas. A mischievous smile tugged at the corners of his lips as he began to explain, his tone infused with pretentiousness yet a hint of humour. "Ah, you see, Maggie, the pasta represents the inherent struggles of human existence. Each strand, twisted and entangled, represents the complexities of our lives, our DNA. And the splattered paint? It symbolises the chaotic beauty that emerges from our darkest moments."

Maggie raised an eyebrow, both amused and bewildered by Thomas's audacious explanation. "And the mould?" she ventured, unable to hide her scepticism. Thomas chuckled, a glint of mischief in his eyes. "Ah, the mould, my dear. It's an ode to the fleeting nature of our achievements. Just as time decays all things, so does the mould decay the canvas, reminding us of the impermanence of our artistic efforts."

Maggie couldn't help but stifle a laugh, her worry momentarily forgotten. "Thomas, your interpretations are... interesting, to say the least.' As they stood amidst the cluttered studio, Her gaze wandered to another canvas tucked away in the corner of the room, this one adorned with a collage of torn paper and fragments of old photographs. The haphazard arrangement seemed chaotic at first, but upon closer inspection, she recognized a hidden story—a narrative waiting to be unveiled. "Maggie, look closely," Thomas urged, his voice tinged with a mix of excitement and vulnerability.

"Each torn piece of paper represents fragments of memories, forgotten moments that shape our existence. And the photographs, well, they capture the essence of human emotions frozen in time."Maggie leaned in, her eyes tracing the lines and contours of the collage.. "Thomas, I believe in your potential as an artist. But art is not just about individual expression; it's about connecting with an audience, evoking emotions, and creating a lasting impact. We need to find a way to bridge the gap between your unique art and the audience's understanding. We need to create an experience, not just an exhibition."

His brows furrowed, a mix of defiance and confusion etched on his face. "Create an experience?you're trying to dilute my vision, to conform it to what everyone else wants. I don't care if my art makes people uncomfortable. Quite frankly, that's the entire point" he said, raising his hands up to heaven like a preacher.Maggie met his gaze, her voice steady but firm. "Thomas, I don't doubt your vision, but art can be both thought-provoking and accessible. We need to find that balance, a language that speaks to both your artistic integrity and the viewers' emotions."

He leaned back in his chair, his features softening with a hint of contemplation. "A language that speaks to both... I suppose there could be something intriguing in that approach." Her eyes brightened with a glimmer of hope. "That's what we're here for, Thomas. Together, we can delve deeper into your themes, explore different techniques, and discover a style that resonates with both your vision and the viewers' emotions. It won't be easy, but I believe we can create something truly incredible."

He sighed, a mixture of frustration and reluctant acceptance. "Alright, let's give it a try. But remember, I won't compromise my artistic integrity." Maggie nodded, a determined smile playing on her lips. "I wouldn't expect anything less. The atmosphere in the room crackled with anticipation as Maggie leaned in, her eyes sparkling with curiosity. With an air of intrigue, she posed the question that had been lingering on the tip of her tongue, eager to unravel the mystery that shrouded the man before her. "So, what's your story? How did you end up in this sun-kissed haven of Crete?"

He shifted in his seat, a flicker of nostalgia dancing across his face as he delved into the depths of his memories. His fingers instinctively reached up to scratch his head, as if seeking solace in the touch of his own thoughts. His gaze momentarily wandered, lost in a maze of recollections, before finding its way back to meet Maggie's inquisitive eyes. With a sigh laced with both resignation and resilience, he began to unveil the intricate tapestry of his life.

"Love, my dear, love brought me to this bohemian paradise," he confessed, his voice carrying the weight of bittersweet experiences. He leaned back in his chair, his fingers absently tapping against the beer bottle, the cool condensation clinging to his skin. "An American woman with dreams as vast as the ocean. We stumbled upon each other amidst the chaotic currents of life, thinking we had found our anchor. But love, it's a tumultuous voyage, and our ship soon sailed into distant horizons, leaving us with nothing but fading memories."

A wry smile curled the corners of his lips, a tinge of self-deprecation adding depth to his words. "You see, my existence has been a wild ride of dashed hopes and failed endeavours," he continued, taking a hearty gulp from the bottle, the bitterness of the beer mirroring the bitterness of past disappointments. "From the beats of DJing in Ibiza, where the nights melted into a blur of euphoria and exhaustion, to the treacherous path of entrepreneurship, where dreams collided head-on with the unforgiving realities of a cutthroat market. Each venture held the promise of triumph, but life had its own script, constantly rewriting my fate."

A moment of sadness washed over him, his eyes drifting towards the window, as if seeking solace in the distant landscape. Then, fueled by an unwavering flame, he leaned forward, his voice resonating with raw passion. "And then, my dear, art found me," he confessed, his words brimming with a newfound sense of purpose. He placed the bottle down with a thud, his hands gesturing with animated conviction. "When all else had failed , from the shipwreck of my life, I was washed up on the shores of art, I discovered my true calling, my raison d'être."

Maggie couldn't help but notice the quirks that made Thomas an odd character to connect with. His scruffy appearance, accompanied by the lingering scent of smoke, further distanced him from the world she knew. As she listened to his tales of unfulfilled dreams, she couldn't help but feel a growing sense of disillusionment."And now, art is my last hope," he continued, taking a swig from his can of beer. "I believe I have what it takes to make it in the art world. This is my time, my time to be recognised."

As the meeting drew to a close, she couldn't help but feel a sinking sensation in her gut. The weight of uncertainty settled heavily upon her, threatening to undermine her confidence. Doubt crept into her mind, and she questioned whether she had underestimated the magnitude of the task before her. Did Thomas possess the necessary focus, skill, or even the ability to create something of true value for the exhibition - or was he going to be an absolute nightmare? She suspected the latter.As they both exchanged uncertain glances, she couldn't help but wonder if there was a glimmer of hope buried within his eccentricity. Perhaps, with her guidance, they could transform his peculiar creations into something that, at the very least, wouldn't send art critics running for the hills.

As she stepped out of Thomas's studio, she found herself navigating the winding alleys of the town, the air carrying a chill that seemed to match the uncertainty in her thoughts. The nagging worry persisted, casting a shadow of doubt over the task she had undertaken. What was the truth about Thomas Evans? Was he simply a middle-aged man seeking redemption, a broken soul searching for purpose, or an arrogant narcissist with a knack for storytelling?

The enigma of his character intrigued her, but she couldn't help but wonder if she had bitten off more than she could chew. In her heart, she contemplated the possibility of helping Thomas unlock his hidden potential, of extracting something extraordinary from the chaos that surrounded him. Yet, a cloud of uncertainty loomed overhead. Could he gather the fragments of his scattered self, focus his energy, and rise to the occasion? Only time would reveal the answer but with 8 weeks to go before the final exhibition time was not on her side.

With a sigh, she acknowledged her fears and also the reality that her plans for an Italian dinner would have to be abandoned. The thought of spaghetti had somehow lost its appeal....In the fading light of the evening, she wandered through the ancient streets of the old town, her mind swirling like a gentle breeze. The city's ambiance embraced her as she strolled, but her tranquillity was interrupted by the melodic chime of her phone. With a tap, the screen came alive, revealing the handsome face of Alex, beckoning her into a video call.

Excitement danced in Alex's eyes, mingled with a hint of nerves, as he shared the thrilling news of his upcoming concert in the UK that very evening. This was no ordinary performance; influential figures from the music industry would grace the event with their presence. The weight of the moment radiated in Alex's voice, blending pride and anticipation, tugging at Maggie's heartstrings. She knew this was the opportunity he had been yearning for, the culmination of his dreams.

Through the pixelated magic of the screen, their connection transcended the boundaries of distance and time. "I want to play something for you," he whispered, perched on the edge of his humble hotel room. The gentle strumming of Alex's guitar spilled into the airwaves, a celestial serenade that wrapped around Maggie's senses. It was "Maggie" by Rod Stewart, a song whose lyrics might not have been conventionally romantic, yet Alex's tender voice wove a tapestry of devotion that stirred her very soul.

Beyond being a mere song, it held memories etched deep within their shared experiences, an ode to their unique bond. With each melodic note, the space between them dissolved, an invisible thread pulling them closer together. Time stood still in the harmonious symphony, transforming the pixels on the screen into a window to their intertwined universe. As the final strum lingered, a quiet stillness settled around them, wrapping them in a cocoon of enchantment. It wasn't just the song itself that captivated Maggie; it was the sentiment woven within each chord, the unwavering connection that transcended physical separation. It was a declaration, whispered softly, affirming their unbreakable bond.

As the echoes of music faded, her eyes widened in astonishment, her gaze fixed on the rose quartz ring adorning her finger. Her heart skipped a beat as Alex's voice filled the air, brimming with a mix of warmth, surprise, and excitement. "You won't believe it," Alex blurted out, a hint of excitement lacing his words. "I've got some big news! I'll be flying in next week!" Her jaw dropped, her face a mix of shock and elation. "No way! Are you serious?" she exclaimed, her voice filled with disbelief and happiness. "I can't believe you're actually coming!" "The weather in Dublin is miserable!! Alex chuckled on the other end of the line. Believe it, darling! We've talked about it for so long, and now it's finally happening. We're going to have the time of our lives!"

A surge of excitement surged through her veins as she envisioned their long-awaited reunion. "Just think of it," she said, her voice brimming with anticipation. "We can finally visit Santorini, we have wanted to go there since we first met" Alex's voice was filled with enthusiasm. "Exactly! We're going to make every moment count. I can't wait to see you again - I've missed you so much." A joyful laughter escaped her lips. "I'm counting down the days until you're here. It's going to be absolutely perfect!" As their conversation winded down, the reality of their upcoming reunion sunk in. "Well, I better start organising myself and getting ready," Alex said. "I'll see you in a week, Maggie. Take care!" Her voice was filled with genuine warmth and excitement. "Safe travels, Alex. See you soon. I love you!!"

Her heart fluttered with joy as she painted vivid mental images of their idyllic rendezvous. The promise of their journey together, immersed in the beauty of Greece, filled her with a sense of enchantment. She could almost feel the warmth of the sun on her skin and taste the saltiness of the sea air on her lips. It was a dream made real by Alex's words, a shared adventure waiting to unfold. Turning a corner, her path collided with another pedestrian, causing both of them to stumble momentarily. A voice, tinged with familiarity, sliced through the disarray. "Maggie Millar, is that you?" it exclaimed.

Her eyes widened like saucers, lifted from the commotion around her, and focused on the spectacle in front of her. And what a spectacle it was – none other than Patrick Kinsella, a relic from her art school days in Dublin. It had been eons since they'd last crossed paths, but the threads of shared lectures, late-night giggles, and memories woven deep surged forth, enveloping her in a sweet wave of nostalgia. "Patrick! I mean, seriously, what are you doing here?" Her voice hit a pitch that only dogs could hear, the disbelief and exhilaration blending in a symphony of surprise. Time curled back like a scroll, and there she was, face to face with a character from her own past, almost like destiny had shuffled its cards just for this moment. "I'm actually in shock! How have you managed to materialise in Rethymnon?"

His response came with a sigh, a glance downward, and then a swift return to meet Maggie's gaze – all executed with the flair of a seasoned actor. "Oh, Maggie dear, hold onto your hat! Michael and I? We've officially called it quits. Our love story had its grand finale, and let me tell you, my heart's like a puzzle with a piece missing." His words hung in the air, laden with a kind of vulnerability that pulled at her heartstrings."Oh, Patrick," she cooed, her hand reaching out as if to catch his confession. "I'm here for you, sweetie." A bittersweet grin tugged at his lips, a blend of gratitude and wistfulness. "Thanks. Life's been a whirlwind, darling. But you know what they say, right? A change of scene is like a shot of clarity." He gestured grandly to the postcard-worthy scene around them – the serene blues of the sea, the golden hues of the sun. "So here I am, chasing some peace and perspective."

In that very instant, they were cocooned in their own bubble amidst the city's clamor, two characters weaving their stories in the tapestry of life. Patrick, draped in a subdued pale grey linen suit, gave off an air of quiet sophistication. His Panama hat cast its suave shadow, adding a touch of enigmatic charm. In the years that had passed, Patrick had risen in the art world, his sculptures now gracing the hallowed halls of galleries like London's Tate Modern.

"Maggie, my dear," he purred, his voice a blend of warmth and curiosity, "what's the scoop? Are you still painting? You were so good." His eyes twinkled with genuine intrigue, as if he was unwrapping a present to discover its delights. Maggie flushed a bit, a touch of sheepishness warming her cheeks as she shook her head. "Gosh, Patrick, I haven't held a brush in ages," she confessed, pushing her oversized sunglasses up onto her head. "Remember? I failed art college half way through my final year ."

Patrick's gaze softened with empathy, soaking in her words like a sponge. "That, I'll never understand," he mused. "You had oodles of talent, darling." Proposing a move to a nearby café, he guided the way to a rustic-charm-infused spot. Maggie ordered a cappuccino, her attempts at Greek impressing Patrick, though she was quick to confess her language struggles. "Goodness, you're a language whiz," he grinned, holding a blue and white menu. 'I'm very lucky that most people on the island speak English, " she replied, "but I'm doing my best to try to pick up some of the language."

They nestled into a cosy nook, the floodgates of art school memories swinging open wide. Laughter danced in the air, weaving the threads of shared experiences. Patrick let out a soft sigh, his gaze drifting in a reverie of days gone by. "Oh, Maggie," he sighed, his voice brushed with gentle nostalgia, "we were such adorable fledglings back then, so green, so innocent." her eyes danced with playful mischief, and she couldn't resist interrupting, her tone dripping with fond ridicule, "Oh, and let's not forget the hideous clothes we wore back then! I mean, seriously, those outfits were just... horrifying!" Patrick burst into laughter, his amusement a symphony of hilarity and disbelief. "And can you believe we actually thought we were the embodiment of cool?" he chimed in, his voice still laced with laughter.

A mischievous glint ignited in Patrick's eyes as he composed himself, ready to unravel the fashion follies of their youth. "Ah, the '90s fashion," he declared with exaggerated exasperation. "We willingly donned the most atrocious garments, my dear... Pleated monstrosities and the vice-like grip of Lycra that defied the laws of comfort." He adopted an almost theatrical tone, as if reciting lines from a comedy routine that mocked their youthful sartorial choices. "And the neon! Sweet mercy, the neon!" Maggie managed to blurt out amidst her giggles, her laughter harmonising with his. "We could have lit up a city block with our fluorescent ensembles. It's a miracle we didn't blind innocent bystanders with our fashion offences."

Their laughter reverberated through the room, a testament to the eccentricities of their former fashion choices and the enduring bond of friendship that had weathered those style mishaps. A mischievous glint danced in Patrick's eyes as he leaned closer to Maggie, ready to spill his confession. "I had my rebellious phase, I must admit," he began. "I even went so far as to dye my hair blue and don black turtlenecks, thinking I was the epitome of avant-garde chic. Oh, the fashion blunders we made in the name of art! We probably should have started a support group for survivors of our sartorial mishaps."

As their laughter gradually subsided, a moment of shared reflection hung in the air. Maggie's voice, tinged with curiosity, broke the silence. "Remember Stephen, the nude model?" she asked with a playful smile. "We painted him so many times, but, well, let's just say his body had its... unique attributes. No matter how hard we tried, it never quite seemed to translate onto the canvas."

"Ah, Stephen, the maestro of dramatic poses," Patrick chuckled, a hint of nostalgia in his voice. "I vividly recall a session where he channelled his inner Greek hero. With his arm outstretched as if holding an imaginary golden shield, a makeshift red cape swirling around him, and his expression fierce and unwavering, we were all completely captivated." A playful glint sparked in Maggie's eyes, her laughter barely contained. "But here's the icing on the cake – in the midst of striking that heroic pose, his foot landed squarely on a rogue paint splatter, and down he went, as if in slow-motion."

Patrick and Maggie dissolved into peals of laughter, their bodies shaking with the sheer hilarity of it all. "He tumbled like a majestic yet wholly ungraceful warrior," Patrick managed to articulate through his giggles. "His makeshift golden shield went airborne, and he ended up flat on his back, legs flailing about in the air. All the while, he was stark naked except for his artistic props." Maggie clutched her sides, tears of laughter streaming down her cheeks. "And, incredibly, he remained in character!" she exclaimed, a touch of disbelief in her voice. "There he lay, sprawled on the floor, fiercely maintaining that heroic expression, while the rest of us were in stitches."

The story of Stephen's ambitious yet ultimately comical attempt at a dramatic pose swiftly ascended to legendary status within the art college. It evolved into a narrative passed down through generations of students, with each retelling becoming more embellished and uproarious than the last. "Ah, they affectionately dubbed him 'The Tumbling Hero,'" Patrick managed to say amid his lingering laughter, a note of amusement in his voice. "He unwittingly became the art school's comic relief, forever etched into our collective memory."

She wiped away her tears, her laughter gradually giving way to a contented chuckle. "Oh, dear Stephen," she sighed, shaking her head with a fondness that transcended time. "While his grace may not have rivalled that of a swan, he brought an immeasurable amount of laughter to our art classes. Those are the moments that truly define our college experience."

Lost in their shared reminiscences, curiosity got the best of them. "I can't help but wonder where he is now," she pondered, her voice tinged with intrigue. Patrick leaned in with a conspiratorial twinkle in his eyes. "You won't believe this," he revealed. "After our art school days, Stephen actually ventured to Milan, where he enrolled in a prestigious institution offering a master's program in the art of nude modelling."

Her jaw practically dropped in astonishment. "No way!" she exclaimed, her eyes widening in disbelief. "I didn't even know such a program existed. How utterly extraordinary!" Their laughter swelled once more, a harmonious chorus echoing through the room as they traded more tales of their art school escapades. The quirks of those unforgettable characters illuminated their conversation, saturating the atmosphere with a blend of mirth and nostalgia.

"Ah, the highs and lows of those times," she mused, her voice bearing a bittersweet undertone. Patrick's tone shifted, a touch of gravity in his words, as he mentioned the enigmatic gothic twin brothers from their past. "Johnny and Robert," Maggie responded, a poignant sigh interlacing with her voice. "I heard the tragic news that one of them passed away from cancer shortly after we graduated. Such a heartbreaking loss."

In the midst of their warm and tender moment, a delicate realisation embraced them both, an acknowledgment of life's fragility and the bittersweet hues that intertwined with their cherished memories. Maggie sighed, her tone a blend of contemplation and yearning. Leaning forward, her eyes locked onto Patrick's, she sought a kindred understanding within his gaze. "Have you ever felt like you're living a life that doesn't quite fit? Like there's a void within you?"

His nod carried the weight of shared experience, his features softening with camaraderie. "Without a doubt," he admitted, his voice becoming a vessel for personal revelation. "It wasn't until a couple of years ago that I found the courage to come out. I know exactly what you mean." Maggie's eyes sparkled with luminous excitement, an exuberant joy that couldn't be contained. "I had a hunch!" she exclaimed, her words infused with a burst of vivacity.

"It was fairly obvious anyway," she continued, a playful smile gracing her lips as she gestured to the pink bloom in his buttonhole. Settling back in his chair, Patrick's hand moved with a graceful flourish, a mischievous grin curving his lips. "Ah, the magic of intuition," he quipped. "Let me assure you, my dear Maggie, embracing your truth is a transformative journey of its own."

But as the weight of past regrets settled upon Maggie's heart, her eyes welled up with tears. "Sometimes," she confessed, her voice trembling with vulnerability, "I can't help but be consumed by my failure at art school." Patrick, his gaze steeped in empathy, extended his hand across the table, his touch gentle as he grasped hers. "Regret can be a formidable companion, my dear friend," he murmured softly. "But remember, life is like a capricious dance. You could have aced your exams and then encountered a random twist of fate that altered everything, just like in that movie, 'Sliding Doors.' Don't let the 'what ifs' overshadow the present."

Their conversation swayed onto gentler shores as Patrick's curiosity led him deeper into Maggie's life. "And what about Rachel, your best friend from art school?" he inquired, his interest genuine and palpable.

A nostalgic smile painted Maggie's lips as she savoured the question, a sip of her coffee carrying the undertones of memories both sweet and sorrowful. "Isn't it peculiar," she mused, a touch of wistfulness weaving through her words, "after we both floundered in our fourth-year exams, we simply... drifted apart." A tinge of sadness tinged her voice as she spoke of the lost connection. "We were both shell-shocked and, perhaps, a little battered. It just sort of... happened, and we lost touch."

Patrick's brows knit together briefly, his mind retracing the footprints of their shared history. "That's a true pity," he commented, a glimmer of nostalgia lighting up his expression. "I have vivid memories of you two, inseparable like a pair of peas in a pod. Oh, yes! The Glippies, that was the affectionate nickname, right? Glamorous Hippies," he pondered aloud, scratching his head in amusement. A radiant smile graced Maggie's lips, a swirl of memories blending with a hint of whimsy. "Yes, the Glippies," she confirmed, her tone kissed with affection. "Flowing skirts, flowers in our hair – a look only art college could embrace," she chuckled.

"You both resembled followers of the Manson family!" Patrick erupted into laughter, though he fell silent as he suggested, his tone gentle, "Maybe it's time to rekindle the connection with Rachel. You two were tight-knit, the best of companions. Reconnecting could provide you the closure and peace you seek from the past." With their coffee cups nearing the dregs, Patrick headed to the counter to settle the bill. Inspired by their heart-to-heart, Maggie delved into her bag and produced a pen. Determinedly, she inked the name "Rachel" in red on the back of her hand. Rachel, her art school confidante, lost in the turbulence of their joint letdown.

"It appears," she began, resolve lacing her voice, "it's time for me to reach out to Rachel. To reconnect, and to find a sense of closure."

Returning to the table, Patrick's gaze flicked to the inscription on Maggie's hand, a smile of acknowledgement playing on his lips. "That, my dear," he pronounced, a swell of pride underscoring his words, "is a stride toward embracing the life you're meant for."

Exiting the charming coffee shop, they emerged onto sun-soaked streets in Crete, the breeze tenderly brushing their faces. The city seemed to animate even more vividly, mirroring the newfound determination brewing within her. They ambled through winding alleys, their dialogue harmonising with the lively pulse of their surroundings. The scent of blooming bougainvillaea intertwined with the waft of fresh pastries, composing a symphony of scents that teased the senses.

Passing a petite art gallery, Maggie's gaze gravitated toward a mesmerising painting of a woman sporting butterfly wings, emerging from a chrysalis. She halted, ensnared by its enchantment, and murmured in awe, "This artwork is extraordinary. The portrayal of transformation is truly captivating." She stepped back slightly to encompass the whole painting and continued, "It's like the woman and the butterfly are one, a testament that change can be both beautiful and empowering." Lost in the moment, she lingered, the painting infusing her with inspiration and a fresh surge of possibility.

Patrick nodded, his attention fixed on the masterpiece. "Absolutely," he concurred, "it's a reminder that our challenges can serve as a cocoon of change, allowing us to discover our genuine selves."Pressing on with their leisurely promenade, the world around them pulsated with vibrant existence, harbouring untold narratives awaiting discovery. The sun began its descent, bathing the city in a golden glow, and Maggie felt a renewed vigour coursing through her veins. Upon reaching a quaint square adorned with timeworn benches and a gently murmuring fountain, she paused and pivoted to face Patrick. Her eyes gleamed with determination. "Thank you," she murmured, her voice quivering with emotion. "For the memories and for helping me remember the person I once was. I miss that younger version of me, so full of hope and optimism."

Patrick's lips curved into a tender smile as he absorbed her words. "You know," he interjected, a gesture encompassing her heart, "that young woman you're describing? She's still tucked away inside you, just waiting to be rediscovered."His smile glowed warmly, the sun's fading rays dancing in his eyes. "It's been an absolute pleasure catching up with you, Maggie," he responded with earnestness. "Promise me you'll reach out to Rachel, alright? I have a feeling it's something you both really need. I recall Rachel being just as devastated as you were when art college didn't pan out for her... reconnecting could truly do wonders."

Extending his hand, Patrick gently squeezed Maggie's fingers. "We'll definitely arrange to meet up again soon. I'm here for the summer, and honestly, a bit of company would be much appreciated." Maggie nodded, a sparkle of anticipation in her eyes. "Absolutely! We'll make sure to catch up again very soon." With a blend of reluctance and hope, they released each other's hands, taking a small step back. As Maggie turned to leave, a newfound lightness infused her steps, carrying with it a surge of inspiration and possibility.

Guided by her curiosity, she wandered into a charming local newsstand. The tinkling bell above the door greeted her entrance, ushering in the invigorating scent of freshly printed papers and the soft hum of conversations. Her gaze was promptly drawn to a neatly stacked pile of newspapers near the entrance, their headlines demanding attention: "Ukraine Conflict Escalates: Kyiv Under Siege." The bustling capital of

Ukraine, home to millions, was now grappling with the onslaught of Russian airstrikes, leaving even kindergartens and orphanages in ruins.

The alarming headlines shocked her, compelling her to move closer to the newspapers for a clearer view. The stories and images within painted a dire portrait of the unfolding crisis. Kyiv, once teeming with life and culture, was now ensnared in a state of siege. With a mix of disbelief and sorrow, she reached for one of the newspapers, her hands trembling slightly. As she unfolded it, her eyes absorbed the front page, a chilling tableau of a city gripped by chaos. The photographs depicted smoke spiralling from shattered buildings, an urban landscape tainted by destruction and the echoes of airstrikes. Buildings lay in ruins, walls crumbled, and windows shattered.

Another image portrayed a kindergarten reduced to rubble, its once-colourful facade now a monument of devastation. Toys and playground equipment lay scattered amidst the wreckage, symbolising the loss of innocence and childhood disrupted by war. Yet another photograph captured the agony of an orphanage, a sombre reflection of the turmoil. The building's facade bore the scars of shelling, windows shattered and walls bearing the marks of violence. It was a heart-wrenching glimpse into the lives of children who had already endured far too much, now grappling with the additional trauma of conflict.

These images served as stark testimonials to the severity of the situation, evoking profound empathy and an urgent call for action. They highlighted the human toll of the conflict, underscoring the immediate need for aid and support to alleviate the suffering of those affected, particularly the vulnerable individuals and communities caught in its grip.

In that poignant moment, the gap between her tranquil seaside haven and the war-ravaged streets of Kiev seemed immeasurable. Compassion surged within her, envisioning the pain and trepidation clutching the Ukrainian people. Her thoughts turned to Kateryna, the spirited Ukrainian fitness instructor she'd come to know through GoFit. A virtual bond had blossomed between them, a kinship born of shared experiences and online friendship. Her heart longed to extend support across the distance, to be a source of strength to Kateryna amidst the havoc.

With the newspaper held in her hands, she continued reading, the mere mention of Putin sending a shudder down her spine. In her mind, he personified a contemporary despot, a power-hungry figure propelled by a twisted nationalism. The motives behind the aggression eluded her grasp, leaving her grappling with the calculated indifference to innocent lives. Echoes of history reverberated in her thoughts, reminding her of the atrocities perpetrated by tyrants of the past.

A deep well of sorrow and impotence engulfed her, and she held the folded newspaper close to her chest, seeking refuge in its tangible presence. The weight of the war's devastation bore down upon her, evoking a sense of insignificance against such monumental suffering. A silent plea for peace escaped her lips, an earnest entreaty for an end to the senseless turmoil.

Stepping out of the store, a heavy cloud of despondency shadowed her. The world appeared cloaked in turmoil and brutality, casting shadows on her ability to effect meaningful change. The scale of the catastrophe bore down on her, causing her to question her capacity to alleviate the agony and usher in an end to the destruction. As Maggie wandered the streets, her mind still entwined with thoughts of the war's heartrending impact, her phone buzzed in her pocket. Retrieving it, she felt a mixture of anticipation and apprehension as her mother's name illuminated the screen. Weary but bracing herself, she answered the call.

"Hello, Mum," she greeted, her voice tinged with the weight of recent events. "Maggie, my love, I've been following the news, and I can't help but fret," her mother's voice conveyed genuine concern. "Considering the situation in Ukraine, wouldn't it be wise for you to return to Dublin?" Maggie sighed lightly. "Honestly, Mum, you must have some sort of sixth sense. I was just reading about it in the newspaper. Things are truly escalating."

Maggie's mother's words burrowed deep into her heart, a testament to the genuine care and protective instincts that defined their relationship. She empathised with the fears that had taken root, both within her mother's concerns and her own swirling doubts. The looming war had cast an uncertain veil over her time in Crete, sowing seeds of hesitation in her mind. With a steadying breath, Maggie deliberated her response, recognizing the intricate dance between safeguarding herself and pursuing her aspirations.

"Mum," she began, her voice tender and thoughtful, "your worry means so much to me, and I get why you're anxious. Your love and support are like a shield around me. I promise, I'll stay alert and cautious, making sure I'm safe above all. If things get worse, if it gets risky for me to be here, I won't hesitate to come back to Dublin. Cross my heart." A pause followed on the other end, as her mother digested Maggie's words. Eventually, her tone softened, revealing a blend of relief and acceptance. "I know you've got a big heart, my darling. I trust you to make the right decisions. Keep checking in with me, okay? And remember, I'm just a phone call away. Your safety is all that matters."

Maggie's heart swelled with gratitude for her mother's understanding and unwavering support. She nodded in response, even though her mother couldn't see her. "Absolutely, Mum. I'll keep you posted, and I'll be careful. Thanks for always having my back." With their conversation winding down, she hung up the phone and inhaled deeply, a renewed determination coursing through her veins. The Ukrainian conflict would remain a heavy weight on her conscience, and being far from home during such a tumultuous period felt disorienting. Striking the right balance between her pursuit of meaningful endeavours in Crete and her responsibility for self-preservation was a tightrope she navigated with care.

As she continued on her path toward the Minoan Arts Alliance office, the ember of hope within her sparked to life again. She refused to surrender to despair, resolved to find a way to contribute, no matter how modest, to the cause she believed in. Gently folding the newspaper, she clung to the belief that compassion and empathy could illuminate even the darkest of times.

Chapter 7: The Unusual Rain

In June, the sun in Crete usually reigned supreme, casting temperatures as high as 35 degrees Celsius. It was the season of sun-seekers flocking to the beaches, basking in the Mediterranean warmth. However, that week, an uncanny event transpired. The sky darkened, ominous clouds gathered, and the heavens wept torrents of rain upon the island. Maggie, confined within her modest apartment, observed this peculiar shift from her window. Immersed in her work, she clacked away at her keyboard, wrestling with the relentless tide of 'New Voices' project tasks. The pounding rain on the rooftop seemed to mirror her sense of captivity, intensifying her feeling of being trapped and unable to break free. Loneliness and isolation crept in, though the prospect of Alex's arrival in just six days provided a glimmer of solace.

Restlessness tugged her chair back, coaxing her toward the balcony. As she slid open the door, a rush of damp air met her and a tableau of rain-drenched streets unfolded. The once-lively beach now lay deserted, its colourful towels and inflatables replaced by vacant sand and shimmering puddles. Tourists sought refuge under restaurant awnings, their vibrant attire a stark contrast against the grey canvas.Standing on the balcony, a profound sadness descended upon her. She watched the hurried pedestrians, their footsteps an accompaniment to the rain's percussion on the pavement. Brightly hued umbrellas, scattered beacons of hope amid the gloom, punctuated the scene. Each step through a puddle seemed to symbolise a fleeting act of defiance against the relentless downpour.

At that moment, she couldn't help but draw a connection between the unusual weather and the turmoil unfolding in Ukraine. It felt as if the world's tears were falling all across Europe, a sombre response to the suffering endured by distant souls. The weight of global troubles, coupled with her personal sense of confinement, tugged at her heartstrings. Helplessness clung to her, an unwanted companion in the face of this brutal tragedy.Returning to her apartment, she peered through the rain-kissed window. She realised that even within such melancholy, glimpses of beauty endured. Raindrops waltzed upon the glass, crafting intricate patterns, while the city's colours appeared more vivid against the grey backdrop. It was a reminder that amid life's tempests, resilience could be found, and beauty could emerge in the unlikeliest places.

After her solitary moment on the balcony, Maggie reentered her apartment, seeking refuge from the dreary scene outside. She shook off the droplets clinging to her clothes and ventured to the kitchen, an intimate sanctuary within the confines of her cosy home. Craving the comfort of a familiar ritual, she filled the kettle with water and placed it on the stove. The gentle hum of the burner and the promise of a warm cup of coffee enveloped the room. As the water heated, the rich smell of freshly ground beans swirled in the air, lifting her spirits and coaxing a small smile to her lips.

With a delicate touch, she reached for her favourite mug, a delicate china cup adorned with pretty pink and green floral patterns depicting Chinese peonies and birds. It had borne witness to countless moments of reflection and solace. She poured the steaming water over the coffee grounds, watching as the dark liquid swirled and mingled, releasing its intoxicating aroma. This simple act of brewing a cup of coffee brought her a sense of familiarity and comfort, anchoring her amidst the uncertainties of the world beyond her window.

Outside, the rain continued its rhythmic serenade on the windows, a constant companion to her thoughts. Yet, within the cosy embrace of her apartment, she found solace in the simplicity of this very moment. Savouring her coffee, she allowed its warmth to permeate her, rekindling her weary soul. The fragrant brew offered a brief respite, a fleeting refuge from the world's worries - and a lingering sense that something was amiss. She'd been grappling with that feeling for days, though she chose to dismiss it; life was already intricate enough without unwarranted bouts of paranoia.

As her tasks unfolded, a spark of curiosity ignited within her. She couldn't help but ponder the lives of friends she'd left behind in Ireland – those familiar faces, both close friends and distant acquaintances. The undeniable truth was that she felt achingly alone in Crete, bereft of friends or family to keep her company. With a sigh, she opened her web browser, ushered onto the familiar blue stage of Facebook.Clicking through profiles, she glimpsed fragmented memories and sporadic updates. She saw friends embarking on new journeys, their smiles immortalised in pixels. A wave of nostalgia rolled through her veins, mingling with a faint longing for her life back in Dublin, where rain held a softer allure.

Her gaze lingered on her sister Catherine's profile, captivated by the vibrant display of fiery red hair and the self-assured posture she assumed in front of her cherished chain of coffee shops, The Daily Grind. Emotions swirled within her, a mixture of longing and an unspoken desire to bridge the chasm that had grown between them over the years. As she gazed at the image, bittersweet memories surged forth, recalling happier moments from their childhood and the strained relationship they now bore.

Her fingertips hovered above the screen, yearning for a tangible connection, a way to reclaim the sisterhood she still craved. Yet, the invisible barriers of their fractured relationship loomed large, preventing her from fully embracing the sisterly bond she desired. It was a profound ache, a yearning for reconciliation that seemed tantalisingly close yet frustratingly out of reach. Still, she couldn't forget Catherine's constant criticism and gaslighting behaviour. She could be such a witch.Continuing to scroll, she stumbled upon life's captured fragments in pixels – a friend's sparkling engagement ring, a heartfelt tribute to a departed pet, a sumptuous meal savoured in an elegant restaurant.

Mixed emotions swirled within her, as envy, sorrow, and longing intertwined in a delicate dance. Then, in a moment of serendipity, Patrick's advice echoed in her mind. He had suggested reaching out to Rachel, her old friend from art college, a connection from a time when creativity flowed freely and friendships were built on shared dreams. The idea flickered within her, igniting a spark of possibility. With determination, she typed "Rachel Murphy" into the search bar, sifting through the numerous profiles that shared the same name. A subtle thrill coursed through her when she found a familiar face, adorned with a sprinkling of freckles and a turquoise necklace that mirrored the hues of the sea.

Her heart raced with anticipation as her cursor hovered over Rachel's profile, a digital portal to the past. Clicking through, she was greeted by a glimpse into Rachel's life—a timeline frozen in time. Simple sketches of flowers, a cat's mischievous grin, and faded photographs from an exotic Egyptian escapade in the distant past. It seemed Rachel hadn't updated her profile in ages. There, among the images, she stumbled upon a snapshot of Rachel from 2017. The heavy-set brown haired woman staring back at her appeared weathered, her youthful vibrance replaced by weariness and a hint of sadness in her eyes.

Her curiosity piqued as she delved deeper into Rachel's Facebook profile. No work history, no relationship status—just a digital canvas waiting to be painted with the hues of her past. Questions swirled in her mind, a puzzle begging to be solved. What had Rachel's life been like? What twists and turns had fate thrown her way? Had she ever gotten over failing art college? The absence of information gnawed at Maggie, igniting a relentless yearning to piece together the fragments of Rachel's story. What twists and turns had time sculpted into her journey?

What dreams had she chased? What formidable hurdles had she faced? The void in Rachel's digital profile became a tantalising enigma, urging her to embark on a virtual quest down the rabbit hole of the internet. With each click, she hoped to unearth a breadcrumb, a tempting clue that would lead her closer to the truth. Yet as minutes melted into hours, she found herself adrift in a vast sea of uncertainty. The emptiness in Rachel's online presence bewildered her—googling her yielded no results, as if Rachel had been erased from the online world it seemed.

"Who, in this day and age, has zero digital footprint?" she mused, her curiosity tinged with a hint of unease.

Curiosity, concern, and an unwavering desire to reconnect tugged at her heartstrings. She couldn't help but wonder if Rachel's absence from the internet was a retreat from the world itself. Had she sought solace in the embrace of solitude, retreating into the depths of her own thoughts? Or perhaps Rachel had charted a different course beyond the confines of social media. As she continued her nostalgic scroll, memories rushed forth like a deluge, transporting her back to the exhilarating days of their art college adventure.

Those late-night conversations, steeped in fervent dreams and unbridled ambition, were fueled not only by their boundless creativity but also by the camaraderie shared over cheap bottles of white wine. With every brushstroke, they breathed life into their visions upon the canvas of reality, fueled by audacious beliefs that they were meant to leave an indelible mark upon the art world, much like their revered idols Basquiat and Warhol.

The '90s, with its rebellious spirit and unbounded creativity, felt like a lifetime ago. She could almost hear the echoes of uproarious laughter and impassioned debates that reverberated through the hallowed halls of the Carlisle College of Art. In those days the mantra "anything goes" resonated within the corridors, casting a liberating spell upon every facet of college life. It was an era of freedom and exploration, captured vividly in her old shoebox which was stuffed with photographs of students exuberantly guzzling beers, puffing on cigarettes— everyone smoked back then - even Maggie.

Art college became a sanctuary of boundless expression, where the focus revolved solely around the creation of art. One might stumble upon giant papier-mâché penises adorned with hypodermic needles or a sculpture made entirely of discarded electronic devices and computer parts, meticulously arranged to resemble a futuristic cityscape.. Amidst this whirlwind of artistic expression, there were teachers who embraced the chaos and pushed the boundaries even further. One actively encouraged students to take LSD as a way to unlock their creative potential. Beyond the classroom, art college became a harbour of liberation for her . It stood as a refuge, a respite from the shackles of conventional education. There, the weight of paperwork dissolved into the ether, replaced by the intoxicating freedom to make choices and revel in the glorious messiness of the creative process.

Looking back, she couldn't help but reflect upon the stark contrast with her present work which seemed to consist of nothing but paperwork. But in those bygone days, she had an unquenchable hunger to create, to express herself unabashedly, without the stifling grip of fear or judgement. As she ventured deeper into the recesses of her art college memories, she could almost hear the clatter of pottery wheels, or smell the scent of freshly mixed paint and turpentine, and feel the unmistakable hum of creativity that filled the air, transporting her back to a time when the world seemed brimming with possibility.

She could almost taste the fervour of their discussions, the fervent belief that they were destined for artistic greatness. In those hallowed halls, they would lose themselves in the rhythm of creation, lost in a symphony of colours and textures that brought their visions to life. Their collective pursuit of artistic mastery bound them together, like kindred spirits dancing to the same creative beat.

As her fingers hovered over the message button, a cascade of emotions surged within her. Would Rachel remember their shared adventures, their laughter-filled nights, and the countless cups of coffee that fueled their artistic endeavours? Doubt clouded her thoughts, threatening to dampen the flame of anticipation. Yet, deep within her, a flicker of hope emerged, urging her to embrace vulnerability and reach out for the connection she so longed for.As she hit the send button, a mix of emotions surged within her—excitement, vulnerability, and a tinge of fear. Would Rachel respond? The minutes felt like hours as she anxiously awaited a reply, her gaze shifting between the screen and the raindrops hammering against her the window of her small apartment.

Just as doubt began to creep in, a notification popped up on her screen. Her heart skipped a beat as she saw Rachel's name. With trembling hands, she clicked on the message, and there it was—a genuine and warm response, filled with enthusiasm and an eagerness to reconnect.Tears welled up in her eyes as she read Rachel's words. In that moment, the rain outside seemed to soften, as if the universe itself was offering a glimmer of hope amidst the storm .With newfound excitement, she began to type her reply. Words flowed effortlessly, bridging the gap that time and distance had created. As she poured her heart out onto the screen, she felt the weight of isolation lifting, replaced by a renewed sense of connection and possibility.

Closing her laptop, she glanced out the window once more. The rain had not ceased, but its relentless downpour no longer felt suffocating. Instead, it served as a backdrop to her journey—a reminder that amidst the unexpected twists and turns of life, there was always an opportunity to seek solace, find connection, and embrace the beauty that lay hidden beneath the surface.

With a newfound sense of purpose, she slipped into her light raincoat, its fabric protecting her from the persistent drizzle, and ventured outside towards the beach. The rhythmic sound of raindrops falling against her hood became a comforting backdrop to her thoughts. As she stood at the water's edge, gazing out at the vast expanse of the sea, her feet sinking into the sand, Her mind wandered to the broken pieces of her artistic aspirations. The dream of becoming an artist, once burning bright within her, had been dampened by the realities of life. With each step she took along the wet sand, the rain steadily drenching her, Maggie's anticipation grew. She didn't mind the discomfort; in fact, it seemed fitting—a physical manifestation of the emotional journey she was embarking upon. The raindrops mingled with her own tears, blending together in a symphony of release and renewal.

As she approached the water's edge, a surge of excitement coursed through her veins. Soon, she would have the chance to reconnect with Rachel, to delve into their shared past and talk about that day, the worst day of her life, when together they received the news that they had both failed their final year 4 assessment. With a glimmer of hope, she yearned for their conversation to bring healing, to help her finally lay that moment to rest and find inner peace. The prospect of rediscovering a kindred spirit filled her with a renewed sense of purpose and ignited a spark of optimism. With every rain-soaked breath, she allowed herself to envision a future where her broken dreams could be mended. The drops of water falling from her coat were like a baptism, washing away the residue of doubt and igniting a flicker of hope for healing and a second chance to begin again.

The following day, she stirred from her sleep, only to be greeted by an unwelcome sight -rain. The rain that had persisted throughout the night had intensified into a tempest, unleashing its fury upon the world outside. The sound of raindrops pounding against the windowpane filled the room, a relentless drumbeat of nature's power. With a mixture of curiosity and concern, she ventured into the living room. There, she discovered the balcony door ajar, swung open violently by the forceful gusts of wind. The room was in disarray, as if caught in the midst of a battle with the elements. The once crisp net curtains now clung to the moisture, their delicate fabric damp and dishevelled. Puddles of rainwater scattered across the floor, silently reflecting the stormy skies above and a vase of pink flowers now lay shattered in a million pieces on the cool tiles of the living room floor.

Amidst this chaos, her attention was drawn to a small, shivering figure huddled on the balcony. A frightened kitten, its fur matted and soaked, cast wide-eyed glances of fear and uncertainty. Maggie's heart swelled with empathy as she approached the tiny creature, her voice soft and soothing. "Hello again, little one," she murmured, extending a gentle hand towards it. She gently cradled the trembling kitten in her arms, feeling its wet fur against her skin and hearing its faint cries of hunger. With a determined stride, she hurried into the welcoming warmth of the kitchen, seeking refuge from the relentless storm.

Carefully placing the famished feline on the countertop, she swiftly poured a small amount of milk into a saucer, a humble offering of nourishment. The kitten's wary eyes locked onto the saucer, its hunger overriding any remaining fear. Without hesitation, it eagerly lapped up the milk, its tiny tongue darting hungrily. Just as the kitten satisfied its appetite, she glanced at her watch and gasped in realisation. She had completely forgotten about the Zoom call with her boss, William!

In a panicked flurry, she closed the balcony door, sprinted to the bedroom, and grabbed a brush to tame her wild, rain-soaked hair. With lightning speed, she pulled it back into a chic ponytail, hastily applied some makeup, and threw on a formal looking white silk blouse. Catching a glimpse of herself in the grainy video call, she couldn't help but burst into laughter.

There she was, the epitome of multitasking madness—a half-madeover professional from the waist up, resembling a news anchor on screen. But the hilarity didn't stop there. As she glanced down, she couldn't help but chuckle at the sight of her lower half—a pair of pink knickers and her fluffy white slippers, the unexpected ensemble providing an unintentional comedic twist. Maggie steadied herself with a mix of embarrassment and amusement before joining the virtual Zoom call. Her top half was polished and put-together, while the bottom half remained her lighthearted secret, a testament to the strange reality of remote work.

As the virtual meeting began, a group of faces appeared on the screen, each person locked in their own little world. Emily sat calmly before an impressive bookshelf, which was impeccably arranged with books competing for attention. Her blonde hair was tied neatly in a bun, giving an air of order and professionalism. William's background seemed like he was in a tropical paradise, palm trees gently moving as if daring to challenge the monotony of the meeting. His suntanned appearance added an element of wanderlust to everyone's day, surrounded by those who had been working tirelessly. Demetris joined from his contemporary villa, providing glimpses of luxury through floor-to-ceiling windows that displayed stunning views of the turquoise sea. And then there was Maggie who joined from her humble apartment.

The meeting felt like it had become bogged down with invisible bureaucracy typical of most virtual meetings. Emily surveyed the team sharply, and her tone hinted at scepticism as they delved into monotonous paperwork. As Emily meticulously reviewed funding applications and EU grants, Maggie attempted to stay focused but her eyelids grew heavy with boredom. The names of artists and numbers on the screen blended into an incomprehensible mess, and she struggled to maintain focus.

As the group talked about Evangeline's performance art, Emily spoke with a voice of experience and caution. "So you're suggesting that Evangeline does some performances?" she asked, opening up the topic to further discussion. "I have to admit, I'm not sure if it has any relevance to the project. We must make sure it is in line with our objectives and doesn't draw unwelcome attention from our EU sponsors."Maggie eagerly chimed in with her thoughts. "I understand your point," she interjected. "It might appear out-there but isn't that what makes art interesting? We must take risks, explore unknown territory, and let Evangeline surprise us!"

William, with his laid-back charm, injected a dose of optimism. "I'm with Maggie on this one," he chuckled, his tropical backdrop adding a touch of whimsy. "We shouldn't be afraid of a little wildness. It could add the spice our project needs!" Emily's lips curved into a faint smile, her scepticism softening. "Alright, let's keep an open mind," she conceded. "But we need to ensure we stay true to our vision and project goals."

Seeking solace from Evangeline's performance art discussion, she discreetly opened a new browser tab hoping to find inspiration that would help her through the meeting. Pinterest called out to her, inviting her into an escape from the dry conversation at hand. Emily voiced caution about Evangeline's performance art as the others chimed in to offer their perspectives. As the meeting continued, Maggie's imagination began to wander away from the tedium of the meeting into her little world she grabbed her pen and notepad, and started daydreaming about her wedding, doodling elegant dresses, hearts, and rings on the sides of the page. In her thoughts, Alex proposed to her as the image of a blissful future together played out in her mind. She glanced down at the ring the street seller had made for her when she first arrived in Crete and smiled: it felt like a sign that he was The One.

But then an unwelcome reminder crept up on her: one of her doodles unintentionally depicted a more robust bride than expected. A wave of self-consciousness overwhelmed Maggie at this sight. With a newfound determination, she quickly texted herself, "Book a fitness class with

Katryna immediately!" The thought of being a plus size bride walking down the aisle in an ugly dress with uncomfortable corsets was too unbearable to even consider.

Suddenly, William's voice broke the silence, bringing her back to reality. "Maggie? Maggie, are you still here?" Blushing and taken aback, she composed herself quickly. She stammered, "Oh, um...sorry, William. I lost the connection for a second. You know how the internet can be in Crete." William nodded gravely. "I understand, Maggie, but let's stay focused during this meeting. It's very important that we all participate actively."

Though virtual meetings are often weighed down by bureaucracy, this one seemed no different. Emily's scrutiny lingered over the participants as they shuffled through endless sheets of paperwork. Maggie found herself growing more and more drowsy from the dull conversation and opened up a new browser tab for escape. Her Pinterest homepage beckoned her with its promise of respite from the tediousness, luring her away with its captivating images.

William, added a dose of optimism. "I second Maggie's opinion," he chuckled. "We should embrace the unpredictable side of art. It might be the spice our project desperately needs!" As the virtual meeting dragged on, Maggie's mind began to drift away, yearning for something more delightful amidst the sea of business jargon. Her pen and notepad became her secret portals to an enchanting world of wedding doodles.

As Emily discussed budgets and timelines, Maggie's pen danced across the paper, sketching elegant wedding gowns with intricate lace patterns, hearts, and rings adorning the margins of her notes. As she absentmindedly crafted intricate designs, her mind drifted back to the fantasy of Alex proposing, the image of a joyful and blissful reunion playing out in her thoughts. She looked down at the beautiful ring that the street seller had made for her that day when she first arrived in Crete and she smiled, she knew it was a special sign, a sign that he was the one. But amidst her daydreaming, a subtle sense of unease crept into her consciousness.

One of her doodles unintentionally depicted a bride who appeared much larger than she had intended. The sight of the plumper figure staring back at her triggered a wave of self-consciousness and distress. Feeling a surge of determination, texted herself a reminder In bold letters, she wrote, "Schedule the next fitness class with Katryna immediately!" The thought of being a fat bride, waddling down the aisle in some hideous dress with a built-in corset, was a nightmare scenario she couldn't bear to entertain.

Suddenly, William's voice called her name, jolting her out of her reverie. "Maggie? Maggie, are you still with us?" Caught off guard, her cheeks flushed with embarrassment, and she quickly regained her composure. Blushing, she replied, "Oh, sorry, William. I must have experienced a momentary lapse. The internet connection here in Crete can be quite unpredictable, you know." William's expression remained serious as he nodded. "I understand, Maggie, but let's try to stay focused. It's crucial to be fully engaged in these meetings."

She gave a shy nod, redness blooming beneath her cheeks. "Yes, William. I'm sorry for the interruption. I'll be sure to check my internet connection before we meet next time," she promised. At last, after what seemed like an eternity, William's voice broke through the heavy air. "Alright everyone, that should do it for today. Let's wrap this up and come back with a clear head next week. Remember to stay on task!"

The never-ending virtual meeting finally came to an end, and a sense of liberation washed over Maggie. With a relieved sigh, she let go of the tension that had been building up throughout the call. Glancing at her notebook, she couldn't help but grin at the playful doodles of wedding dresses and hearts that adorned the margins. It had been a creative escape from the mundane discussions that seemed to drag on forever. As she closed her laptop, her mind shifted to the exciting possibilities ahead.

The anticipation of a potential marriage proposal sent a delightful shiver down her spine. Maggie couldn't stop daydreaming about the moment when Alex might pop the question. The thought of taking their relationship to the next level filled her with a mix of happiness and excitement. And beyond her personal life, her mind buzzed with plans for the upcoming art exhibition. Bringing the artists' creations to life in a vibrant display had been a long-standing dream, and now it was finally happening. The prospect of collaborating with Evangeline, the performance artist, ignited her enthusiasm even more.

The morning sun peeked through the curtains, coaxing Maggie out of her slumber. Reluctantly, she opened her eyes to a brand-new day. Reaching for her smartphone on the nightstand, the blinding white light of the screen momentarily stunned her. With a grumble, she tapped the device and was greeted by a notification urging her to "Schedule an appointment with Kateryna." Her mind wandered back to the events of the previous day—the excitement of a possible proposal and the buzz of the upcoming exhibition lingered within her thoughts. Those sparks of excitement added a splash of colour to her morning contemplations. Swiftly, she set up the appointment and gathered her notes, neatly organising them in a black folder. The day ahead held a mix of personal aspirations and professional commitments. The anticipation of her meeting with Evangeline later fueled her drive. The exhibition felt like an intricate puzzle, and she couldn't wait to bring all the pieces together, crafting a captivating showcase that would shine a spotlight on the talents of the artists.

Standing before the mirror, Maggie scrutinised her reflection with a blend of frustration and determination. She yearned for those instant transformations she often saw on Instagram, but she knew that real change took time and effort. It required a good deal of patience and perseverance. With a sigh of acceptance, she smoothed down her black dress, flattering her curves, and slipped into her trusty silver trainers. Imperfect but resolute, she was ready to face the world.

Stepping outside, the city greeted her with its usual chaos—a symphony of car horns, bustling pedestrians, and snippets of conversation drifting through the air. Maggie's heart pounded in her chest, a mix of excitement and nerves intertwining within her. She navigated the urban jungle, heading towards the heart of the city where Evangeline, the enigmatic artist, awaited their encounter for the 'New Voices' project. After an hour of diligently following her Google Maps directions, she found herself in the heart of a forgotten neighbourhood on the outskirts of Rethymnon. This place was a far cry from the charm and glamour the town had to offer. It was like stepping into a time warp, where every building stood abandoned and crumbling, carrying the weight of the forgotten stories of the people who had once lived there.

As she continued to explore, she stumbled upon an old industrial estate that seemed frozen in time. The walls were adorned with vibrant graffiti, a rebellious clash of colours and powerful messages that the frustrated youth of Greece had defiantly scrawled across the surfaces. She pulled out her phone and opened a translation app, capturing the Greek words and phrases to uncover their meaning.One message caught her attention, boldly spray-painted in striking red letters: "Οι άνεργοι είμαστε η φωνή," which translated to "The unemployed are the voice." It was a powerful statement, echoing the frustration and struggles of a generation grappling with high unemployment rates and economic hardships.Further down the wall, Maggie discovered another poignant message: "Το σύστημα μας πνίγει," which meant "The system is suffocating us."

As she stood before the vibrant graffiti, she couldn't help but be moved by the messages etched on the walls. The raw emotions and frustration of the young people resonated with her, tugging at her heartstrings. She imagined the faces of those who had sprayed their emotions onto those walls, their voices echoing through the vivid strokes of spray paint."I wonder where they are now?" Maggie pondered, her gaze shifting from the faded graffiti to her phone once again, seeking directions to her destination.And then, as if the universe had conspired to grant her wish, she looked up from her phone and there it was—Studio 23.

As she carefully navigated the debris, she eventually came across an inconspicuous door. Pushing it open, it groaned as it revealed a surprisingly vibrant space. Adorned with colourful murals, the walls contrasted starkly with the ruins outside. In the centre of the room stood a woman wearing a robotic costume, glowing with intricate electronic parts. A futuristic soundtrack filled the air, exuding creative energy and boundless innovation.

Summoning her courage, Maggie cleared her throat and announced herself over the rhythmic symphony of mechanical sounds. "Hello, Evangeline! I'm Maggie Millar... from Artists Connect!" Her voice struggled to be heard amidst the noise. The woman turned to face her, anything but ordinary. Eva stood tall and slender, around 28 Maggie guessed, her presence commanding attention. With a daring smile, she greeted Maggie, her words infused with challenge and a hint of mischief. "Welcome to my den of rebellion," she proclaimed theatrically, her voice carrying an almost tangible sense of exhilaration.

A chill ran down her spine, a mixture of excitement and trepidation at the enigmatic energy that surrounded this woman. Uncertainty gripped her for a moment, but she pushed it aside, intrigued by what lay before her. "Call me Eva," she suggested, her voice dripping with an alluring coolness. She placed a large metal and glass headpiece onto a nearby table, its intricate design gleaming in the ambient light.

Eva glided across the room, exuding a rockstar chic vibe with her cropped sweatshirt and frayed denim shorts. Her white sneakers completed the look, but it was her neon-coloured hair that truly captivated Maggie. The ombre of yellow and green shades flowed in mesmerising waves around her head, a bold display of individualism.Taking in her surroundings, Maggie noticed large fabric sheets hung from the ceiling, each one with its own unique texture and design. The breeze from an open window created an ethereal dance as the fabrics swayed gracefully.

 She followed Eva's gaze to a large video screen in the corner of the studio, and her eyes lit up with excitement. "I'm really curious to learn more about your work, Eva," she said, her voice genuinely intrigued as she stepped towards the makeshift seating. Eva clicked on a big, glowing remote control, and the lights dimmed, revealing a giant television screen."This is a piece I recently performed in Berlin," Eva said, handing Maggie a booklet filled with words and images that hinted at the depths of her artistic vision. "I think you'll find it... challenging," she added with a mischievous twinkle in her eyes.

The video began to play, immersing she into a world where boundaries dissolved, and inhibitions were left behind. Eva's performance was a visceral experience, and Maggie watched with a mix of shock and horror as she poured animal blood upon herself, the vivid liquid cascading down her skin. The performance was designed to provoke and challenge.Struggling to find the right words, Maggie hesitated before offering her thoughts. "I have to say, Eva, your work is... daring," she said cautiously, attempting to conceal her unease. But the truth was, she found the performance to be disturbing rather than enlightening.

Eva's smirk seemed to mock her response, mischief dancing in her eyes. "Daring is an understatement, my dear," she replied, her voice dripping with playful sarcasm. "I've always believed that art should shake you to your core, but it seems it didn't quite resonate with you, did it?"

Before Maggie could respond, another video began to play, this time revolving around environmental degradation and its impact on marginalised communities. Evan nude again, but this time drenched in paint, flung it haphazardly onto a colossal canvas, passionately shouting phrases about saving the planet. The spectacle didn't end there; at the climax, she dramatically lifted a glass globe filled with glittering sand, releasing it to create a surreal spectacle.

While Maggie recognized the importance of environmental awareness, she couldn't help but question whether Eva's dramatic gestures were merely for show, lacking the depth and nuance necessary to truly engage the audience. Curiosity tugging at her, Maggie couldn't resist asking, "So, Eva, how did you find yourself in the world of performance art?" Leaning back, Eva's gaze wandered to a nearby canvas, her thoughts drifting back to the fragments of memories that shaped her. "It was a moment of rebellion, really," she began, her voice a tapestry of nostalgia and determination.

"I needed an outlet, a sanctuary, to channel the raw emotions and frustrations that come with being a woman in a world that often silences us. Performance art became my refuge, a medium through which I could break free from the constraints of societal expectations and make a bold statement." "Some of it is quite shocking," she nervously interjected, her words trembling like leaves in a gust of wind.

Eva's eyes blazed with a righteous fire, her voice filled with unwavering conviction. "Shocking? Ha! That's the whole point, Maggie," she scoffed, her words dripping with disdain. "The world needs to be jolted out of its complacency, out of its apathy. My art is a rallying cry, a wake-up call for those who choose to ignore the suffering and injustice that plague our society. If it makes people uncomfortable, then it's doing its job."

Maggie's worry intensified as the weight of the unknown bore down upon her. "But Eva, won't it be too provocative?" Eva's laughter reverberated through the studio, exuding a combination of confidence and self-awareness. "My dear, the purpose of art is not to please everyone or conform to expectations," she countered. "It is meant to ignite a fire within, to stir the depths of the soul, and to challenge the status quo. If it rattles a few cages along the way, then it has served its purpose."

Maggie looked at Eva, her eyes wide with admiration and curiosity. She could sense there was more to Eva's passion than met the eye. With a deep breath, Eva began to open up, her voice tinged with sarcasm and a hint of superiority. "You see, Maggie, my work is not for the faint of heart," Eva said with a smug grin. "It takes a certain level of intellect and understanding to appreciate the depths of my art. Clearly, it might be too much for someone like you to grasp."

Her jaw clenched, but she refused to be intimidated. She had encountered difficult artists before, and she wasn't about to let Eva's pompous attitude get under her skin. "Well, I may not fully comprehend your artistic vision, Eva, but I believe that art should also connect with its audience and evoke emotions beyond shock," she retorted, her voice steady.

Eva raised an eyebrow, unimpressed by Maggie's response. "Connecting with the masses is not my goal," she stated dismissively. "I create art for those who can appreciate its complexity and meaning, not for the masses who seek mindless entertainment."Maggie's frustration grew, but she remained composed. "True art has the power to both challenge and connect," she said firmly. "It's not about excluding people; it's about touching souls and sparking conversations. But I suppose your approach is one way of doing things."

Eva's lips curled into a smirk, her superiority complex evident. "Ah, you're just like the rest of them, afraid to embrace true art and revel in its audacity," she quipped, her tone dripping with condescension. he took a deep breath, refusing to let Eva's arrogance get the best of her. "I appreciate that you have a unique perspective, Eva," she replied, her voice measured. "But I believe that art should have a purpose beyond just satisfying the artist's ego. It should have depth and meaning that can resonate with a wider audience."

Eva chuckled, clearly amused by Maggie's stance. "Depth and meaning?" she scoffed. "You're missing the point entirely. My art is meant to challenge the status quo, to make people uncomfortable, to disrupt their complacency. I'm not here to hold their hands and provide easy answers."Maggie felt a surge of frustration but remained determined to stand her ground. "I'm not suggesting you should provide easy answers," she countered. "But alienating your audience with a holier-than-thou attitude will only isolate you as an artist. True creativity lies in finding a balance between pushing boundaries and connecting with others."

Eva's eyes narrowed, her ego bruised by Maggie's words. "You think you understand my art?" she retorted, her voice dripping with sarcasm. "You, with your safe and conventional approach to creativity? You wouldn't know real art if it slapped you in the face." Maggie's patience was wearing thin, but she refused to stoop to Eva's level. "I may not fully understand what you are trying to get across, Eva," she said calmly, "but I do know that true art doesn't require belittling others to make a point. If you want your message to be heard, you might consider being more open to different perspectives."

Eva scoffed, dismissing Maggie's words with a wave of her hand. "I don't need validation from someone who can't appreciate the depth of my work," she said haughtily. "You can stick to your safe, mediocre art, and I'll continue to challenge and inspire those who understand what true creativity is." Maggie took a deep breath, trying to maintain her composure in the face of Eva's arrogance. "I never claimed to be the ultimate authority on art," she said firmly. "But I do believe that art should have the power to unite and inspire, not just divide and alienate."Eva rolled her eyes, clearly uninterested in continuing the conversation. "Well, if you're done wasting my time with your shallow opinions, I have work to do," she said dismissively.

Feeling both disappointed and relieved, Maggie decided to take her leave. "Very well, Eva," she replied. "I hope your part in the exhibition goes well, and I wish you all the best with your art."As she walked away,

Maggie couldn't help but feel a mix of emotions. Eva's arrogance had left a bitter taste in her mouth, but she also couldn't deny the impact of Eva's work. It was undeniably provocative and daring, even if she disagreed with Eva's approach.

Deep down, Maggie knew that art came in many forms, and while Eva's attitude might be difficult to stomach, her commitment to pushing boundaries was undeniable. As she left the vibrant studio behind, Maggie couldn't help but wonder about the complexities of art and the different ways it could impact people.As the days passed, Maggie found herself grappling with Eva's words and her own beliefs about art. She was excited about Alex's impending arrival in Crete, and yet, the encounter with Eva had left a mark on her - and an eerie feeling of dread - one that she just couldn't shake.

After the tense and disheartening meeting with Eva, Maggie felt her spirits plummet like a deflating balloon. The excitement she had carried before now lay dormant, replaced by a cloud of doubt and scepticism hovering over her. Thomas and Eva had left a bitter taste in her mouth, but she knew she had to soldier on, hoping to find a glimmer of artistic hope amid the storm.

Next on the list was Atticus, the hat-loving painter, and a wave of worry crashed over her. The memory of the previous encounters left her on edge, wondering if this meeting would be just as challenging. Doubts swirled like a tempest in her mind: Would he be open to collaboration, or was she destined to face another uphill battle on this seemingly cursed project? The uncertainty weighed heavy on her heart as she stepped into the unknown, bracing herself for whatever lay ahead.

Chapter 8: The Long Wait is Over...

The next Saturday morning, Maggie stood amidst the lively bustle of the crowded bus station, her heart brimming with excitement and anticipation. The Mediterranean sun blazed overhead, urging her to cling to her elegant straw hat, a shield for her fair complexion against the scorching rays. Her wispy pale pink dress fluttered in the **simmering** heat, and beads of sweat formed on her forehead, yet she remained spellbound by the vibrant energy enveloping her—the station alive with the buzz of travellers from different corners of the world, chatting in various languages, laughter weaving through the air.

Brimming with excitement, Maggie wandered over to a nearby kiosk at the bus station, her thirst calling for relief from the scorching heat. She reached for a bottle of water and grabbed a newspaper, eager to catch up on the latest world events as she waited for the bus. As she sipped the cool water, she scanned the headlines, her eyes drawn to the stories of climate change and its impact on the world. Finally, the bus arrived, and as Maggie stepped aboard, families excitedly planned their adventures, couples shared loving glances, and solo travellers captured the essence of their journey through their camera lenses. The cool blast of air conditioning offered a welcome respite from the Cretan heat, and Maggie found a seat by an open window, savouring the refreshing breeze.

Amidst the scenic beauty and camaraderie of fellow travellers, her mind drifted back to memories of Alex—their first meeting 5 years ago when she went to see his band, Ramshackle, play in Dublin, his habit of buying flowers for her every Thursday, the shared laughter, the warmth of his touch. Their bond felt like an invisible thread weaving their hearts together, and a mix of excitement, uncertainty, and hope filled her as the bus carried her forward. Alex was her North Star, guiding her, and the thought of their reunion was the wind propelling her forward.

As the bus rumbled along, its worn-out appearance seemed insignificant compared to the picturesque landscape unfolding outside the dusty windows. Each turn of the winding roads revealed a new wonder—the shimmering olive groves, like a sea of silver leaves, glistening under the sun's caress. The expansive blue ocean stretched like a vast canvas, brushed with hues of turquoise and aquamarine. Charming villages nestled against rugged cliffs looked like blurred paintings brought to life.

Inside the bus, the air carried a distinct scent—a blend of sweat and sunblock, a testament to the determination of passengers braving the unseasonably hot temperatures. Despite the discomfort, some still wore their COVID masks, a lingering reminder of a time when the world stood suspended in uncertainty, a time that had shaped their journeys.

As Maggie's eyes scanned the pages of her newspaper, her attention was drawn to a headline that hit her like a punch to the gut. "Rhodes Wildfires: British Tourist Says Trying to Escape the Flames 'Was Literally Like the End of the World.'" The words weighed heavy on her heart as she read on. The scorching temperatures, reaching up to 44°C, had caused chaos, leading to the largest wildfire evacuation in Greece's history, with 19,000 people forced to leave their homes.

The article served as a stark reminder of the changing climate and its devastating consequences. She imagined the tourists at the Acropolis, seeking shade and respite from the scorching heat. She pictured the elderly, seeking solace indoors, away from the unforgiving rays of the sun. It all seemed almost unreal, a sobering glimpse into the impact of environmental shifts on people's lives.

As the bus continued its journey, the contrasting scenes outside and the news within the paper created a dissonance within Maggie. The beauty of the landscape clashed with the harsh reality of natural disasters, leaving her feeling both captivated and troubled. It was a poignant moment that made her reflect on the fragility of the world and the need for collective action to protect it.

Another headline drew her gaze, "Venice's Last Stand: City Crumbling into the Sea." The picture of eminent scientists, their worried expressions mirrored her own concerns. Venice, a symbol of beauty and history, was facing its own existential crisis. The news painted a grim picture, predicting that the city might have only 10 more years before it succumbed to the rising waters.

With trembling hands, Maggie turned to the next page of the newspaper, and her heart sank as she was confronted with horrifying images from the war in Ukraine. The stark reality of human suffering, the devastation, and the sheer brutality of it all were too much to bear. She quickly shut the newspaper, unable to stomach any more of the heart-wrenching images. It was a painful reminder of the harshness of the world, a world where countless lives were torn apart by conflict, climate change and violence.

Seeking solace, she lifted her gaze from the distressing print on the page and directed it towards the breathtaking views beyond the dusty bus windows. The picturesque landscape seemed almost surreal, a stark contrast to the darkness she had just witnessed. The shimmering olive groves, bathed in the golden rays of the sun, offered a sense of tranquillity amidst the chaos of the outside world. The expansive blue ocean stretched endlessly, inviting her to lose herself in its vastness, if only for a moment.

The weight of the world's problems bore down on Maggie's heart. The world seemed to be crying out for action, demanding a collective effort to address the challenges at hand. She wondered how she, as an individual, could make a difference in the face of such overwhelming global issues.

Her thoughts were drawn back to Eva's powerful performance, a simple yet impactful message about saving the planet. Eva's heartfelt plea resonated in her mind, urging everyone to take responsibility for the world they inhabited. In stark contrast, Thomas appeared to be spiralling down a different path, seeking solace in self-destruction. Both of them were seeking a second chance at life, and somehow, she felt a sense of responsibility for helping them find it..As the bus journey continued, the outside landscape seemed to mirror the turmoil in Maggie's mind. The earth, kissed by the sun, stretched out with shimmering olive groves, presenting a picture of both beauty and fragility. It served as a poignant reminder of the delicate balance that needed to be preserved in the world.

The bus journey continued, the landscape outside becoming a blur, but inside the bus, time stood still for Maggie. In this suspended moment, she found herself lost in thoughts of Alex, reminiscing about their laughter, the tender moments they shared, and the profound connection they had forged. The bus eventually glided to a stop, its mechanical hum blending with the symphony of the airport terminal. As Maggie stepped off, her excitement palpable, she maintained a composed exterior. The scorching sun cast shadows on the concrete, and the distant sound of luggage wheels echoed like a rhythmic melody. She was ready to embrace the joyous reunion that awaited her

The arrivals board shimmered with enticing destinations—Madrid, Mariselles, Lisbon, and Scotland—a captivating array of potential journeys and cultures awaiting discovery. Maggie checked her notepad, and the time read 6:30 PM. She verified it against the digital clock on the arrivals screen, her heart pounding with excitement. Standing at the arrivals gate, she couldn't help but be enthralled by the diverse tapestry of characters emerging from the plane. Each person seemed to carry a unique story etched upon their faces and expressed through their body language, like living books yearning to be read.

In the bustling arrivals gate of the airport, a sea of taxi drivers eagerly held up signs with names written in bold letters. Each sign represented a unique story—a tale of a traveller's journey, their destination, and the connection that awaited them on the other side. Among the crowd, one person stood out—the first to disembark—an attractive young woman adorned with cornrowed hair, radiating confidence with her enhanced pout and false lashes. Her bold attire, featuring flesh-coloured yoga pants hugging her curves and a daring bra top in the same shade, left little to the imagination. The sight captured the attention of several nearby men, who gazed with awe.

Following closely behind was a man whose stern countenance reminded Maggie of the strange scientology leader, David Miscavige. Dressed sharply in a sleek black suit and gripping a briefcase, he navigated through the bustling crowd with determined focus, shouting loudly into a smartphone : "I need those numbers by yesterday!" he barked, his tone enough to make anyone shudder. His eyes remained fixed on his destination, never wavering from his purpose, giving him an air of authority and arrogance.

As more passengers emerged, each with their unique style and energy, Maggie couldn't help but be fascinated by the human tapestry unfolding before her. A group of giggling friends huddled together, sharing inside jokes and unforgettable memories from their journey. An elderly couple, hands intertwined, exuded a profound sense of comfort and companionship.

In stark contrast, a teenage girl emerged from the plane, a vibrant vision in her neon pink dress that seemed to defy the sea of muted colours around her. Obsessed with capturing the perfect angle, she was in a world of her own, engrossed in taking incessant selfies, seemingly oblivious to the wonders unfolding in the world beyond her screen.

With each person that emerged from the plane, Maggie's heart skipped a beat, hoping that the next one would be Alex. Her eyes darted from face to face, trying to catch a glimpse of his familiar features. At one point, a man with similar curly hair and a backpack on his shoulder appeared, and for a moment, her heart leaped with excitement. But as he drew closer, Maggie's hopes deflated, and she realised it wasn't him.

As the crowd gradually thinned, Maggie's anxiety grew. Doubt gnawed at the edges of her mind, wondering if she had somehow missed him or if there was a delay. Her heart ached with each passing second, and she tried to stay patient, reminding herself that he would be here soon.Amidst the lively commotion, Maggie's focus remained fixed on the arrivals board, her anticipation building with every passing second. Maggie's heart sank as the trickle of passengers finally ceased, and Alex was still nowhere to be seen. Panic threatened to overwhelm her, and tears welled up in her eyes. Her mind raced with worry and doubt, and for a fleeting moment, she felt a wave of hopelessness wash over her. Just as she was on the brink of giving in to despair, her eyes caught a glimpse of a familiar figure in the distance. Like a ray of sunlight breaking through the clouds, she saw him. There he was, strolling confidently out of the plane with that warm smile that made her heart skip a beat.As their eyes met, a sense of relief

As the bustling airport crowd swirled around her, Maggie's heart quickened its pace, and time seemed to slow to a crawl. And then, there he was—the man she had been yearning for, with blue jeans that clung to his lightly tanned skin, a mop of curly brown hair tousled in the breeze, and a T-shirt boasting the iconic Rolling Stones open mouth emblem. The sight of him sent a jolt of electricity through her veins, igniting a fire that had been smouldering in her heart during their time apart.

Their eyes locked, and without a second thought, Maggie ran towards him, drawn by an invisible force that defied the distance between them.

As she reached him, he flung his arms around her in a tight embrace, and their lips met in a passionate kiss that ignited the world around them. It was as if time stood still, leaving only the two of them in the universe, entangled in a love that transcended everything else.

"My sweet girl," he whispered in her ear, his voice a tender caress. "I love you so much. I have missed you so much."His words enveloped her like a warm blanket, and she felt her worries and doubts melt away in his arms. Her gaze met his, and in that moment, everything they had endured seemed insignificant compared to the overwhelming joy of being reunited."I thought that you'd never come," she admitted, her voice soft but filled with a mix of relief and vulnerability. "But you are here now, and that is all that matters."

Their eyes locked, and in that moment, the world around them seemed to fade away, leaving only the two of them in their own little universe.The guitar pressed between them, a tangible symbol of his presence and the music that connected them. The airport noise seemed to dull to a hushed murmur as they held each other, lost in the comfort of being together again. " Sorry I couldn't come sooner, but I couldn't turn up the chance at Counterflows" he said, looking deep into her eyes."I know," she said, burying her face in the crook of his neck, inhaling his familiar scent that instantly calmed her nerves. "But the wait felt like an eternity.""I promise, I'll never make you wait that long again," he said, his voice filled with sincerity.

As they finally pulled away from their passionate embrace, the air crackled with electricity, and an exhilarating sense of euphoria enveloped them both. It was as if their souls had been set on fire, ignited by the intensity of their love. With bright smiles adorning their faces, they intertwined their fingers and began to wander out of the bustling airport.Hand in hand, they navigated through the sea of people, their connection palpable to anyone who caught a glimpse of them. Each step felt like a new adventure, a journey they were embarking on together. They exchanged glances, laughter bubbling between them like a symphony of joy.

Finally free from the confines of the airport, they hailed a taxi, its blue and red paint standing out in the sea of vehicles. The driver, a warm and friendly local, greeted them with a welcoming smile as they hopped into the backseat."Where to, lovebirds?" the driver asked with a hint of playfulness in his voice."Take us to the heart of Chania," Alex replied, a glimmer of excitement in his eyes. "We've got some exploring to do.

As the taxi pulled away from the airport, Maggie and Alex sat close together, their fingers intertwined, as they watched the world outside the window pass by in a blur of lights and colours. In that moment, they felt like they were the only two people in the world, wrapped up in the cocoon of their love and the promise of what lay ahead. They were two souls, entwined and destined to explore the world together, hand in hand, and heart to heart.

They watched through the window as the cityscape unfolded, a blend of history and modernity. Ancient ruins whispered stories of the past, coexisting harmoniously with bustling shops and lively cafes."I wonder if they'll still be holding hands a year from now," he thought to himself, a hint of sarcasm in his mental remark. He had seen countless couples come and go, their passions fizzling out like sparklers on a damp night.But Maggie was totally oblivious, she had never been happier in her entire life. She felt a surge of gratitude for the twists and turns that had led her to this very moment. Life had a funny way of working out, and in that moment, she knew that all the waiting, the doubts, and the distance were worth it.

The taxi ride was an exhilarating dance through the bustling city streets. The driver weaved through traffic with expert skill, yet there was a hint of recklessness in his manoeuvres that added a dash of excitement to the journey. The city lights streaked by like shooting stars, casting fleeting shadows on the couple seated in the backseat. Throughout the ride, their words were scarce, but their desire for each other spoke volumes. Their eyes locked, and a palpable tension filled the air, each stolen glance intensifying the anticipation.

Alex's hand, bold and daring, ventured up Maggie's skirt, sending a lightning bolt of desire straight to her core. The heat between them was palpable, a magnetic force pulling them closer with every passing moment. The taxi seemed to move in slow motion as they neared her apartment. Maggie's heart raced, the rhythmic thumping echoing in her ears. She felt almost overwhelmed by the longing that surged within her, the delightful tension lingering unspoken between them during that long journey home.

As the taxi came to a stop, their eyes met once more, and they shared an unspoken understanding. The driver's presence felt like a mere afterthought as Alex helped Maggie out of the car, their hands interlocked in a tight embrace. The anticipation was electrifying, the air charged with the promise of what was to come. With trembling fingers, Maggie fumbled for her keys, her heart pounding in her chest. As they entered the dimly lit apartment, a sense of intimacy enveloped them. The outside world faded away, leaving only the two of them in their private sanctuary.

Without a word, Alex lifted Maggie's chin, and their lips met in a searing kiss that ignited their souls. It was a kiss that tasted of desire and longing, of all the months they had spent apart, finally coming together in this moment of passion and intimacy. Time seemed to stand still as they explored each other's lips, the intensity of their connection growing with each passing second. Maggie's fingers traced the contours of Alex's body, feeling the warmth of his skin beneath her touch. He let out a low moan, and in that sound, she sensed that he was just as overcome with desire as she was. Their bodies pressed together, a symphony of desire and longing merging into one. In that intimate space, they surrendered to each other, their bodies moving in perfect harmony. The night was filled with a crescendo of passion and pleasure, a dance of two lovers reunited after so many months apart. Their love was a wildfire, consuming them both in its fiery embrace.

As dawn broke, they lay entwined in each other's arms, their bodies glistening with a sheen of sweat. In the warm glow of the morning light seeping through the sheer white curtains, Maggie savoured lying close to Alex, listening to the steady rhythm of his breath as he drifted in and out of sleep. She felt grateful for this man, whom she believed was sent to her by destiny. The apartment seemed like a chaotic tsunami of their passionate encounter, with embroidered pillows strewn around, flowered sheets and a blue-striped duvet carelessly tossed at the bed's foot. Her patchwork quilt lay in a heap, and clothing—jeans, a brown leather jacket, a pink lace bra, a light pink dress, and a sunhat—decorated the floor.

As Alex stirred and pulled her close, she felt the warmth of his body, and he whispered softly, "What makes you so special then?" In her drowsy state, she murmured, "W-What?" He immediately apologised, wondering why he woke her. But she reassured him that she cherished these intimate moments, nestling her head into his chest. The golden rays of the Mediterranean sun streamed into the cosy apartment, but they failed to dispel the growing unease in Maggie's heart. Alex's hand gently moved down to her stomach, giving it a playful pat. "It looks like you've been enjoying the Cretan food," he laughed with a hint of sarcasm. His words hit her like a cold gust of wind, and her heart sank. "Do you think I've gained weight?" she asked, her voice trembling with embarrassment. Her cheeks flushed with a rosy hue, feeling exposed and vulnerable.

"Your weight, Maggie, goes up and down, it always has," he replied, attempting reassurance, but it only added to her confusion and hurt." I prefer it when it is down, but you're certainly larger than when I last saw you in Dublin," he added. His words left her grasping for understanding, unsure if it was a compliment or a veiled criticism. Internally, she struggled to process his comment. She wanted to brush it off and pretend it didn't bother her, to hide her vulnerability. But the ache of hurt lingered, haunting her like a shadow in the back of her mind.

The room that once felt so warm and intimate now seemed distant, the laughter and passion fading away, replaced by an awkward silence filled with unspoken emotions and insecurities. Maggie tried to shift the conversation away from her body, dismissing his comment as innocent teasing. But the pang of insecurity persisted, the memories of past judgments about her appearance resurfacing and deepening the weight she already carried.

As the morning light painted patterns on the walls, Maggie struggled to push the sad thoughts away. She attempted to muster unwavering conviction that today would be a good day, but beneath the facade, doubt and self-consciousness still prevailed, casting a dark cloud over her emotions.

She lay there, seeking refuge in a distant memory of visiting the temple of Aphrodite with Pangotis. His words echoed in her mind, "No one is perfect, not even the goddess of beauty. And anyway, it's really our flaws that make us beautiful. Perfection is cold." But those comforting words couldn't silence the whispers of insecurity, especially after Alex's comment. She yearned to confide in him, to share her vulnerability and seek solace in his arms, but the fear of misunderstanding and rejection held her back.

With a conflicted heart, she mustered the courage to gently brush her fingers against his cheek, savouring the warmth of his skin. In that moment, she wanted to hold onto the intimacy they shared the night before, but the weight of his words remained, creating an invisible barrier between them. As the jarring sound of the alarm clock shattered the tranquillity, the silence that hung between them was abruptly broken. She let out a soft groan, realising with regret that she had an appointment at half ten. As she dressed, a sense of sadness settled over her. Alex's comment about her weight still weighed heavily on her mind, leaving her hurt and confused. She knew that one remark couldn't define their relationship, but the uncertainty lingered, clouding her emotions.

With resolve, Maggie made her way to the door, a lingering glance back at Alex, who was suffering from jet lag and had decided to sleep in, as she stepped into the outside world the taste of their bittersweet reunion clung to her like a delicate perfume. The door closed behind her, she couldn't shake the memory of Alex's warmth and the whispered words that left her heart in disarray. The world outside beckoned with its promises, but doubt and confusion simmered just beneath the surface. She knew she had to face her insecurities head-on, but the path ahead seemed foggy and uncertain.

With tears in her eyes, she turned on Spotify, seeking solace in George Michael's 'I knew You Were Waiting,' a song that perfectly captured her current emotional state. As the music enveloped her, she clung to the melody like a lifeline, vowing to keep her faith intact. The lyrics became an anthem of perseverance, reassuring her that their love story would unfold in its own time and place. "Nothing can stop me, no, Knew you were waiting for me." The song breathed life into her hopes and dreams, reminding her that love would find a way, no matter the obstacles.

Chapter 9: Scars of the Past

The scorching sun blazed high in the sky as Maggie made her way through the labyrinth of bustling streets in the heart of Rethymno. The city seemed to pulse with energy, and the air was thick with a medley of scents from street vendors selling their delicacies. She couldn't help but feel the excitement building within her, knowing that she was about to meet Atticus, the third artist she would collaborate with on the project, "New Voices."

Her heart pounded with anticipation, and she kept checking her phone for any last-minute updates from the cafe where they were scheduled to meet, just in case there was a last minute change of plans. As she scrolled through her notifications, a message from her old art college friend,

Rachel, caught her eye. "Hey Glippie, do you want to Facetime sometime this week? " The nickname "Glippie" brought a nostalgic smile to her face. It had been almost 15 years since they last spoke, and she was thrilled at the prospect of catching up with Rachel filled her with excitement. "I'd love to catch up, Rachel! It's been way too long. Let's definitely Facetime this week," Maggie replied, her excitement evident in her quick typing. She felt a sense of warmth knowing that amidst the hectic art project, she would have a chance to reconnect with an old friend.

As she continued on her way, the narrow streets of Rethymno seemed to come alive with vibrant colours and captivating sounds, the clinking of glasses from nearby cafes added to the symphony of life around her and the cool sea breeze was a welcome relief from the blistering sun. The city's charm enveloped her, momentarily easing her nerves about meeting Atticus. Her heart raced as she stepped into "Kafenio Chromata," a captivating coffee shop nestled in the enchanting labyrinthine streets of the old town - the most charming part of the city. The air was thick with the aroma of freshly brewed coffee, intermingled with the unmistakable energy of creativity that filled the space.

Her eyes darted around the coffee shop until they landed on him, tucked away in a corner as if he were a secret waiting to be unravelled. She recalled Demetris mentioning his fondness for hats, and there it was—a striking red fedora perched atop his head. The hat seemed to add an air of mystery, casting a shadow over his soulful eyes, which looked tired and sleep deprived. .He sat there with an air of quiet confidence, dressed in a long-sleeved blue linen shirt that draped casually over his lean frame. Despite his poised exterior, she couldn't help but notice the subtle fidgeting with his shirt cuffs, a telltale sign of nervousness lurking beneath the surface.

As he glanced around the room, a subtle blush warmed his cheeks, almost as if he were unsure of being noticed. Yet, there was an undeniable magnetism in his presence, a pull that drew her closer to uncover the essence of his enigmatic presence."Hi, you must be Maggie," he said with genuine warmth, extending a hand adorned with multiple rings that seemed to reflect his creative personality.A genuine smile graced her lips at the sight of his infectious enthusiasm. "Yes, I am. It's great to finally meet you, Atticus. I've heard so much about your work."

The café seemed to fall away around them as they settled into their conversation, flowing effortlessly like old friends catching up over coffee. As the conversation unfolded, her curiosity intensified, and she couldn't resist the burning question in her mind. "Atticus, I'd love to see some of your art. Do you have anything you could show me?" For a moment, hesitation and excitement danced in his eyes, before he nodded with a hint of vulnerability. "Sure," he replied, opening his old laptop. The slideshow began, and Maggie's breath caught in her throat. Skillfully painted male figures graced the screen, their embraces and expressions painting a tapestry of emotions.

The fusion of realism and modern artistry, reminiscent of the great Hockney, breathed life into each piece, making them wholly Atticus's own. Intricate brushstrokes danced across the canvas, infusing the paintings with a raw intimacy and vulnerability that stirred her soul. Each artwork was a vivid story, with delightful colours like pale lemons, icy blues, and vibrant oranges and reds. The nudes, confident and bold, expressed passion and vulnerability in every brushstroke. Emotions whispered through the vibrant pigments, drawing the onlookers into the soul of the artist. Colours spoke louder than words, creating a symphony of emotions on canvas.

At the other end of the coffee shop, a tempest of emotions exploded as a couple found themselves caught in a passionate and tumultuous argument. The atmosphere thickened with tension, and onlookers couldn't help but be drawn to the spectacle about to unfold.Maggie, her eyes filled with a mix of amusement and intrigue, chuckled softly, appreciating Atticus's witty perspective amidst the dramatic scene. "Well, this is one way to spice up our first meeting," she said, her eyes twinkling with amusement.

The girl, with fiery eyes and flushed cheeks, fixed her partner with an intense gaze. In a fit of unbridled rage, she unleashed a torrent of words in Greek, her voice echoing through the café, "Ξεπατίσεις χοίρους, σε εμπιστεύτηκα!" Her gestures were wild, hands animatedly gesturing in the air as she poured out her fury.In a dramatic flourish, she hurled her coffee cup to the floor, unleashing a cacophony of chaos as the ceramic shattered into a thousand fragments, sending splashes of steaming coffee in all directions. The people in the coffee shop gasped in surprise, jumping out of their chairs to avoid the sharp pieces of china and scalding liquid that danced perilously across the room.

Amidst the chaos, Atticus, a keen observer, took it upon himself to translate the girl's heated words to his friend Maggie. "She just said: 'You cheating swine, I trusted you!'" he relayed, his voice tinged with intrigue. As they watched the couple's emotions continue to erupt like a volcanic eruption, Atticus couldn't resist adding another playful remark, "I hope their love wasn't as fragile as that coffee cup!"The overweight owner of the coffee shop rushed over to the quarrelling couple, his face red with anger. "Enough of this madness! Get out of my café!" he bellowed, his voice booming over the commotion.

As the dramatic scene continued to unfold, Atticus leaned in, eagerly sharing the juicy backstory behind this passionate confrontation. "He's been cheating on her," he revealed, a mischievous gleam in his eye. "She checked his smartphone while he went to the bathroom." Maggie and Atticus were thoroughly enthralled by the unfolding drama. A knowing smile played on hia lips as he made a witty comment to lighten the mood, though the tension in the air remained palpable. "Well, it seems like they've brewed up quite the storm," he remarked, his eyes glinting with amusement.The couple, now chastised by the owner's outburst, reluctantly made their way to the exit, their argument still simmering, but subdued. The people in the coffee shop watched in a mixture of relief and curiosity as the door closed behind the departing pair, leaving behind a shattered coffee cup and scattered emotions.

In the aftermath of the dramatic outburst, the coffee shop slowly returned to its usual tranquillity, but the incident left an indelible mark on the atmosphere. Whispers of the scene circulated among the patrons as they returned to their seats, exchanging curious glances and hushed discussions about the unforgettable spectacle they had just witnessed. As Maggie and Atticus resumed their exploration of the paintings, they couldn't help but laugh about the drama they had just witnessed.

As they looked through more of the artwork, Atticus's vulnerability came to the fore. He leaned in, his voice softer, sharing the struggles of an emerging artist trying to navigate the treacherous waters of financial uncertainty. "I've been pouring my soul into my work, but the financial aspect is tough. This month, the studio rent has me on edge," he admitted, his fingers absentmindedly tapping on the edge of his coffee cup. His admission struck a chord within her, and Maggie's empathy deepened as she understood the battles he fought silently. "I can't imagine how challenging that must be. Your art is extraordinary—it deserves to be seen and appreciated by the world," she reassured, reaching out to gently place her hand on his arm in a gesture of comfort.

A hint of weariness played across his face, as though the weight of his journey had momentarily settled upon him. "Thank you for saying that. I've been at a crossroads lately, considering getting a normal job just to make ends meet. But my passion lies here. I don't want to go back to waiting tables. Rethymno is a beautiful place, but jobs are scarce, and I want to keep pursuing my dream," he confessed, his eyes searching hers forconnection.Her heart swelled with understanding, knowing the struggle of choosing between practicality and one's passion. "I get it. The road of an artist is rarely smooth, but I believe in you and your unique talent. The funding from Artists Connect could be a turning point for you," she encouraged.

Hope shimmered in Atticus's eyes, a glimmer of light in the darkness of uncertainty. "You really think so?" "Absolutely," Maggie affirmed. "Your art carries a soulful depth that resonates with people. With the right exposure and support, it will find its audience." A cocktail of emotions danced across Atticus's face—hope, doubt, and a flicker of determination. "It's a tough road, but I can't let go of my dream. I need this funding to keep going, to have the space and resources to create."

Hours passed like minutes, and the coffee shop began to empty as the day waned. As their meeting came to a close, Atticus picked up his laptop to put it back into his bag. In that moment, his long-sleeved shirt shifted, revealing a myriad of scars on his wrist and arm. Maggie's eyes widened in shock and concern, the revelation striking her like a thunderbolt. "Oh, Atticus," she whispered, her hand automatically covering her mouth. "I had no idea..." Her heart ached for the pain he must have endured,A flicker of vulnerability passed over him, but their gazes locked, and a moment of truth flowed between them.

"It was a long time ago, I was just really, really lonley" he said, clearly embarrassed, trying to explain it away, but the vulnerability in his eyes spoke louder than any words.Even though he was a complete stranger, she reached out and hugged him as tightly as she could.He hesitated for a moment before surrendering to the comfort of her presence, and then the tears flowed—a testament to the burden he had been carrying alone."It's okay," she whispered, her touch reassuring. Her voice was gentle as she said, "Don't worry, I'm not going to say anything about this, okay?" She wanted him to know that she accepted him as he was, and that she would protect his vulnerability with the utmost care.

"Thanks," he responded, choking on his words and fighting back tears. "And, for heaven's sake, don't worry about the rent. We can release some of the funding to help you out—you don't have to struggle alone." The weight that had burdened him for so long was now being shared, and it brought a sense of relief he hadn't known was possible. In that moment, the coffee shop seemed to fade away, leaving just the two of them connected in a profound moment of understanding ..

As she bid him farewell and left the coffee shop, Maggie was in a state of shock and sadness. She couldn't help but feel pained for Atticus, someone so incredibly talented yet haunted by past scars. But she also felt a newfound sense of purpose—to support him and help him in any way that she could. Their encounter had changed something within her, igniting a fierce determination to stand by him, no matter what challenges lay ahead.

After her meeting with him, Maggie was still in a state of shock, her mind haunted by the image of his scarred arms and wrists. She felt an overwhelming sense of heartbreak for him, wondering what could have driven him to harm himself in such a disturbing way. A motherly urge to protect him surged within her as she found herself aimlessly wandering through the cobbled streets, trying to process the emotional encounter.

Amidst her thoughts, her phone buzzed with an incoming call from Alex. "Hey, Maggie! I'm out sightseeing, but how about we meet for dinner at around 8 PM?" Alex's voice carried excitement and enthusiasm. "You know that spot 'Taverna Athene'? It's got a fantastic view of the sea. Let's make tonight special!" Despite the lingering comments from that morning, she pushed them aside. The thought of seeing Alex again brought a smile to her face, and she eagerly agreed, "Sounds perfect, Alex! I'll be there."

After a scenic yet somewhat sombre bus ride along the sun-kissed coast of Greece, Maggie stepped off the local bus near the Aegean Breeze hotel and made her way to her cosy apartment. The vibrant energy of the seaside town seemed almost surreal, a stark contrast to the weight that had been pressing on her shoulders. She shed her denim jacket at the entrance and, with a sense of purpose, quickly changed into her workout gear. Today's session with Kateryna on the GoFit Platform wasn't just about fitness; it was a much-needed escape from the events of the afternoon.

As Maggie logged into her GoFit account, the screen came to life, revealing Kateryna on the other end. Something seemed amiss about her today—she appeared thinner, with more stress lines etched onto her face than Maggie remembered. Concern flooded her heart, and she greeted her with warmth, "Hi, Kateryna. It's so nice to see you again. Is everything okay on your end?"Kateryna responded with a half-smile, her voice tinged with weariness, "I'm hanging in there. I live at the Dnipro Elysium apartments, in a safe part of town. It's been tough, but we're managing."

Maggie nodded, recalling a bit of architectural trivia, "I've heard of those, I think. Weren't they designed by a famous architect?"Kateryna's eyes brightened a little, appreciating the diversion. "Yes, it's an Art Nouveau style building designed by V. Gorodetsky in 1903. I feel lucky to live here."Maggie's eyes lit up at the mention of Art Nouveau. "Art Nouveau is my absolute favorite style of architecture. It's incredibly beautiful."Kateryna's face softened, but the weight of her troubles still lingered. "It truly is," she agreed. "Anyway, I'm grateful for this class. It's a welcome distraction and a chance to connect with familiar faces."

They commenced their workout, but an unspoken heaviness filled the virtual room. Moments passed, accompanied only by their synchronised movements. Then, Kateryna broke the silence, her voice carrying a wisdom that seemed beyond her years.

"Maggie," she began, her tone gentle yet profound, "life has a way of tossing us into unexpected storms. We find ourselves battling against relentless tides, struggling to stay afloat." Her movements took on a graceful quality as she spoke, akin to a dancer lost in her own rhythm. "But it's in these tempests that we discover the depth of our strength." Maggie listened with rapt attention, captivated by Kateryna's words.

Kateryna continued, "Strength isn't just about physical endurance, although that's important. It's about the power to endure, to persevere, no matter how fiercely the winds blow, you know?" Her eyes met Maggie's through the screen, forging a profound connection. "It's about finding that inner light that guides us through the darkest of nights." Maggie's breaths fell in sync with her instructor's, and the digital room seemed to blur away.

"As we confront our struggles," Kateryna concluded, her voice steady, "we must remember that even amidst chaos, we hold the power to choose our response. We can choose strength, to keep moving forward, one step at a time." Maggie whispered, her voice laden with emotion, "Thank you." Kateryna responded with a serene smile, her eyes reflecting an unwavering resilience. "Always remember, Maggie, you're far stronger than you realise. We all are."

As the virtual exercise class came to an end, Maggie felt a renewed sense of purpose and strength. She thanked Kateryna sincerely for the workout and the wisdom she had imparted. However, even as she bid farewell and closed her laptop, a lingering sense of admiration and inspiration clung to her heart. She couldn't help but feel a deep respect for the young woman, whose words had resonated far beyond their virtual fitness class.

As she got ready for her dinner date with Alex, she found herself unable to shake the weight of the world that seemed to rest heavily on Kateryna's shoulders. The feeling of helplessness gnawed at her, and she hated the overwhelming sense of powerlessness that washed over her. The images of conflict and suffering that Kateryna must be witnessing haunted her mind, and she couldn't bear the thought of her enduring such turmoil. The weight of her meeting with Atticus had also taken its toll. It had been an emotional day, and she yearned for an evening of solace and comfort with Alex.

As Maggie stood before her bedroom mirror, her long brown hair cascaded in gentle waves down her shoulders, and a feeling of empowerment washed over her with each pass of the curling iron. The vintage-inspired Betty Paige-style fringe she fashioned allowed the process to consume her thoughts, offering a brief respite from the lingering worries that had haunted her day. With steady hands, she applied a touch of red lipstick, the bold hue adding a touch of glamour to her look. A precise stroke of eyeliner accentuated her eyes, adding a touch of allure to her appearance. As she reached into her jewellery box, her fingers found the lovebirds necklace that Alex had given her. She fastened it around her neck, grabbed a pair of shades and closed the door of her apartment.

Stepping out into the late evening sun, she felt the gentle breeze brush against her cheeks, as if nature itself was trying to console her. The city seemed to sense her mood and responded with a slower pace, matching the rhythm of her heart. As she walked through the city streets, she embraced the distraction of her surroundings, observing the play of light and shadows as the sun dipped lower. Each passing moment allowed her to be present in the here and now, and she savoured the simple act of putting one foot in front of the other.

As she made her way towards "Taverna Athene," the stunning restaurant perched above the azure sea, a sense of serenity washed over her. The rhythmic sound of waves below seemed to synchronise with her breathing, calming her mind and allowing her to be fully present in the moment.

Entering the restaurant, she was immediately captivated by its cool blend of modern and traditional Greek elements. Her eyes traced the intricately designed wooden beams that adorned the ceilings, infusing the space with a warm and inviting ambiance. The soft glow from the glass lanterns, each adorned with a shimmering candle, added a touch of enchantment to the surroundings, casting dancing shadows on the walls that seemed to tell their own stories.

Her eyes scanned the horizon for any sign of Alex and there he was leaning against the balcony, his face illuminated by his mobile phone. He seemed to be engrossed in something, and a subtle pang of curiosity crossed her mind. Her heart fluttered at the sight of him, his mop of curly brown hair catching the last rays of the setting sun, creating a halo-like aura around him. His lightly tanned skin added a touch of warmth to his already handsome features. Something about the way he held himself, though, gave her a slight sense of intrigue.

As she drew nearer, Alex looked up from his phone, and she noticed a fleeting expression of surprise quickly replaced by a smile. "Hey, you," Alex greeted softly, his voice carrying a hint of cheerfulness. "You look stunning." A blush crept across Maggie's cheeks, and a soft smile played on her lips as she greeted him. "Thank you, Alex. You look quite dashing yourself." He chuckled, the sound tinged with a touch of lightheartedness, and slipped his phone into his pocket. As he reached out to pull her into a warm embrace, she couldn't shake the feeling that something was slightly off, but she couldn't quite put her finger on it. It was almost as if he was holding back something, a secret or a surprise.

Their gazes met, and Maggie tried to read his emotions, but he skillfully masked whatever was on his mind. She couldn't help but wonder if there was more to this evening than he was letting on. But as quickly as the suspicion arose, so did her trust in him. She knew he had a flair for surprises, and perhaps he was simply excited about the plans he had in store for the night. With a soft smile, she decided to let go of her worries and embrace the moment. They made their way to their cosy corner table, serenaded by the gentle melody of the sea, and his demeanour seemed to relax as they engaged in easy conversation.

"Wow, this place is absolutely stunning," she remarked, her eyes sweeping over the picturesque view of the azure sea. "How on earth did you find it?" A mischievous glint sparkled in Alex's eyes as he leaned back in his chair, a secretive smile playing on his lips. "Oh, just a little recommendation I stumbled upon on a travel blog," he replied, relishing the anticipation in Maggie's expression. "It's quite a hidden gem." The waitress gracefully handed them the menu, each page filled with delectable Greek dishes that made Maggie's mouth water. "You should try our Greek salad," she said with a warm smile.

"We use tomatoes grown on the island, and they're really sweet and juicy and the feta cheese is locally sourced from a nearby farmer. To top it off, we use local olive oil that adds a nice touch to the whole dish. Let me know if you'd like to try it." Alex took a moment to peruse the options before decisively nodding. "Alright, we will go with the Greek salad then," he said, his eyes briefly meeting Maggie's for agreement before continuing, "and let's also have a bottle of Pinot Grigio."

"You know me so well," she said, her voice filled with warmth."Of course," he replied with a playful wink. "After all, I am an expert in knowing what my girlfriend loves.""So, let me tell you about my day! His eyes sparkled with enthusiasm as he recounted his experiences. "Rethymno is something else, Maggie! The old town is like this perfect blend of history and modern vibes. I stumbled upon some incredible street musicians; it's like the whole town is alive with music."

Maggie leaned in, captivated by his storytelling, her artistic soul resonating with every word. "Tell me more," she urged."I couldn't resist getting lost in the musical magic," Alex continued animatedly, his green eyes shining. "There was this amazing guitarist, man, he was painting the air with these intricate melodies. And then there was a violinist, and her music, it just hit you right in the gut. I couldn't help myself, grabbed my harmonica, and joined in the jamming session. It was amazing."

Maggie's eyes gleamed with appreciation. "That sounds like an unforgettable moment."

"Totally," he nodded, relishing the memory. "It's one of those experiences that stick with you, you know? Makes you feel alive." As the waitress approached their table, she deftly uncorked the wine bottle and poured a generous amount into Alex's glass. He swirled the wine, savouring its aroma before taking a sip and nodding with approval. The waitress then turned her attention to Maggie, pouring her a glass as well.

As she observed this interaction, Maggie couldn't help but notice the subtle assumptions that lingered in such moments. The waitress seemed to automatically defer to Alex, presuming his opinion mattered most, perhaps assuming he was the one with the means to pay for the evening. Yet, those who truly knew Alex understood that he lived a more modest lifestyle, hand to mouth, and had always struggled with money.Nevertheless, Maggie decided to take this moment in stride. She looked and took a mouthful of the chilled white wine, knowing that it was common for societal norms to play out in such ways.

He turned to her with concern. "So, how was your day, Maggie? You seem a bit off."
She took a deep breath, her mind still filled with the weight of the day's encounters. "It was intense," she replied, her voice tinged with emotion. "I met with Atticus,that artist I told you I was meeting and it was... different. He opened up to me, and I saw scars on his arms and wrists. It was heartbreaking"

Alex reached out and gently squeezed her hand, offering comfort. "That sounds awful. Must've been tough."It really was," she continued, her eyes reflecting a mix of sadness and compassion. "I just wanted to protect him, you know? But I felt so powerless, like there was nothing I could do to help."

He nodded understandingly, listening attentively. "Sometimes, all we can do is be there for someone, lend a listening ear. It means more than you think.""Yeah, I guess you're right," she said, her fingers fiddling with the lovebirds necklace around her neck. "And then there's Kateryna," she added, her voice now carrying worry. "She's going through so much with the war in Ukraine. It's just awful, Alex. The conflict feels so senseless, and I can't stop thinking about it."

He reached for his glass and took a sip, thoughtful. "It's heartbreaking, I know. The world seems to be in absolute chaos." She nodded, her eyes drifting to the horizon. "And it's not just the wars," she said, her tone growing earnest. "Greece is burning, and the temperatures in Europe are hitting record highs. The environment is changing, and it's scary."

As they continued talking, Alex skillfully led the conversation to lighter topics, making Maggie smile and laugh amidst her concerns. He called the waitress over and ordered a traditional Baklava dessert to finish their meal. "And a fruit salad for the lady," he added, flashing a warm smile at her .

She leaned back in her chair, her mind still preoccupied with the weight of the day's encounters. Alex could sense her lingering worries, but he was determined to lift her spirits. "I know, I know," he said, trying to reassure her, "but hey, I have a surprise for you, something that I think will cheer you up." With a hint of excitement, he reached into his knapsack and pulled out a collection of brochures, waiting for the perfect moment to reveal his surprise.

"Check this out. A weekend trip to Santorini," he finally said, offering the brochures to her. Her face immediately lit up with delight as she flipped through the pages. "Santorini? Wow, that's been on my bucket list forever," she exclaimed, her eyes glowing with anticipation.Intrigued, Maggie opened the brochure, and her breath caught at the sight that greeted her. Pictures of Santorini adorned the pages, showcasing the stunning caldera of Oia with its iconic white and blue buildings perched on the cliffs, overlooking the sapphire Aegean Sea.

The brochure transported her to a world of breathtaking sunsets, where the sky and the sea blended into a mesmerising canvas of hues, painting the horizon with warm shades of orange and pink. It was as if she could feel the salty breeze on her skin and hear the gentle lapping of the waves against the rocks.His grin widened as he watched her reaction, delighted to have caught her off guard with his surprise. "Well, it's no longer just a dream. I've already booked it for us this weekend," Alex said, a glint of excitement dancing in his eyes. Grateful for the thoughtfulness and love behind his gesture, she reached across the table, gently squeezing his hand. "Thank you for this wonderful surprise. I'm so excited to explore Santorini with you."

As they stepped out of the restaurant, the world around them seemed to hush, creating an intimate bubble where they were the only two souls under the vast, clear night sky. The moon, like a radiant silver pearl, hung high above, casting its gentle glow upon the city below.Chatter and laughter spilled out from the open doors of the nearby bars, blending harmoniously with the hum of the streets, as if the city itself were alive and breathing in the warm embrace of the evening. Despite the late hour, the air still clung to the sweltering heat of the day, wrapping around the couple like a comforting blanket. The world seemed to slow down as they walked hand in hand, their hearts entwined in a tender moment of togetherness.

In the midst of this enchanting backdrop, Her s eyes caught a sight that made her heart skip a beat. Amidst the crowd, a man stumbled out of a nearby bar, his unsteady gait and dishevelled appearance revealing the effects of too many pints. A familiar figure emerged from the haze of the night—Thomas, the painter she had met in his studio not long ago. His tousled hair and clothes adorned in vibrant paint stains were unmistakable, and a silver hoop earring glimmered in his ear like a touch of rebelliousness.

"That guy seems really wasted," Alex remarked, breaking her from her thoughts. "Yes," Maggie replied, her voice tinged with a mix of worry and regret. Alex, sensing her distress, gently squeezed her hand, offering a silent gesture of support. But the comforting touch felt distant, unable to bridge the chasm of doubt that had taken root within her. The city, with all its vibrant colours and bustling life, offered no solace. It was as if the universe itself conspired against her, underscoring the daunting truth that some battles couldn't be won.

In the midst of it all, a distant memory flickered in her mind—Demetris's words of caution about Thomas being a "wildcard." She wished she had heeded the warning, but hope and ambition had blinded her to the darkness that lurked beneath the surface.

As they walked on, the moon's glow seemed to wane, the city's liveliness fading into a hollow echo. Maggie's heart felt heavy with defeat, knowing that the project she had poured her soul into was now teetering on the precipice of failure. She couldn't help but wonder if her desire to ignite Thomas's artistic spark was nothing more than a naive dream. Perhaps, some souls were destined to be consumed by their own demons, and all her efforts were nothing more than futile brushstrokes on a canvas destined to remain empty.

Chapter 10: Rachel's Return

The next morning, Alex sprang out of bed with a burst of energy, ready to kickstart the day with a refreshing swim in the sea, which was just seconds from the beachside apartment. His enthusiasm for the water was infectious, and he couldn't resist the allure of the waves that beckoned him from the bedroom window. With a splash, he dove into the cool embrace of the Aegean, relishing the sensation of the salty water against his skin. "this is living!" he thought to himself as his arms sliced through the water, feeling a sense of liberation with every stroke.

Meanwhile, Maggie stretched lazily under the warm sunlight streaming through the window. Her mind felt a whirlwind of thoughts, but she chose to take a moment for herself before diving into the day's tasks. Deciding to head to the Olympus Minimart, she ventured out into the lively streets, her senses alive with the sights and sounds of Greece awakening. As she strolled along the cobblestone pathways, a hint of nostalgia washed over her as she thought back to her art school days and the phone call she had scheduled later that morning with her old pal, Rachel.

Continuing on her path, she arrived at the Olympus Minimart, where the shopkeeper welcomed her with a warm smile. He playfully teased her about her fair complexion, "Why you so pale?" he teased in a friendly manner " You need to get outside into the sunshine, pretty lady!". He gestured towards the shelves stocked with sunscreen and beach accessories. "You should hit the beach, feel the sand between your toes, and soak up the sun!"

"I'll keep that in mind," she replied with a smile, picking up a bottle of sunscreen from the shelf and throwing it into her basket, along with a fresh loaf of bread, a carton of milk, and a bag of coffee. As she made her way to the cashier, she noticed a little cat sitting by the entrance, its bright eyes staring up at her with curiosity. She couldn't resist bending down to give the furry creature a gentle pat on the head. The cat purred contentedly for a moment before scurrying away to explore other corners of the store.

"Ah, you've made a friend," the shopkeeper chuckled, amused by the interaction. "Cats are like the unofficial guardians of my business. They come and go as they please, but they always find their way back." she smiled, charmed by the idea of these feline guardians watching over the Olympus Minimart. "They must enjoy the lively atmosphere here," she remarked. "Oh, they certainly do, we keep them well fed too. " the shopkeeper agreed, his eyes twinkling with affection for the feline visitors. " I'm glad, " she replied,"there are so many strays on the island."

"Now, anything else I can get you?""Do you stock any Irish newspapers?" she asked on a whim, thinking that she was probably out of luck."Actually, yes," he replied with a surprising grin, gesturing to a newsstand that had a range of newspapers from many different countries. Amidst the array of international papers, Maggie spotted a familiar sight

– The Irish Times. A smile of appreciation spread across her face, grateful for this unexpected touch of home. With her shopping bag full, Maggie made her way back to the apartment, where she felt a sense of purpose settle upon her. She was eager to dive into the curatorial work that lay ahead – the report on each artist and their proposals for the upcoming exhibition.

Before getting started , she brewed her favourite coffee, the rich aroma filling the air like a comforting embrace. Carrying the steaming mug out to the balcony, she settled into a wicker chair, ready to savour a few moments of solitude. The soft breeze danced with the leaves of the nearby trees, creating a gentle symphony as her phone came to life - and just like that, on the screen, appeared Rachel O'Driscoll - a face she hadn't seen in over 15 years. As she looked at the woman sitting in front of her, Maggie couldn't help but be taken aback. Gone was the fresh-faced college student she once knew, with an angelic face and a smattering of freckles, replaced by a weary figure adorned with deep lines and a look that spoke of a hard-lived life. The contrast between the image in her memory and the reality before her was stark.

"Oh, Maggie, it's amazing to see you after all this time," Rachel said, her voice cracking with emotion. "You look amazing," she added, trying to offer a compliment, but the sadness in her eyes betrayed her true feelings. "You have not aged one day." "You too," Maggie replied with a gentle smile, trying to be diplomatic. Inside, her heart ached for her friend. She wanted to reach out and erase the years of pain etched on Rachel's face, but she knew she couldn't.

Rachel had a vape pen in hand, and she seemed to take constant drags from it, a nervous habit that had replaced her once carefree demeanour."Hey, Maggie," Rachel greeted, her voice a bit jittery. She took another puff from her vape and sighed. "It's been way too long. I can't believe how much time has passed."Maggie smiled warmly, her heart reaching out to her old friend. "I know, right? It's been ages since we caught up. How have you been?"

Rachel's eyes darted around, avoiding direct eye contact. She seemed uncomfortable, and her words spilled out with a hint of frustration. "Well, life hasn't exactly been a smooth ride, you know? After college, I thought things would be different, but it's been tough. I struggled to find a job, and... I don't know, everything just feels so overwhelming sometimes."

Maggie nodded sympathetically, trying to provide a listening ear. "I can imagine. Life can throw unexpected challenges our way. But remember, I'm here for you, Rach."

Rachel's fingers fidgeted with the vape pen, a sign of her anxiety. "I know, I know. It's just... I feel stuck, you know? Like everyone around me is moving forward, and I'm just here, treading water.".

The weight of sadness settled upon her shoulders. She couldn't help but feel the enormity of Rachel's struggles and the gulf that now separated them. Her friend seemed so different from the young girl she had known—full of life, talent, and potential. It was a sobering reminder of the unpredictable nature of life and the myriad paths it could take. Yet, amidst the hardships, there was a glimmer of hope in Rachel's voice. She shared her involvement in a community art exhibition and her newfound passion for sketching flowers and nature scenes.

As the call came to an end, she couldn't shake the bittersweet feeling that lingered within her. She felt a mixture of shock and heartache for her friend, knowing that life had taken them on different journeys. Rachel's dreams of grand exhibitions in New York and LA now seemed like distant fantasies, but Maggie hoped that somehow her friend would find her way back to the path she had once dreamed of.

It would have been easy to get lost in a reverie about the past but Maggie had work to do.
As she scanned her inbox, an email from Eva emerged like an unexpected detonation, demanding answers about her delayed funding. Simultaneously, an urgent message from Emily Winsor sought a financial report, adding to the mounting pressure. And just when she thought she had seen it all, a typically flaky email from her boss, William, arrived. He was searching for the original application they had submitted months ago. Maggie couldn't help but roll her eyes as she thought of William's tendency to misplace important documents.

With a sigh, she embarked on a search-and-rescue mission for the elusive application, navigating through the labyrinth of files on her computer. Each minute seemed to stretch like an eternity as she tried to untangle the digital chaos.After five hours of battling with spreadsheets, emails, and files, her body had grown sore from inactivity. The office chair that had once been comfortable now felt like a prison, chaining her to her desk. A deep longing for fresh air and movement tugged at her like an irresistible magnet. With relief Maggie shut her laptop, grabbed her keys and headed outside into the blistering Cretean sun.

As she set forth on her four-mile walk down the coast road, memories of her college days with Rachel resurfaced like a vivid reel of film coming to life. They were inseparable back then, two young women brimming with dreams and aspirations. Her heart yearned for that sense of closeness once again, but as she recalled the phone call from Rachel, a sense of melancholy washed over her.

The image of her friend on the screen lingered in her mind, a stark contrast to the vivacious, freckled young woman she once knew. Rachel's auburn hair, once flowing with fiery enthusiasm, now with streaks of grey, seemed burdened with the weight of life's hardships. The deep lines etched on her face told stories of struggles and battles fought, leaving Maggie with a lingering ache for the happiness her friend deserved.Rachel's words replayed in her mind like a haunting melody. The dreams they once shared, of conquering the art world, seemed like echoes from a distant past. Instead, reality had carved a different path for

Rachel, one filled with setbacks and obstacles that had altered the course of her journey.

As she ruminated on the phone call, she passed by charming little shops, their colourful facades a reflection of the vibrant energy that pulsed through the town. The aroma of fresh seafood from the market stalls, mixed with spices, ground coffee and blooming flowers filled the air, mingling with the chatter of locals and tourists alike.

Amidst the cheerful ambiance, her thoughts lingered on Rachel's life. The vintage store where Rachel worked part time must have held stories of its own, a repository of memories from times gone by. Maggie pictured her amidst the treasured garments and trinkets of the past, standing as a guardian of history, while the world outside rushed on, leaving her to grapple with unfulfilled dreams. The town's beauty couldn't dispel the heaviness that settled in her heart. She couldn't help but wonder how life had led them on such different paths.

On her way, she happened upon a delightful little boutique called "Grecian Goddess Brides," and like a moth drawn to a flame, she couldn't resist peeking through the window adorned with stunning wedding dresses. The gowns seemed to dance with ethereal beauty, each one a masterpiece of lace, silk, and tulle. Their intricate designs captured her imagination, as if they were whispering sweet promises of love and new beginnings. The dresses seemed to carry the dreams of countless brides, woven into every stitch, as if each one had a story to tell, just waiting for the right woman to bring it to life. She felt like a character in her own fairy tale, where everything was aligned, and destiny was calling her towards a beautiful future.

In that moment, her concentration was abruptly shattered by the shrill ringtone of her phone. "William" flashed on the screen, and she sighed before picking up the call. "Hey, Maggie," William's voice sounded exasperated. "Thomas still hasn't done his paperwork, and it's holding up the funding for the entire project." Her brow furrowed. "Seriously? He's had days to get it done. I'll give him a nudge and sort it out." "Please do," William said, his tone a mix of annoyance and urgency. "We can't afford any delays."

"No worries, I'll handle it," Maggie assured him, feeling the pressure building up. "Anything else?" "Yeah," William continued, "Have you made progress with the venue for the exhibition?" Maggie hesitated, feeling the weight of the task at hand. "I'm working on it," she replied truthfully. "It's been a bit tough, though. I'm not well-connected in the art scene here, and language barriers are a thing." "I get it," William said sympathetically. "Just do your best. We need a great venue to make this exhibition a success."

"I know," Maggie said with determination. "I'll keep pushing and see what I can come up with."

As she hung up, Maggie felt the weight of the responsibilities on her shoulders. She was no stranger to challenges, but this project felt like a mounting marathon of obstacles...

Chapter 11; Santorini

Two days had flown by, and now, Maggie and Alex found themselves at the pretty harbour of Chania, brimming with anticipation for their adventure to Santorini island. The warm sun enveloped them, adding to the excitement that surged within as they took in the sight of the boundless horizon which was scattered with little white sailing ships and massive cruise liners, some the size of vast shopping centres.

Their eyes scanned the harbour until they spotted the **Olympus Princess**—an unfortunate sight among the pristine boats lined up. Its worn-out hull and peeling paint spoke volumes about its neglect and dilapidated state. "This can't be it?" Maggie exclaimed in dismay. "It's dreadful, it looked much better in the brochure" Alex agreed, sporting a shocked expression. Clearly, the ship had endured far more than its fair share of journeys, but instead of gaining character, it had become a symbol of neglect. Yet, they had no choice but to proceed; turning back was no longer an option.

With a curious blend of apprehension and intrigue, they stepped aboard, only to be greeted by a somewhat tragic interior. The carpets, a peculiar blend of green and peach, looked like they had time-travelled straight from the '80s. And an odd scent lingered in the air, reminiscent of a forgotten bathing suit left in a car trunk for way too long; a mixture of mildew, rusty metal, and regret, as if the boat itself had given up on life

The ship's dated decor unfolded before them, with uncomfortable plastic chairs in an odd magnolia shade and 'luxurious' pastel sofas that had likely seen better days in their distant past.Maggie couldn't help but find humour in the situation, she rolled her eyes, "This ship's decor needs a one-way ticket to the past." she laughed, "I feel like we're on a bad '80s sitcom set," he added, clearly unimpressed. Despite the ship's quirks and questionable aesthetics, they were determined to make the most of their journey to Santorini.

The crew's lacklustre welcome made it clear that they were anything but thrilled to receive more tourists. With forced smiles, they directed Maggie and Alex to a secluded corner near the cafeteria, where they settled onto the uncomfortable fitted seating. Despite the less-than-ideal start, the gentle rocking of the ship soon worked its magic, lulling them into a peaceful slumber. As they drifted off, they couldn't help but surrender to the tranquillity of the journey ahead. Hours passed by in a dreamlike state as the **Olympus Princess** navigated the turquoise waters of the Aegean Sea.

As Maggie stirred from her sleep a few hours later, the ship's clock had stealthily ticked its way to lunchtime, and through the window, she caught sight of the approaching island, gently coming into focus in the distance. Her eyes sparkled with excitement as she nudged Alex, her voice vibrating with eager anticipation, "Come on, we're nearly there!

Let's head up to the deck and get the view!" Without hesitation, they gathered their belongings, adrenaline coursing through their veins, and ascended the metal staircase with a sense of urgency, aiming for the ship's highest point.

As the Minoan Princess glided smoothly into the bustling Santorini Cruise Port, they felt an electrifying rush of anticipation. Their eyes widened in amazement as they stood before the very place that had filled their daydreams for what felt like forever."Oh my God, look at this!" she exclaimed, her voice tinged with excitement. "It's even more beautiful in reality than all the pictures we've seen online!" He nodded, equally captivated by the stunning view. "I know, right? It's like we've stepped into a postcard or something. Absolutely breathtaking!"

With eager anticipation, they stepped off the ship, ready to embrace the enchanting allure of the picturesque island that lay ahead. As their feet touched the shores of Santorini, their eyes lit up with wonder, and Maggie couldn't hold back her excitement, exclaiming, "I can't believe we're finally here!" The port teemed with an invigorating energy, a symphony of travellers from every corner of the world, all irresistibly drawn to Santorini's magnetic charm. Ferries gracefully arrived and departed, creating a living tapestry of journeys beginning and ending, with each wanderer carrying tales as unique as the islands themselves.

As they bid farewell to the **Olympus Princess**, they embarked on the walk to their Air BNB through the picturesque streets of Santorini. With each step, the salty sea breeze kissed their cheeks, while the soft murmur of locals conversing in Greek filled the air, creating a harmonious atmosphere of its own. Their excitement was palpable, and they happily snapped pictures along the way. She checked the Google Maps app on her smartphone with a determined look, "Alright, we're almost there. Just a few more turns." he smirked, his eyes scanning the surroundings, "Piece of cake. We got this." Their journey continued, but the labyrinthine streets of Santorini had other plans, and soon, they found themselves lost in the charming chaos.

Scratching her head, Maggie remarked, "Wait, this doesn't look right."
He squinted at the map, "Are we going the wrong way?"
They attempted to course-correct, but each attempt seemed to lead them deeper into the maze.
With a laugh, she couldn't help but jest, "I swear we just passed that café!" Grinning, Alex retorted, "I think Google maps is playing a game

with us." Unfazed, they recalibrated their route, only to stumble into a bustling market square, alive with vibrant stalls and a kaleidoscope of colours. As they wandered through the picturesque streets of Santorini, their initial excitement began to wane as they found themselves going around in circles.

Frustrated, she said, "I don't understand, according to Google maps, it should be just around this corner." Alex, trying to stay positive, replied, "Well, let's keep going. It has to be around here somewhere." But with every turn they took, they seemed to end up in a different dead-end or back to where they started. The once-charming streets now felt like a maze designed to confuse them, and all those whitewashed houses looked exactly the same after a while.

Maggie struggled to drag her heavy suitcase along the narrow and confusing streets, while he effortlessly carried a guitar case and a backpack. The weight of her luggage made each step feel like a battle, and despite her exhaustion, he didn't offer to help. "Maggie, are you sure you're reading the map correctly? This can't be that difficult," he remarked, a hint of frustration in his voice.

Feeling flustered and irritated, she shot back, "Of course, I am! It's not my fault the streets here are like a riddle!" They attempted to retrace their steps once more, but the fatigue was evident in Maggie's face as she persisted, determined not to admit defeat. "We just need to find a different route," she insisted, trying to mask the strain in her voice.

His impatience grew with each unsuccessful turn. "We've been walking in circles for ages! Can't we just ask someone for directions?" But Maggie's pride got the better of her, and she clenched her jaw, unwilling to give in. "No, I can figure this out. I don't need help from a stranger." The tension between them escalated with every wrong turn they took. The initial excitement of their adventure now lay buried under layers of irritation and stubbornness. As they strolled along the bustling streets, their contrasting styles started to rub each other the wrong way. "We should head towards the waterfront first," Alex suggested, pointing in a direction he deemed fit.

She hesitated, looking longingly towards the charming, narrow alleys that beckoned with a sense of mystery. "I think we should explore those cobblestone streets over there. They seem intriguing," she countered, her adventurous spirit not easily subdued. He sighed, his patience wearing thin. "Maggie, we can't just wander aimlessly. We have a limited time here, and I'd rather not waste it getting lost. Let's stick to the plan."Her excitement dampened, Maggie reluctantly agreed to follow Alex's lead. But as they walked, the tension between them simmered, both feeling like they were missing out on the experience they had envisioned.

Finally, after taking a few more wrong turns, Alex's patience reached its breaking point. "Enough! You're clearly lost, and your stubbornness is making it worse. I'm going to ask for help," he declared, frustration dripping from his words.He stormed off, leaving her standing there, torn between her pride and the undeniable realisation that they desperately needed assistance. As he disappeared into the distance, her heart sank, weighed down by the gravity of both the suitcase and the situation.She swallowed her ego and called out to him, "Wait! I'm sorry, alright? I shouldn't have been so stubborn. Let's ask for directions together."He turned back to her, a hint of reluctance still present in his expression. "Fine," he replied tersely, "but we better find someone who knows these streets better than Google maps."

As they walked through the winding alleyways, they came across a friendly-looking local sitting outside a quaint café. He had a warm smile that instantly put them at ease. Maggie mustered up the courage to approach him, her pride now overshadowed by the desire to find their AirBNB and salvage their day ."Excuse me," Maggie said, her voice tinged with a mix of frustration and hope, "We seem to be a bit lost. Could you please help us find our AirBnB?"

His eyes twinkled with kindness as he studied the digital lines and circles. "Ah, I see you've taken a few detours," he said in a soothing tone. "You just need to take a left at the end of this street, and then the second right. Follow that road for a few minutes, and you'll reach your destination."

Maggie and Alex exchanged glances, silently relieved that their search was finally coming to an end. "Thank you so much," Alex said sincerely, grateful for the local's assistance. "We really appreciate your help." The old man nodded, his smile widening, revealing a few wrinkles around his eyes that spoke of a life well-lived. "It's my pleasure," he replied warmly.With newfound hope, Maggie and Alex followed the directions they had been given. As they walked together, the weight of their previous disagreement seemed to lessen, but the tension still simmered beneath the surface.

They soon found their accommodation, a charming whitewashed house tucked away on a quiet street, exactly as described in the listing. Entering the cosy space, they put down their luggage and let out a collective sigh of relief. The squabble that had plagued them earlier slowly dissipated, replaced by the excitement of exploring a new place together. "Look at this place," she said with genuine awe, "It's like stepping into a beautiful chapter of Greek history." Alex nodded, appreciating the authenticity, "Yeah, it really captures the essence of Santorini. I love traditional architecture."

The living room exuded warmth with its plush cushions and handwoven rugs, creating an inviting space to relax after a morning of exploration. The soft lighting from antique lanterns gave the room a comfortable atmosphere. The bedroom was equally enchanting, with a wrought-iron bed adorned with crisp white linens and billowy curtains that gently swayed with the breeze. A small window framed by wooden shutters allowed a glimpse of the cloudless blue sky. Maggie ran her fingers over the intricate patterns of a decorative vase, "I can't get over the charm of this place. It feels like we're living in a Greek tale." "Let's hope it's not a Greek tragedy," Alex replied with a hint of sarcasm.

As they settled into their accommodation, Maggie couldn't shake off the lingering feeling of annoyance from earlier. She tried to push it aside, reminding herself that travel often came with its share of ups and downs. But as they sat in silence for a moment, she decided to address the elephant in the room. Taking a deep breath, she spoke softly, "Alex, I just want to say that I felt a little hurt by how annoyed you got with me back there." Alex looked genuinely surprised, "I'm sorry, Maggie. I didn't mean to hurt you. I was just as frustrated with the situation, don't make a big deal out of it. OK?"

Maggie's shoulders relaxed, and she offered a genuine smile, "You're right. We're in one of the most beautiful places in the world, and I don't want anything to spoil it for us." Changing the topic, Maggie leaned against the windowsill, her gaze fixed on the breathtaking view before them, "This view is incredible. I could stare at it all day." Alex wrapped his arm around her, enjoying the moment, "Hey," he whispered, his voice barely above a breath, "you are incredible, you know that?" Maggie smiled, the weight of the argument dissolving, "Right back at you."

As the sun bathed the room in a warm, golden glow, Alex's gaze fell upon his guitar resting against the nearby wall. A gentle melody began to form in his mind, and he couldn't resist the urge to bring his music into the moment. "Would you mind if I played something?" he asked, running his fingers gently over the strings. Maggie's eyes lit up with curiosity and anticipation. "Of course not," she said, her voice tinged with excitement, "I'd love to hear you play." With that, he began to strum a mellow tune, his fingers dancing effortlessly across the frets. The soft, melodic notes filled the air, creating a soothing backdrop to their intimate surroundings.

She closed her eyes, allowing the music to wash over her, each note wrapping around her heart like a warm embrace. The world outside faded away as they both became immersed in the magic of the moment. She leaned in closer to him, feeling the rhythm of his music reverberate through her entire being. The soft strumming of the guitar stirred a bittersweet nostalgia within her, and her mind travelled back to a moment five years ago.

The familiar tune took her back to Dublin, where she first saw his band, Ramshackle, play in a small, dimly lit pub. It was a night filled with youthful excitement and laughter, where the crowd swayed to the music, swept away by the raw passion and energy of the performance. In that distant memory, she saw a younger version of Alex, his eyes ablaze with passion as he poured his heart and soul into the music. He was the same person, yet somehow different, as time had shaped them both and brought them to this moment.

As Alex played the final chords, the last echoes of the melody lingered in the air. He set his guitar aside, and they sat together in silence for a moment, savouring the lingering magic of the music and the connection they had with each other. Maggie finally opened her eyes, her heart overflowing with gratitude. "That was beautiful," she whispered, her voice barely above a breath.
Alex smiled, his eyes shining with affection, "Not as beautiful as you."

Time seemed to slow down as they savoured the tenderness of the moment. The outside world ceased to exist as they immersed themselves in the comfort of each other's arms. With every touch, their bodies communicated a language of desire and adoration. The weight of their earlier disagreements had melted away, leaving only a sense of belonging and ease in each other's presence. "Thank you for being patient with me earlier," Maggie said softly, her fingers tracing circles on his arm.Alex kissed her forehead, his voice filled with warmth, "It's okay. We're in this together, right? Ups and downs, the whole package."

As they lay there, basking in the afterglow of their connection, Maggie felt a surge of energy and excitement. She looked into Alex's eyes and suggested, "You know what? We should head out and explore the town. I heard the sunset in the old town is incredible."

Alex's face lit up with enthusiasm, "That sounds like a great idea. Let's do it!"

As the sun began its graceful descent towards the horizon, painting the sky with hues of pink and orange, they set out to explore the enchanting streets of Oia. The town's white-washed buildings with their distinctive blue-domed roofs surrounded them, creating a postcard-perfect scene that seemed almost surreal.The narrow streets were lined with charming boutiques, art galleries, and cafes, each one inviting them to discover the treasures hidden within.

With every turn they took, the view of the dramatic caldera cliffs unfolded before them, bathed in the warm glow of the setting sun. The cliffside houses seemed to cling to the edge, defying gravity, and the azure sea below sparkled with a mesmerising allure. As they continued their exploration, they found themselves in a small square, where a group of talented musicians filled the air with the melodic strains of traditional Greek music. The lively tunes immediately caught their attention, and they couldn't resist swaying to the rhythm, swept up in the infectious energy of the island.

Maggie's laughter danced through the warm Santorini air, her eyes sparkling with delight as she twirled in Alex's arms. "It's like we're in a movie, isn't it? This is amazing!" she exclaimed, her energy infectious. Alex's grin widened, mirroring her enthusiasm. "Lovin' the dance moves," he teased, spinning her around once more. A playful glint danced in her eyes. "So, are you up for the challenge of finding the best spot to watch the sunset?" she asked, a hint of mischief in her tone.

"Absolutely! It's a mission we can't fail," he replied, rising to the occasion with a laugh. Hand in hand, they set off, their eyes scanning the horizon for the perfect vantage point. They strolled along the gentle slope of the streets, passing charming terraces and balconies adorned with cascading flowers, each spot seemingly vying for their attention. "That terrace over there looks promising," she pointed out.

He shook his head with a grin. "Nah, the view from there is beautiful, but it's not quite what we're looking for."

Their quest continued, the golden sun casting a warm glow over the white-washed buildings as it slowly descended. With every passing moment, their anticipation grew, fueling their determination to find the perfect spot.Finally, they arrived at a panoramic viewpoint, a hidden gem offering an unobstructed vista of the caldera. The sight took their breath away. "Alex, look at this! It's incredible!" she gasped, her eyes wide with wonder.

He nodded in agreement, his voice filled with awe. "This is it. This is the spot we've been searching for."
They settled comfortably on a nearby ledge, both of them drawn to the horizon where the setting sun painted the sky with a mesmerising display of colours. The sea shimmered like a sheet of liquid gold, and the caldera came alive with a mysterious allure in the twilight.

Maggie reached into her bag and pulled out her old canon camera. "I can't miss this moment," she exclaimed, eagerly adjusting the camera settings to capture the scene perfectly."You've got an eye for beauty, sweetheart . Your photographs have a way of stealing a piece of a moment and making it timeless," Alex complimented, leaning in closer.

Pride and humility mingled in her smile. "Thank you, darling. Santorini is such a picturesque place; it's hard not to get lost in its beauty." Focused on framing the perfect shot, she was unaware of Alex's movements behind her. As she lowered her camera, she turned to share her excitement with him, only to find him on one knee, a mixture of nerves and affection in his eyes.

In that tender moment, he clasped her hand gently, his voice soft yet firm. "Maggie, my sweet, cat-loving, George Michael obsessed and brilliantly artistic partner in crime, from the moment we met, I knew you were one of a kind. You may be hopeless with directions and couldn't find your way out of a paper bag, but I wouldn't have you any other way. You're the light of my life, and I can't imagine a future without you."

With trembling hands, he opened a small, velvet box, revealing a beautifully crafted vintage ring with a delicate sapphire at its heart. Tears of joy glistened in her eyes as she looked at the ring and then back at him, her heart bursting with love and happiness. She managed a choked, "Yes, Alex, my darling, yes."

As Maggie whispered her acceptance, a wave of joy swept through the crowd nearby. Strangers, caught up in the heartfelt moment, couldn't help but cheer and applaud, their excitement echoing through the narrow streets of Oia. It was as if the town itself joined in the celebration, embracing their love.

The musicians, inspired by the happy atmosphere, played with renewed energy, creating a symphony that harmonised with the beating of their hearts.In that magical moment, time seemed to slow down. The world around them transformed into a canvas of emotions, where love painted the landscape in shades of euphoria. Maggie and Alex felt cocooned in happiness, as if the universe itself blessed their union.

With a mixture of anticipation and excitement, Maggie dialled her mother's number, her heart pounding as she waited for the call to connect."Hello?" her mother's voice sounded, a blend of surprise and warmth.

"Hi, Mum," Maggie greeted, her own voice carrying a hint of nervousness. "I have some news."

There was a pause on the other end of the line, followed by an expectant, "Go on, dear. I'm listening."

Maggie took a deep breath, her fingers tightening around the phone. "I'm engaged," she announced, a rush of emotions surging within her.

Silence reigned for a moment before her mother's voice erupted in joy. "Oh, Maggie! Finally! I'm so happy for you, darling. It's about time." A genuine smile tugged at Maggie's lips as she soaked in her mother's happiness. Despite the distance that separated them, the warmth of her mother's support enveloped her like a comforting embrace.

Tears of joy shimmered in Maggie's eyes, reflecting the colours of the setting sun. Alex, filled with elation, gently wiped away her tears, his touch tender and reassuring. They stood there, locked in each other's gaze, feeling the depth of the love that brought them to this unforgettable moment. The onlookers, moved by the sincerity of the proposal, showered them with cheers and well-wishes. Some clapped, while others raised their glasses, toasting to their newfound journey together. Strangers became allies in love, connected by the simple yet profound magic of two people saying "yes" to a future filled with endless possibilities.

As the cheers subsided, Maggie and Alex wrapped their arms around each other, savouring the embrace that symbolised the beginning of their forever. The old town of Oia, adorned with its whitewashed walls and blue domes, became a witness to a love that felt as timeless as the ancient island itself.

With the sun now resting below the horizon, the town was illuminated by soft, flickering lights that resembled stars descending to earth. Hand in hand, they continued their walk through the enchanting streets of Oia, but now, everything was different. They were no longer just two people exploring the wonders of Santorini—they were now bound by a love that would endure, like the eternal dance of the sun and the sea, forever and always.

It was the best day of her entire life.

The next morning, the soft glow of dawn filtered through the curtains, gently rousing Maggie and Alex from their peaceful slumber. As they slowly opened their eyes, a rush of happiness washed over them, a reminder of the new chapter they had just begun together as an engaged couple. Maggie couldn't contain her excitement and joy as she sat up, the velvet box with the ring resting on the nightstand catching her eye. With a grin that stretched from ear to ear, she glanced at Alex, who was watching her with a mix of love and contentment. "We're engaged," she whispered, her voice filled with awe and wonder. Alex chuckled, "Yes, we are," he replied, reaching out to brush a stray strand of hair away from her face. "And I couldn't be happier."

They shared a tender moment, their fingers interlocking, sealing their love with a silent promise. The prospect of spending the rest of their lives together filled them with a sense of peace and excitement that seemed to transcend time. As Maggie tiptoed to the window, she gently pushed aside the curtains, revealing the breathtaking view of the sun-kissed ocean stretching out before them. The sea sparkled like a treasure trove of diamonds, its waves whispering tales of ancient mythology and timeless romance.

She took a deep breath, the salty scent of the sea filling her lungs. The air was tinged with the promise of adventure for the day ahead and happiness - pure innocent sweet happiness. With giddy anticipation, they decided to start their day with a traditional Greek breakfast, immersing themselves in the local flavours and culture. Hand in hand, they strolled through the charming cobblestone streets of the village, greeted by the warm smiles of the locals who had caught wind of their engagement. The quaint cafes and shops were beginning to come alive, each one contributing to the vibrant tapestry of the town.

As they walked toward the charming café perched on the cliff's edge, the irresistible scent of fresh pastries and strong Greek coffee beckoned, wrapping them in a soft embrace. Greeted by a friendly waiter with a hearty "Kalimera!" and a genuine smile, they felt an immediate sense of familiarity. "So, what can I get you for breakfast?" he asked in his melodic Greek accent. Opting for a traditional breakfast, they dug into a delectable spread – olive bread that looked like a piece of art, creamy feta cheese that practically melted in their mouths, ripe tomatoes that burst with flavour, and plump olives that added a satisfying twist. And to elevate the experience, a generous dollop of tangy tzatziki sauce. It was a plate that perfectly captured the essence of the Mediterranean.

Maggie flipped open her phone, her curiosity piqued as she read through the flurry of jumbled messages from Rachel. The texts were like a collage of their shared past, sprinkled with mentions of bands they adored—Radiohead, Nirvana, REM. Yet, there was an unsettling disjointedness to them, as if Rachel was wrestling with her thoughts, trying to piece together fragments of memories and emotions.

"Hey, remember that time we danced in the rain after that art show?" one message reminisced.
Another followed, "Found my old sketchbooks. Wish I could turn back time and actually finish something. Regrets, you know."

Maggie frowned, attempting to decode the cryptic messages before her. More texts appeared, "Those days when we turned anything into art, girl? Our creativity knew no bounds!" Memories of their wild art school escapades brought a smile to her lips, but beneath the fondness, a knot of worry tightened in her chest. The messages hinted at Rachel texting under the influence, and she suspected her friend might be struggling with her past drinking habits. A pang of concern tugged at her heart; something felt off.

With a deep breath, she typed back, "Hey, Rachel. How have you been?" Almost instantly, a reply buzzed, "Maggie, my partner in art and chaos! I'm swimming in a sea of missed chances and shattered dreams. Art school failure keeps haunting me." she sighed, her heart heavy with worry as she gently probed further, "Rachel, these messages are really intense. Is everything okay?"

There was a brief pause, then Rachel's reply appeared, "Nah, don't sweat it. Just caught up in my own maze of thoughts. You know how it goes, old demons and all." Her unease was palpable. Maggie sensed a storm of emotions brewing beneath the surface of her words, a cloud cast by the influence of alcohol.

Setting her smartphone on the table, she took a casual sip of her orange juice, her gaze drifting towards the horizon. Lost in her musings, she observed the rhythmic ebb and flow of the sea, its cadence mirroring the currents of her thoughts.

Nearby, a young woman with long blonde hair caught her eye, a modern echo of Joni Mitchell. The woman meticulously crafted a watercolour, capturing the essence of the scene – the meandering streets, the cascade of pink blossoms, and the blue-domed buildings set against a backdrop of pristine white facades.

Noticing her contemplative expression, Alex spoke with a touch of curiosity, "Lost in thought, my dear?" After a brief hesitation, she opened up, her voice tinged with nostalgia. "Seeing that girl paint took me back to my art school days. It's been ages since I held a paintbrush myself." He responded with an encouraging smile, his arm draped casually over her shoulders. "You were a true artist back then; your passion for painting was real."

She let out a soft sigh, her gaze still captivated by the young artist's work. The strokes on the paper seemed to resonate with her own artistic past, reigniting memories of a time when creativity flowed freely. "Maybe," she murmured, vulnerability seeping into her voice, "but I also faced the sting of art school failure. Unmet expectations knocked me down a peg, and I let those setbacks dent my confidence. Felt like I fell short," she added, as she added milk to her coffee.

"You know, Alex, I often think about what would have happened if I hadn't failed art school. I might be a successful artist today, living an entirely different life." A solitary tear escaped the corner of her eye, glistening like a diamond in the soft morning light. Alex reached out, his hand brushing against hers gently. "There's nothing wrong with being an arts administrator, Maggie," he said, his tone soothing and reassuring. "You're brilliant at it," he said, taking a leisurely sip of his freshly squeezed orange juice. "Some of us have to settle for more practical paths. Not all dreams are meant to come true."

She sighed, her fingers absentmindedly drizzling olive oil over a warm piece of bread. The kitchen was filled with the aroma of freshly brewed coffee, mingling with the earthy scent of olive oil. "But look at you," she said, her voice wistful, as if trying to grasp the intangible. "Living this amazingly creative life as a musician. I want that. I want that life."

Alex's touch on her hair was tender, a caress filled with unspoken understanding. "We can't all live the creative life, you know," he said, his voice carrying the weight of experience. "I mean, everyone desires it, but it's a difficult journey. I've been chasing a record deal for years. You should stick to your lane, do what you're good at. And there's nothing wrong, Maggie Miller, with being an arts administrator," he declared, his hands rising up to the heavens in a gesture reminiscent of a preacher's sermon. "Live in the moment! Appreciate what you have! "

The gentle rhythm of the sea continued its soothing melody, enveloping her in contemplative silence. As the young artist's brush danced across the canvas, each stroke seemed to mirror a page from her own history. She glimpsed a reflection of her former self, a self unburdened by doubts and insecurities, basking in the freedom of creativity. "Everything good?" his voice brought her back to the present, a lifeline breaking through the tides of memory. She turned her focus to him, offering a reassuring smile to allay his concern. "Yeah, just a fleeting moment of reflection," she responded, shaking off her reverie with a subtle shake of her head. "But let's not dwell on that. Any thoughts on how we should make the most of today?"

Both of them seemed momentarily adrift, caught in the uncertainty of their plans. Seeking guidance, Alex motioned to the waiter, who approached with a friendly demeanour. "Excuse me, could you suggest a great place for us to explore around here?"The waiter's eyes lit up with enthusiasm. "Ah, absolutely! You can't miss out on Fira Skala," he replied warmly. "It's a nearby port known for its breathtaking views and laid-back atmosphere – the perfect getaway." Intrigued, Maggie leaned in, her curiosity ignited. "That sounds fascinating. How do we get there?"

The waiter's demeanour took on a playful edge as he leaned closer, his voice hushed in a conspiratorial tone. "Well, brace yourselves for a bit of an adventure. To reach Fira Skala, you'll need to conquer the 587 steps down to the port. But trust me, the journey is worth every step."Alex raised an eyebrow, a mix of surprise and amusement in his expression. "587 steps? You're serious?"The waiter chuckled, a twinkle in his eyes. "Absolutely! It's a bit of a challenge, but the breathtaking views along the way make it unforgettable. Take your time and enjoy the scenery."

Thwy shared a glance, a blend of excitement and a touch of nervousness passing between them. "Sounds like an experience," she mused, her adventurous spirit coming to the forefront.
Embracing the idea, they began their journey by foot, bidding farewell to the charming village as they set out towards the famous steps. The path led them through narrow winding streets, past whitewashed buildings adorned with vibrant pink flowers that contrasted beautifully against the blue-shuttered windows. Local shops lining the streets offered an array of unique souvenirs and traditional crafts, adding to the allure of the

journey ahead. As they descended the steps, their excitement grew with each passing moment. The breathtaking views of the caldera and the Aegean Sea unfolded before them, making the journey down all the more rewarding.

"I can't believe we get to experience this together," she said, her voice filled with wonder.

Alex squeezed her hand, his heart full of gratitude. "Me neither. It's moments like these that you remember when you are old." With each step, they felt a sense of closeness to the island, as if Santorini was revealing its secrets to them. They passed by friendly locals who greeted them warmly and exchanged smiles with fellow travellers making the same descent.

Finally, they reached Fira Skala, and their eyes widened in awe. The small port was a picturesque scene, with colourful fishing boats gently swaying on the clear transparent waters, and the surrounding cliffs creating a serene atmosphere. As they sat by the water's edge, watching the waves dance and hearing the sounds of the sea, they felt a sense of peace wash over them. The view from Fira Skala was like a painting come to life, and they were grateful to witness its beauty.

Taking the lead, Maggie boldly forged ahead, seeking out a hidden alcove for themselves. With a mischevious grin , she shed her dress and stood in her underwear, then fearlessly plunged into the welcoming coolness of the water. The liquid enveloped her body, a refreshing embrace that wrapped around her like a soothing caress. As the initial shock of the water's chill subsided, she couldn't help but release a spontaneous cry of delight, the sound merging harmoniously with the gentle rhythm of the waves. "Oh, this feels absolutely amazing!" she proclaimed, her voice carrying an undeniable note of liberation "Come in!"

Alex seamlessly followed suit, shedding his T-shirt and jeans with swift enthusiasm, his wide grin mirroring the infectious excitement of the moment. With a graceful dive, he immersed himself in the water's embrace. "You're right. Feels like a whole new world down here." Beneath the water's surface, it was as if gravity had relinquished its hold, allowing them to glide effortlessly with the gentle currents. Sunlight pierced through the crystal turquoise water, casting an ethereal radiance that bathed everything in an otherworldly glow.

Her fingers grazed a strand of seaweed, her laughter ringing out. "Can you believe how surreal this is?" Her eyes were wide with wonder. Alex nodded, his gaze tracing the interplay of light and shadow. "It's like our very own underwater kingdom." As they ventured deeper, the underwater depths unfurled before them in a vibrant tapestry of colours and intricate designs. Her delighted gasp mingled with the gentle rush of bubbles as a school of fish darted past, their scales shimmering like molten silver. "Did you catch that?" Her excitement was palpable. Alex's grin mirrored her enthusiasm. "Absolutely, it's as if they're performing just for us."

Their gazes locked amidst the crystal-clear expanse of the turquoise ocean. The swirling currents embraced them as Alex reached for Maggie's hand, their fingers entwining. The world faded, leaving just the two of them in a watery haven. He drew her closer, and they moved together in a timeless dance. Amidst the vibrant waves, their lips met in a gentle kiss, a blend of saltwater and sweetness. Time seemed to pause as their love flowed freely in the ocean's embrace.

They swam in the cool Aegean waters for nearly an hour, but the relentless midday sun took its toll. She wiped her forehead, her cheeks flushed. "This is incredible, but I can't handle much more of this sun." he agreed, sweat glistening on his brow. "I'm with you. Let's head back to the apartment and escape this heat.

As they faced the daunting challenge of ascending the 587 steps, an unexpected scene stirred both compassion and unease within Maggie. A cluster of fatigued donkeys lingered nearby, their coats dusted with a fine layer of dirt. The animals bore saddles that showed signs of wear, and weariness emanated from their eyes, evidence of the toll their labour had taken.Alex's gaze shifted from the weary donkeys to Maggie, his brow furrowing in thought. "Perhaps taking a donkey could make this climb easier?" he suggested.Maggie's focus remained on the animals, her voice tinged with empathy and sadness. "It doesn't sit well with me, Alex. The sight of these donkeys struggling in this intense heat is just heartbreaking." He reluctantly nodded in agreement and began the ascent.

10 minutes into the climb, smiles were replaced with determined expressions as they forged ahead on the unforgiving path. Sweat drenched Alex's forehead, and each breath came in ragged gasps. "This... this is brutal," he managed, his words punctuated by shallow breaths.Concern and exhaustion etched her features as she fanned

herself, her voice trembling. "I didn't expect it to be this demanding. It's like we're trekking through a scorching desert." The initial lightheartedness waned, replaced by an intensifying sense of desperation. The weight of the heat bore down as they ascended, every step an uphill battle against their own limitations.

"Going down felt like a breeze compared to this," Alex admitted, wiping his forehead. Agreeing, Maggie fanned herself and quipped, "Yeah, the heat adds a whole new level of challenge. But hey, we're creating unforgettable memories, right?" The path grew steeper, unrelenting. Breaks became more frequent, offering brief refuge in sporadic patches of shade. "Guess this is Santorini's version of a stairmaster workout," Alex attempted to lighten the mood. Maggie's chuckle was accompanied by a visible struggle against the heat. "I didn't sign up for a marathon," she joked, though weariness laced her voice.

But as they pressed forward, the heat's unyielding grip began to take its toll on Maggie. Energy dwindled, and dizziness set in. Concern etched Alex's features as he noticed her struggle. "Are you alright?" he asked, his hand resting gently on her shoulder. Managing a strained smile, Maggie admitted, "Feeling lightheaded. The heat is getting to me." He swiftly took action. "Let's find some shade, rest for a bit, and take it slow."

A small alcove provided respite from the sun's intensity. She sat, her back against the cool stone wall, Alex offering support by sitting beside her and wrapping his arm around her.Flushed and faltering, Maggie clung to the stone railing. "I can't do this, Alex. I feel sick." Frustration tinged his response, his tone harsh. "Seriously, Maggie? You didn't think twice about this before rejecting the donkey ride?"

Her eyes blazed with a mix of anger and disbelief. "You're blaming me for this? You wanted the easy way out to avoid a little discomfort?" His retort was sharp, his annoyance evident. "It's not just discomfort, Maggie. It's a brutal climb, and you're making it harder by refusing to be practical."Her voice quivered with hurt and anger. "I thought you understood why I didn't want to support animal mistreatment. But apparently, your comfort matters more."His frustration reached a boiling point, his voice raised. "This isn't about some moral high ground, Maggie. It's about making smart choices. Look at you now, struggling and ruining our entire experience."

Amidst the tension, two compassionate German tourists materialised like a reprieve, momentarily breaking the escalating tension. The taller of the two, her eyes carrying warmth, approached Maggie with concern. "Are you okay? Do you need any help?" Swallowing her pride, she looked back at the German woman and nodded appreciatively. "Yes, I could use a hand. Thank you." With unexpected strength, the German woman extended her arm to Maggie, while her companion put his hand around her waist. Their silent support spoke volumes, transcending language barriers as they helped them navigate the remaining ascent.

With the ascent conquered, Maggie and Alex shared a mixture of relief and newfound appreciation. Santorini's unspoiled beauty sprawled before them, untouched by the echoes of their recent argument. As the German tourists bid their farewells, a palpable calm settled in, a temporary respite amidst the tension.

In the fading aftermath of their disagreement, Alex pulled her close, their embrace a silent testament to shared triumph and a fragile sense of reconciliation. "We made it," he exhaled, his arms providing a blend of comfort and victory. Maggie met his gaze, a soft smile gracing her lips. "Their help was a stroke of luck," she acknowledged, a touch of gratitude infusing her words, a nod to the role of chance in their journey. Alex's fingers brushed her cheek, his expression tender but uncertain. "What's on your mind?" She drew a breath, steadying herself for the candid vulnerability that was about to unfold. "I was thinking about us, our path ahead. Sometimes, I find myself wondering where we're truly headed. Your impatience, the frustration that boils over... it can be a lot to bear."

A slight frown appeared on his face, and his eyes showed a hint of vulnerability. "Wait, what's really bothering you? Is this about that donkey thing?" he asked, looking a bit confused. She absentmindedly played with the rose quartz ring on her finger, her tone a mix of uncertainty and determination. "Nah, Alex. It's not about that. It's about those times you get all snappy out of nowhere. Love isn't just about getting through tough stuff. It's about being patient, getting each other, you know? Not just dealing with occasional grumpiness. I want us to be the kind of love that sails through the calm and the crazy, where we handle our differences without getting all frustrated."

He kept his hand on her cheek for a moment, like he was torn between emotions. "Maggie, you know I've got feelings for you. The crap we've been through has only made us tougher. And looking ahead... I really believe in us, in our ability to handle whatever comes." Her eyes locked onto his, uncertainty and hope mixed in her gaze. "I want to believe that too, Alex. I really do." He leaned in, their lips meeting in a heartfelt kiss that said a whole lot. "Then we'll take it one step at a time, facing whatever comes together."

Exhausted from their eventful day, they tumbled back to their small whitewashed house, their bodies yearning for the embrace of rest. With a collective sigh of relief, they collapsed onto the inviting bed, limbs heavy and minds finally at ease. Yet, beneath the surface of their weariness, a subtle unease lingered, like a distant whisper of uncertainty that refused to be silenced. As they held each other close, a quiet doubt tiptoed through their minds, casting a shadow over their otherwise peaceful slumber.

The following morning, as the sun cast a warm glow over their room, she stirred from her sleep. With a sense of purpose, she rose from the bed and began to pack their belongings, the events of the previous day etched into her memory. The weight of unspoken thoughts hung heavy in the air, a left over tension that she tried hard to ignore. Determination fueled her actions as she carefully folded clothes and stowed away memories, a silent contemplation settling within her.

Soon, their bags were neatly packed and ready by the door. Maggie and Alex exchanged a glance, their eyes betraying a mixture of excitement and apprehension. As they left their Airbnb behind, they made their way to the old port of Santorini, the air tinged with a bittersweet blend of anticipation, excitement and doubt. The Olympus Princess cruise ship awaited them, a vessel that would carry them back to Crete, yet the journey ahead seemed to mirror the uncharted territories of their own hearts. Hand in hand, they embarked on this new adventure, ready to navigate whatever challenges lay ahead, uncertain yet resolute, their future a canvas waiting to be painted

Chapter 12; The One

Upon her return to Crete, Maggie wasted no time immersing herself in the whirlwind of her wedding preparations. With a swipe of her fingers, she dialled Patrick's number, a smile playing on her lips as the call set their plans into motion, locking in a meet-up for the upcoming Tuesday.

A mere blink later, it seemed, she found herself on the bustling streets outside Grecian Goddess Brides. A clear blue sky hung overhead, and her heart danced with expectation. And then, like a scene straight out of a film, there he was: Patrick, a vision of undeniable grace, strolling toward her. His pale pink linen suit was a modern nod to sophistication, a statement that whispered confidence in an unconventional choice. A Panama hat perched jauntily atop his head completed the look, a wink of style that only he could pull off with such ease.

And then, as if time had scripted its own poetic pause, his arms found their way around her. "I can't believe Maggie Millar is getting married," his exclamation rang out, a perfect blend of disbelief and humour that hung in the air like a melodic chime. "It's hard to believe, isn't it?" Maggie's replied, a reflection of the sentiment that swirled within her, carried a mixture of excitement and amazement.

With playful grins, they entered the ornate doorway, crossing into a world woven with lace, silk, and dreams. The boutique exuded an enchanting vibe, as if each gown held a story eager to unfold, and secrets waiting to be revealed. As Maggie explored the collection of wedding dresses, her eyes sparkled with excitement and anticipation. The air was filled with the alluring scent of satin and chiffon, coaxing her fingers to gently explore the delicate fabrics, envisioning herself gliding down the aisle in a true fairy tale masterpiece.

Approaching with a sense of curiosity, the saleswoman's eyes gleamed as she inquired, "Can I help you?" Her voice held the mystique of secret adventures. Maggie's grin lit up mischievously. "Do you happen to have this gown in a size 12?" she asked, pointing to an exquisite creation adorned with intricate beading and a flowing train. Intrigued by their playful energy, the saleswoman disappeared into the depths of the shop, akin to a treasure hunter on the hunt for a prized gem. Maggie's excitement was practically palpable as she continued her exploration, her fingers tracing gowns that seemed to breathe out tales of love and romance.

In a sea of tulle and satin, his eyes widened with delight as he unearthed a dazzling tiara among the accessories. A cheeky grin danced on his lips as he crowned himself and struck a pose, evoking laughter and delight from Maggie. The boutique hummed with activity, a whirlwind of excitement embodied by soon-to-be brides. Laughter and dreams intertwined as each woman sought "the one" within the racks of bridal opulence. They revealed in the rich tapestry of brides, each weaving a unique thread of style and persona. From timeless ball gowns to bold silhouettes, the boutique beckoned to brides-to-be who dared to challenge tradition.

As they meandered through the gowns, Maggie's eyes widened with wonder. Each dress seemed to tell a story of love and optimism, inviting her to step into it on a momentous day. With every gentle touch on the delicate fabric, a surge of anticipation coursed through her, envisioning herself as the radiant bride she aspired to be. Within the dressing room, a haven of dreams unfolded. She slipped into one gown after another, twirling and admiring her reflection in the mirror. Some dresses whisked her into a fairy tale realm, while others exuded modern elegance—each offering a fleeting glimpse of the woman she longed to transform into on her wedding day.

With each new dress, Patrick's gaze radiated admiration. "You are a vision, Maggie," he effused, genuine awe infusing his voice. Together, they reveled in the enchanting moment, luxuriating in the fantasy of unearthing the perfect dress, one that would capture her heart. Amidst this bridal odyssey, time seemed to suspend its march. The world beyond receded as Maggie and Patrick delved into a realm where reality intertwined with dreams. With each gown, they ventured deeper into the enchantment of love, believing that amidst the satin and lace, they would unearth a dress potent enough to transform her special day into an indelible memory.

"Is this available in a larger size?" she inquired, her fingers tracing the delicate contours of a silk duchess gown adorned with fleur-de-lis embroidery and a regal chapel-length train. The salesgirl nodded, "I'll check in the stockroom," and vanished amidst the tapestry of satin, sparkles, and tulle that surrounded them. Patrick, the candid commentator, raised an eyebrow and quipped, "Looks a bit Kardashian, don't you think?" A playful smirk graced his lips as he wrinkled his nose in mock disapproval. She then slipped into a simple dress in an A-line style. "I've seen potato sacks with more flattering silhouettes. Maybe we should just tie a ribbon around you and call it a day." Maggie's eyes sparkled mischievously. "Well, there's no harm in trying it on," she retorted, her laughter resonating in the air.

With the enthusiasm of a wild boar uncovering truffles, she combed through the sale rail, retrieving a tiara adorned with tiny, twinkling butterflies. The bridal haven buzzed with activity, brimming with brides-to-be navigating an ocean of dresses, trailing trains, and preening reflections in mirrors. The biannual sale at Grecian Goddess Brides drew brides from every corner of Crete, each aspiring to discover their dream gown at this grand event. Amidst this throng, the chant of "Need a size 6, or 8, or 10?" resonated like the call of novice auctioneers.

"Grab and snatch anything," Maggie commanded, her determination propelling her onward. Patrick, however, sighed, checked his watch, and elegantly slumped onto a crimson velvet chaise longue opposite the changing room. Maggie, her eyes lit with a near feverish fervour, scanned the dress rack with wild intensity. Amidst the flurry, a pause ensued, and Patrick posed a candid question, his voice a gentle whisper in the air, "Are you sure he's your soulmate?" her response was soft, tinged with uncertainty, as she bit her lip and cast her gaze downward. "Yes," she whispered, offering a white lie cradled in a wedding magazine she clutched like a security blanket.

"The sale rail isn't exactly brimming with choices," she deflected, steering the conversation. Patrick's ever-supportive voice chimed in with reassurance, "Don't fret, honey. I have a feeling today is the day we uncover your dream dress." she responded with a hopeful chuckle. "I certainly hope so," she mused, a hopeful smile tugging at the corners of her lips. "I've been imagining this moment for so long." A sea of gowns beckoned, each silhouette and embellishment vying for her attention. Patrick, the quintessential fashion cheerleader, accompanied her with exuberant gestures, punctuated by effusive praises of "gorgeous" and "beautiful," or their counterparts "hideous" and "vile," delivered with theatrical flair.

A dress emerged, draped across the sales girl's arms like an ivory flag, and she couldn't contain her excitement, emitting a joyous yelp. With boundless enthusiasm, she darted into the changing room, akin to an exuberant pup. "I adore this one," she exclaimed, her hands clapping together in delight, just before she disappeared behind a luxurious curtain of pink velvet. After a few minutes, a voice echoed from behind the dressing room door, Patrick inquiring, "How's it going?" Her response carried a hint of breathlessness. "Fantastic," she gasped, her voice exuding both exhilaration and a touch of complexity. "It's just... a tad complicated to slip into."

Emerging from the dressing room a short while later, she slipped into an opulent satin gown that boasted an enormous train cascading behind her. Her presence elicited a symphony of laughter from Patrick, his chuckles reaching a crescendo that verged on snorting territory. "This one would be perfect if it weren't for the gigantic bow on my bottom," She sighed, her tone a blend of admiration and constructive critique. Patrick's wry humour waltzed through the air as he quipped, "It's like a mutant butterfly decided to plant a kiss on your behind! You're practically floating in a sea of whipped cream!" Her laughter bubbled forth uncontrollably, a joyful response to Patrick's lightning-fast wit.

After a triumphant exit from the tulle monstrosity, Maggie finally managed to catch her breath, holding the dress before her like a conqueror's trophy. "Well, that was certainly an adventure." Leaning in conspiratorially, Patrick couldn't resist adding his own comedic touch, "And just think, if we ever run out of tablecloths at the reception, we know who to call."

Undeterred by the playful banter, she pressed forward with her mission, determined to unveil the dress that resonated with her heart. The dynamic duo seamlessly navigated through a kaleidoscope of options, oscillating between the luxurious caress of silk and the sophisticated allure of satin. Their discussions meandered from the practicality of sleeves to the enchantment of off-the-shoulder designs, and even ventured into the realm of spirited debates over pearls versus the dazzling allure of diamante.

With a burst of excitement, she emerged once again, radiant in a ballerina-style dress that seemed to whisper of ethereal grace. "This one, Patrick! What do you think?" she beamed, a touch of anticipation in her eyes. Patrick's gaze sparkled with a sardonic gleam as he offered his commentary, "Absolutely captivating, darling. Is the dress rehearsing for a Swan Lake revival?" A mischievous glint danced in Maggie's eyes as she teased, "You might have missed your calling as a fashion critic."Patrick's response was swift, delivered with a grin that could only be described as infectious, "Well, as long as I get to indulge in free Champagne at every wedding I critique, sign me up!"

Maggie's gaze drifted toward the bargain rack, where a sheer sequined creation with a daring plunging neckline beckoned. Patrick's critique didn't falter, likening it to something Cher might wear, his impatience palpable.In the midst of laughter and deliberation, a sense of time wasted cast its shadow. "This was futile," she sighed, a hint of dejection tinging her voice as she surveyed the racks, her eyes betraying a touch of teary disappointment. Jacket donned, she cast one last glance at the sale rail, the allure of each dress still tantalising, though none had captured her heart.

Then, an exclamation of awe escaped her lips. A sequined tulle masterpiece adorned a mannequin at the room's edge, a gown that seemed to emit a magnetic pull. "I think this is it!" Maggie gasped, her heart racing as the curtain fell on the moment of truth. Eyes alight, Patrick clapped his hands, his praise effusive. "Gorgeous! Fabulous! Amazing! Wonderful!" he sang, each word infused with genuine enthusiasm.

A mere five minutes later, she stood before a mirror, her breath held in anticipation. As she emerged from behind the dressing room door, a collective gasp echoed. The vintage style Swarovski-studded tulle gown enveloped her like a shimmering cloud, her veil cascading elegantly. A rush of delight surged through Maggie as she beheld her reflection, her hand instinctively touching her lips in awe. "I love it," she whispered, a radiant smile gracing her features. Patrick's jubilant voice rang out, his words a crescendo of affirmation, "It's the best thing since sliced bruschetta, darling!"

Amidst the joyous laughter and the gentle flutter of tulle, Maggie twirled and danced, her heart aglow. The tulle seemed to melt around her, its ethereal embrace lifting her beyond the mundane, into a realm where dreams converged with reality. As the tears brimmed in her eyes, Patrick hummed a joyful tune. "You look beautiful," he gasped, his hand covering his mouth in astonishment, erasing any lingering doubts. The inexpensive dresses that had initially caught her eye seemed insignificant now compared to the gown that had stolen her heart. It was located in the designer section, priced at a steep £10,000, but her determination remained unwavering.

A mixture of disbelief and concern crossed Patrick's face as he gawked at the price tag. "I didn't realise it cost THAT much!" he exclaimed, his voice echoing like a wake-up call. Maggie responded with a smile so wide it almost seemed painful. "Every girl dreams about their wedding day," she explained, as if that sentiment could justify the splurge. "YOU CAN'T AFFORD IT!" Patrick hollered in response. Undeterred by his protest, Maggie fixed the sales assistant with an intense stare, questioning, "It is very expensive. I'm not sure. What would you do?" The sales assistant responded without hesitation, "I think you should buy it. You never know what could happen. You could die in a minute. A meteor could come through this ceiling and kill you right now."

"In that case, I think that I absolutely have to get it," Maggie declared with a twinkle in her eye, her resolve unshaken. As Maggie handed over her Visa card, a sensation of pure relief washed over her. The shop assistant scanned the tags on the expensive wedding dress, tiara, and veil, and Maggie felt as if a giant hot air balloon was inflated inside her head, filling the space where her brain was supposed to be. Walking out of the store with a suit bag and pink shopping bags in hand, Patrick whispered, "I think the dress is beautiful - but are you sure you've found 'the One'?" Her response was a heartfelt affirmation, "I've never been more sure of anything in my entire life."

As the sun dipped below the horizon, casting its golden hues across the landscape, Maggie returned home from her shopping expedition. A sense of relief washed over her as she stepped into the tranquillity of her apartment. The soft glow of the lights played gently on the walls, creating a cosy sanctuary that seemed to welcome her back with open arms. With a knowing glance toward the clock, she realised that Alex was still out, immersed in his sightseeing adventures. A smile tugged at the corners of her lips, a secret she held close as she embarked on her own covert mission.

Moving with a practised grace, Maggie carefully extracted the precious cargo from her shopping bags. The wedding dress, a masterpiece of lace and silk, seemed to emanate a radiant energy that pulsed with the promise of her future. Her heart fluttered as she held it, her fingers dancing over the delicate fabric as if tracing the contours of her dreams. In the quiet confines of her bedroom, Maggie's gaze shifted to the closet, an alcove of secrets and memories. With a sense of purpose, she ascended to the very top shelf, a realm reserved for treasures and forgotten keepsakes. There, behind a row of neatly arranged shoes and sunhats, she found the perfect sanctuary for her bridal masterpiece.

All of a sudden, Alex stormed into the apartment like a gust of wind, the door swinging open to reveal his eager grin. "Hold on to your seat," he exclaimed. The air buzzed with suspense, a melody unsung. Maggie swivelled around, her eyes bright with curiosity. "Spill it," she said, a hint of intrigue in her voice. Excitement electrified Alex's expression as he spilled the news. "Got a call from Indie Jam Records," he announced, his voice tinged with a mix of disbelief and awe. "They want a sit-down with me and the band."

The weight of his words hung in the air, each syllable a tribute to the years he had spent chasing his dreams. Memories of the electrifying Counterflows performance reverberated through the room, the applause and cheers of the audience echoing like a defining beat that had captured the attention of those who held the power to shape his future. " Oh my God," that's amazing, she responded, raising her hands up to heaven like a preacher.

His gaze held hers, determination sparking like a wildfire in his eyes. "This is what we've been working toward all these years," he declared, his voice steady with conviction.Her heart expanded with a joy she couldn't contain; she enveloped him in a hug, sealing the moment with a fierce kiss. Their embrace felt like a victory lap, an acknowledgment of their dedication and the promise of a new beginning. But underneath it all, a shadow lingered.A moment later, the room's aura shifted, as his excitement wavered, replaced by a flicker of apprehension. She sensed the shift, her pulse quickening.

"But," he started, his voice trailing off, eyes locked onto hers . A hush settled over the room, his next words heavy.Maggie's gaze sharpened, her own apprehension rising. "But what?" she asked, a quiver in her voice.His fingers danced along the edge of a nearby table as he chose his words. "The catch is, the meeting's in London on Tuesday," he revealed, his words a delicate balance between hope and uncertainty. Her eyebrows furrowed, surprise flashing across her features. "Tuesday?" Her tone held disbelief. "Like, this upcoming Tuesday?"

A solemn nod confirmed Maggie's suspicion. "Exactly," he affirmed, his eyes locking with hers, silently imploring her to understand the weight of his decision. Between them, a sea of unspoken emotions swirled—a blend of longing, hope, and the fear of what lay ahead."But you were supposed to stay for another six weeks," she murmured, her voice laced with disappointment that coloured the air between them like a fading sunset.His touch softened, his fingers tracing a delicate path along her jawline, a touch that spoke volumes without words. "I know, Maggie," he murmured, his voice a soothing melody meant to calm the storm within her. "I promise, I'm doing this for us, for our future."

His words carried a mix of sincerity and determination, but all Maggie felt was pain, a deep familiar pain in her chest, which felt as if it might overwhelm her. As the echoes of conversations lingered in the air, she exhaled, caught between the tides of separation and the allure of the unknown. She traced her finger along the edge of a photo frame on the table, her picture of George Michael innocently smiling back up at her.

Time seemed to blur as Alex moved with a sense of urgency, his hands working swiftly to pack his belongings. Clothes folded and essentials stowed away, he paused, his brow furrowing in frustration as he searched for his passport amidst the scattered papers on the desk. Panic flitted across his features, his fingers flipping through documents in a frenzy, the room suddenly feeling too small to contain his growing anxiety.

"Where did I put that thing?" he muttered, his voice tinged with a touch of exasperation and desperation. Drawers were opened and closed, papers shuffled, and a sense of urgency filled the air as his search became increasingly frantic. She watched, her heart aching for him, the weight of their impending separation heavy on her chest. "I'm flying out at 11pm," he declared, his voice tinged with both determination and a hint of disbelief at the time constraint.

Her concern was palpable, her eyes searching for reassurance. "You sure about that?" Her voice held a delicate balance of worry and a glimmer of hope, her fingers subconsciously clutching at the lovebirds pendant around her neck. She knew that every moment counted, every delay potentially altering the course of their farewell.

A flicker of panic crossed his face as he continued to rummage through his belongings, his movements growing more frantic as time ticked away. His breath caught in his throat as he realised the passport was nowhere to be found. His fingers ran through his hair in frustration, a mixture of anxiety and desperation clouding his features. "I can't find it," he muttered under his breath, his voice a raw admission of defeat, his eyes scanning the room in desperation as if hoping the elusive document would reveal itself.

Maggie's heart went out to him, a mixture of empathy and concern flooding her. She moved closer, her own sense of urgency mirrored in her actions. The daze that had settled over her moments ago was now replaced by a turbulent mix of emotions—confusion, shock, and a growing sense of resentment.

"Alex, it's lost," she urged, her voice laced with a touch of desperation. Her eyes scanned the room, her mind racing to think of where the passport could possibly be. She felt a knot forming in her stomach, the weight of their situation settling heavily upon her. With a renewed sense of determination, she began to help him search. Drawers were pulled open with a sense of urgency, papers shuffled and tossed aside. Each passing moment felt like an eternity as they scoured the room, their breaths coming faster, their hearts pounding.

"Check the desk again," she suggested, her voice urgent. "Maybe it slipped beneath some papers." Her hands trembled slightly as she continued to search, the tension in the room growing with every passing second. He nodded, his movements frantic as he pulled open the desk drawer once more. Papers were rifled through, shuffled, and then... a gasp of relief escaped his lips. "Found it!" he exclaimed, his voice tinged with a mixture of triumph and relief.

Her heart clenched as she turned to him, her eyes meeting his with a mixture of emotions. She wasn't triumphant as she had hoped she would be, but rather, a sense of sadness and resignation settled over her. She forced a small smile, trying to push aside the growing resentment that threatened to consume her.

He held up the passport, a small smile playing on his lips. "I can't believe it was right here all along," he said, his words a mix of disbelief and relief. The tension that had filled the room seemed to dissipate, replaced by a sense of shared accomplishment. Maggie let out a shaky breath, her gaze dropping to the floor for a moment before meeting him once more. "I'm glad you found it," she said softly, fighting back the tears.

A knock announced the taxi's arrival, a stark reminder of their impending parting. Their eyes locked, emotions exchanged without words. Guitar slung over his shoulder, suitcase in hand, he said, "Don't worry." His voice was a gentle promise. "I love you, Maggie Millar - with all my heart. I'll be back…soon." As he settled into the taxi's backseat, the door closing quietly, her heart hung suspended. The driver met her gaze, understanding passing between them. A nod, a gear shift, and the taxi pulled away. Leaning against the doorframe, she watched the lights below fade into the distance. The city's symphony continued, the rhythm of life in stark contrast to her stillness.

Stepping back into the apartment, her gaze still held the echo of the taxi's departure. The world outside felt distant, a blur of city lights and fleeting moments. The air within the apartment seemed heavier, carrying the weight of her solitude. She moved through the familiar room, the silence a stark contrast to the laughter and conversations that had once filled it. The remnants of their shared moments together lingered—a forgotten jacket draped over a chair, a half-empty coffee mug on the table—as if the room itself held its breath, waiting for his return.

She sank onto the couch, her thoughts a swirl of memories and emotions. She hugged a cushion to her chest, seeking solace in its familiar embrace. The image of Alex's departing smile played on a loop in her mind. She traced her fingers along the fabric of the cushion, her touch a gentle caress as she held onto the traces of his warmth that still lingered. Finally, fatigue tugged at her, the emotional rollercoaster of the day leaving her drained. Slowly, she rose from the couch and made her way to the bedroom. The soft glow of a bedside lamp illuminated the room, casting a warm, subdued ambiance.

She slipped beneath the covers, her body sinking into the mattress. The sheets felt cool against her skin, a stark reminder of the absence she felt beside her. She closed her eyes, willing herself to find rest despite the ache that throbbed within. As she drifted into sleep's slumber, her consciousness embarked on a wild dance between reality and fantasy. And there, standing before her, was George Michael himself—an embodiment of effortless coolness and irresistible charisma. He was wearing a black leather jacket, oozing the same iconic vibe that graced the cover of his legendary album "Faith." His stubble was meticulously groomed, adding a touch of rugged charm to his debonair persona. But it was those magnificent wings, ethereal and resplendent, that truly stole her breath away, casting a soft, radiant glow in shades of peach and pink.

"Well, well, well," he greeted with a mischievous glint in his eyes. "Seems like the cosmos decided to have a little fun with your dream tonight." Her heart skipped a beat, torn between disbelief and intrigue. "George? Are you... is this real or just a trick of my mind?" The enigmatic figure chuckled, his laughter a cascade of notes that seemed to resonate in the very air. "We're in a dreamscape, love. A playground for the imagination, where reality gets a bit... twisty."

George's eyes sparkled with a knowing glint as he replied, "Ah, Maggie, my dear, dreams are a bit like songs—sometimes they carry messages we need to hear." He stepped closer, a warm and reassuring presence. "I'm here to offer you a bit of guidance, a gentle nudge in the right direction."

Maggie's brow furrowed, a sense of curiosity overcoming her initial surprise. "Guidance? But George, what could you possibly have to tell me?" Just as George was about to respond, a ripple of energy seemed to fill the air, and the dream's atmosphere shifted. A second George Michael emerged, his presence carrying an aura of wit and wisdom. Dressed in a crisp white shirt and relaxed jeans, he leaned against an imaginary lamppost, a bemused smile playing on his lips.

"Well, well, well," the second George quipped, his voice a melodic blend of amusement and sagacity. "Seems like you're getting a double dose of me tonight, darling." Her eyes widened as she took in the sight of the two Georges, her surprise giving way to a mixture of astonishment and curiosity. "Who... who are you?"

The second George chuckled, his eyes dancing with mirth. "Think of me as the director's cut, the unfiltered version of George Michael, if you will. Here to add a touch of wit and wisdom to our little tête-à-tête."

The original George nodded in agreement, his smile warm. "Indeed, love. Sometimes, I even need a bit of guidance from the wiser version of myself." Maggie blinked, trying to process the surreal situation. "So, you're both here to help me?" The second George winked. "Absolutely, sweetheart. Think of me as the voice in your head that makes you smile and say, 'Ah, that's a clever thought.'" The original George chuckled. "And I'm here to remind you that life's a dance, even when you're waltzing through dreams. "

She felt a sense of comfort settling over her, the presence of the two Georges creating a unique blend of reassurance and amusement. "Okay, then. What should I do about Alex?" The second George leaned forward, his expression thoughtful. "Listen, the heart can be a tricky thing. But remember, a song isn't just about the notes; it's about the feeling behind them. If something doesn't quite harmonise, it's time to rewrite the tune."

Sunlight spilled into the room when she awoke, eight hours later, a new day unfurling before her. Lying still for a moment, her gaze remained fixed on the ceiling. A weight settled within her chest, the memory of Alex's departure lingering like a dull ache. It was as if the air itself held the residue of his absence, casting a sombre veil over the dawn. With a resigned sigh, Maggie swung her legs over the side of the bed, her fingers grazing the cool sheets. She sat upright, as if in search of a lingering echo of his touch. The remnants of last night's dream tiptoed along the fringes of her consciousness, fragments of a puzzle begging to be assembled into a coherent picture.

As she walked into her kitchen, her fingers danced over her phone's screen. A quick search confirmed the date—June 25, George Michael's birthday. A shiver coursed through her as she glanced at the calendar on her wall, the same date staring back at her. What was the dream trying to say? The answer remained elusive, like Alex himself.

As she prepared her cup of coffee, the gentle hum of the coffee machine filled the air, offering a familiar rhythm that brought a sense of comfort amid the swirling uncertainty. The dream echoed in fragments within her mind, a puzzle of memories – George's enigmatic smile, his words rich with both wit and wisdom. It was as though his presence lingered, an ethereal specter haunting the edges of her consciousness.

With her steaming mug cradled in her hands, Maggie remained in the cosy confines of her kitchen. Sunlight filtered through the windows, painting warm patterns across the tiled floor. The dream's narrative intertwined with Alex's abrupt departure, creating a tapestry of emotions that left her feeling adrift in her own thoughts. She took a quiet sip of her coffee, the taste mirroring the mingling bitterness of her musings.

"What am I to make of all this?" Her voice was a whisper, carried on the air like a secret shared with the walls. The dream had left behind an undercurrent of fatalism, a reminder that life's threads sometimes lay beyond one's grasp. Her fingertip traced the rim of the mug absentmindedly, lost in contemplation. The uncertainty of the future loomed large, a landscape of possibilities that was simultaneously exhilarating and daunting. George's message, the dream's enigmatic insight – they seemed to nudge her toward embracing the unknown.

Walking through her home, she entered her bedroom, a space filled with the traces of her life – a scattering of books on the nightstand, the soft comforter invitingly spread across the bed. She stood by the window, gazing at the same sun-kissed sea that had graced her thoughts moments ago. The waves whispered a soothing cadence, a backdrop to her introspection. Dreams, departures, and an uncertain future wove together in a complex tapestry of emotions that she struggled to untangle.

"Que sera, sera," she murmured softly to herself, the phrase a mantra that carried a blend of acceptance and resignation. With a final glance at the ever-present horizon from the vantage of her bedroom, Maggie turned away from the window and allowed herself to sink into the embrace of her bed. The mix of trepidation and a quiet, lingering sadness echoed within her, a reminder that amidst life's uncertainties, her own journey continued to unfold in the haven of her personal space.

Chapter 13: The Girl in the Picture

Maggie's apartment felt suffocating, the walls closing in on her as she buried herself in paperwork, desperate to escape the sadness that lingered like a ghost after Alex's departure. For hours, she had been glued to her computer screen, her eyes weary and her head pounding with a persistent ache. The weight of the unspoken words between them hung heavily in the air. With a sigh, she pushed her chair back and rose, her legs stiff from hours of sitting. She made her way to the balcony, hoping the fresh air might clear her mind. As she stepped outside, the sunlight hit her like a blinding wave of white. She shielded her eyes, momentarily blinded by the brilliance of the day.

Below, people dotted the beach, their laughter and chatter carried on the gentle breeze. The sea stretched out endlessly, a vast expanse of shimmering blue. Despite the ache in her head, the scene before her seemed to whisper promises of peace and solace.

In that moment, Maggie decided she needed a break. She needed to step away from the confines of her apartment and the weight of her thoughts. With determined steps, she descended the stairs and set foot on the warm sand. The grains shifted beneath her feet, grounding her in the present. She walked along the edge of the water, the gentle waves lapping at her toes. The sun kissed her skin, warming the places where sadness had taken residence. With each step, the tension in her shoulders eased, and the ache in her head began to fade.

The rhythmic sound of the waves became a soothing melody, and the salty breeze carried away the remnants of her worries. As she walked, she allowed her mind to wander, to drift away from the paperwork and the heartache. For a brief moment, she felt weightless, as if the burdens of the world had been lifted from her shoulders.

In the midst of the vastness of the sea and the endless sky, Maggie found a glimmer of peace. The world was so much bigger than her worries, and in that realisation, she discovered a newfound sense of perspective. The sadness didn't vanish entirely, but it became more manageable, a distant ache rather than an overwhelming storm.

As she walked, the world around her seemed to melt away. The air carried the briny scent of the ocean, and the soft caress of the breeze played with her hair, teasing strands across her face. The sand moulded itself beneath her steps, yielding to her presence as if the beach itself offered a gentle embrace. Each footprint she left behind was a fleeting mark of her existence, a momentary testament to her journey.

In the distance, the quaint silhouette of a beachside cafe materialised. Its facade exuded an aura of cheerful simplicity, a stark contrast to the tempest that had just unfolded within the confines of the studio. The allure of its promise drew her in, the melodic chatter of patrons and the strains of music carrying the promise of respite. The worn wooden sign swayed gently in the breeze, inviting her to step into its embrace.

Crossing the threshold, the warmth of the cafe enveloped her like a hug from an old friend. Polished seashells adorned the walls, casting delicate shadows in the soft lighting. The aroma of freshly brewed coffee mingled with the salty tang of the sea, creating an intoxicating blend that awakened her senses. She made her way to the counter, her eyes scanning the menu until she settled on a comforting cup of chamomile tea.

A small corner table, bathed in gentle sunlight, beckoned her. Settling into the worn chair, she gazed out of the window, her gaze fixed on the vast expanse of the sea. The waves danced and shimmered like liquid gold under the sun's tender caress, their eternal rhythm a reminder of nature's ceaseless embrace.Just as she began to drift away into her own thoughts, her phone, a jarring intrusion in this moment of tranquillity, vibrated on the table. With a sigh, she picked it up, her heart momentarily lifted by the possibility of a friendly message or a comforting connection.

"Hello?" Maggie answered, her voice a mixture of curiosity and a hint of caution, as if the world beyond her current haven was an uninvited guest. On the other end of the line, Catherine's usually vivacious tone carried an unexpected gravity. "Maggie, I need to talk to you about something... something important."

Her fingers tensed around the phone. "What's wrong, Catherine? You sound serious."

There was a palpable pause, a weightiness that hung between them. "I heard you got engaged to Alex, and, well, I think it might be a mistake." Maggie's grip on the phone tightened further, her knuckles turning white. "What? Catherine, you have no right to say that."

Catherine pressed on, undeterred. "I was scrolling through Facebook earlier, and I stumbled upon a photo. It was... Alex" The world seemed to hold its breath as her pulse quickened. Alex. The man who had promised her forever, who had captured her heart on this very island. "What photo?" Her voice trembled, uncertainty bleeding into every word. Catherine took a deep breath, her tone solemn. "It's a photo of him, Maggie. He's at the Counterflows Festival, and there's a woman – a woman in a bikini and a pink cowboy hat – sitting on his knee."

Her world teetered on the edge of upheaval. The sand shifted beneath her feet, mirroring the instability within her heart. "That's impossible," she shot back, her voice tinged with a mixture of desperation and denial. "I checked his Facebook earlier today, there's nothing like that on there."Catherine's voice remained steady, despite the revelation she was delivering. "The band's page," she clarified. "Ramshackle. The photo was posted there."

The words hung heavy in the air, an indictment of the reality that had crashed into her sanctuary of thoughts. The waves outside continued their eternal ballet, and yet the tranquillity she had sought felt like an illusion shattered."What... what are you saying?" her voice trembled, a mix of dread and disbelief weaving through her words like a haunting melody.Catherine's tone softened, a gentle current of empathy flowing through her words. "I'm saying that Alex is with someone else, Maggie. And from the looks of it, it's not just a casual acquaintance."

Maggie's heart skipped a beat, her breath catching in her chest. Tears threatened to spill from her eyes, and she clutched the phone as if it were a lifeline, the cold device grounding her in a world that had suddenly turned uncertain."He... he's cheating on me?" her voice cracked, a lump forming in her throat that seemed impossible to swallow.

For a moment, a heavy silence hung in the air – a silence that was laden with truth, confirming the fear that had crept into her heart. As reality settled like an anchor, she felt a whirlwind of emotions churn within her: anger at the betrayal, sadness for the love she thought they shared, and a searing humiliation that cut deep.

Catherine's voice broke through the stillness, offering a lifeline of compassion. "Maggie, I'm so sorry you had to find out this way." She brushed away a tear that had escaped her eye, her hand trembling as she navigated to her smartphone's Facebook app. The weight of the impending revelation pressed down on her, yet she felt a compelling need to confront the truth head-on.

As the photo loaded on her screen, her heart sank further. There, captured in pixels, was the visual evidence of the betrayal. Alex, her Alex, with a woman she didn't recognise, his arm casually draped around her waist. Their smiles, so carefree and oblivious to the world, felt like cruel jesters, mocking the love she thought they had shared.

The photo, frozen in time on her smartphone's screen, bore witness to a betrayal that cut deep. Every pixel seemed to magnify the deceit, amplifying the pain that radiates through her heart. Shattered trust stared back at her in the form of a captured moment – a man she had believed in, a love she had invested in, and the stark reality that it had all been a facade. It was a crushing realisation, like a punch to the gut, a reminder that the life she had built was perched on the fragile foundation of illusion.

Her sister's voice cut through the heavy silence, a lifeline to reality amidst the turmoil. "I wish you didn't have to find out this way," she offered, her words carrying genuine sympathy. She could feel the warmth of her concern, a glimmer of light in the darkness.

"But, you know, he has been gaslighting you for years," her voice held a comforting softness, as if seeking to cushion the blow. "It might not seem like a good thing now, but this is probably a lucky escape." The reassurance was like a fragile thread of hope, a reminder that sometimes pain can pave the way to something good, something…better.Tears clung to Maggie's lashes, falling unchecked onto her cheeks as her world crumbled. "I can't, I just can't," her voice trembled with the weight of her distress, the impact of the revelation.

The photo had triggered a landslide of doubts, of past instances that now took on a sinister hue. She remembered the restaurant night, the subtle shift in Alex's demeanour, the way he had hastily hidden his phone the moment she entered. Had he been texting the other woman then, right under her nose? The pieces of the puzzle clicked with painful precision. And Santorini, the dreamy getaway that had been the backdrop of their love story – had it all been a lie? Her mind raced, unravelling threads that had been woven with care and affection. The laughter, the stolen glances, the shared dreams – had they all been staged, part of a grand illusion?

With her conversation with Catherine winding down, her gaze drifted from the screen to the view before her. The sea stretched out, its vastness mirroring the expanse of emotions within her. Her world felt broken, the foundation of her reality shaken. As she stared at the waves that danced to their own rhythm, she grappled with the enormity of the deception that had shattered her trust and left her stranded in a sea of uncertainty.

With trembling fingers, Maggie's gaze shifted from the painful image on her smartphone's screen to the contact labelled "Alex." Her heart performed an erratic dance in her chest, a cacophony of emotions swirling within her. She longed for an explanation, some miraculous revelation that would shatter the nightmare that had engulfed her life. But at the same time, a part of her braced for the cold, unvarnished truth that the damning photo spoke more loudly than words ever could. Summoning a reservoir of courage she never knew she had, she tapped on the image and selected the option to send it to Alex. The message bar displayed the "Sending" status, a digital embodiment of her vulnerability laid bare. Seconds stretched into infinity as she waited for the notification that would signal his acknowledgment.

And then, it came, a subtle chime that pierced the silence, and Maggie's heart performed an uneven rhythm. The message notification read "Seen" beneath the image. He had seen it. The weight of that realisation descended upon her like an anchor, dragging her into a turbulent sea of emotions. Her pulse raced, and her eyes remained locked on the screen, desperate for his response, praying against reason for a rational explanation.

Minutes ticked by, each one a torturous eternity, yet there was no reply. The silence on the other end of the digital connection became deafening, echoing the chasm that had torn open within her. Thoughts whirled in her mind like a tempest. Why hadn't he responded? Was his silence a cloak of shame, shielding him from the truth? Or was it a tacit admission of guilt, a confirmation of her deepest fears?

The lack of a response was an unanswered question that hung in the air, louder than words. As the truth of his silence took root, Maggie experienced a tumultuous blend of anger, sorrow, and reluctant acceptance. It was a painful acknowledgment that their once-vibrant love story, now stained by betrayal, had reached its bitter end.

With a heavy sigh, she set her phone down on the table, her fingers trailing over its cold surface. The unspoken words, the absence of explanation, carved a raw wound in her heart. She slumped into her chair and began to cry, her tears flowing freely and unchecked. It was a rare moment of vulnerability for Maggie, a stark contrast to her usual composed self. She wept loudly and unashamedly, her sobs wracking her body. It was a catharsis, a release of the pent-up anguish that had consumed her.

In that solitary moment, as she wept, Maggie realised she stood at a crossroads. The path ahead was shrouded in uncertainty, an uncharted journey into the unknown. The map of her life had been torn to shreds, and she had no choice but to navigate the fragments and build a new path from the ruins. As she continued to stare at her phone, the absence of a response confirming her worst fears, Maggie felt a flicker of strength rise within her—a determination to confront the pain, face the truth, and rebuild her life on her own terms.

Chapter 14:Chapter Title: Whispers of Archanes

The morning sun streamed through the kitchen window, bathing the wooden countertops in a soft, golden hue. Maggie lingered by the table, a delicate swirl of her coffee spoon in the cup capturing her absentminded attention. Beside the bowl of fresh fruits, her smartphone lay silent, its screen an unspoken collage of emotions. The absence of Alex's reply reverberated like a haunting echo, an unspoken testament to the ever-widening gulf that now separated them. She had called his number more times than she could count, each call an unvoiced plea for reconnection, for some kind of understanding, yet his response remained elusive, leaving her aching for a bridge to span the deepening abyss of silence.

Between sips of her coffee, she idly shuffled through a stack of brochures that Pangotis, the affable guide from the hotel, had handed her upon her arrival in Crete. In the weeks gone by, they had hardly captured her notice, her focus consumed by the thrill of her novel surroundings. Now, they lay before her like a beckoning light, a glimmer of possibility to shift her focus from the tempestuous waters of her troubled relationship. With a soft exhale, she set her coffee aside and picked up the glossy pamphlets, their pages flipping in a soothing rhythm until a headline emerged, "Archanes: Unveiling the Soul of Crete." The vivid images of a quaint village nestled amidst the embrace of nature held her gaze, offering a fleeting escape from the storm within her mind.

Archanes, a village that seemed to exist in a different rhythm, whispered promises of serenity and exploration. Its traditional architecture, narrow streets, and the embrace of vineyards and olive groves all seemed like a sanctuary of authenticity and the photographs transported her to a world far removed from her current gloom. A decision formed in her mind – a spontaneous choice to embrace the allure of Archanes and escape the weight of her sadness, if only for a day. Setting the brochure down, she reached for her essentials –a hat, a camera and a small backpack. Her smartphone, a symbol of her connection to the outside world, and Alex, remained untouched. It was a deliberate choice to find peace and break away from the confusion that consumed her.

The sun's rays enveloped her as she stepped out of her apartment, and as she walked, the distant echo of her smartphone's notifications seemed to fade, replaced by the anticipation of discovering a village that held the promise of new experiences and a chance to find herself once again. She embarked on a bus journey that wound through the picturesque Cretan countryside, the gentle hum of the engine lulling her into a sense of calm. Through the window, she watched as the landscape unfold before her, revealing rolling hills, vineyards, and olive groves that stretched as far as the eye could see. The journey itself was an adventure, a chance to absorb the beauty of the island's heart.

Arriving at the village of Archanes, she stepped off the bus and found herself in the middle of a charming world of vibrant colours. Houses painted in pastel shades, as if picked from an Easter basket, lined the streets, their terracotta roofs providing a warm contrast against the expanse of cobalt blue sky. Each house seemed to hold a story, a piece of the village's history preserved in its architecture. A blush-pink house adorned with cascading wisteria caught her attention, and she couldn't resist taking a moment to capture its beauty in a photograph.

Wandering through the labyrinthine streets of the village, the symphony of scents filled the air, a tantalising blend of Cretan delicacies that beckoned from every corner. The aroma of grilled seafood, oregano and garlic from local tavernas mingled with the earthy notes of local wine and the rich essence of olive oil. As she strolled, the town's soul revealed itself in artful displays of blooming flowers, vivid against the whitewashed walls of houses. Orange, lemon, and mandarin trees adorned yards, terraces, and balconies, their vibrant splashes of yellow and hesperidium an ode to the island's fertile soil.

Amidst the picturesque serenity of the village, her gaze was drawn to an older woman, her age gracefully etched in the lines on her face and the silver strands of her hair that gleamed like threads of wisdom in the sunlight. The woman was engrossed in tending her garden, a haven of vibrant life and colour that seemed to flourish under her experienced touch. Intrigued by this scene, Maggie felt an irresistible pull to approach, to unravel the secrets held within both the garden and the woman herself.

"These flowers... they're more than amazing. What are they?" Maggie asked, her tone a mix of genuine curiosity and awe. The woman's eyes lit up with a contagious enthusiasm, like a secret about to be shared. "You'll spot these all around Crete. Jerusalem Sage and orchids—those are close to my heart too. And guess what?" Her finger extended toward a vibrant pink blossom, excitement practically radiating from her. "That's the Anemone—a real standout, if you ask me." she nodded, captivated by the moment. "Anemone? That's an unusual name. Why's it called that?" she inquired, eager to dive into the story behind the vibrant petals.

"The name comes from the Greek word for wind, 'anemos'," Iris explained, her fingers skillfully tending to a nearby rosebush as she spoke. "In ancient Greek belief, it was the gentle touch of the wind that encouraged these blossoms to bloom." "I'm Iris," she added, her tone embracing warmth and hospitality. Maggie reciprocated with a handshake."Maggie," she replied, her eyes sparkling with interest.

"Am I detecting an Irish accent?" Iris remarked , as her gaze shifted towards the sun-kissed freckles that adorned Maggie's cheeks. Maggie's response was swift, accompanied by an infectious grin, "Yes, from Dublin."As the conversation wove its tapestry, her curiosity mirrored her intrigued expression. "And what about you?" she inquired, her interest an open book waiting to be read. "I've been a local for most of my life," came the proud response, her lips forming a smile that held a familiarity etched with time. "Though there were a few years spent in England during my twenties." she added a touch of nostalgia adding colour to her words.

"So, what brings you here?" Iris inquired. Maggie took a deliberate, unhurried breath, allowing the weight of recent events to linger in the air like a silent echo. "I…I needed a change of scenery, a break from the usual," she replied, her words infused with a touch of vulnerability, her gaze drifting pensively. "Escaping it all?" Iris added, her voice a gentle murmur, like a breeze that carried understanding.

"I was actually just engaged, you know?" Maggie shared, her fingers absently adjusting the brim of her straw sunhat to shield herself from the midday sun. "It was supposed to be this incredible moment, but recently, I found out he's been cheating," she confessed, her voice catching as her eyes welled with tears, like raindrops tracing delicate paths down her cheeks. "Or... well, at least that's what it seems like." She paused, a breath suspended in the air as she wiped her eyes with the back of her hand, her gaze finding a distant point beyond. "I'm just... so confused."

Amidst her pruning, Iris observed her with the empathetic gaze of someone who's navigated life's complex terrain. Drawing a little closer, her presence acted as a gentle anchor amidst Maggie's swirling emotions. "Your story," Iris began, her voice a river of wisdom borne from years of lived experiences, "it resonates deeply with me." Leaning in, her curiosity ignited like a spark in the night. "Really?" she inquired, her fingers tracing the delicate edges of a nearby leaf as if in tune with the rhythm of their conversation.

Iris's nod carried the weight of her own journeys, her eyes becoming a bridge that spanned generations and lives. "Divorce, distance, grown kids—I've found my own way through all of it," she confessed. Maggie's nod was accompanied by a soft smile, a silent recognition that they were treading a similar path. "You really get it." There was an unspoken comfort in discovering a kindred spirit, a connection that transcended mere words.

"You see, my dear," Iris began, her words weaving a delicate symphony that harmonised with the rustling leaves and the distant melody of a bird, "this garden has been my confidante through the seasons of life." Her fingers brushed against the velvety petals of a rose, the touch infused with a lifetime of tenderness and understanding. "In spring, when the world awakens from its sleep, these blossoms emerge as if from a dream. They remind me of the innocence of beginnings, the beauty of unfolding, and the potential that resides within every bud."

Her attention was fully captured, her gaze following Iris's gesture as it swept towards the resplendent colours of the garden. "And then comes autumn, with its gentle wisdom. The leaves transform into a kaleidoscope of fiery hues, reminding me that change is inevitable. Even in letting go, there's a kind of beauty that only time can unveil."

As Iris spoke, Maggie's voice interjected softly, "It's like the leaves are painting a portrait of transformation." She exchanged a knowing smile with Iris, feeling the connection deepen.Iris's steps guided them to a quiet corner, where delicate snowdrops swayed gracefully in the breeze. "Winter becomes a time of introspection, of finding solace in simplicity. The snowdrops endure the harshest cold to emerge as symbols of resilience, whispering that even in the harshest moments, grace can be found."

"That's truly inspiring," she responded, a note of appreciation in her voice. The weight of her recent struggles seemed to lessen as she absorbed Iris's wisdom.Her gaze turned skyward, capturing the hues of a summer sunset and the commencement of a nightly cricket serenade. "Ah, summer—the season of vibrancy and life in full bloom. These flowers are like fleeting moments of joy, vibrant and precious, reminding us to savour the present, for it too shall pass."

As Iris spoke, her voice carried a gentle cadence, as though she were weaving a tapestry of time and seasons with her words. "Much like this garden, our lives mirror these seasons. From innocence to discovery, from change to letting go, from resilience to jubilant celebration. Each phase has its rhythm, its purpose, and its beauty." Iris's gaze returned to Maggie, brimming with the depth of her understanding. "Embracing these life seasons, both in the garden and within ourselves, is where we find the true essence of existence. It's in understanding that every petal, every leaf, every experience is a part of the whole. Our lives, like this garden, are enriched by the diversity of its seasons."

She continued, gently placing her gardening tools on a nearby wooden chair , a pause settling like a fleeting thought in the conversation. "I'm actually planning to visit the church," she mentioned casually, retrieving her bouquet of flowers from the basket with her weathered hands, "You're more than welcome to join me... I have a feeling it might offer some peace."

Leaving the pretty garden behind, Maggie and Iris's footsteps led them to a village treasure, the Saint Nicholas Chapel. Nestled within the village's charm, the building's weathered stone walls bore the marks of time, a testament to eras long past. Stepping inside, she was embraced by a serene quietness that seemed to exist outside the confines of time. The cool air, faintly scented with the lingering touch of incense, enveloped her like a soothing embrace. Sunlight streamed through stained glass windows, casting a vivid mosaic of colours onto the ancient stone floor, an artistic interplay of reverence and awe. Her footsteps resonated softly, echoing alongside the whispers of countless prayers that had graced this sacred space.

As her gaze wandered, Maggie's eyes were captivated by the icons that adorned the walls. Each one depicted faith and devotion in mesmerising detail. The painted eyes of saints held a depth of understanding that seemed to reach out to hers, conveying a timeless wisdom that transcended generations. A sense of kinship with those who had found solace and connection within these walls grew within her, their hopes and sorrows reverberating like quiet echoes reflection. Choosing a seat toward the rear, Maggie surrendered herself to the enveloping stillness. Settling onto the bench, she allowed her heart to open to the tranquillity of the present moment.

Her gaze lifted to the intricate patterns adorning the chapel's ceiling, inviting her thoughts into a contemplative dance. Amid the chapel's serene embrace, her whispered prayers mingled with the reflections of her troubled heart. "Why hasn't he replied to my texts?" she whispered under her breath "How could he simply vanish? Who is the girl in the picture" The emptiness within her reverberated through the solemn halls, an unvoiced plea for clarity amidst the uncertainties of life. In a poignant moment, Maggie approached a small cluster of flickering candles. Choosing one, she struck a match and watched as the flame sprang to life. With a silent prayer for insight, she placed the candle among its companions, its glow casting a warm flicker of hope within the chapel's tranquil hush.

Maggie watched as Iris placed her bouquet at the base of a statue, and mouthed a silent prayer. As they stepped into the daylight, Maggie's curiosity found its voice "I couldn't help but notice the beautiful flowers you left there. Is there a special meaning behind it?"Her smile was tinged with reverence, her eyes carrying a deep understanding. "Those flowers are an offering to St. Nicholas," she explained, her voice gentle and soothing. "He's revered as the friend and protector of those in trouble or need. Leaving flowers is a way of seeking his guidance and support, especially during times of uncertainty."

Maggie nodded, a glimmer of comprehension illuminating her eyes. The gesture mirrored the struggles she held within. "It's beautiful, isn't it? How faith and tradition can provide comfort when things get tough," she mused, her words a product of contemplation. Iris's smile widened, the mutual comprehension bridging the gap between them. "Absolutely," she replied, her tone tender, the unspoken link between them almost tangible. "For me, it's always been a source of comfort, especially through my divorce." They strolled on, their pace unhurried, as the resonance of their shared encounters enriched the burgeoning bond that was forming between them.

Their footsteps meandered, leading them to a charming taverna where the tantalising scent of traditional Greek cuisine hung in the air like an invisible song, beckoning them to indulge in both flavours and moments. "I'm absolutely famished," she declared with a playful grin, her anticipation evident. "Care for a bite?" she invited, to which Iris responded with an affirming nod. Settling at a corner table, they found themselves surrounded by the warmth of a space that seemed to embody the very essence of Greek hospitality. As their easy conversation flowed, they settled into the cadence of the taverna's lively ambiance. Their words intertwined like old friends catching up, their fingers tracing the menu, as if exploring a treasure map of Greek delights.

Amid the culinary adventure, Iris leaned in "You're at a crossroads," she observed, her voice carrying the weight of her own journey's wisdom. Her words were spoken with the steady grace of someone who had learned to navigate life's unpredictable tides.She nodded, her gaze briefly lifting from her plate to steal a glance at the village outside."Walking the line between what's past and what's yet to come," Iris continued, her voice a gentle stream amid the taverna's lively chatter. "The beauty lies in rediscovering yourself, even when the world seems distant." A single tear glistened in Maggie's eye – a release, an acknowledgment of the emotions swirling within her. "Moving forward, even when the path is unclear," she added, her voice carrying both vulnerability and determination.

As they tasted an array of Greek dishes, Iris's words flowed like a gentle stream, weaving words of wisdom that seemed to echo through the flavours of their meal."You know," she began, pausing as she savoured a forkful of moussaka, "there's an ancient Greek philosophy called Stoicism that might offer you some solace during these challenging times." Maggie's curiosity was piqued, and she looked up from her plate, her interest evident in her eyes. "Stoicism?" she inquired, her tone inviting her to continue.

"Yes," she nodded, her gaze reflective. "Stoicism is about recognising what's within our control and what isn't. It teaches us to focus on our thoughts, emotions, and actions, while letting go of things beyond our control, like the actions of others or external circumstances." She nodded thoughtfully, her fork tracing patterns on her plate. "So, it's about finding a sense of inner peace and resilience?" "Exactly," Iris replied with a warm smile. "It's about acknowledging that challenges and difficulties are inevitable, but our response to them is what truly matters. We have the power to choose our attitudes, our perspectives, and our actions, regardless of the situations we find ourselves in."

Iris's words seemed to add depth to the flavours dancing on their taste buds and as they shared bites of spanakopita and exchanged stories, she expanded on the philosophy of Stoicism ,"You see, it encourages us to embrace adversity as an opportunity for growth," she continued. "Just like the olive trees here in Crete. They endure harsh conditions, rocky soil, and intense sun, yet they produce some of the finest olive oil. Similarly, we can transform challenges into sources of strength." Her eyes sparkled with newfound understanding. "So, it's about finding our own resilience and using difficulties as stepping stones?"

Iris's smile was like a sunbeam breaking through the clouds. "Exactly, Maggie. And by practising Stoicism, we can find a sense of inner calm even in the worst situations. It's about embracing life with open arms and a steady heart." As their meal progressed, their connection deepened, each bite of food accompanied by words of insight and understanding. Their conversation became a lifeline, guiding Maggie through the labyrinth of her emotions and offering her a glimpse of the path ahead. In the warm glow of the taverna's ambiance, she found herself feeling nourished not only by the delicious food but also by the shared wisdom and companionship of her new friend. It was as if the weight of her heartbreak was being lifted, piece by piece, with each shared joke and heartfelt moment.

As the sun embarked on its descent, casting its golden glow upon the village, a bittersweet realisation crept in - their day was drawing to a close. Iris, her eyes holding a glint of something profound, rose gracefully from her seat. With a fluid motion, she extended a pendant towards Maggie, a small yet meaningful token of their newfound bond. The pendant bore an image of Saint Nicholas, a protector and a friend to those in need."I hope this little medal carries a piece of the village's serenity with you," she spoke, her voice imbued with the depth of their shared connection. Holding the pendant in her palm, Maggie felt an overwhelming surge of gratitude for the unexpected friendship that had unfolded over the course of the day. She looked up, her gaze meeting Iris's, and the unspoken words of thanks seemed to shimmer between them.

As the moments ticked by, they found themselves on the precipice of parting ways. Her words hung in the air, like a promise woven into the tapestry of the moment. "Paths have a way of crossing again," she said, her tone carrying an air of mystery, as if hinting at the intricate tapestry of fate that interwoven lives."Remember, dear, the world is your garden," Iris's parting words resonated with a deep resonance, echoing in the chamber of Maggie's heart. "You hold the power to tend to it, nurture it, and find beauty even in the midst of challenges." With these gentle words, Iris left a legacy of encouragement that lingered like the fragrance of blooming flowers.

With a final exchange of smiles that carried a depth of unspoken understanding, Maggie stood there, watching as Iris gracefully moved away, her silhouette melding into the vibrant tapestry of the village. As solitude settled around her once again, her gaze remained fixed on the horizon, a space where the mountains and sky interwoven in a breathtaking dance of colours. This harmonious convergence was a poignant reminder that even the most contrasting elements could create a mesmerising symphony of beauty. As she threw her backpack over her shoulder, Maggie's thoughts turned inward. She couldn't help but reflect on the chance encounters that had coloured her day. That connection she'd shared with Iris, even if it was brief, had really left a mark on her. It was like a ray of hope that cut through the challenges life had thrown before her.

With the village slipping into the embrace of twilight, and the world around her slowly fading into shades of dusk, she knew it was time to say goodbye to Archanes. The bus back to her hotel was waiting, ready to transport her back to her small apartment. As she glanced back one last time at the village that had unfolded its stories to her, she couldn't help but feel a mix of nostalgia and gratitude.

Stepping onto the bus, the doors closing behind her with a soft sigh, Maggie carried with her the memories of a day that had woven its threads into the fabric of her journey. Every moment, every connection, had become a part of her adventure, a chapter in her story that she'd always remember.

Chapter 15: Stories from the Shore

The dawn's first light tiptoed through Maggie's bedroom window, casting a soft, hopeful glow upon her tangled sheets. Sleep had been elusive, her restless night filled with questions left unanswered, and she finally succumbed to the morning at 5 AM. Her gaze remained locked on the ceiling, as though it held the secrets to her unspoken emotions. The air carried a sense of anticipation, caught between the promise of a new day and the weight of unspoken feelings.She hurriedly dressed, carefully applying her signature black eyeliner and coaxing her hair into a Bettie Page-inspired style. Each step quickened her heartbeat, a nervous rhythm of anticipation propelling her forward. The city stirred to life as dawn broke, and Maggie's destination was the Minoan Arts office, a refuge amidst the city's awakening.

Inside, the office exuded an aura of efficiency that masked the underlying tension. It was as though the very walls whispered of unrest. Her meeting with Demetris and Emily was a whirlwind of topics, but among them, the impending encounter with Nadir and the pressing need for funds to support Atticus loomed largest. The air buzzed with discussions, every financial detail scrutinised with unwavering precision.

Yet, beneath the surface of immediate demands, Maggie's thoughts wove a parallel narrative. Her broken engagement remained an unsolved puzzle, a silent orchestrator in the background. The untouched white wedding dress remained etched in her memory, a bittersweet relic of a path diverged. As the meeting unfolded, her reflections merged seamlessly with the ongoing discussions, like threads weaving together to form an intricate tapestry of her thoughts and the challenges before her.

Stepping out of the office hours later, the town unfolded before Maggie like a vibrant tapestry of life. She found herself at the mercy of her digital world as her phone chimed with a message from Alex, its bittersweet plea resonating in her heart: "I know you're hurting, but I need you to trust me." Each word struck a poignant note, tugging at the strings of her emotions. A surge of determination propelled her to explore the Ramshackle Facebook page, and there it was—a frozen moment of uncertainty. The sequined bikini, the pink cowboy hat, and beneath it all, a name that blazed like a neon sign—Cathy O'Driscoll.

Leaning against a nearby bike shop, the world seemed to hold its breath, waiting for Maggie's next move. Her fingers trembled as she sent a virtual friend request. Acceptance came swiftly and silently, forging a digital bridge to a reality she hadn't quite anticipated. Summoning every ounce of courage, she dialled the woman's number, each ring echoing like the frantic beat of her heart, a pulsating rhythm of anticipation. And then, Maggie's voice broke the silence, a fragile melody of determination woven with vulnerability.

"Hello," she ventured, her words a delicate dance between seeking and hoping. "I hope this isn't too forward, but do you happen to know someone named Alex Peterson?" A breathy pause, pregnant with unspoken truth, lingered on the line. "Yeah, he's my boyfriend. Who's asking?" The words landed like a stone dropped into a still pond, sending ripples of tension across the line. Her heart raced, the moment poised like a held note in a haunting melody.

An echo of silence embraced the call, the weight of revelation enveloping her in its grasp. "Hello...hello," a whisper emerged from the other end, carrying a truth too heavy to ignore. Reality, once elusive, now stared her down—the person she had confided in, the one she had cherished, was enmeshed in another's life. Tears swelled, emotions surged like a tempest of pain, betrayal, and disbelief. The urge to confront Alex surged within her, yet the shroud of doubt clouded her every thought.

Stepping onto the bus that would carry her home, Maggie's heart appeared to dance to its own erratic rhythm, mirroring the whirlwind of emotions that swirled within her. Holding her feelings close like fragile treasures, she resolutely barred the floodgates of tears from breaking in public. Amidst a sea of unfamiliar faces on the bus, she surreptitiously gauged her fellow travellers, yearning for a glimmer of shared empathy amidst the crowd. And then, in a serendipitous instant, it occurred—a fleeting connection, a shared understanding with a fellow passenger. In that unspoken exchange, it was as though a secret pact had been forged, uniting them against the adversities of the day.

Once she returned to the sanctuary of her apartment, Maggie released the morning's weight with a heavy exhale, the very air seemed to carry the weight of her emotions, as if the room itself held a deep empathy for her struggles. Summoning a blend of apprehension and determination, she delved into her handbag, retrieving her smartphone. Anticipation and anxiety waged a silent battle within her. Slowly, carefully, Maggie began to craft her message, each tap of the keys punctuated by the emotions swirling within her. "I've just had a conversation that shattered my world," she typed, her fingers hesitating briefly before continuing. "I just spoke to a woman, Cathay O'Driscoll and something that I never expected. She says she's your girlfriend. You can't lie your way out of this...." Her gaze remained fixed on the screen, her heartache and confusion transferred into the digital words.

The room held its breath as she took in the message. With a blend of hope and fear, she hit "send," releasing her words into the digital realm. Instantly, her phone hummed to life, displaying Alex's response: "I can explain." His words dangled, a plea for understanding. "Explain? Are you saying there's a reason behind this?"

Then another message popped up: "You should know me better. I'd never do something like that to you" It hovered, a fragile connection strained under the weight of betrayal. "Understand you better? I believed I did, but I was wrong."

With resolve and uncertainty warring within her, she left the kitchen table, her heart pounding. In her room, she opened the window overlooking the tumultuous sea. Its waves mirrored her inner turmoil. The ocean breeze brushed her skin as she typed her final message: "Never contact me again!" The words hung there, a mixture of strength and pain. Silence settled like a heavy fog, smothering any glimmer of hope. The room felt smaller, heavy with choices made and the sting of his betrayal. The distant crash of waves became a distant soundtrack to her inner chaos, a reminder of the storm raging within.

As she sat there, the truth pressed down on her like a heavy fog, the room shrinking and the air growing thin as the enormity of it all settled in. She had given him her trust, believing in the bond they shared, only to have it shattered by a photograph of some slutty girl in a sequined bikini. The aftermath left behind a deafening silence, a suffocating weight that snuffed out any lingering glimmers of hope. The walls seemed to close in, the room tightening around her, amplifying the weight of her decisions and the brutal reality of Alex's betrayal.

She sat for a few moments in complete shock until a sudden jolt ripped Maggie from her musings. The impending meeting with Nadir rushed to the forefront of her thoughts, a stark reminder of duties that couldn't be evaded. After a lukewarm shower that barely brushed away the emotional residue, Maggie stepped out into the world. The sunlit path led her to Rethymno's Venetian Harbor, a tapestry of vibrant seafood tavernas and cosy cafes overlooking the well-worn fishing boats. Amid the echoes of betrayal and lingering sadness,, her focus shifted to the impending meeting with Nadir—the final artist chosen by William, her boss, for the innovative New Voices project. Anticipation and curiosity intertwined within her, offering a temporary reprieve from her personal struggles.

The Venetian Harbor burst with a vibrant symphony of life. Fishing boats twirled in harmony with the sea's dance, while the waitstaff along the promenade choreographed an enchanting performance, their voices a melodic lure for culinary delights. Settling at a table beside the water's edge, she exhaled softly, the whispers of the waves becoming a backdrop for her contemplation. As she awaited her coffee's arrival, a sudden vibration pierced the air, illuminating her phone with Alex's name. The text message unfolded before her, a latent explosion of apology and denial. Her fingers trembled, the phone a conduit for the tempest of feelings swirling within her. Memories of Santorini's golden days clashed with the harsh reality she was slowly embracing. A part of her yearned to respond, to pour her heart into words, but with a quivering breath, she chose otherwise. The delete button was a hesitant release, erasing the message yet leaving behind its impact—a palpable aftershock that left her feeling both rattled and raw.

With a soft thud, her phone landed on the table, momentarily diverting her attention from thoughts of Alex and the mysterious deleted message. The atmosphere shifted as a presence drew near, and when Maggie looked up, her gaze met that of a man who seemed to exude an air of tranquil strength. Draped in layers mirroring the colours of the coast, he appeared like a living embodiment of the seaside itself.

Her phone landed on the table with a soft, distant thud, drawing her attention away from the enigma of Alex's deleted message. Approaching her was a man dressed simply, in a crisp white t-shirt and jeans. He bore an air of reserved strength, his presence magnetic yet veiled, like a novel with hidden chapters."Are you Maggie?" His voice flowed like a tranquil stream, its melody evoking distant memories of waves kissing a distant shore. Maggie met his gaze with a polite smile, extending her hand. "You must be Nadir."

Their handshake held a hint of distance, an unspoken chasm that hovered in the silence between them. He settled into his seat with graceful poise, a piece of art caught in the dappled sunlight that filtered through the window. Her notebook lay open, poised for their conversation. "I've been looking forward to this," she admitted, her voice tinged with anticipation.

Nadir's gaze briefly flitted to the bustling fishing boats in the harbour, finding a momentary respite in the tranquil maritime scene. When he turned his attention back to Maggie, a mixture of vulnerability and guarded reserve coloured his gaze."It's a pleasure to finally meet you," he replied, extending his hand.Sensing there was more beneath the surface, Maggie inquired, "Could you tell me about your work?"Nadir's gaze briefly flicked to the bustling fishing boats in the harbour, finding a momentary respite in the tranquil maritime scene. When he turned his attention back to Maggie, a mixture of vulnerability and guarded reserve coloured his gaze. "It's a pleasure to finally meet you," he replied, extending his hand. Sensing there was more beneath the surface, Maggie inquired, "Could you tell me about your work?"

Nadir's story began to unfold in a more conversational tone, "Well, it all started here in Crete, back in 2016. I came on a rubber dinghy, you know, escaping the horrors of Syria. It wasn't an easy journey." His voice carried the weight of his experiences, and he paused for a moment, lost in thought. As he continued, Nadir shared, "I guess being here made me realise how powerful stories can be. They're like threads in the fabric of life, holding us all together, especially in times of chaos. So, I decided to pick up a camera and start capturing these stories, these moments."

From a weathered leather knapsack, he produced a laptop, its surfaces softened by the hands of time. With a practised grace, he unveiled the screen, unveiling a gallery of photographs from the Moria refugee camp on Lesvos, snapshots from his arrival. The images portrayed a sea of life jackets strewn across the shoreline, remnants of a perilous journey teetering between the promise of hope and the looming spectre of uncertainty. "Do you see these life jackets?" His words resonated with a depth that hinted at concealed wounds, yet his gaze remained an enigmatic veil. "They embody courage, the audacity it takes to face that treacherous voyage," he explained, his voice straddling the delicate line between admiration and sorrow.

With a resolute keystroke, another image materialised on the laptop's screen. It showcased a shoreline adorned with an assortment of footwear—sandals, sneakers, well-worn boots, and pint-sized shoes—all scattered upon the sands. Each pair of shoes narrated stories of journeys undertaken, a testament to the unwavering spirits of those who had pursued safety and the glimmer of a brighter tomorrow across turbulent waters. Nadir's demeanour stayed composed, yet Maggie couldn't shake the feeling of a concealed wellspring of anguish beneath his stoic exterior.

"With each click of the shutter, I'm making a promise—to remember, to honour, and to create an everlasting tribute to the lives that were lost." he said, staring out to sea. "It's my way of making sure they're never forgotten, that each single person, each life, meant something." Maggie's eyes glistened, touched deeply by the story behind the powerful images she had witnessed. "I understand," she responded softly, her voice carrying the weight of sympathy and respect for his journey.

"You see," he began, "the thing is, the world tends to keep moving, news cycles shift, and these pictures—the faces behind them—they tend to fade into the background," he continued, his voice tinged with a touch of melancholy. "But it's become my mission, my responsibility really, to keep these stories alive through my lens." She listened intently, her heart weighed down by the gravity of his words. Within his photographs, she discerned more than just images; they were fragments of lives, fragments of human experience that transcended the boundaries of time and space.

Maggie's voice intertwined with the conversation, a blend of relief and authentic curiosity. "So, everything's sorted now, isn't it? People aren't making those perilous journeys anymore?" Nadir's response carried a composed gravity, a touch of sadness evident beneath his words. "Not quite," he replied, his tone measured but laden with a quiet weight. "Just last June, we lost 78 lives," he revealed, a sombre note entering his voice as he delved into the tragic incident. "Off the southwestern coast of Pylos, near the Peloponnese. It happened close to one of the deepest points in the Mediterranean." The heaviness of his words lingered in the air, a stark reminder of the ongoing challenges. "There were over 500 people on that vessel," he added, emphasising the scale of the heart-wrenching loss. "Others arrive on flimsy plastic dinghies, held together by tape and glue. It's heartrending," he continued, his voice tinged with a mixture of compassion and sorrow.

Her brow furrowed in response. "That's truly horrifying," she murmured, leaning in as if to grasp the weight of the conversation. Her fingers idly traced patterns on the tablecloth, a gesture that mirrored her contemplation. "Currently, Greece is providing refuge for around 22,000 displaced individuals from Ukraine," he disclosed, his gaze momentarily shifting downwards before meeting Maggie's again. "Mostly women and children," he added, his voice carrying the compassion he felt for those whose lives were intertwined with the numbers. "Your work is truly significant, " she responded, her voice gentle and sincere. In the backdrop of their conversation, the serene sounds of the sea seemed to echo her sentiment. "You've managed to capture the heart of their struggle."

The distant cries of seagulls and the relentless rhythm of the waves—seemed to underscore the gravity of their discussion. "We're all running towards safety," He leaned back slightly, his hands resting on the edge of the table, his gaze distant yet resolute. "Greece becomes a sanctuary not just on maps, but in the hearts of those who seek refuge," he continued. "My purpose now is to give them a voice—their stories, a mosaic of bravery, sorrow, and above all, hope," he declared, the words carrying the weight of his conviction.. "Hope," he stressed, his finger punctuating the air, "it's the heartbeat that courses through my images." Maggie found herself compelled to lean in slightly, her elbows resting on the table, her gaze fixed on him. "But how do you capture something as intangible as hope?" Her voice held a note of curiosity, a yearning to understand more.

Nadir's lips curved into a thoughtful smile, his hands gesturing as if to illustrate his point. "It's like catching a fleeting sunbeam," he began, his fingers intertwining and then releasing into the air. "In the midst of darkness, it's that sliver of light that pierces through, that reminds us there's a way forward." His gaze remained fixed on her, the harbour's gentle waves shimmering behind him as if in silent agreement. "But with every image I capture," he continued, "hope reveals itself. It's in the eyes of those who persevere, the smiles shared despite the odds." "It's the essence of humanity, distilled into moments that transcend the frame."

Maggie's curiosity persisted, her own fingers tracing invisible patterns on her napkin. "And does sharing these stories really make a difference?" His eyes softened, as if remembering a thousand faces he had captured through his lens. "It's the ripple effect," he said, his gaze distant for a moment before refocusing on her. "One story touches another, igniting empathy, inspiring action. A single photograph can be a catalyst for change, a reminder that behind each statistic is a life—a story that matters."

As the conversation drew to a close, a sense of camaraderie settled between them, accentuated by the soft clinking of dishes being cleared from neighbouring tables. She looked at him, a genuine warmth in her eyes. "Your photographs are important." she said softly, her words punctuated by the laughter of children playing by the harbour. "Thank you for sharing them with me."

His smile was a blend of gratitude and humility, his gaze briefly drifting to the harbour before returning to her. "And thank you for listening," he replied, his voice gentle yet resolute. "It's not often I get to speak about these things."As they exchanged parting words, the sun began to dip below the horizon, casting a warm, golden hue over the water. Maggie felt a sense of reverence for the courage Nadir possessed and the creativity he channelled into his art.

As she meandered through the old part of the town, with its pretty balconies and baskets of flowers, images of the perilous crossing from Turkey to Lesvos played out vividly in her mind. Departing from the bustling embrace of the Venetian Harbour, a whirlwind of emotions churned within her—a potent concoction of revelation and humility. It was as though she had been granted a brief yet profound glimpse into a parallel world—one teeming with stories of agony, bravery, and unyielding resolve.

Maggie stepped onto the cobbled streets of the old town, feeling an instant connection to the history embedded within each weathered stone. The sparkle of jewellery shops lined her path, their displays guarding the whispers of time. It was as if the streets themselves were inviting her into their secrets.

Guided by an invisible hand, she found herself drawn to the open doors of a charming bookstore. The shelves were a symphony of stories, each one an adventure waiting to unfold. Greek bestsellers beckoned with promises of distant worlds, while political exposés stood as a reminder of the world's complexities.

Amidst the enticing titles, a cover caught her eye, one that seemed jarringly out of place—a loud depiction of celebrity culture dominated by the Kardashians. She couldn't help but frown at the stark contrast between this spectacle and the weight of Nadir's narratives. Doubt crept in, questioning the values of her culture, the obsession with trends overshadowing stories of human resilience.

Then, like a hidden treasure, she stumbled upon the English section—an escape into a broader literary universe. A book titled "On the Greek Philosophy of Stoicism" practically leapt into her hands. Its promise of ancient wisdom resonated deeply. Holding it close, Maggie felt as if she stood on the edge of something profound, a chance to break free from her constraints.Stepping back into the daylight, book cradled in her arms, she felt a shift within herself. Gratitude blossomed—an opportunity to glimpse Nadir's world, to step beyond her own boundaries. With each step, she embraced the unknown, where questions danced without easy answers.

Memories of her past relationship with Alex resurfaced—a mosaic of her history, its fragments still poignant. The stories of Nadir, Atticus, Eva and Thomas wove together, revealing life's intricate tapestry. The road ahead was uncertain, but she was determined to seek understanding, connection, and her own revelations. Clutching the book to her chest, she sought not just answers, but also solace for her wounded heart.Each tale within those pages echoed a common desire: the wisdom to navigate life's challenges and the chance for a fresh start. Unexpectedly, Maggie found herself yearning for her own second chance.

Chapter 16: The Shadows of the Past

In the wake of her encounter at the harbour in Crete, Maggie found herself cocooned in a sense of disillusionment that clouded her days. The ruins of her relationship with Alex cast long shadows over her, a once-promising vision now fragmented like shards of glass after a tempest. The nights were heavy with solitude, her apartment's silence amplifying her isolation into an insurmountable abyss, a vast expanse of loneliness that seemed to echo back her heartache.

One evening, a glass of wine cradled in her hand, its rich hue mirroring the swirl of her thoughts. The soft glow of her laptop illuminated her surroundings, creating an intimate space for introspection. Her fingertip hovered over Rachel's name in her contact list, the memory of their Santorini exchange hanging in the air like an unfinished melody. With weeks having slipped by since that conversation, she gathered her courage and pressed the call button. The phone rang out, each chime carrying a note of anticipation until Rachel's voice finally broke through, tentative yet open. "Hello?"

A fragile smile graced Maggie's lips, the sound of Rachel's voice rekindling a connection that had lain dormant. "Rachel, it's Maggie," she spoke, her voice tinged with nostalgia and a longing to bridge the temporal gap. A pause lingered, heavy with unspoken words and a shared history that neither time nor distance could erase. "Maggie? Is that really you?" Rachel's voice trembled with a mixture of surprise and a hint of hope.

She exhaled softly, her words carrying a blend of relief and longing. "Yes, Rachel, it's me," she affirmed, her words weaving the strands of their intertwined past and the present moment. "I've been meaning to talk to you. When we last spoke in Santorini, you seemed troubled. How have you been?" Rachel's reply held a fragile vulnerability, her voice a thread connecting their shared experiences. "I'm managing," she whispered, her words bearing the weight of battles fought. "Life's full of twists and turns." A pause followed, as if the words held a world of unspoken thoughts.

"But you know what? Amid all the struggles, we did have those moments that sparkled, didn't we?" Rachel's voice, now warmer, reached across the miles, pulling them back to the heart of their bond. "Remember our 'glippes' phase back in art school? " Maggie's laughter danced in the air, a timeless echo of their connection. "Oh, the Glamorous Hippies! I remember it vividly," she responded with a fond chuckle, her voice carrying the echoes of their shared adventures.

Rachel's voice warmed, as if the mere mention of their art college days had whisked her away to a distant era. "God, I've missed you," she admitted, her words heavy with longing. "Remember that crazy art college ball?" Maggie's heart somersaulted within her chest, memories flooding in at the mere utterance of that night. "Oh, how could I ever forget?" she replied, her voice laced with the zest of reminiscence.A chuckle danced in Rachel's tone, reminiscent of the laughter they once shared. "The night we transformed ourselves into these over-the-top French courtiers, remember?"

She burst into laughter, vivid scenes of their outlandish costumes playing before her mind's eye. "Yes, yes! We were in charge of the door and handling the money, can you believe it?"Rachel's laughter rang through the air, a joyful echo of the past. "And, I admit, I got completely hammered that night," she confessed, their shared amusement evident. "But honestly, it's still one of my best memories from art college." her laughter chimed in harmony with Rachel's, the years melting away as they relived those carefree moments. "I can't forget that," she agreed with affection. "You were the life and soul of every party, no doubt about it."

"I was a mad bitch back then!" Rachel laughed, hysterically. Her tone turned playfully mischievous, an air of secrets shared between them. "Do you want to hear the rest of the story from that night?" she asked, a teasing note in her voice.

Her curiosity piqued, her mind ready to unfurl the pages of old anecdotes. "Oh, absolutely! Spill the beans," she encouraged, leaning into the conversation as if they were conspiring once more.

With a playful glint in her eye, Rachel continued, "So, you know how we were in charge of the cash, right? Well, I sort of managed to sneak a chunk of it into my bag." Maggie gasped, a mixture of shock and amazement escaping her lips. "You did what?" she exclaimed, her voice a crescendo of disbelief.

Her laughter tinkled like wind chimes, a medley of guilt and amusement. "And that little haul," she confessed, her words veiled in humour, "lasted me for months." More giggles followed, a blend of recklessness and mirth. Emotions surged within Maggie like waves, each crashing against her composure. "You actually stole money from the art college ball?" she repeated, her voice carrying a mix of incredulity and astonishment. Her laughter faded, the echoes of their shared joy diminishing into a sheepish pause. "I know it sounds wild," she replied, her tone apologetic, "but it was all just a bit of harmless fun, Maggie. Lighten up."

"'Lighten up'?!" her retort brimmed with frustration, her exasperation simmering to the surface. "You seriously expect me to 'lighten up' when your little stunt effectively derailed my future? The life I was meant to have. And you think that warrants a casual response?!"

Rachel attempted to offer an explanation, her voice faltering as she tread on the delicate ground of their shared history. "You're blowing this entirely out of proportion," she said, her words hesitant. "It was just a harmless prank, a bit of fun." As Maggie took a sip of her wine, the taste seemed to mirror the bitterness of betrayal that lingered in her mouth. "So, you're telling me that you're the reason behind my art school failure," Maggie's voice quivered with a potent mix of accusation and realisation. "You took that money, and I paid the price for it," she asserted, the weight of their shared secret palpable in her words.

"Nobody ever found out, for heaven's sake," Rachel responded, attempting to defend herself. Maggie's comeback was swift and cutting, laced with anger. "You thoughtless idiot!" she snapped back, her fury unabated by Rachel's attempts to downplay the situation. Rachel's patience wore thin as she countered, her own frustration beginning to show. "Alright, fine," she replied, her tone tinged with exasperation. "I'll admit it was a stupid decision on my part. But you're blowing this whole thing way out of proportion." She took a gulp of wine, the bitterness of her actions mingling with the lingering bitterness of old wounds.

"Yes, I took the money, and yes, we both ended up failing art college exactly two weeks later. But don't act like my actions were the sole reason for our failures. It's not as simple as that," Rachel retorted, her voice tinged with a mixture of regret and defensiveness.

"They were two separate things," Rachel protested, her own frustration simmering beneath her words. But her heart pounded, realisation flooding in like a dam breaking. "Do you even understand what that did to me, Rachel?" Her voice trembled, heavy with years of buried pain. "Failing art college, abandoning my dreams... becoming the 'black sheep' of the family. It crushed me. And all these years, I've carried the burden of that guilt."

Tears shimmered in Maggie's eyes, a whirlwind of emotions spinning in her gaze. Long-held resentment, the release of truth, and the bitter sweetness of closure mingled within her voice. "You changed the entire course of my life, Rachel. I was destined to be an artist, yet because of your actions, I ended up in some dull administrative role." A poignant sob echoed through the phone, a poignant echo of the emotions their conversation had ignited. "Maggie, you're making it sound so much worse," Rachel tried to explain, her words a fragile defence against the overwhelming feelings. "It was just a bit of money..."

"Just a bit of money?" her voice surged with unleashed frustration. "You just said that it lasted you... for months!" Rachel's tone faltered, "You can't pin your failure on me. You just have to face the truth Maggie.Perhaps you...we...were just not good enough?" Amid the whirlwind of emotions, Rachel's voice softened, carrying a fragile sincerity. "I never wanted things to turn out this way, I..." A solitary tear traced down Maggie's cheek, her finger tenderly wiping it away. "Goodbye, Rachel," Maggie murmured, her voice carrying both finality and an undertone of lingering ache.

Hanging up, Maggie retreated to her bedroom, her dresser offering refuge. Her reflection gazed back, from the mirror seeking answers within her eyes. Emotions stormed, an unspoken query lingering – "Who are you, Maggie Millar? Who the fuck are you?" Stripped down, she studied herself in the mirror, a mosaic of emotions etched upon her features – vulnerabilities, choices, and an unexpected ache. With a trembling breath, heavy as the cosmos, she removed her engagement ring, placing it gently on the dresser. It became a symbol – love's journey from hope to heartbreak. Beside it, George Michael's photograph stood like a silent guardian, resonating beyond the visual. As silence enveloped the room, memories flooded back, the dream's echo haunting her: "A song isn't just notes; it's the emotion they hold. If something's out of tune, it's time to rewrite the melody."

Chapter 17: A New Canvas

Amidst the convoluted maze of her emotions and the tattered remnants of her once-vibrant dreams, Maggie found herself ensnared in a situation that unravelled like a poorly knitted scarf. It was as if every stitch of her life had been pulled loose, leaving her stranded in a sea of confusion. The initial weeks post-breakup and Rachel's jaw-dropping revelation had been a whirlwind of emotional turbulence, a tempest navigated with a combination of tears, copious ice cream, a marathon of questionable romantic comedies and George Michael's ' I Can't Make You Love Me,' playing on a loop.

Maggie slouched on her bed, cocooned in self-pity, her entire universe confined to a luminous computer screen. Next to her, an abandoned pizza slice shared space with an empty Chardonnay bottle, a Pringles canister, and a small mountain of crumpled chocolate wrappers. She rubbed her eyes wearily, then reached for her bedside table and grabbed her mobile. There it was—the text she had impulsively fired off to Alex at an ungodly hour: "imissss*%# u! WHHHHYYY???" A sigh escaped her lips, and a deep pang of regret.

"Stupid, stupid, stupid," she muttered, each spoonful of ice cream serving as an exclamation point in her internal monologue of self-chastisement. How on earth had her life veered into this chaotic tailspin? Her once-promising relationship with Alex had crumbled, her career had hit the skids, and now she had to grapple with Rachel's jaw-dropping revelation. It was as though she'd unwittingly landed a starring role in a melodramatic daytime soap opera.

A discarded copy of Vogue lay within arm's reach, its pages teeming with impossibly glamorous models living lives of impossibly beautiful splendour. Irony hung in the air, almost palpable. Her own life felt like it belonged to a different dimension altogether compared to the airbrushed perfection paraded across those pages. She cast a rueful glance at her burgeoning midsection and sighed—everything seemed utterly futile.

With another weighty sigh, she reached for her phone, hoping for a digital escape into the realm of social media. However, her quick scroll through friends' overly filtered snapshots of enviable existences only served to magnify her feelings of inadequacy. It was as if the universe had conspired to pile on her misfortunes.

Just as she was about to toss her mobile aside in resignation, a sharp knock on her door jolted her from her scrolling stupor. Her heart leaped in surprise. Who in the world could be calling on her at this ungodly hour? She reluctantly set her phone aside and shuffled toward the door, her sock-clad feet making a soft swishing sound against the floor. Upon flinging open the door, Patrick stood before her, his expression a curious blend of exasperation and determination. Without missing a beat, he sauntered in as if he owned the place—a human whirlwind in action.

"Maggie Millar, I've had it up to here with this gloomy cloud you've been holed up under!" Patrick declared, his hands defiantly planted on his hips. "It's been weeks, and you're still drowning in a pool of self-pity." Her eyes widened in sheer astonishment as his directness hit her like a splash of icy water. "But, Patrick, I—"

"No more excuses!" Patrick interjected, waving his hand dismissively. "I'm here to rescue you from this emotional quicksand. I was as shocked as you when I heard about Alex and Rachel—the audacity of that woman. But that's beside the point! A breakup and a career setback do not define you. Remember, you're Maggie Millar, the woman who wore a tiara to lectures and danced to her own imaginary music in supermarket aisles!"

"It's been three long weeks, darling - high time you brushed off that foul Alex creature," he announced, striding over to the window and flinging back the blue shutters, bathing the room in glorious golden sunlight. "Now, I'm going to do some tidying up," he declared, eyeing the messy bedroom. "Are you planning to submit this chaos for the Turner Prize?" he quipped, winking at Maggie. She lowered her gaze, crossed her arms tightly, and shook her head in silence.

"Chin up, sweetie, it's not the end of the world, you know," he reassured her while picking up an empty pizza box. "Well, it certainly feels like it," she responded, a lump of sadness lodged in her throat like indigestion. "Alex was an emotionally stunted, commitment-phobic..."

"But I loved him," Maggie whined, leaning forward to grab a tissue from a box on the table. "Don't talk nonsense," Patrick retorted. "It's a lucky escape, Maggie Millar. A lucky escape!" he said, pushing her glasses up the bridge of his nose. She clutched a photograph of Alex from her bedside table and gazed at it with a mix of sadness and longing, tears streaming down her cheeks. Patrick watched her for a moment, then asked softly, "Do you think he was cheating all these years?"

"I don't know. Now I realise I really didn't know him at all," Maggie mused, her voice tinged with confusion. "Honestly, I don't know if he ever loved me, if he never loved me, if he even hated me. I don't know, and I'm sure I never will," she continued, her lips devoid of a smile.

"Right!" Patrick announced, springing to his feet and marching purposefully into the kitchen. "Time to start fresh," he declared, reemerging with a pair of scissors. Maggie stared at him, her expression one of pure shock. "You don't expect me to..." "Yes," said Patrick, shooting her a piercing look. "It's time to cut that man out of your life for good." With a deep breath, Maggie raised the scissors and, with a shaky hand, decisively snipped off Alex's head.

A faint smile flickered at the corners of her lips, a glimmer of amusement breaking through her emotional fog. "But what about the wedding dress?" she suddenly remembered, a note of desperation in her voice. "I spent a fortune on it..."

Patrick's eyes sparkled with mischief. "You know, we might be able to return it or even sell it on eBay," he suggested, adopting a thoughtful tone. "'Wedding gown, never used.' It could be the first line of a country song." He responded with a grin. "Get up from that sofa, there's no room for wallowing!" he exclaimed, pulling Maggie to her feet.

In that moment, Maggie realised she was in for a ride—an idiosyncratic, unpredictable, entirely Patrick-inspired journey. While the world around her was a tumult of emotions and shattered dreams, she had a sense that his unwavering determination might just be the lifeline she needed to navigate her way through the chaos.Maggie blinked, taken aback by Patrick's sudden pep talk. She hadn't expected this at all. "I... I guess I just don't know where to start," she admitted, her voice tinged with vulnerability.

Patrick's eyes softened, and he crossed the room to sit next to Maggie on the couch. "You start by taking one step at a time. Remember those dreams you had before Alex? Remember the passion you had for your art? Who you were, who you dreamed that you could be? Well, it's time to dust off those paint brushes and start capturing life again," Patrick said, his voice unwavering. "And as for Alex? He's history, a chapter you're better off without."

Maggie managed a small smile, feeling a glimmer of hope stir within her. Patrick had a way of cutting through the darkness and injecting a dose of reality and humour into any situation."Tonight," Patrick continued with a conspiratorial twinkle in his eye, "we're embarking on a grand adventure, one that will take us to the uncharted waters of a brand-new art gallery opening. And you, my dear, are my trusted companion for this escapade. Who knows? Perhaps you'll discover inspiration, or at the very least, an exhilarating diversion from the chaos."

She couldn't suppress a chuckle at Patrick's boundless enthusiasm. Maybe, just maybe, this was the nudge she needed to begin piecing her life back together. With newfound resolve, she set her ice cream aside and rose from the couch."All right, Patrick, you win. Let's do this," she declared, a glimmer of excitement twinkling in her eyes.Patrick beamed triumphantly. "That's the spirit! Now, let's transform you into a vision of elegance, ready for a night filled with art, adventure, and who knows what else!"

Guided by Patrick's infectious zeal, she embarked on a mini makeover session. Her hair was coaxed into the perfect style, a touch of makeup applied with finesse, and the vibrant dress he'd selected clung to her like a second skin. As she gazed at her reflection in the mirror, she couldn't help but marvel at the transformation. For the first time in weeks, she felt a glimmer of her former self—the Maggie who embraced life with open arms and fearless determination.

As they stepped into the lively art gallery, there was an undeniable buzz of excitement in the air. Laughter and animated conversations melded with the gentle clinking of glasses, weaving a harmonious symphony of anticipation. The gallery's walls served as vibrant canvases, each one telling its own tale through masterful brushstrokes. Patrick spotted Maggie gazing at a painting that was, to put it kindly, utterly abysmal. It looked as though a toddler had gone on a wild paint-flinging spree. "Maggie, that's just awful," Patrick declared, unable to contain his amusement. Atticus joined them, and upon seeing the atrocity on the wall, he couldn't help but concur. "Terrible. Absolutely terrible." Patrick, never one to shy away from a bit of encouragement, jumped in. "If this can get exhibited, I bet you could get some of your work up here on these walls."

"I'm not sure I've got it anymore. It's been fifteen years since I last picked up a paintbrush." Patrick, determined to boost her confidence, insisted, "You were talented, Maggie." Maggie mustered a faint smile. "Thanks, Patrick, but it's been too long. I missed my chance." Intrigued by her perspective, Patrick raised an eyebrow. "Why's that, Maggie?" She sighed softly, her gaze still locked on the vibrant canvas. "Without a degree or a master's, these galleries don't even consider you," she explained, a touch of resignation in her voice. "Vincent van Gogh was largely self-taught," Patrick began, his enthusiasm igniting. "And Frida Kahlo never attended art school. They followed their passion, honed their skills, and created masterpieces. It's not about diplomas; it's about the art itself."

Maggie's attention shifted to a nearby painting adorned with neon dollar signs, her thoughts racing. "I get what you're saying," she replied thoughtfully. "But the gallery system is manipulated by the wealthy and influential. It's supposed to be democratic and open, but in reality, it's exclusive and elitist, making it nearly impossible for people like me to break through. It's like your destiny is defined by your family's social status."

Patrick's smile remained firm, as if he welcomed this intellectual exchange. "You're absolutely right, Maggie. At the last group show I did in London - there were a mix of artists - and the only common denominator they had was that they all seemed to have come from the most unbelievably privileged backgrounds - lots of Tarquin's and Felicity's . There's nothing fair about any of it."

Maggie nodded, her eyes now fixed on a sculpture of a golden ladder leading to nowhere. "It's not just about talent anymore; it's about connections, wealth, and who you know. Lots of really incredible artists are overlooked while a select few dominate the scene." A nearby couple, impeccably dressed and sipping champagne, seemed oblivious to the conversation around them as they whispered about their latest art acquisitions. Maggie couldn't help but observe, her voice tinged with frustration. "Look at them, Patrick. They treat art like an investment, not as a form of expression or emotion. It's all about market value."

Patrick's gaze followed hers, and he couldn't hide his exasperation. "It depresses me, " he said, shaking his head. " It's become a commodity rather than a source of inspiration. And worse, it perpetuates a cycle of inequality. Artists without the right connections or means to attend prestigious art schools are pushed to the margins.

Maggie leaned closer, her voice conspiratorial as she delved into the discussion. "You know, it's not just the lack of representation for women and people of colour in the art world," she confided, "but the whole system seems like an old boys' club." Patrick nodded in agreement, his eyes reflecting deep thought. "You're spot on, Maggie. The art world is filled with complexities, and we won't see a transformation overnight."

"Enough of these heavy subjects for now," he suggested, guiding her away from the sombre conversation. They meandered toward a waiter carrying a tray of glistening champagne flutes. Patrick offered one to Maggie with a charming smile. "To embracing the pleasures of the present," he toasted, his grin infectious, "and savouring every sip."

As Maggie reached for her glass, she gracefully avoided tripping over another guest's foot, averting a potential catastrophe that might have sent the delicate flutes shattering. "Apologies!" she exclaimed, regaining her poise. Maggie's eyes then landed on Atticus—a distinctive figure with his flamboyant red fedora and an array of captivating rings. "Atticus!" she greeted him with a lighthearted chuckle,

Atticus responded with a heartfelt hug. "Wonderful to see you again. And thank you for your support with the funding for my studio rent. You can't imagine how much it means to me." Maggie's gracious smile mirrored the sparkling chandeliers of the gallery. "It was my pleasure. I'm thrilled to have been able to help." Turning to her companion, Maggie introduced them with a mischievous smile. "Atticus, meet Patrick." "Are you Patrick Evans?" Atticus inquired, his eyes filled with curiosity. "The sculptor?" Patrick beamed with pride. "That's me! The one and only." Atticus leaned in earnestly. "I admire your work. It's truly powerful."

As the champagne flowed, Atticus and Patrick engaged in a spirited conversation about their favourite contemporary artists. Maggie couldn't help but be entertained by their animated exchange. Atticus leaned forward, his eyes sparkling with enthusiasm. "You know, Patrick, Jeff Koons's art is like a burst of pop culture fireworks! It's like he's saying, 'Look at this shiny, colourful world we live in!'"

Patrick nodded vigorously, mimicking the explosion of fireworks with his hands. "Absolutely! Koons takes everyday objects and turns them into these larger-than-life sculptures. It's like he's challenging us to see the extraordinary in the ordinary." Atticus leaned back, gesticulating with his hands as he spoke. "And then there's Yayoi Kusama, the queen of polka dots! Her work feels like stepping into another dimension." Patrick laughed, his own hands mimicking the dance of polka dots in the air. "Oh, Kusama's immersive installations are a trip! You enter her world, and suddenly, you're surrounded by endless dots. It's like being lost in a dream."

Maggie watched with delight as their conversation flowed seamlessly, their expressive gestures and laughter painting a vivid picture of kindred spirits bonding over their shared love for art. She couldn't help but observe in awe the magnetic connection between Patrick and Atticus, two souls who had seemingly been searching for each other in the vibrant gallery.Her mother's old saying reverberated in her mind like a comforting melody, "For every old sock, there is an old shoe." Atticus and Patrick were like two puzzle pieces that had finally found their perfect fit. Their connection felt as natural as the ebb and flow of the tide, as if destiny had guided them to this serendipitous meeting.

Maggie's heart swelled with happiness, her enthusiasm bubbling over as she reached for another glass of champagne. The effervescent liquid sparkled like liquid joy in her glass, casting a warm, golden glow over her slightly tipsy state. The gallery's vibrant art seemed to come alive, its colours dancing in perfect harmony with her newfound exhilaration."Here's to us!" she declared with a merry giggle, raising her glass once more. Patrick and Atticus, equally swept up in the festive spirit of the evening, clinked their glasses with hers."To new beginnings!" Patrick chimed in with a playful wink.Atticus held his glass aloft, the night's revelry evident in his eyes. "To art, friendship, and unexpected connections!"

Exiting the art gallery, Maggie, Patrick, and Atticus teetered arm in arm through the enchanting streets of Rethymno. The night air felt crisp against their flushed cheeks, and their laughter, punctuated by an occasional hiccup, echoed through the cobblestone lanes. Each step seemed like a dance, guided by the rhythm of champagne-induced jollity.

"Oh, look! Stars!" Maggie exclaimed, tilting her head back dramatically to admire the twinkling constellations. Her words bubbled out amidst a fit of giggles, and she swayed slightly, nearly toppling over, causing Patrick and Atticus to erupt in laughter.Patrick leaned in, his eyes sparkling with drunk amusement. "Do I see Uranus?" he teased, winking at Atticus. "You should be so lucky!" The three of them collapsed into laughter, their giggles echoing through the quiet streets. Atticus, equally amused by the situation, chimed in, "It's like they're celebrating with us."

He stumbled over a cobblestone, but Maggie and Patrick grabbed his arms to steady him, and they all laughed like a group of mischievous teenagers.

Pointing towards the night sky with exaggerated flair, Atticus declared, "That one there, the brightest one in the entire sky. I think it's Sirius!" Patrick burst into laughter. "Sirius? Are you sure you're not mistaking it for a UFO?"Maggie, who was still swaying gently and trying to focus on the stars, chimed in, "No, no! It's definitely Sirius. I read about it in a book once—Sirius is like the rock star of the night sky!"

They walked on, their tipsy banter interspersed with snippets of fond memories from the gallery and grand plans for their future artistic escapades. The narrow streets seemed to embrace them, arms linked and hearts light, it was as if the universe had conspired to bring these three kindred spirits together. For in that drunken moment, amidst laughter and dreams, they had painted a masterpiece of their own—a canvas filled with the beauty of art, attraction, and the promise of new beginnings.

The next morning, she awoke with a pounding headache and a parched throat, her memories of the previous night's revelry flooding back. She groaned, burying her head under the pillow in a futile attempt to escape the relentless sunlight streaming through her bedroom window. Dragging herself out of bed, she shuffled into the kitchen in search of some much-needed relief in the form of water and aspirin. As she sipped the water, her phone chimed with a new message. Blinking away the haze of her hangover, she squinted at the screen, trying to make sense of the message from Patrick. "Open your front door," it read.

Confused yet intrigued, she shuffled to the front door and swung it open. To her astonishment, there on the doorstep was a blank canvas, pristine and waiting. A note accompanied it, simply saying, "Begin anew." Her headache momentarily forgotten, she couldn't help but smile. Patrick, always the bearer of surprises, had left her this unexpected gift. The blank canvas seemed to hold endless possibilities, a symbol of second chances and untapped potential. Though she felt a bit intimidated by the thought of painting, Maggie was incredibly grateful for Patrick's thoughtfulness.

She decided to place the canvas in the corner of her small apartment as a reminder that sometimes, it's the unexpected gestures from friends that can inspire us to explore new horizons. As the day unfolded and she looked at the blank canvas, she couldn't help but feel a sense of hope and curiosity about what the future might hold. Even in the midst of a hangover, Patrick's gift had given her something to look forward to—a chance to begin anew. She ran her hand nervously over the pristine white surface, the possibilities stretching out before her like a blank page in a story waiting to be written.

Chapter 18: The Evil Eye

Several sun-soaked days had gently slipped by since the whirlwind of the art gallery soirée, leaving Maggie in a contemplative and introspective mood. The canvas in the corner remained untouched, like a silent sentinel awaiting the right moment to reveal its secrets. Yet, as each day passed, she never quite found the inspiration or courage to put brush to canvas. Instead, she often found herself drawn back to that unforgettable day in Archanes, where the village's charming streets seemed to resonate with laughter, and the Mediterranean air whispered mysteries that tickled her curiosity. But, above all, it was the profound conversation on Stoicism with Iris that had sparked a fire within her, a desire to dive deeper into this ancient Greek philosophy.

One quiet Sunday morning, an inexplicable yearning awakened within her. Stretching out her arm, she reached for the well-thumbed volume on Stoicism, its pages slightly worn and adorned with ink-stained passages. It held the echoes of conversations with Iris, the imprints of wisdom, and the promise of self-discovery. With the book cradled in her hands, Maggie ventured outside, the salty breeze tousling her hair. The rhythmic crash of waves against the shore serenaded her thoughts. She walked barefoot to the nearby beach, each step sinking into the cool, welcoming embrace of the sand, as if the Earth itself were reaching out to guide her.

Pausing to savour the vast expanse of the glistening sea before her, her fingers delicately turned the pages of the book. She opened it to a random passage, as if an old friend had been waiting patiently for her return. "Think of the life you have lived until now as over and, as a dead man, see what's left as a bonus and live it according to Nature. Love the hand that fate deals you and play it as your own, for what could be more fitting?" With each barefoot step along the shoreline, the waves lapped at her feet, a gentle reminder of the ever-moving, ever-changing nature of life.

The quotes pirouetted through her consciousness, weaving a tapestry of understanding. Stoicism was no longer a distant philosophy; it had become a comforting companion on her journey through life's uncertainties. She turned to another page, and the words spoke to her with uncanny precision: "If a man knows not which port he sails, no wind is favourable."

She gazed out at the horizon, where the azure sky met the turquoise waters in a tender embrace. In the distance, an old man stood by a boat, its hull adorned with vibrant reds and blues. He was meticulously repairing fishing nets, each knot and stitch a testament to his resilience against the unforgiving sea. "Isn't it a beautiful morning?" she greeted him with a warm, genuine smile, her eyes mirroring her admiration for the boat's craftsmanship. "Indeed, it is," he replied in a raspy voice, bearing the wisdom of years spent at sea. "Perfect for mending nets and preparing for the next catch."

She leaned in a little closer, her curiosity as bright as the Greek sun. "Catch many fish this morning?" The old fisherman retrieved a cigarette tucked behind his ear, lighting it with the grace of a practised ritual. A small flame momentarily illuminated the contours of his weathered face.

He took a deep drag, exhaling a plume of smoke that mingled gracefully with the salt-tinged air. "No, very bad actually," he admitted, a hint of resignation in his voice."Really?" Maggie responded with an inquisitive arch of her brow. The old man met her gaze, "There are no controls in Greece," he confessed with bluntness, a truth etched in his voice. "A fisherman might haul in 150 kilograms of fish, but when it comes time to declare the catch, he will only admit to fifty. No one is there to inspect and check you."

"That is terrible," she said, with empathy. "For generations, my family fished, " he continued "It's more than a livelihood; it's a way of life, a deep connection to the sea, to this place." His gaze shifted to the shimmering waters, reflecting the uncertain future of an ancient tradition. "But it seems that way of life, my way of life," he paused, his voice tinged with sorrow, "is fading."

As they chatted, her gaze was drawn to a striking blue and white amulet hanging from the boat's prow. "What's that?" she asked, curiosity overcoming her."The Mati," he responded, "it protects from the evil eye."Maggie leaned in, captivated. "The evil eye?"

"Yes," he confirmed with a nod. "It's a superstition that's been part of Greek culture for generations. It's said that if someone looks at you with hatred and envy in their heart, it can bring you misfortune." Her fascination deepened. "And how do you protect yourself from it?"

The fisherman chuckled, his eyes crinkling with amusement. "There are various ways. Some recite ancient incantations, others might cast a protective spell by spitting, and many wear an evil eye charm." He gestured to the striking blue amulet adorned with a painted "mati" or eye. "Just like that one."

She admired the charm, its cerulean hues glistening in the sunlight. "It's beautiful. Does it work?"He shrugged, a hint of mystery in his gaze. "Who's to say? But it's a part of our culture, a tradition passed down through generations. It's our way of protecting ourselves from the unseen." In that fleeting moment, amidst the ageless wisdom of the sea and the mystique of ancient traditions, Maggie felt a profound connection to the world around her. It was as if the whispers of tradition were imparting their secrets to her, urging her to embrace the rich tapestry of life.

As the two continued to chat at the edge of the shore, the fisherman shared more about the island's customs and superstitions. He spoke of festivals celebrating the changing seasons, of dances that echoed through the village streets, and of olive groves that had stood for centuries, their gnarled trunks testaments to the passage of time. She listened with rapt attention, absorbing every word as if it were a treasure trove of cultural riches.

After she said goodbye, she continued her leisurely stroll along the sun-kissed beach, passing by charming little shops filled with the alluring scents of Greek soap, intricate handmade pottery, and an assortment of trinkets and souvenirs that whispered tales of this coastal town's rich history.However, it was the glimmering window display of a quaint shop that stopped her in her tracks. There, right before her eyes, was a pendant that seemed like destiny itself had placed it in her path—an enchanting blue glass eye, just like the one hanging from the fisherman's boat. The pendant held an inexplicable allure, like a piece of the island's soul captured in glass.

Without a second thought, Maggie decided to make it her own, her fingers dancing over the smooth surface of the glass as she held it in her hand. It was a tangible connection to the traditions and mystique of Greece, something to hold close to her heart. Stepping back out into the warm embrace of the Greek sun, she felt a rush of emotions as she unclasped the delicate lovebirds necklace that Alex had given her so many years ago in Dublin. The pendant held countless memories, but it was time to let it go.

With a mix of nostalgia and determination, she removed the new pendant of The Mati from its paper bag. The glass eye seemed to shimmer with an inner light as she fastened it around her neck, a symbol of protection and a promise of new beginnings.Finding a secluded spot overlooking the glistening sea, Maggie gently gripped the lovebirds necklace, its significance now a memory.

A tear trickled down her cheek as she softly whispered, "Goodbye, Alex."
With a sense of release, she let the necklace slip through her fingers. It twirled gracefully in the air, catching the sunlight in a final, poignant farewell, before disappearing beneath the clear turquoise waves.As the necklace sank into the depths of the sea, she felt a deep sense of closure. The pendant of The Mati hung proudly around her neck, its ancient

protection mingling with her hopes for a brighter future. Turning her gaze back to the horizon, she embraced the warmth of the sun on her skin, ready to step forward into the next chapter of her life, wherever that may take her.

When Maggie returned to her apartment, she powered up her laptop, eager to start her fitness class through the GoFit platform. The familiar blue screen blinked to life, and there, on the other side of the digital divide, stood Kateryna, her long blonde hair tied up in a tight bun. Normally, she exuded positivity but today was different. Her smile was replaced by a weariness that weighed down her pretty features.

Maggie's heart sank at the sight of her. Kateryna's eyes glistened, betraying the tears she had tried to conceal, and it was painfully evident that something was amiss. As they began their exercise class, Maggie couldn't ignore the palpable shift in her mood. The vibrant energy that usually filled their virtual sessions was replaced by an underlying heaviness that tugged at her heartstrings. Her usually cheerful instructions were delivered with a hint of melancholy.

"Are you okay?" Maggie asked gently, as she moved out of a body stretch. Kateryna seemed momentarily taken aback, as if no one had asked her that question in a while. "I'm fine," she replied, but her voice quivered slightly, giving away her true feelings. "It's just... difficult." She hesitated, and her gaze drifted to somewhere beyond the screen. "They're bombing near my home, and... I'm...I'm scared."

Her heart ached as she watched Kateryna, her radiant spirit now clouded with sorrow and it was impossible for her to ignore the pain etched across her instructor's face. "Kateryna," Maggie's voice trembled with empathy, "I wish there was something, anything, I could do or say. We all feel so helpless, and I can't even begin to fathom what it's like for you and your people. It's so wrong."

Kateryna, unable to contain her emotions any longer, slowly sank to the floor. Her slender frame folded, and she buried her head in her hands, her shoulders heaving with deep, sorrowful gasps. It was a raw, powerful display of vulnerability that tore at her soul.

"I have to continue," she whispered between sobs, her voice muffled by her trembling hands. "What else can I do?" With great effort, she wiped the tears from her face, her determination shining through her despair. "I have to work, you know, to keep going. The gym I used to work in is now rubble. Everything is gone."

Maggie's heart sank at her words. She had been drawn into the very real and terrifying world that she was living in, and the weight of the situation pressed heavily on her chest.

"Is your family okay?" Maggie asked, her voice trembling with concern. The distance between them seemed insurmountable, but the digital connection made their conversation strangely intimate. Kateryna nodded, her eyes glistening with unshed tears. "Yes, thank goodness," she replied, her voice quivering. "But it's hard, Maggie. Every day, it feels as if the war, the bombs, are getting closer."

Maggie's mind raced with worry, her thoughts consumed by the danger her friend Kateryna and her family faced in war-torn Kiev. "Can you get out of Kiev, somewhere safer?" she implored, her voice filled with genuine concern, a lifeline of empathy extended across digital space. Kateryna's response was a fragile admission of uncertainty, her words barely above a whisper. "It's just... everything is so uncertain right now."

her heart ached, the distance between them seeming insurmountable. "My cousin lives in Chernivtsi, one of the towns in the western region," she offered, a glimmer of hope in the darkness. "It might be safer there."

Through the screen, she tried to convey a reassuring smile, her voice soft but firm. "You should go," she said, the words filled with genuine concern. "Please, stay safe."

Tears welled up in Kateryna's eyes, tears of gratitude for the friend who cared so deeply for her well-being. "You know, we can stop the class," Maggie offered gently, her compassion flowing through the digital connection.Kateryna, her face etched with the weight of the world's troubles, hesitated briefly. "No," she replied, her voice resolute. "It is helping to keep me sane. I need to focus on something positive."As the virtual exercise class continued, both women found solace and strength in each other's virtual presence. Each stretch and movement became a channel for their fears and hopes, blurring the screens that separated them. In that moment, it was as though they stood side by side, confronting the world's challenges together.

As the virtual fitness session concluded, Kateryna's face, though shadowed by the weight of her dire circumstances, began to glimmer with newfound strength. The soft, muted light in Maggie's room cast a gentle glow on Kateryna's weary yet determined expression. It was the face of a warrior, someone who had stared down hardship and refused to surrender to despair. Maggie couldn't help but be moved by her instructor's unyielding spirit, recognizing the immense courage it took to keep teaching amid such heart-wrenching turmoil.

"Thank you, Kateryna," she whispered with genuine sincerity as they wrapped up their virtual fitness class. Her voice held a depth of gratitude that words alone could scarcely convey. "For today, for everything." Kateryna managed a small, genuine smile, a fragile yet heartwarming gesture that defied the burden she carried. Her eyes reflected a complex mix of emotions – gratitude, weariness, but also a glimmer of hope. "It's good to have this class," she replied softly, her voice quivering slightly. "And to have a friend out there somewhere."

With her laptop gently closed, Maggie found herself engulfed in an overwhelming sense of helplessness. The world beyond her window, her usual tranquil haven in Greece, now felt like an insurmountable fortress, shielding her from the agonising realities unfolding in Ukraine. Her gaze drifted beyond the glass, where the cerulean sky stretched limitlessly, a reminder that some challenges refused to yield to simple resolutions. She felt ensnared in a web of despair and frustration, emotions that lingered long after her laptop screen had dimmed.

In a world interconnected by the wonders of technology, Maggie couldn't evade the haunting truth of her profound powerlessness in the face of overwhelming human anguish. It was an ache that clung to her, an unwelcome companion whose relentless presence whispered even in the hushed solitude of her room. Her heart bore the heavy burden of it all.

Leaving her apartment behind, she ventured out into the open air, the salt-tinged breeze of the Aegean Sea enveloping her. She walked briskly, seeking the freshness of the beach and the vastness of the horizon to clear her mind.

As she reached the shore, the waves stretched out before her like an endless canvas, each crest a blank page yearning for stories. Maggie's thoughts drifted back to Rachel, to their shared art college days, and to the betrayal that had altered the course of her life. For years, she had allowed that betrayal to fester within her, like a wound that refused to heal.But now, gazing at the expanse of the sea and feeling the cool misty rain on her skin, she realised it was time to let go of the past. The bitterness and anger that had ensnared her for so long no longer served her. They were shackles she had willingly worn, and she was finally ready to cast them aside.

The rain fell gently, a tender hand brushing away the traces of old wounds. She closed her eyes, letting the raindrops create a symphony on her skin. A sense of liberation washed over her, cleansing her soul of past regrets and pain. The words of the quote reverberated in her heart: "While we wait for life, life passes." Maggie had waited in the shadows for too many yesterdays. "It will be different this time," she declared, the raindrops merging with her tears. "It has to be."

Chapter 19:Egos and Easels

Maggie strolled along the winding streets of Rethymnon, her steps leading her to the quaint Kafenio Chromata tucked away in a charming courtyard. She settled at an outdoor table surrounded by vibrant flowers, where the distant melody of chirping birds danced in the air. A gentle breeze kissed her cheeks, carrying the tempting scent of coffee and freshly baked pastries. It was a serene day, perfectly tranquil, yet her heart pulsed with anxiety.

She noticed an abandoned sandwich on the table, attracting bold, feathered opportunists. Watching the birds pull at pieces of cheese and crust, she managed a wistful smile that momentarily eased her nerves. The cafe, usually a peaceful haven, felt different today. She was about to meet the artists from the New Voices project, and the weight of their expectations and diverse creative energies made her palms clammy. Maggie inhaled deeply, reminding herself why she had come to Crete; she had a mission, no matter how daunting it seemed.

A quick glance at her smartphone reminded her they would arrive soon. She signalled the waiter for an iced tea, its cold glass comforting in her grip as she observed the mix of tourists and locals absorbed in their own worlds. Her solitude was short-lived as Patrick and Atticus appeared, their cheerful presence bringing warmth to her heart. Atticus, with his distinctive red fedora, exuded a bohemian style, while Patrick, in a Hawaiian shirt and shorts, showcased his creative spirit.

Patrick waved as they approached, taking their seats at the table next to Maggie. "It's been a few weeks since the gallery opening," he noted, concerned lacing his words. "How are you holding up?" Maggie sighed, her gaze wandering to the sandwich which had now attracted 8 birds who were in the midst of a violent battle for the very last piece of cheddar. "Diving headfirst into my work," she replied, determination in her voice. "And have you heard anything from Alex?" Patrick asked, leaning on her arm. "Not a word," she replied with a sigh. Atticus leaned back, casting an empathetic gaze at Patrick before focusing on Maggie.

"We know it's been tough," he said kindly, "but you've got a real talent for this, Maggie. You're doing something incredible with the project." Patrick nodded, offering his support. "Absolutely. You've gathered a fantastic group of artists, and this exhibition will be a great success, mark my words." Maggie's spirits lifted at their words of encouragement. "Thank you, guys," she said, touched by their unwavering support. "I just hope we can all agree on a theme for the exhibition; I'm a little worried."

As they continued chatting, Eva made her entrance, exuding an air of detached coolness. With a dramatic sigh, she approached the table, the rhythmic click of her cowboy boots on the cobblestones adding an unexpected rhythm to the scene. Maggie greeted her warmly, undeterred by her less-than-enthusiastic demeanour. "Eva, glad you could make it," she said, offering a handshake. Eva eyed her hand before giving it a half-hearted shake. "Yeah, yeah," she replied, tossing her vibrant hair dismissively. "So, what's this meeting all about, anyway?"

Atticus, always the peacemaker, explained, "We need to decide on a theme." The cafe's courtyard seemed to hold its breath as they awaited the arrival of the remaining artists. Moments later, Nadir approached, his steps hesitant yet filled with hope, his well-worn leather knapsack thrown over his shoulder. Maggie's heart warmed as he introduced himself, gratitude evident in his voice for the chance to be part of something new. The camaraderie was short-lived as Thomas, the final member of their artistic ensemble, stumbled toward their table, slightly dishevelled and trailing the unmistakable scent of alcohol.

"Maggie, my dear!" Thomas declared with an overly familiar hug that invaded personal space. Alcohol emanated from him, and Maggie couldn't hide her disappointment. "How's our fearless leader doing today?" he asked, his eyes betraying a hint of mockery. Suppressing her frustration, she responded with a strained smile, "I'm good, Thomas. "

She playfully nudged him, hoping to steer the conversation away from his inebriation. "Can you try to keep it under control?" she added, irritation tingling her tone.

When all the artists had finally gathered, Maggie leaned forward in her chair, offering a nervous yet hopeful smile. "First off, thank you all for coming," she began, anticipation in her voice. "Today's meeting is to introduce everyone and, hopefully, find common ground." Though Eva seemed preoccupied with distant thoughts, Maggie continued, "And, of course, we need to decide on a theme for the exhibition, which might be a bit challenging given the diversity of your work." Atticus chimed in enthusiastically, "Sounds wonderful!"

Eva, leading the discussion, declared, "Our theme should be 'Urban Chaos.' It's edgy, contemporary, and demands attention." Patrick, never one to mince words, chimed in, "Eva, that's the most worn-out idea I've ever heard. 'Urban Chaos'? Really? It's a cliché that's been run into the ground."

Trying to mediate, Maggie ventured, "What about 'Urban Renaissance'? It's inclusive, positive, and offers endless interpretations." Eva and

Thomas exchanged smirks, as if they were sharing a secret joke. "Maggie, dear," Eva began condescendingly, "your ideas are so... safe."

Thomas added, "She's right, you know. 'Urban Renaissance' sounds like something straight out of a corporate art manual." Unfazed, Maggie challenged, "Well, what brilliant concepts do you both have?" Eva, relishing the spotlight, leaned back confidently. "How about 'I Don't Belong'? It's bold, gritty, and strikes at the heart of our generation's struggles." Nadir chimed in, eager to support Eva, "Yes, 'I Don't Belong' captures the essence of our art, our struggle. It's what we need."

Atticus, the voice of reason, disagreed. "It's very negative," he said, his tone firm. "Sorry, but I don't like it at all." Tension hung thick in the air as the search for a theme turned into a battlefield of opinions. Maggie sensed the need for a change, a shift beyond their artistic differences to a larger purpose. She cleared her throat and suggested tentatively, "What if we considered something more impactful, like something around climate change? It affects us all, and our art could raise awareness."

Her proposal was met with strong resistance. Thomas scoffed dramatically, "Oh, Maggie, it's a bit... expected, isn't it? Climate change?

It's like beating a dead horse." Eva, growing impatient, joined in, "I have to agree with Thomas. We're artists, not activists. Let's focus on something that excites us creatively." Frustrated, Maggie retorted, "At least I'm trying to find middle ground instead of stubbornly clinging to my own ideas."

Just when it seemed like all was lost, Atticus surprised everyone. Leaning in with an ironic smile, he suggested, "How about 'Visions of My Mortality'? It's deep, thought-provoking, and bound to make people ponder the meaning of life."

Silence fell upon the courtyard like a heavy mist. Maggie and the others stared at Atticus, a mix of confusion and amusement on their faces. Trying to keep her composure, Maggie asked, "Atticus, could you please explain your idea?" Undeterred by sceptical looks, Atticus launched into an impassioned explanation. "It's about exploring the human condition, the fragility of life, and the urgency of living in the present. Our art could provoke deep introspection and resonate profoundly with our audience." Instead of thoughtful consideration, Atticus's suggestion was met with bursts of laughter. Eva couldn't contain her amusement and burst into giggles. Thomas, a few drinks in, laughed loudly, drawing the attention of diners at a table nearby.

"Visions of My Mortality? Seriously, Atticus?" Eva managed to choke out between laughs. Patrick, trying to ease the tension, joined in with a playful grin. "Well, it's certainly a unique take." Nadir, the peacemaker, offered a polite smile. "It's intriguing, but perhaps a bit too... existential for our exhibition." Atticus, though slightly crestfallen, chuckled along with the others. "Alright, alright," he said, raising his hands in surrender, "I guess 'Visions of My Mortality' might be a bit heavy for our first exhibition."

As the meeting continued, fueled by an increasing flow of alcohol, Thomas became progressively more intoxicated. Eva couldn't resist challenging him on various points, their voices growing louder, arguments more intense. The once-promising atmosphere of collaboration eroded before Maggie's eyes.

Desperate to restore order, she implored, "Guys, can we please focus on finding a theme that works for all of us?" But Eva and Thomas were beyond diplomacy, their verbal sparring now threatening to turn into a full-blown showdown. The courtyard, once a haven of creativity and potential, had transformed into a battlefield of egos. Maggie wondered if they could ever find a theme that truly represented their collective vision.

Realising the situation had spiralled out of control, she leaned back, exhaustion and frustration wearing on her. Patrick abruptly rose from his chair, scraping the cobblestone floor with a sound like distant thunder. "I can't take this anymore; it's too much. I'm sorry, Maggie." Atticus, mirroring Patrick's exasperation, stood with a heavy sigh, his resolve fragile as a butterfly in a storm. "I agree, Patrick. I'm sorry too." With one last shared look of exasperation, they departed swiftly, leaving behind a chaotic scene.

Thomas sat alone at his table, nursing his wine with an amused expression, cigarette smoke curling upward like a solitary question mark in the smoky haze. Nadir, his compassionate eyes filled with understanding, placed a reassuring hand on Maggie's shoulder as they watched the artists disappear into the bustling crowd. His touch was a lifeline in a turbulent sea. "I'm sorry it turned out like this," he said as they surveyed the scattered papers and remnants of their once-promising brainstorming session strewn across the cafe table. "Sometimes, creative minds clash, and egos take over."

Maggie sighed deeply, her shock still palpable. "I never imagined our meeting would descend into such chaos," she admitted, disappointment colouring her voice. "I had hoped we could all come together and create something beautiful." Nadir offered her a gentle smile, his eyes mirroring the concern she felt.

"Don't worry, we'll regroup; everyone just needs some time to cool down." He glanced over at Thomas, lost in thought, nursing his beer. The cafe's atmosphere, once a backdrop for creativity, now bore the weight of a turbulent meeting and an uncertainty that loomed over the entire exhibition like a heavy, dark cloud.

As Maggie stepped out of the cafe, a chill breeze rustled through her hair, carrying the scent of distant rain. She pulled her coat tighter around her, the evening air carrying a sense of foreboding. She turned back for a moment, catching Nadir's eye. There was a silent understanding between them, a shared acknowledgment of the challenges ahead."Goodnight,

Nadir," she said, her voice carrying a mix of exhaustion and determination.

"Goodnight, Maggie," he replied, his tone filled with reassurance. "We'll find a way through this, together."

With a final nod, Maggie walked away, her footsteps echoing on the cobblestone street. Each step felt heavy with the weight of the evening's events, yet she couldn't shake off the flicker of hope Nadir's words had ignited within her. The night was dark and uncertain, but somewhere in the shadows, there was a glimmer of possibility.

That night, as she lay in bed, her mind was a whirlwind of thoughts, doubts swirling around like a stormy sea. She tossed and turned, trying to find a comfortable position amidst the sea of uncertainties, her mind feeling adrift in a turbulent ocean of reflection. The soft sound of the Aegean Sea outside her window, which had once been a soothing lullaby, now served as a constant reminder of the ongoing challenges she faced. "Why am I here in Crete?" Maggie whispered into the darkness, her voice barely audible, like a fragile echo in a vast cavern. Her friend Pamela, back in Ireland, had always believed strongly in fate, often saying that "everything happens for a reason."

But in the depths of that restless night, Maggie couldn't help but question that belief, her faith in fate flickering like a lone candle in the night. Maggie had come to Crete with a dream, aiming to unite four artists for what was supposed to be a groundbreaking project. It had felt like a calling, a purpose worth pursuing. However, as time passed and the project encountered setbacks, doubts crept in. She couldn't shake the feeling that she was battling against the tide, her dreams adrift in uncertainty.

Leaving behind her life in Ireland, including family and friends, for this endeavour had been a bold step. Now, as she lay awake in the darkness, she questioned whether it had all been a mistake. She longed for Pamela's comforting presence and wisdom. Maggie pondered her mantra, "everything happens for a reason." Did she still hold onto that belief? Was there a purpose behind the turmoil and trials in Crete? Or had she been naive to think her journey would be smooth?

As dawn broke, Maggie found no clear answers, her doubts clouding her thoughts. She knew the road ahead would be challenging, demanding resilience she hadn't known she possessed. Perhaps she'd uncover the reason for her journey or craft it herself, her destiny awaiting her touch. One thing remained certain: Crete's trials were shaping her in unforeseen ways.

Chapter 19: Eva's Escape

The morning sun tiptoed into Maggie's room, casting a gentle glow on the remnants of a turbulent night. Her head pulsed with a relentless ache, a cruel reminder of the stormy meeting that still echoed in her thoughts. Stumbling into the kitchen, her movements resembled a sleepwalker's, her mind caught in a chaotic tempest.The coffee machine, forever cheerful, seemed to taunt her with its perky gurgles as it brewed her morning salvation. The aroma of freshly brewed coffee wafted through the air, a fragrant lifeline amidst the chaos.

"Come on, coffee," she muttered, her voice laced with desperation, "fix my life, please." She poured herself a cup, the warmth seeping through her fingers like a reassuring embrace. It wasn't a magical solution, but it did offer a momentary respite, clearing the fog in her mind just a little.

With her hands wrapped around the mug, she peered out of the window. The cerulean sea shimmered under the morning sun, a tranquil contrast to the turmoil within her. "Alright, Maggie," she said to her reflection in the windowpane, determination burning in her eyes, "time to face the wreckage of your dreams."

Setting the cup down, she pulled out a dress from her closet and a pair of the biggest, darkest sunglasses she could find, as if preparing for battle against the world.

After savouring the last sip of her morning coffee, Maggie ventured into the bustling heart of town. With a sense of purpose, she made her way to the Aegean Arts Alliance, clutching the final paperwork in her hands like a precious artifact.. The office, usually a hub of creativity, appeared different today — a touch less welcoming, its atmosphere tinged with an undercurrent of tension.

As she pushed the door open, doubts and worries swirled in her mind. Would her submission be accepted? Had she done enough to salvage the project after the turbulent meeting? The questions hung in the air, almost tangible.

Approaching the reception desk, she cleared her throat, her voice sounding small in the vast, echoing space. "I have the final paperwork," she said, her words barely audible above the hum of activity around her. The receptionist, eyes glued to her computer screen, barely glanced in her direction. "Just leave it there," came the indifferent reply.

With a sinking feeling, Maggie placed the paperwork on the desk, her dreams and aspirations now reduced to a mere folder of documents. Just as she was about to leave her eyes met with Emily Winsor."I've been hearing quite a lot, Maggie," Emily said, her voice heavy with accusation. "Rumours, whispers about your performance, or lack thereof. People are questioning your ability to lead this project."

Maggie felt a surge of anger, her grip on the coffee cup tightening. "And what have you heard, Emily?" she shot back, refusing to let the woman's words shake her resolve. "Gossip and half-truths, I presume?"Emily's lips curved into a sly smile. "Oh, it's more than just gossip. Artists talk, Maggie. They talk about commitment, about passion. They doubt your dedication to this project."

Maggie took a deep breath, attempting to steady her rising temper. "Doubt is natural, Emily. But I am fully committed to this project. I won't let baseless rumours tarnish what we're trying to create here."Emily's eyes narrowed, the tension between them palpable. "Actions speak louder than words, Maggie," she said, her tone condescending. "We need results, not excuses."

Frustration surged withinher, mingling with a burning desire to prove her worth. "I don't need to prove myself to you or anyone else," she declared, her voice unwavering. "I believe in the power of art, and I believe in the potential of this project. If you're looking for a fight, Emily, you'll find one. But don't mistake my determination for weakness."

With that, Maggie turned on her heel and walked away, leaving Emily Winsor standing there, momentarily with a look of shock on her face. The encounter had ignited a fire within her, a determination to prove her critics wrong. She would channel her frustration into fuel, using it to propel herself and the project forward.

Stepping out of the office, Maggie was momentarily blinded by the brilliant sun, its golden rays washing over her like a reassuring embrace, as if nature itself was endorsing her newfound determination. Her steps quickened as she realised her fitness class with Kateryna awaited—a vital respite from the surrounding chaos. The nearby bus stop beckoned, and she could already spot the approaching bus on the horizon.

As she boarded, her mind replayed the confrontation with Emily Winsor. A giggle, unexpected and liberating, bubbled up from within her. Shocked at her own audacity, she couldn't help but find a strange sense of pride in the way she had stood her ground. The old Maggie might have crumbled under Emily's scrutiny, but this version of herself was different—stronger, fiercer.

The bus rattled along the coastal road, the cerulean sea winking at her from beyond the window. The sunlight danced on the waves, casting a golden glow that seemed to mirror the fire in her spirit. She gazed out, her thoughts a whirlwind of defiance and determination.

A chuckle escaped her lips, surprising the elderly woman sitting next to her. She hastily covered her mouth, eyes wide with the realisation that she had made a sound far louder than intended. The woman, however, just smiled kindly, perhaps recognizing a fellow warrior in the battle of life.

Returning home, with seconds to spare, she set her bag down and headed to the cosy nook in her apartment where she had her yoga mat and fitness ball. A few clicks later, she was logged in and ready for her scheduled fitness class. However, as the page loaded, an eerie silence filled the room—no sign of Kateryna, no video feed, no cheerful greeting. Anxiety clawed at her chest.

Kateryna had never been late or absent from their virtual fitness sessions before. An uneasy wait began, with minutes stretching into what felt like hours. Perhaps there had been a misunderstanding about the class time? Yet, as the clock on her wall marked a half-hour of waiting, her concern deepened - she was nowhere to be found

Her eyes lingered on the familiar green and blue header of the GoFit website, its cheerful images of people exercising felt painfully out of place, out of sync with her emotions. A lump formed in her throat, and she couldn't shake the feeling of helplessness. With trembling hands, she closed the laptop, her thoughts consumed by worry for her virtual friend.

Kateryna's well-being consumed her thoughts, casting a shadow over everything else in Maggie's world. Amidst her own heartaches and struggles, she couldn't help but ponder the fragility of life and the capriciousness of destiny. As she peered out of her apartment window, the turquoise ocean beyond offered no solace.

The days that followed unfolded as an agonising wait, each passing moment amplifying her anxiety. She relentlessly scoured the internet for any sign of Kateryna. News from Ukraine remained disconcerting, and her apprehensions for her friend's safety deepened. Hours turned into days, and before she realised it, a whole week had slipped away with still no word.

As the weekend arrived, it bore a heavier burden than usual. The New Voices project had encountered an unforeseen hurdle, careening into chaos after a tumultuous meeting. Discord among the artists had intensified, and she felt her grasp on the very dream that had brought her to Crete slipping away. Loneliness hung in the air like a thick fog, and the once picturesque beauty of the island now felt like a distant mirage.

In this small corner of the world, Maggie's circle of true friends was confined to just Patrick. Her existence had become a monotonous cycle, a relentless loop of work, sleepless nights, and an unyielding yearning for the familiar comforts of Ireland. As she lay in bed, a profound sense of desolation draped over her like a heavy quilt, suffocating her hopes. She yearned for guidance, a glimmer of hope to illuminate her path through the tumultuous journey of her life. And she knew precisely where to find it.

With a sudden burst of determination, Maggie snatched her worn denim jacket, its frayed edges testament to countless adventures, and slung her backpack over one shoulder. The plan, if you could call it that, was as hazy as the morning mist over the Cretan hills. Yet, an irresistible pull tugged at her heart, guiding her steps toward Archanes. There, in the winding alleys and ancient charm, she believed she might discover Iris, the enigmatic woman who held the key to the answers she so desperately sought. The uncertainty of it all hung in the air, but Maggie's heart beat to a compelling rhythm that whispered, "Go, find the truth."

As she made her way to the bustling bus stop, the lively rhythm of Rethymnon surrounded her. Conversations and laughter blended into a melodic symphony, a backdrop to her contemplative thoughts. The door hissed open after a 20-minute wait, inviting her into the familiar embrace of locals and tourists. Finding solace by a window seat, she observed the passing landscape, picturesque villages and olive groves flashing by like frames in a film.

Maggie's mind wandered as the bus journeyed onward, retracing the events of recent weeks — the turmoil of the project, the shards of a broken engagement, and her newfound resolve. Her thoughts were a whirlwind, a chaotic puzzle demanding to be solved. She clung to the hope that Iris, with her stoic wisdom and mystical connection, could offer the clarity she desperately sought.

After hours on the bus, Maggie disembarked in Archanes, her eyes wide with anticipation and the echo of her steps bouncing off the cobbled streets. The village, steeped in history and mystery, sprawled before her, its ancient buildings whispering tales of ages past. Clutching her backpack, she ventured deeper into the labyrinth of alleys, the fading sunlight casting elongated shadows on the ground.

Armed with only the name 'Iris' and a vague description of her house, Maggie's search turned into a quest. She asked locals for directions, but the responses were as winding as the streets themselves, leaving her more lost than before. Frustration gnawed at her determination, and for a moment, she contemplated abandoning her mission.

Just as the idea of giving up started to settle in her mind, a glimmer of hope reignited her resolve. With renewed determination, she turned one last corner, her eyes scanning the unfamiliar facades. And there, bathed in the soft glow of the dying day, was a scene straight out of a fairytale.

An old woman, her back slightly bent with age, tended to a garden that seemed to burst with every colour nature could offer. Flowers of all shapes and sizes stretched toward the sky, their vibrant petals painted by the setting sun. Maggie's heart skipped a beat; she knew, in that instant, that she had found Iris.Destiny, it seemed, had orchestrated their meeting, as Iris casually turned her head, and their eyes locked.

"Maggie, dear, whatever wind has brought you to my doorstep today?" Iris's words were akin to a comforting embrace, and Maggie's eyes welled up with tears as she closed the distance between them."Oh, Iris, I'm feeling utterly adrift," Maggie confessed, her voice trembling beneath the weight of her troubles. "This project, my life here... it's all unravelling, and I'm beginning to think I should return to Ireland. After all, I don't really know anyone here, and I don't have any friends."

" You have me", Iris responded with a warm smile, ushering Maggie into her charming whitewashed home. Sunlight filtered through the kitchen window, casting a comforting glow that whispered reassurance. "How about a cup of Shepherd's Tea?"Intrigued, Maggie's curiosity piqued as she watched Iris prepare the tea. "Shepherd's Tea? I've never heard of it before. What's it like?"

Iris poured hot water into a delicate china cup adorned with graceful blue and pink motifs featuring birds and flowers, then placed the cup gently in front of Maggie. "The proper name is Tsai tou vounou, but we call it Shepherd's Tea or Mountain Tea. It's made from the dried flowers, leaves, and stems of the sideritis plant. It will warm your spirit and gently ease your mind."

Appreciative of Iris's gesture, Maggie offered a grateful smile. "It's wonderful," she said, her fingers tracing the delicate curve of her teacup. Iris paused, her gaze softening with serene wisdom. "My dear, in the grand tapestry of life, we are rarely truly lost. Sometimes, we're simply navigating uncharted waters."

Maggie nodded, her eyes brimming with a newfound understanding. "I see where you're coming from, but this Crete project has turned into a real whirlwind. And my friend, the Ukrainian girl I mentioned earlier, she's... she's vanished without a trace. Honestly, I'm feeling quite lost, and I'm not sure which way to turn."

Iris offered a warm, comforting smile. "Maggie, dear, you mustn't carry the weight of the world on your shoulders. Sometimes, you just have to trust yourself and believe that everything will fall into place in the end." Maggie, her eyes glistening with vulnerability, confessed, "It's just that I've poured so much of my heart and soul into this project, leaving my old life behind. I'm terrified it might all crumble away before I even get a chance to find my footing here."

Her eyes were drawn to a large bunch of pink and purple Anemones in a vase on the kitchen table, their delicate petals swaying gently in the breeze that drifted through the open window.

Iris, sitting across from Maggie, noticed her gaze and smiled knowingly. "You see those flowers, Maggie?" She gestured towards the vibrant bouquet with a graceful sweep of her hand.

Maggie nodded, her eyes still fixed on the colourful blooms. "Yes, Iris, they're beautiful."

Iris's smile deepened as she reached out and picked up one of the Anemones, cradling it in her hand. "Each of these flowers is like a voice, Maggie. Just as unique and precious as your own."

Maggie leaned in, captivated by Iris's words, and nodded in agreement. "I've been thinking a lot about the power of one voice lately." Iris placed the Anemone back in the vase and leaned forward, her eyes locked onto Maggie's. "You see, dear, history is filled with stories of individuals who, with the strength of their convictions and the power of their voices, have changed the world. One voice can start a movement, can challenge the status quo, and can make an impact that ripples through generations."

Maggie's fingers lightly traced the rim of her teacup, her thoughts swirling. "But sometimes, it's hard to believe that my voice, one voice, can make a difference amidst all the noise and chaos."

Iris reached out and placed her hand over Maggie's, a comforting gesture that spoke volumes. "That's where you're mistaken, my dear. Every voice matters, and every voice has the potential to be a catalyst for change. Just like these Anemones, standing tall amidst the other flowers, your voice can stand out and make a difference."

Maggie's eyes met Iris's, filled with a newfound sense of determination. "You're right, Iris. I may be just one person, but my voice can make a difference." Iris nodded in agreement, her eyes twinkling with pride. "That's the spirit, Maggie. Embrace your voice, for it carries the potential to create positive change, even in the most challenging of times."

As Maggie prepared to leave, she couldn't help but glance back at the Anemones, now standing tall and vibrant in their vase. She knew that, just like those flowers, her voice had the power to bloom and inspire.

Waving goodbye at the gate, Maggie felt her spirits lift like a sail catching a favourable breeze. As she prepared to leave, she turned to Iris with heartfelt gratitude. "Iris, thank you, for the tea, for the conversation, and for just listening…" Iris placed a reassuring hand on Maggie's shoulder. "My door is always open to you."

Touched by her's words, Maggie gave her a warm embrace before making her way out of the inviting whitewashed house. Stepping back onto the cobbled streets of Archanes, she carried with her a renewed sense of purpose.

As the sun dipped below the horizon, painting the picturesque town of Archanes with a rosy glow, Maggie found herself lost in the timeless allure of the Cretan landscape. The rhythmic hum of the bus engine and the gentle swaying of the vehicle lulled her into a contemplative reverie, her thoughts twirling like dappled sunlight on ancient stone walls.

But, like a beacon cutting through her musings, Maggie's phone chimed, shattering the enchantment. She fumbled for the device, her fingers gliding over its sleek surface before finally retrieving it. An unexpected message from Eva, the enigmatic performance artist, lit up the screen—an invitation for a rendezvous at a wine bar later that evening. Caught off guard by the proposition, Maggie hesitated briefly before accepting, a newfound curiosity piqued her interest.

Forty minutes later, Maggie walked into the Bohemie rooftop bar, a hidden gem that seemed to exist in its own whimsical realm. Tiny fairy lights sprinkled a magical glow, classic lampshades lent a nostalgic air, and an assortment of colourful cushions created cosy enclaves for conversations.

Eva, perched on a cushioned seat, spotted her and beckoned her over with a smile. Her presence exuded confidence and charm, seamlessly blending with the enchanting surroundings. "Sorry for storming out of the meeting," she began, her voice a sultry melody accompanied by the subtle clinking of ice in her cocktail glass. "It wasn't very professional of me. I've had a lot on my mind, and that guy, Thomas? He was driving me nuts!"

Maggie replied with empathy, her voice carrying understanding. "He drives all of us nuts," she added with a knowing smile. "Thomas is a handful." Eva nodded in agreement, her elegant fingers tracing the rim of her cocktail glass, candlelight dancing on the jewels adorning her fingers. "I don't like people stealing my ideas," she added, dismissing the topic with a wave of her hand.

Maggie leaned in, her eyes filled with determination and sincerity. "Let's forget about that meeting," she declared, her voice brimming with conviction. "It was a disaster, but what matters is that we all create meaningful artwork, something worthwhile." She responded with a nonchalant shrug, her fingers brushing a few strands of green hair from her face. "I have my doubts," she admitted, her tone thoughtful. "I'm not great at working in a group, you know. I've always been more of a solo artist."

Worry creased Maggie's brow, her fingers tapping the table nervously. "Is that why you invited me here?" Her voice quivered with anxiety. "Are you thinking of backing out of the exhibition?"
Eva hesitated, her gaze dropping to her cocktail as she swirled it absentmindedly. "Well," she began cautiously, choosing her words carefully, "I can't deny that the thought has crossed my mind."

Their conversation took on a more serious tone as Eva continued, and the rooftop bar, with its enchanting ambiance, faded into the background. "The project lacks direction. I can't create art if I don't know the theme, the direction, or even what it's about. And that's not me being difficult. We only have three weeks..."

A blush of embarrassment coloured Maggie's cheeks. She gazed out at the city bathed in the gentle, golden hues of twilight. "I get it," she began, "It's been a challenge to align everyone's perspectives. And, to be completely frank, you've seemed distant and reserved. Is there something more to this?"

Eva took a deep breath, her emerald eyes meeting Maggie's with a rare vulnerability. "You're right," she admitted, her voice gentler now, stripped of its usual armour. "The truth is, I've built this image as a defence mechanism. It's a shield against getting hurt again."

Maggie listened intently, empathising with Eva's confession. "Hurt from what?" she asked softly.

Eva hesitated before continuing. "My aloofness shields me from the pain of my past, and the years I spent in a controlling and abusive relationship when I was living in Germany. It became my defence, protecting me from vulnerability."

Eva's normally steady and assertive voice quivered with raw emotion. "My 'feminist art,' as I like to call it, was a response to that." A shiver ran down Maggie's spine, and she leaned in, captivated by Eva's story. "Tell me more," she urged gently.

Her narrative gained momentum. "My fiancé Severin wanted me to wear long, conservative dresses and forbade makeup or dyeing my hair. We were part of a Christian group, but looking back, it was more of a cult than anything."

Eva paused, as if selecting a memory from the maze of her past. Then, she began, "We were expected to embrace a strict code of conduct, which included complete obedience to the leader's every command."

Maggie leaned in, her curiosity piqued. "Can you give me an example?" Her gaze turned inward as she delved into another harrowing anecdote from her life within the cult. "One of the most unsettling rituals they had was called 'The Purification,' where they believed cleansing the body would purify the soul."

Maggie's curiosity was piqued. "What did this purification entail?" She sighed deeply, her voice filled with a mix of bitterness and resilience. "It involved long periods of fasting, extreme physical exertion, and even self-flagellation. We were made to believe that enduring these trials was a way to atone for our sins and draw closer to their twisted version of spirituality." Maggie's heart ached for the young woman sitting in front of her.

"That sounds absolutely horrific," Eva nodded, her eyes filled with the haunted memories of that time. "It was. The breaking point for me came during one of these purification rituals. We were supposed to go without food or water for three days while working in the fields, under the scorching sun. I saw members collapsing from exhaustion and dehydration, and something inside me snapped."

Maggie listened in stunned silence as Eva continued her story. "I decided that I couldn't endure it any longer. I secretly shared some water and food with those who were suffering the most. It was a small act of defiance, but it was the beginning of my awakening." Tears welled up in Maggie's eyes as she grasped the enormity of Eva's courage. "You risked everything to help others." Eva's lips curled into a determined smile. "Yes, Maggie. That moment made me realise that I had to break free from that oppressive life and find a way to help others escape too."

Maggie couldn't help but admire Eva's resilience and compassion."Once I escaped, I booked a flight—the first available to Crete. I dyed my hair green and became a new person." Eva's eyes glistened with gratitude."You're an incredible person, Eva. Your strength is truly inspiring." Maggie asked softly, her voice filled with compassion.Eva nodded, her gaze distant as she looked off into the middle distance. "That's kind of you," she said, her eyes unfocused as she relived those tumultuous moments.

As Maggie listened to Eva's story, she felt an undeniable connection, not just to the fellow artist sitting before her, but to the resilience and power of the human spirit. It was a reminder that life's most challenging experiences could be transformative, shaping individuals into forces of inspiration and change.

Their conversation continued, deepening the bond between them. "I want to be part of this exhibition, Maggie," Eva declared, her voice filled with newfound determination. "But you need to take control of this project before it falls apart , and, most importantly, you need to do something about Thomas."Maggie met her words with unwavering resolve. "We're in this together, and I won't let you down."

Eva's eyes softened, a genuine smile gracing her lips. "Thank you, Maggie," she said sincerely. "Women should support each other—I don't want to see you fail."

With those words, Maggie's heart swelled with a sense of purpose. She realised that their shared experiences and the stories of resilience they carried could infuse their art with a profound depth and meaning. As she left the enchanting Bohemie rooftop bar that night, she walked through the labyrinthine streets of Reythemon with a newfound clarity.

Underneath the canopy of the starlit Cretan sky, she made a vow to herself to use her voice and to paint, to paint as if her life depended on it.As she ventured further into the night, Maggie's heart swelled with newfound purpose. The enchantment of the city at night seemed to embrace her, offering its blessings to the journey that lay ahead.

Chapter 20: A Painful Revelation

The following day, bathed in the serene glow of a Sunday evening, Maggie found herself strolling through the picturesque streets of Heraklion, a charming town nearby. The gentle breeze whispered through the leaves of ancient olive trees, and the air was saturated with the sweet fragrance of jasmine. It was a tranquil moment of solitude, a world away from the challenges of her everyday life.

As she meandered along the quaint cobblestone streets, she stumbled, quite literally, into the heart of the most significant religious celebration on the island—the Dormition of the Virgin Mary. In a place where evenings typically were quiet, tonight was an exception. The atmosphere crackled with excitement and anticipation. Vibrant banners, adorned with intricate designs, swayed in the warm breeze, and the sound of traditional bouzouki music hung in the air.

And right there, amidst this vibrant tapestry, her path intertwined once more with Pangiotis, the amiable hotel tour guide who had become her friend earlier in the trip. His grin stretched as wide as the horizon, when he spotted her amidst the crowd and he waved with an infectious zeal to catch her eye."Maggie! What a fantastic twist of fate to find you here," Her face lit up, grateful for the familiar face amid this whirlwind of celebration. "Pangiotis, I had no inkling there was a festival today. What's it all about?"

With a nod, Pangiotis began to explain. "So, in every church and chapel dedicated to the Virgin Mary, who we fondly call the Panagia here, they throw an annual celebration. Town squares light up with group gatherings and traditional dances that go on until the early hours. This festival lasts four whole days and is basically the biggest party you'll ever see on this island!"

Encouraging her to join him in the heart of the festivities, Pangiotis led Maggie through the lively streets. Their journey eventually brought them to a lively square. Here, a magnificent church stood aglow with the soft, otherworldly light of numerous candles.

Pangiotis gestured to the old building, his voice lowered in reverence. "Right here, Maggie, you'll see the Panagia . It's truly special; they adorn her in exquisite gowns and jewellery, then carry her out of the church in a grand procession through the town. Look, I believe they're preparing for it right now..."

As she gazed around in wonder, the locals moved with graceful reverence, their devotion palpable as they lifted the statue of the Virgin high onto a plinth that seemed to reach for the heavens. Garlands of fresh flowers adorned the statue, their vibrant colours a breathtaking contrast against the pale stone of the church. Whispered prayers and hymns filled the air, creating an atmosphere of serenity and enchantment.

Maggie found herself utterly captivated, not only by the sight but also by the intoxicating aroma that enveloped her, a rich and musky scent that seemed to transcend the senses. She leaned in closer to Pangiotis, her voice a hushed whisper. "What is that incredible smell?"

Pangiotis smiled, his eyes reflecting the deep reverence of the moment. "It's a blend of Frankincense, Myrrh, and Rose. It's traditionally used in all the Greek religious festivities."

Maggie nodded in understanding, her gaze returning to the procession before her.. "It's truly beautiful," she murmured, taking it all in.

As the statue continued its solemn journey along the winding cobblestone streets, the air grew heavy with the fragrance of incense and the delicate scent of roses. Even the cobbled roads themselves seemed to participate in the celebration, with locals scattering rose petals in the path of the event. Amidst the procession, Maggie's thoughts turned to Kateryna, her online friend who she'd become close to since her arrival in Crete. She couldn't help but wonder about her current whereabouts and safety. A silent prayer escaped her lips, carried away by the fragrant breeze, as she sent her words somewhere up above a cloud.

Pangiotis, always the gracious host and guide, noticed the pensive look on Maggie's face. He gently squeezed her hand and said, "Maggie, in moments like this, it's truly special, isn't it? It makes you feel connected to everyone here and something bigger." She smiled, grateful for his understanding. "You're right, Pangiotis. This place, this celebration, it's all so... magical."

As they continued to follow the procession, the cobblestone streets unfurled before them like a winding, ancient river. The procession eventually led them to a small square adorned with flickering candles and fragrant rose petals. Here, the locals gathered to pay their respects to the Panagia, their faces illuminated by the warm, golden glow of the candles. Pangiotis leaned in and whispered, "This, Maggie, is the heart of Crete—a place where faith, tradition, and community come together to create something wonderful." Touched by the sincerity of his words, she nodded in agreement.

At precisely 8PM The grand procession had concluded its majestic journey, leaving behind nothing but a trail of scattered rose petals adorning the cobblestone streets and the sweet scent of incense that still caressed the evening breeze. With a wistful farewell to the vibrant festivities, she began her leisurely stroll homeward, meandering along the picturesque coast road. Here, the seaside eateries buzzed with laughter, beachfront restaurants hummed with diners relishing their meals, and bars echoed with clinking glasses and lively conversations. The infectious rhythm of traditional music compelled even the most reserved to sway and dance under the clear blue sky.

As Maggie ambled along, the enchanting sights and sounds of the coastal promenade enveloped her. She passed by a charming newsagent, its exterior illuminated by a mesmerising, flashing neon sign that beckoned both locals and travellers alike. Her gaze was irresistibly drawn to the wire stand adorned with a colourful array of international newspapers, each offering a portal to distant corners of the world.

The word "Kiev" stood out in bold, like a glaring spotlight in the dim room. Her fingers quivered as they reached for the newspaper, a sense of foreboding gripping her. Her eyes darted nervously across the front page, and the words practically jumped off the paper, striking her like a bolt of lightning: "Kiev Bombings - A Week of Unrest. Combat Drones Target Zhytomyr, 25 Lives Lost." Her heart sank, a leaden weight settling in her chest, while an unsettling lump lodged itself firmly in her throat.

As her pulse quickened, she delved further into the grim details, her breath hitching with each word. "Combat drones ruthlessly targeted the core of Zhytomyr's central region." Her face, etched with concern, absorbed the chilling implications of this audacious assault—an unsettling prelude to the horrors that lay within.

Her quivering gaze descended down the page, where a haunting image materialised: a once-majestic Art Nouveau building, now reduced to a desolate heap of rubble. Her heart constricted, and tears welled in her eyes as she fixated on the heartrending caption, "Renowned Dnipro

Elysium Apartments, designed by V. Gorodetsky." Her breath hung suspended, ensnared in the grip of her constricting throat.

In a heart-wrenching whisper, she compelled herself to read on, absorbing the harrowing truth unfolding before her eyes. "Everything has been destroyed," the mayor declared with crushing finality. The weight of those words crashed upon her like a merciless tsunami, dragging her thoughts into a relentless whirlpool of unrelenting anguish.

A memory surfaced—a name, a name that sent shivers down her spine. Kateryna had spoken of the Dnipro Elysium Apartments, the period building she called home, now reduced to rubble. With a sudden, gut-wrenching realisation, Maggie choked back a sob. Tears streamed down her cheeks as she clutched the newspaper to her chest.

Overwhelmed by grief and despair, she sank onto a nearby bench, her tears flowing freely. Alone, she sat with the newspaper open on her lap, her face frozen in a shocked expression amid the quiet Cretan night, surrounded by the remnants of a festival that now felt a world away from the devastation she had just discovered. At that moment, all the charm of the festival and the enchantment of Crete seemed like distant memories.

As she mourned for her friend, the world carried on around her, oblivious to the turmoil within her heart. The sweet fragrance of jasmine and incense still lingered in the air, a bittersweet reminder of the tranquillity shattered by the harsh realities of the news. The destruction of the Dnipro Elysium Apartments, a building she now knew was Kateryna's home, was the confirmation she had dreaded. Kateryna was gone.

Amidst the whirlwind of celebrations, Maggie moved through the city like a spectre, her steps heavy with the weight of grief. The colourful banners overhead and the lively folk music faded into a muffled hum, drowned out by the deafening silence of her loss. She was an outsider looking in, a solitary figure in a crowd of jubilant faces.

The Dormition of the Virgin Mary, with its vibrant colours and jubilant processions, was now forever intertwined with the memory of her friend, a bittersweet testament to the fragility of life. And as the city revealed in its festivities, Maggie carried the heavy knowledge of Kateryna's fate in her heart, a burden she would bear as a testament to their friendship, forever.

In the days following that damning newspaper article, she found herself adrift on a turbulent sea of sorrow and anger. The news of the Ukraine bombings had hit her with the force of a wrecking ball, a visceral reminder of the cruelty and chaos that swirled beyond the tranquil streets of Crete. Each night, sleep eluded her, her mind haunted by vivid images of destruction and the agonising uncertainty of her friend's final moments.

Her cosy apartment, usually an oasis of solitude in the bustling city, now bore the visible marks of her life's tumultuous currents. The room whispered tales of change, not in the clichéd glow of sunlight streaming through the window, but in the subtle shift of energy. The blinking cursor on her blank document was a silent witness to her mounting deadlines, yet her thoughts roamed far from the mundane spreadsheets and reports clamouring for her attention.

A craving for a cigarette, a habit she had long forsaken, gnawed at her. It wasn't about the nicotine; it was about the fleeting escape, that stolen moment of respite. She resisted, reminding herself of the years she had put between herself and that old vice. The ashtray that once claimed a prominent place on her desk had been replaced by a vase of fresh fruit, a testament to her healthier choices.

But as her gaze remained fixed on the unyielding screen, her concentration waned. Thoughts of Kateryna surged into her mind, carrying with them a profound, gnawing ache that seemed to permeate her very being. It was a pain that defied quantification or explanation, an emotional tempest that left her feeling utterly adrift in a sea of hopelessness.

The recent breakup with Alex, which had once felt like the end of the world, now appeared utterly insignificant. The mundane tasks of her daily life—emails, meetings, responsibilities—seemed pointless, mere distractions in the face of the devastating news about Kateryna.

Maggie sighed deeply, running her hands through her hair in frustration, and that's when her phone pierced the silence with its insistent ringtone. Startled, she reached for it, and the name "Catherine" flashed on the screen. Her sister rarely called at this hour. With trembling fingers, Maggie answered the call. "Catherine?" Her sister's voice came through the line, laced with concern. "Maggie, darling, I've been trying to reach you. Are you okay?"

Catherine's voice carried a peculiar blend of sympathy and a hint of superiority. "Hello, Maggie. I'm sorry to hear about you and Alex... I did try to warn you."

Maggie's knuckles tightened on the phone, her emotions a turbulent mix of anger and humiliation. "I don't want to— I can't talk about this right now," she managed to reply through clenched teeth. "I'm dealing with something else.""What is it now?" Catherine replied, her tone theatrically exaggerated. "Well, if you must know, I think a friend of mine from Ukraine has been killed..."

Maggie's voice cracked as she struggled to maintain her composure. "The Ukrainians?" Catherine interjected, her tone dismissive. "They're over here in droves, we don't need all of these refugees. Ireland has enough problems of its own..."Maggie had had enough. The anger, grief, and frustration boiled over as she cut her sister short. "Catherine—fuck off!" She slammed the phone down, the resounding click echoing through the room.

In the midst of her emotional tempest, Maggie felt an overwhelming need to channel her emotions, to give voice to the rage that consumed her. Her eyes scanned the room, desperately searching for something—anything—to bridge the chasm of despair. And then, they landed upon the canvas Patrick had bought her, nestled in the corner. It beckoned to her like a long-lost friend, an urgent plea to express the maelstrom of emotions swirling within her.

With newfound determination, she retrieved the canvas, unzipping the accompanying bag.

Inside, an assortment of paintbrushes awaited, each a potential conduit for her emotions. The palette of acrylic paints lay before her, a vibrant spectrum of colours eager to be set free. They would become her voice in this moment of turmoil, a means to articulate the inexpressible.Guided by an unseen force, she made her way to the kitchen. Selecting a well-worn dish, she filled a glass with water. The gentle clinking of glass against porcelain felt like a reassuring melody, a prelude to the emotional symphony she was about to compose.

With deliberate care, she blended various paints, each stroke purposeful and urgent. Her hands, once trembling with frustration, now moved with unwavering resolve. Each brushstroke extended her soul, a cathartic release of the pent-up turmoil that had threatened to consume her. It was as though a storm raged within her, and the canvas was the sole vessel capable of containing its fury.

As she began to paint, the image took shape on the canvas. It was a woman, dressed in the vibrant colours of traditional Ukrainian clothing, a Vinok adorning her head. But this was no idyllic portrayal; this was a raw and powerful depiction, s a symbol of the country itself, wounded and bloodied. Her clothing was torn, her face marked by the scars of conflict, and her eyes, though weary, held a fierce resilience.

Aroundher, hands reached out to her in desperation, some bloodied, some trembling. They were the hands of the innocent, the voices of the oppressed, and the cries of a nation torn apart by war. Her strokes were bold and unyielding, each one a testament to the pain and anger that surged within her.

Days turned into nights, and she poured herself into her work. She hardly noticed the passage of time as she painted, her emotions bleeding onto the canvas. The image she created was a stark reflection of the world's injustices, a cry for compassion and understanding. When she finally stepped back to examine her creation, she felt a strange mix of exhaustion and catharsis. "Mother Ukraine," she whispered, her voice barely audible in the quiet room. It was a name that held both reverence and sorrow, a symbol of a nation's strength and its enduring struggle.

It was her first painting in fifteen long years, and it filled her with awe and wonder. She knew her painting couldn't change the world or bring back Kateryna. Yet, it stood as her tribute—a humble offering of empathy and unity. A reminder that amidst darkness, art could be a guiding light, reflecting humanity's unyielding spirit. As she gazed at her creation, she embraced the pain and fury of the Ukraine conflict, finding the resolve to speak out against injustice. In a world filled with countless voices, she finally understood the power of her own.

Chapter 21:The kiss

The next morning, Maggie woke up with a cloud of frustration hovering over her, a creative block casting a gloomy shadow on her enthusiasm. With a mix of hope and desperation, she dialled Nadir's number, seeking a lifeline amidst the storm. His voice, when he answered, was a comforting melody in her chaos. "Nadir," she said, the words tumbling out, "I'm stuck. Seriously stuck. Any chance you've got a magical cure for a creative block?"

"Maggie," he replied, his voice a soothing balm, "I do have ideas, but I don't want to just tell you. I want to show you something, something that might reignite that creative spark within you. Meet me at the old community centre by the harbour. Come alone. Trust me, it'll be worth your while." Maggie bit her lip, uncertainty mingling with curiosity. "Alright," she replied, determination lacing her tone, "I'll be there. But it better be good."

Exiting her apartment, the door clicked shut behind her, sealing the past like a letter sent and lost to time. Her destination beckoned: the community centre nestled beside The Venetian Harbor, its boats adorned in vibrant shades of blue and red. Maggie meandered through the labyrinthine streets until she discovered the unassuming whitewashed edifice, distinguished by its cheerful yellow door—just as he had vividly described.

As she approached, her gaze met Nadir's, and in his hazel eyes, she detected a fusion of gratitude and anticipation, radiating like the sun overhead. "Thank you for coming," he uttered, with a sincere smile. "I have a hunch this might be precisely what you've been looking for." In response, Maggie reciprocated his smile, a potent blend of excitement and optimism gleaming in her eyes. "Well, I'm here to find out!"

Amidst the vibrant energy of the community centre, Maggie stepped over its threshold and found herself breathless, her senses instantly overwhelmed by a riot of colours and shapes adorning the walls. Paintings, drawings, and sculptures whispered tales of resilience, loss, and hope. At her side stood Nadir, his eyes ablaze with a fervent passion. "Art is the universal language of the soul," he declared, pointing towards a mural. "It transcends borders, languages, and cultures. These creations are not just artworks; they are fragments of these refugees' souls, stitched together with hope and strength."

Maggie's gaze shifted to a striking woman in a vibrant kimono, her eyes deep and soulful. As Nadir introduced them, Sophia's voice, though soft, resonated with authority. "Thank you for coming today. This place is special. It's more than just a building; it's a sanctuary woven from the dreams and hopes of people who've overcome unimaginable challenges. Despite our small size, our mission is vast: we mend broken spirits, breathe life into those who've suffered, and offer hope in the darkest times."

Maggie nodded, her eyes drawn back to the artworks. "These creations are astounding," she said in genuine awe. "They speak volumes without uttering a single word." Sophia's gaze turned to a painting depicting a solitary figure gazing at a distant horizon, her words landing softly in the room like delicate brushstrokes on a canvas. "Our strength comes from community, from people like you, who join hands with us, making our mission, our dreams, and the dreams of those we serve, come alive."

In the soft glow of the sunlit room, Maggie felt a stirring within her, ignited by the passion in Nadir's eyes. "How can I help?" she ventured, her voice gaining newfound strength, her eyes glimmering with resolve. Nadir's lips curved into a gentle smile, a spark of anticipation dancing in his gaze. "You can be their voice, magnify their tales, and share their narratives with the world through this project," he said earnestly. "Let's not just offer them comfort; let's offer them a platform, a chance not only to mend but to resonate far beyond these walls."

Amidst the serene ambiance of the art-filled room, Maggie and Nadir exchanged a meaningful glance, a shared understanding passing between them. "I've got it," Maggie exclaimed, her voice bubbling with excitement, as if she had uncovered a precious gem. "Resilience: Art in the Face of Adversity." Nadir's eyes sparkled with agreement, his face reflecting her enthusiasm. "It's perfect," he declared, his voice resonating with conviction. "A tribute to refugees everywhere, a celebration of art's incredible power to unite us all."

Sophia, standing nearby, couldn't help but be moved by the profound idea taking shape before her. Her eyes shimmered with appreciation, reflecting the genuine admiration she felt for the concept. "It's a theme that not only honors their journey but also showcases the strength of the human spirit," she chimed in, her words landing softly in the room like delicate brushstrokes on a canvas. In that moment, amidst the vibrant atmosphere of creativity, they knew they had stumbled upon something wonderful – a theme that would not only inspire the artists but also touch the hearts of everyone who experienced the exhibition.

As they left the community centre, the vibrant energy of the space humming around them, Nadir and Maggie strolled through the bustling streets of the old town, and for the first time in ages, Maggie felt different, lighter. "What's this feeling? Ahhh... I feel happy," she realised, astonished. It was the first time she had felt this way in the longest time. Beside her, Nadir's passion for the project was palpable, his eyes alight with fervour. As he delved into the impact and future possibilities of the exhibition, Maggie found herself not just admiring his intellect but also noticing, perhaps for the first time, the depth of his charisma. His words flowed naturally, like a storyteller weaving a captivating tale, painting vivid scenes of his experiences. She was captivated not only by the project but also by the man standing beside her.

"I hope you don't mind me asking," she ventured as they passed stalls of vibrant flowers in the village square, "but how did you manage to survive that treacherous boat trip to Lesvos?" Nadir's expression softened, his eyes carrying a weight of sadness, momentarily clouded by haunting memories of the past. "It was a harrowing journey," he began, his voice steady, each word carefully chosen.

"My sister," he continued, his voice softening, as if he were caressing the memory. "She didn't make it," he paused, his gaze drifting to a distant, haunting horizon. "She drowned with her son, Nael."

Maggie felt her heart constrict with the pain that laced Nadir's words. The depth of his loss was unfathomable, and in that moment, she wished she could bear some of his burden. Her hand, almost of its own accord, found its way to his arm, a gesture of comfort and understanding. "I'm so sorry," she whispered, her voice breaking with the weight of empathy. "I can't imagine what you have been through."

Nadir's eyes, normally vibrant and full of life, now seemed to hold the echoes of a grief that ran immeasurably deep. "They were everything to me," he confessed, his voice barely above a whisper. "Tulane was the embodiment of kindness, and Nael... he had his mother's smile." His voice wavered, the memories threatening to consume him. "I create, I photograph, I paint... all of it is to keep their memories alive, to honour them in the only way I know how."

Maggie felt a lump forming in her throat, the ache of Nadir's loss reverberating within her own heart. In that shared moment of raw vulnerability, she realised the extraordinary strength it took for him to transform his pain into art, to weave their memories into the fabric of his creations. She admired him, not just for his talent but for his resilience, for his ability to channel grief into something so beautiful and profound.

"You're honouring them in the most beautiful way possible," Maggie said, her voice filled with a mixture of awe and tenderness. "Through your art, their light continues to shine, and their love touches the hearts of those who witness your creations." She squeezed his arm gently, hoping to convey the depth of her understanding and admiration. Nadir looked at her, gratitude and a glimmer of hope flickering in his eyes. "Thank you," he whispered, his voice hoarse with emotion. "Your understanding... it means more to me than I can express."

Maggie felt a surge of emotions – admiration, empathy, and something else, something unspoken yet powerful. It was a connection that went beyond the shared project; it was a shared understanding of the resilience of the human spirit.

As they continued their walk, she found herself stepping closer to Nadir, the space between them shrinking until it was almost nonexistent. Their hands brushed against each other, a fleeting touch that sent shivers down Maggie's spine. It was as if the universe itself conspired to bring them closer, intertwining their fates in a delicate dance of destiny.

The old town, with its winding alleys and ancient secrets, bore witness to this silent exchange between two souls finding solace in each other. In that moment, amidst the echoes of history, Nadir turned to Maggie, his eyes searching hers as if seeking permission. Without a word, he reached out, his fingers gently tracing the outline of her cheek, a gesture filled with tenderness and unspoken promises.

Maggie's heart raced, the world around her fading into insignificance. In Nadir's touch, she felt a thousand emotions – the weight of their shared experiences, the anticipation of unexplored possibilities, and the gentle whisper of a connection that defied explanation. It was a moment suspended in time, a chapter in their story that had only just begun, but one that held the promise of something extraordinary.

In that fleeting kiss, under the canvas of the universe, Time stood still, the world hushed into a serene stillness, giving them the opportunity to savor the sweetness of the moment. As they pulled away, their eyes met, reflecting the certainty of their newfound bond. The world around them slowly came back into focus, but the magic of that moment lingered, leaving an indelible mark on their hearts. The moment their lips parted, Nadir's eyes widened in realisation, his expression a mix of surprise and regret. "I'm sorry," he stammered, his voice filled with genuine remorse. "I shouldn't have... I don't know what came over me.'

Maggie, her cheeks flushed, felt a sudden wave of awkwardness wash over her. She looked down, avoiding his gaze, and managed to say, "Yes," her voice barely audible, not quite knowing what to say. Her agreement hung in the air, heavy with unspoken sentiments.

"It was a mistake," Nadir continued, his tone carrying a heavy weight of disappointment in himself. He took a step back, creating a physical distance between them, mirroring the emotional chasm that seemed to have opened up in the wake of their shared moment. He cleared his throat, his eyes searching for words to mend the situation. "I value our friendship, Maggie. I didn't mean to complicate things."

Maggie nodded, her heart aching with an odd mixture of relief and regret. "It's okay," she replied, her voice gentle yet laced with sadness. "Let's just forget it happened, alright? We have a project to focus on, after all."Nadir took her hand in his, his grip firm yet gentle. "Friends," he agreed, a hint of gratitude in his eyes.

As they reached the end of the street, Maggie cleared her throat, trying to dispel the awkwardness. "I should get going," she said, her voice lacking its usual warmth. "I'll call you tomorrow about your funding."Nadir nodded, his expression pained. "Yes, tomorrow," he replied, his eyes searching Maggie's face for something she couldn't quite comprehend.

With a forced smile, Maggie turned away, her heart heavy with confusion and disappointment. She walked away, each step echoing the ache within her, the magic of the moment now tainted with regret and confusion. Behind her, Nadir stood still, his own turmoil mirrored in his eyes, his hand reaching out involuntarily as if to grasp something that had slipped away. But it was too late. The opportunity had passed, leaving them both with a lingering sense of what could have been, lost in the shadow of an ill-timed kiss.

The next morning, she awoke with a jolt, the remnants of a dream fading like mist in the morning sun. For a moment, she lay there, her thoughts a chaotic swirl of emotions and half-formed memories. Then, like a sudden gust of wind, the memory of the kiss rushed back to her, stealing her breath away. She sat up, her heart pounding in her chest. The room was bathed in the soft hues of dawn, and everything seemed hushed, as if the world outside was holding its breath. Maggie ran a hand through her tousled hair, trying to make sense of the tangled mess of feelings inside her.

The kiss had been a mistake, they had both agreed on that. But why couldn't she shake off the lingering warmth of his touch, the way his lips had felt against hers? It was as if that fleeting moment had imprinted itself on her soul, leaving an indelible mark.

As she stared at the ceiling, a whirlwind of thoughts consumed her. Nadir's eyes, warm and searching, haunted her thoughts. She remembered the way he had looked at her afterward, the regret in his voice when he apologised. But there had been something more in his gaze, something unspoken that left her heart in turmoil. With a sigh, she swung her legs out of bed and padded to the window. The world outside was waking up, the first light of day painting the sky in hues of pink and gold. It was a new day, a fresh start, and yet, Maggie couldn't shake off the sense of longing that had settled in her chest.

She shook her head, as if trying to dispel the confusing thoughts. "It was just a kiss," she whispered to herself, hoping the words would make it easier to believe. But deep down, she knew it was more than that. The kiss had awakened something inside her, a yearning for a connection that went beyond friendship.

As she got ready for the day ahead, her mind kept drifting back to that moment. She tried to focus on the tasks at hand, the exhibition, the project, but Nadir's presence lingered like a ghost in the corners of her mind. She wondered if he was feeling the same way, if he, too, was wrestling with the aftermath of their shared moment.

With a deep breath, Maggie resolved to push the thoughts aside. There was work to be done, a project to complete. She couldn't afford to let her emotions cloud her judgement. And yet, as she stepped out into the new day, a subtle ache in her heart reminded her that some things, once felt, could not be easily ignored or forgotten.

Chapter 22: Confronting the Past

Two days had come and gone since that unexpected kiss, and Maggie found herself trapped in its aftermath. Her office was awash in sunlight, yet her thoughts were a turbulent storm of confusion. Her laptop sat open before her, but the emails and work reports had faded into inconsequence. The paramount enigma occupying her thoughts, intricate and unresolved, was Thomas.

Atticus and Eva, her colleagues, had embraced the new project direction, "Resilience: Art in the Face of Adversity," with eagerness, providing a much-needed respite from her inner turmoil. Yet, the looming conversation with Thomas was an ominous cloud on her horizon, casting shadows over her day. While Atticus and Eva had been receptive, Thomas remained an elusive phantom.

Her fingers traced the rim of her coffee mug in an absentminded dance as she wrestled with a tangle of emotions. Her hopeful gaze fell upon her phone, yearning for a message from Thomas, yet the screen stubbornly remained void of any communication. Thomas, ever the master of elusiveness, had once more slipped through her grasp. Days had unfurled into a relentless string of unanswered attempts to reach him, each message vanishing into a disquieting abyss of silence. Eva's instruction to "Do something about Thomas" resonated in her mind, intensifying the urgency of the matter.

The desk before her bore the marks of her ongoing skirmish with paperwork—a battlefield strewn with sketches, contracts, and proposals in disarray. They sprawled chaotically, reminiscent of a complex mosaic she was desperately trying to decipher.

She couldn't understand why Thomas was chosen for the project, given his track record of inconsistency. Yet, her determination stood firm; she refused to let Thomas's unreliability jeopardise the entire exhibition. With a sigh that mirrored her mingled apprehension and optimism, she dialled his number once more, the phone ringing in a slow, hesitant rhythm. Each ring seemed to stretch time, a heartbeat of uncertainty, until it finally succumbed to voicemail. Suppressing her disappointment, she left another message, her tone retaining its professionalism but tinged with the growing strain of exasperation.

Strangely, her busy workload became a shield and armour against the lingering sense of abandonment Alex's betrayal had left in its wake. It also served to distract her from the confusion she felt about the stolen kiss with Nadir. The ceaseless cacophony of tasks became both a refuge and a distraction, a way to sidestep the ache that gnawed at her core. In the whirlwind of responsibilities, she found solace, albeit temporary, from the emotional storm swirling within her.

After a week of missed phone calls, her frustration had reached a boiling point and she couldn't shake the feeling that Thomas was avoiding her, dodging her calls and messages. The upcoming exhibition loomed over her like a storm cloud, and his absence had left a void that threatened to swallow her determination whole. With her heart pounding and her patience wearing thin, Maggie decided to take matters into her own hands. She knew where his studio was, a hidden workspace tucked away in a quiet alley. Clutching her resolve like a lifeline, she set out on a mission to find him, hoping to unravel the mystery of his sudden disappearance.

The afternoon sun cast long shadows as she made her way through the narrow alley. Whitewashed walls and the distant hum of traffic formed a backdrop to her determination. She reached the weathered door of the studio, hesitating only briefly before pushing it open. With a determined exhale, she pushed open the door and stepped into the dimly lit room.

The sight that met her eyes was a shock to her system, a jolt that reverberated through her entire being. The studio was now a chaotic mess and the floor was littered with crumpled paper, discarded paint brushes, and half-empty cans of paint. Canvases leaned against the walls in haphazard arrangements, some still bearing the faint traces of incomplete strokes - there were bags of uncooked pasta, glue, and old cans nailed to a wooden board. But it was the state of Thomas himself that struck her the hardest. There he was, slouched on a stained and worn sofa, his clothes rumpled and hair dishevelled. Empty bottles were scattered around him, like silent witnesses to his unravelling. His eyes were closed, and the rhythm of his breath was uneven and laboured.

Her gaze swept over the disarray, her heart pounding in her chest. How could this be happening? The exhibition was mere weeks away, and there was no trace of any work having been completed."Thomas!" Her voice was a sharp, almost accusatory, exclamation. His eyes fluttered open, and he blinked in surprise as if he hadn't expected to see her there. A pang of anger surged within her. "What on earth is going on here?" He winced, as if her words were a harsh ray of sunlight exposing his shortcomings. "Maggie," he rasped, his voice carrying a mixture of guilt and fatigue. "I... I didn't expect you."

Her frustration boiled over. She gestured around the studio, her voice laced with incredulity. "Clearly! Look at this place! The exhibition is around the corner, and what do I find? Chaos, Thomas. Utter chaos!" He sat up slowly, his movements sluggish and heavy. "I know. I've been struggling.""Struggling?" Her voice dripped with sarcasm. "Is that what you call this?" She swept her arm in a dramatic arc, indicating the disarray that surrounded them. "Do you realise the magnitude of what's at stake?"

She paced back and forth, her frustration coursing through her veins like a wildfire. "We've put everything into this exhibition. Countless hours, sleepless nights, and for what? To have it all unravel because you can't get your act together?" His eyes flickered with a hint of defiance. "It's not that simple, Maggie. I've hit a creative wall. I can't force inspiration."

"Force?" She nearly spat out the word. "This isn't about inspiration anymore, Thomas. This is about commitment, about professionalism. We made a promise to ourselves and to each other."

Maggie's patience had eroded like the edges of a weathered cliff. The studio, once a place of artistic potential, now bore the scars of neglect and frustration. With a deep breath, her voice cut through the air like a determined wind. "Right, I've had enough."

Her words hung there, a declaration of her resolve. She strode over to the table cluttered with artistic detritus, her eyes narrowing on the bottle of vodka that seemed to embody Thomas's recent downward spiral. Her hand shot out like a lightning strike, gripping the bottle's neck with unwavering determination.But just as she was about to tip the bottle, a desperate voice broke through her intent. "No! Wait!"Startled, Maggie turned to see Thomas stumbling to his feet from the threadbare sofa, his dishevelled appearance a stark contrast to his usual artistic grace. His eyes were wide, pleading, and the scent of alcohol wafted from him like a bitter perfume."Please,," he implored, his voice a raw plea. "Don't pour it out."

Maggie's grip on the bottle tightened, her frustration warring with her compassion. "Thomas, look at yourself," she said, her voice tinged with a mix of exasperation and concern. "You're drowning your talent in a sea of self-destruction." Thomas's gaze faltered, his shoulders slumping as if under the weight of her words. "I know," he whispered, his voice carrying the weight of regret. "But it's... it's the only way I can quiet the chaos."

Maggie stood there, her grip on the vodka bottle loosening slightly. His words, desperate and filled with regret, hung in the air between them like a fragile thread. She could see the battle within him, the struggle against the demons that threatened to consume his talent and drown him in self-destruction. Her heart ached with compassion, but her determination remained unyielding.

"You have to find another way, Thomas," she urged, her voice softening, edged with a mix of compassion and frustration. "This isn't just about you anymore. We have an exhibition coming, and your art – your talent – is a crucial part of it.""You have to get your act together," she said firmly, her voice carrying the weight of their shared dreams. "If you continue down this path, if you let your demons control you, we'll lose everything – the exhibition, our chance at success."

Thomas's eyes blazed with anger, his voice dripping with sarcasm. "Oh, now you're the saviour, huh? Coming to rescue the exhibition from my supposed incompetence?" her voice was a thunderous retort. "If that's what it takes, then yes. I won't let your self-destructive behaviour destroy everything we've worked for." He shot to his feet, frustration igniting his eyes, and his voice reverberated with defiance. "You don't get to decide what I do with my life, Maggie Millar."

Her gaze remained unyielding, her voice steady, cutting through the charged air like a knife. "You're damn right I don't. But I won't stand by and watch you ruin everything we've tried to do."Their words hung in the air, an electric storm crackling between them, filling the studio with palpable tension. The weight of their confrontation settled heavily, a battle of wills and emotions. With a final, seething glare, she turned on her heel and strode away, leaving Thomas to grapple with the chaos he had unleashed. The studio seemed to exhale in relief as she stepped outside, the fresh air washing over her like a cleansing wave. The sun caressed her skin, a gentle reminder that amidst the turmoil, there was still beauty to be found.

Maggie, her heart still pounding from the clash with Thomas, sought solace on the beach. Urgency fueled her steps as she slipped off her shoes, the velvety warmth of the sand embracing her feet. Each grain was a reminder that amid life's chaos, pockets of serenity could be discovered. The rhythmic melody of waves crashing against the shore called to her, inviting her forward.

The salty breeze whispered through her hair as she stood on the beach, her eyes fixed on the boundless expanse of the sea. The confrontation with Thomas had left her shaken, emotions churning within heras her fingers traced the outline of the blue glass pendant that hung around her neck. The smooth surface, cool against her skin, anchored her in that moment of turmoil. She scanned the horizon, hoping to spot the old fisherman she had met on this very beach not long ago. His wisdom had been a beacon of clarity then, but he was nowhere to be found now. With a heavy sigh, she turned her attention back to the sea, hoping to find a moment of calm in its turquoise depths.

Just then, her mobile chimed, its sound cutting through the crash of the waves. Her heart skipped a beat as she read the message from Thomas. It was concise yet pregnant with an apology, "I'm sorry." her eyes lingered on the screen, her mind a whirlwind of conflicting emotions.

The first raindrops splattered on her screen as she typed out her response, "I believe in second chances and I'm here to support you, but you have to be willing to fight for your own talent." She pressed send, her heart pounding in anticipation of what the future might hold.

She halted, drawn by the allure of a seashell glistening in the wet sand. Its intricate spirals were like nature's poetry, a masterpiece carved by the sea. Cradling it gently in her hand, she marvelled at its elegance and the intricate patterns that adorned its surface. The gentle percussion of raindrops on the sand serenaded her as she continued her stroll away from the shore.

As she walked, she passed by elegant boutiques, their windows adorned with sparkling jewellery and exquisite evening wear. The rain turned the reflections in the glass into shimmering, distorted images, like fragments of a surreal painting.

In the midst of the deluge, she swiftly shrugged off her denim jacket and raised it above her head, attempting to create a makeshift shield against the torrential rain. In the distance, her apartment building stood like a beacon, its lights flickering amidst the rain's haze. Through the blurred curtain of water, the building's glow remained warm and inviting, promising refuge from the stormy night.

As she approached her front porch, soaked to the bone, she spotted a figure, dressed in black, hunched in the doorway. Suddenly, she recognized the face coming towards her in the darkness and felt a bolt of electricity course through her body like a shock.

"A-Alex, what are you doing here?" she stammered, her voice barely above a whisper, her heart hammering in her chest. He looked up, his eyes filled with remorse, rain-soaked hair clinging to his forehead. His eyes, once warm and familiar, were now clouded with remorse.

"I messed up, Maggie," he pleaded, his voice raw with emotion. "I can't even explain how it happened. It was a moment of weakness, a terrible mistake. I never meant for it to happen, but I need you to believe me." Maggie's hands clenched into fists, her nails biting into her palms as she glared at him. The image of the girl in the sequined bikini and pink cowboy hat seared into her mind like a brand, igniting a fury that roared through her veins.

Her arms were crossed tightly over her chest, her gaze icy. "A moment of weakness,?" she retorted, her tone laced with bitterness. "I spoke to Cathy O'Driscoll," she spat, her voice trembling with anger. "She said she was your girlfriend. There's no way you can lie your way out of this, Alex. And two months of silence? Absolutely nothing from you for two months!"

Alex's eyes darted, guilt etched across his face. He looked like a man who had weathered a storm, his exhaustion evident in the dark circles under his eyes. "I'm so sorry," he stammered, his voice catching. He took a step closer, his hands reaching out as if to touch her, but he stopped midway, realising the futility of the gesture. "I made a huge mistake," he continued, his voice cracking. "But Maggie, you mean everything to me. I can't imagine my life without you."

Her eyes softened for a moment, a flicker of the love they had shared evident in her gaze. But then, her expression hardened again. "Love is more than just words, Alex," she said, her voice steely. "It's actions. It's respect. It's honesty. And you've shattered all of that."

Raindrops tapped against the windowpane like a melancholic melody, matching the rhythm of Maggie's heavy heart as she faced Alex's persistent plea. His desperation hung in the air, palpable and thick, the echo of his love lingering like a haunting whisper.

"I'm not leaving Crete until you take me back," Alex declared, his voice threaded with desperation. He ran a hand through his wet hair, his frustration etched across his face. "I don't know what else to say," he admitted, his voice barely a whisper. "I'm lost without you. Please, Maggie, give me another chance. I'll do anything to prove that I can change, that I can be the person you deserve."

Maggie's gaze bore into his, searching for sincerity amidst the chaos of their emotions. For a moment, she wavered, her resolve flickering like a candle in the wind. The pain of their history tugged at her heartstrings, threatening to weaken her resolve. But then, with a determined shake of her head, she found her voice, steady and unwavering. "No, Alex. I can't do this anymore. I can't be with someone I can't trust. It's over."

His shoulders slumped, defeat etched across his features. "I came all the way from London…" he trailed off, his voice trailing into emptiness, the weight of his own mistakes pressing down on him. "Well, go back to London," she responded, her voice firm, her words slicing through the tension that hung between them. "You are not welcome here." He turned away, a broken man in the wake of his own actions. The sound of the door closing echoed through the hallway as Maggie stepped inside her apartment, shutting the door behind her. It was a final punctuation mark on a relationship that had once held promise but had now crumbled under the weight of betrayal.

As the rain continued to pour outside, casting a somber ambiance over the city, she sank to the floor, her heart heavy with sorrow. The love she had once felt for Alex now mingled with a profound sense of loss. Yet, amidst the pain, there was a glimmer of something else—strength, resilience, and the promise of a new beginning. She knew it wouldn't be easy. The wounds he had inflicted were deep, and trust, once broken, was not easily mended. But as the rain beat against the windows, Maggie felt a cleansing sensation, as if the storm outside was washing away the remnants of a love that had turned toxic.

In the silence that followed, she closed her eyes, allowing the sounds of the rain to cocoon her, embracing the catharsis it brought. The chapter with Alex had ended, painful yet necessary. With each raindrop, she felt the weight lifting, making room for healing and the possibility of a future where trust and love could bloom once more. It was a bittersweet moment, but in the midst of the storm, she found a flicker of hope, whispering promises of brighter days ahead.

Chapter 23: Shadows and Light

Under the tender caress of the Wednesday morning sky, Maggie stirred from her slumber, wrapped in the cocoon of her duvet. Her eyes fluttered open at the soft murmur of the clock, signalling the approach of 9:50 a.m. The room glowed in a golden luminescence, sunlight filtering through her curtains. A palm tree cast its shadow upon her wall, its branches swaying delicately in the morning breeze, a silent dance to the rhythm of the wind's whispers.

With a contented sigh, she stretched her arms wide, savouring the leisurely dance of dawn that tiptoed through her window. Her laptop, a faithful companion privy to the quiet moments of her life, lay within arm's reach. Tracing her fingers along its familiar contours, she drew it closer, the screen blinking awake, mirroring her gradual ascent into the day.

In the sanctuary of her room, she clicked open her email, half-expecting the mundane influx of work-related messages. Yet, amid the ordinary hum of her inbox, one stood out "Apologies and Amends." The subject line possessed a mysterious allure, tugging at her curiosity like a moth to flame. Intrigued, she clicked on it, her heart echoing the rhythm of the unfolding narrative.

Rachel's words flowed like a meandering brook, a heartfelt confession winding through the bends of remorse. The email bore the weight of truth, each syllable heavy with the burden of past misdeeds. Rachel laid bare her soul, confessing the theft of money, the art college ball, and the far-reaching consequences that had marred both their lives and regret - four long pages of regret. As she read, her fingers hovered over the keyboard, suspended in time, caught between empathy and anger.

Since the moment she discovered the truth, the weight of Rachel's deception had settled heavily upon her heart, the ache a constant companion reverberating through the corridors of their shared college memories. The friendship they once cherished, vibrant and untarnished, now tasted as bitter as spoiled milk, leaving a lingering aftertaste of betrayal.

Yet, amidst the unexpected waves of remorse emanating from Rachel, a flicker of forgiveness began to kindle within her, as if a long-dormant ember had stirred from its deep slumber. Bathed in the soft morning glow, a moment of sweet liberation washed over her, dissolving the bitterness that had consumed her for so long. In the quiet cocoon of her apartment, her gaze turned to five canvas's in the corner of the room reminding her that her dreams were still possible even if a nagging doubt still clawed at the edges of her confidence.

She closed her eyes, attempting to silence the relentless doubts. Patrick's words, his unwavering faith in her abilities, flashed in her mind. But those words were drowned out by the relentless chant of self-criticism.

The fear of inadequacy, of her art being disregarded, threatened to crush her spirit.

The day swept by in a whirl of work calls and paperwork, the Mediterranean sun casting its warm, golden glow outside her window. Laughter and cheerful chatter floated up from the beach, vividly contrasting her quiet solitude at the kitchen table. Each cup of coffee marked the passing hours, until finally, at 5:30 pm, the sweet relief of closing her laptop washed over her. "I need fresh air," she mused, a deep yearning for the outdoors pulling at her.

With swift movements, she dressed in a vintage-patterned sundress, its vibrant colours echoing the spirit of the seaside town. Stepping outside, she was embraced by the cool caress of sea air against her skin. Her feet guided her into the heart of the town, where the promise of inspiration beckoned. Turning down a charming side street, she caught sight of an art gallery, its windows filled with intriguing displays. With a sense of anticipation, she ventured inside, ready to immerse herself in the world of creativity and beauty.

Inside the gallery, her eyes widened with anticipation as she was drawn to a mesmerising exhibit featuring surreal paintings that seemed to dance with otherworldly magic. Each stroke of the brush told a story, and the vibrant colours spoke of emotions that resonated deeply within her. Curiosity piqued, she approached the paintings, her eyes tracing the contours of each surreal scene. Lost in the fantastical imagery, she felt a gentle tap on her shoulder. Turning around, she found herself face to face with a familiar figure, a warm smile playing on his lips.

"Nadir," she greeted him, her voice tinged with genuine surprise. "It's so good to see you here."

He, too, seemed pleasantly taken aback. "Thank you," he replied, his eyes reflecting genuine humility. "I've been meaning to call you—about the kiss. I couldn't get it out of my mind." Maggie flushed with embarrassment, attempting to downplay the moment. "It's okay," she stammered, trying to brush it off. "We just got carried away, it was a mistake."

Nadir gently shook his head, his eyes locking onto hers with newfound intensity. "No, Maggie," he said, his voice tender yet firm. "That kiss wasn't a mistake. It was something I've been feeling for a long time, something I should have said before." Her eyes widened, a glimmer of hope replacing her earlier awkwardness. "Nadir, I..." she began, her words faltering as she searched for the right response, her heart racing with vulnerability.

Nadir took a step closer, closing the distance between them once more. "Maggie, you're ... you're...so beautiful," he confessed, his voice soft as a caress, his sincerity enveloping them like a warm embrace. "I feel this undeniable connection, something that goes beyond words. I can't deny what I feel any longer."

In that moment, their shared uncertainty dissolved into a profound realisation that their connection ran deeper than they had dared to admit. The world around them faded away, leaving only the two of them in a suspended moment of vulnerability and truth.

"Would you like to take a walk?" he asked, his voice gentle as a soothing melody. She nodded, silently grateful for his calming presence. Together, they strolled towards the beach, the golden hues of the setting sun casting a warm glow over the coastline.

They settled on the soft sand, the sound of the waves creating a comforting background melody. Nadir's touch was like a healing balm to Maggie's wounded heart as he gently took her small hand in his. In the fading light, he began to share the intricacies of his own journey as a Syrian refugee—the struggles he had faced, the resilience that had kept him going, and the flickers of hope he had discovered in unexpected places, like the connection they were forging.

Maggie listened, her heart swelling with empathy and admiration for the strength Nadir exhibited. Amidst the chaos of her own life, she realised she had found something real and profoundly meaningful with him. It was a second chance at love, an unexpected gift bestowed upon her.

He leaned in, his lips meeting hers in a gentle, tender kiss. In that moment, beneath the canopy of stars, their kiss held the essence of newfound love, a beautiful beginning neither had anticipated. In the tranquil serenity of the beach, under the vast expanse of the night sky, they found solace in each other's arms. It was a moment of profound connection, where past sorrows faded, making room for the promising dawn of a shared future.

Yet, in the quiet corners of Maggie's mind, where thoughts whispered like distant echoes, there lingered the unshakable awareness of Alex's presence in Crete. She hoped against hope that he had boarded a plane back to London, leaving behind the fragments of their broken relationship amidst the Mediterranean breeze. Yet, beneath her optimism, there was a gnawing feeling, an unsettling intuition that their paths might cross again.

She tried to bury this feeling beneath layers of newfound confidence and the warmth of Nadir's affection, seeking solace in the embrace of a love that was kind and true. But the spectre of Alex, with his haunting words and the memories they shared, haunted the recesses of her thoughts. It was as if a part of her knew that their story was not yet concluded, that there were chapters left unspoken, waiting in the wings of fate.

In the fleeting moments of silence, when the world around her grew still, she would catch herself wondering about him. Was he wandering the ancient streets of Crete, contemplating the ruins of their relationship as she did? Did he, too, carry the weight of their shared past, the echoes of their laughter and the residue of their tears?

As much as she longed for closure, there was a peculiar ache in her heart, a mixture of fear and curiosity. The island of Crete, with its azure waters and sunsets dipped in gold, had been a witness to their love story's rise and fall. It held the echoes of their whispered promises and the shattered remnants of their trust.

In the quiet of the night, as stars adorned the canvas of the sky, Maggie found herself lost in these contemplations. She hoped for the strength to face whatever the future held, to confront the ghosts of her past, and perhaps, find a way to bid Alex a final farewell. But for now, all she could do was wait, caught between the echoes of yesterday and the uncertain melodies of tomorrow, her heart aching for resolution.

Chapter 24: A Canvas of Dreams

The first light of dawn stretched lazily over Rethymno, painting the town in hues of soft pink and gold. Down in the bustling heart of the Old Town, Galero Café buzzed with life, a vibrant blend of laughter, chatter, and the clinking of coffee cups. Patrick, his eyes alight with purpose, savoured his coffee at a secluded corner table, the rich aroma mingling with the electric buzz of anticipation that hung in the air, promising something extraordinary.

With his coffee drained, he stepped out into the lively streets of the old town, where the morning sunlight caressed the cobblestones, and whispers of ancient stories floated in the bre eze. He moved with determination, his footsteps echoing off weathered walls, passing by the Rimondi Fountain, a sentinel amidst the bustling energy of the town.

Its water glistened in the sunlight, a testament to the enduring beauty of the town and its rich history. The air was filled with the tantalising aroma of freshly baked pastries and the cheerful chatter of locals going about their day. Arriving at the Minoan Art Alliance, he squared his shoulders, ready to use his powers of persuasion to the max.

The receptionist, a sharp-eyed woman with a haircut as sharp as her gaze, regarded him sceptically. "May I speak to Emily Winsor, please?" Patrick requested, his voice steady, a current of anticipation running beneath his words. The woman, with a disdainful curl of her lip, checked Emily's schedule on her computer, her fingers moving with deliberate precision.

"Ms. Winsor is in a meeting at the moment. Do you have an appointment?" inquired the receptionist, her tone laced with thinly veiled impatience. Patrick, undeterred, looked her directly in the eye. "No," he said earnestly, attempting to win her over. "But it's very important."

Eleni gestured to a red plastic chair, positioned neatly opposite the desk.

"Wait there; she should be free in around 10 minutes." Despite his initial optimism, 35 seemingly endless minutes passed as Patrick waited, reading outdated magazines that hadn't seen the light of day in years. Just as he was starting to lose hope, the door swung open, revealing Emily Winsor, a vision of professional poise. She was dressed in a crisp white shirt, pressed navy jeans, nude-coloured stilettos and a tight blonde bun which only emphasised the perfect symmetry of her features. Patrick stood and introduced himself, his voice resonating with unwavering conviction, ready to lay out his plans with the hope that she would see the importance of his cause.

"I'm Patrick Evans, and I'm here to talk to you about the New Voices project, " he said, leaning forward. " I've stumbled upon a brilliant new artist you might be interested in." With a flourish, he retrieved his smartphone, a treasure trove of Maggie's art waiting to be unveiled.

"We've already selected all the artists for the project," Emily responded dismissively, her voice dripping with haughtiness and condescension. She turned away, the sharp click of her heels emphasising her determined strides. Yet, after just a few paces, she came to an abrupt halt, her cheeks flushing with sudden realisation. With a mix of curiosity and a hint of self-consciousness, she pivoted back around, her nonchalance shattering like delicate glass under Patrick's unwavering gaze. Recognition sparked in her eyes, and her voice, though composed, was tinged with newfound awareness.

"Wait," she stammered, her tone now laced with embarrassment and awe, "are you Patrick Evans? The sculptor with the sell-out show in the Tate Modern? Who just won the de Laszlo Medal" Her initial disbelief dissolved into a blend of astonishment and self-consciousness, her cheeks deepening in hue as she processed the significance of the encounter. "The very same," Patrick confirmed, a playful grin tugging at his lips. "I've long admired your work," Emily confessed, quickly changing her tone. "So, what did you want to discuss? " she beckoned, leading him into a sunlit room, the glass walls inviting the warmth of the day inside.

Seated across from Emily, Patrick opened the gallery on his smartphone, each image, stealthily captured in Maggie's apartment, unfurling like petals in bloom. The painting of Mother Ukraine, its colours a riot of political fervour, made Emily gasp in awe. The portrait, akin to Picasso's crying woman, resonated with raw, unspoken loss. With each revelation, Emily found herself speechless, her breath caught in the emotions woven into every brushstroke.

"W"Who is this artist?" she breathed, her voice tinged with wonder. "Do you think they'd consider joining our show? They're clearly immensely talented." Patrick leaned back, savouring the moment, his eyes dancing with mischief, before revealing the clandestine brilliance he had uncovered."Oh, you might be familiar with her," he teased, his grin widening. "Does the name Maggie Millar ring a bell?"

"What?" Emily exclaimed, her shock reverberating in the room. "That administrator woman!?" Her eyes widened in disbelief, and she gasped, her world momentarily tilting on its axis.

"Yes, that Administrator woman," Patrick affirmed, his eyes alight with the thrill of discovery.

Emily sat there, her astonishment clear in her expression, her hand involuntarily reaching to her chest as if trying to steady her racing heart. "I didn't even know that she painted?" she said, her surprise evident. She realised that she had always underestimated Maggie from the moment they met, believing her to be nothing more than a secretary with an elevated job title. Now, she understood how very wrong she had been.

Patrick nodded, a triumphant smile on his face. "Yes," he said, leaning back in his chair. "You're right, Emily. There's something very special here, and she absolutely has to be included in the exhibition. These works need to be seen. After all, the exhibition is called 'New Voices,' and hers is a voice that needs to be heard."

Emily hesitated for a moment, her pride warring with the undeniable talent displayed before her. With a reluctant sigh, she conceded, her voice laced with grudging acknowledgement, "Fine, include Maggie Millar in the exhibition. If her art is as exceptional as you say, we can't afford to overlook it."

Patrick nodded, a sense of triumph gleaming in his eyes. He had achieved the impossible, breaking through Emily's haughty exterior and forcing her to acknowledge the brilliance she had initially dismissed. The room buzzed with the weight of this decision, and the anticipation of what was to come hung in the air, transforming the atmosphere into one charged with possibility.

As the two of them discussed plans and strategies for reaching out to Maggie and including her in the exhibition, Patrick's phone buzzed with a message from her. She had woken up and was eager to meet with him, unaware that her dreams of becoming an artist and having her work seen and appreciated were about to become a reality. Patrick couldn't help but smile at the serendipity of it all, realising that he would be able to help his old art college friend achieve some of her dreams, even if it was 15 years later than expected.

An hour later, Patrick stepped out into the blistering sun, leaving behind the bustling energy of The Minoan Arts office. He looked back at the building, a place where their artistic journey had taken a thrilling turn.

With a renewed sense of purpose, he made his way to the nearest bus stop, the promise of a brighter future propelling him forward.

The bus arrived, its door hissing open in invitation. Patrick boarded, his heart pounding with anticipation. As the vehicle rumbled along the vibrant streets of Rethymno, he couldn't help but feel a surge of hope for what lay ahead. Each passing street seemed to whisper a promise, and with every moment, he grew more eager to share the incredible news with Maggie.

Finally, the bus came to a stop near her apartment building. Patrick stepped off, his excitement palpable as he walked the cobbled path leading to her door. With a quick breath to steady himself, he pushed the door open, which was slightly ajar, ready to deliver the life-changing news that awaited Maggie on the other side. The hinges creaked softly in the warm breeze, a sound that seemed to echo the anticipation building inside him.

She sat at her cluttered kitchen table, surrounded by stacks of paperwork and spreadsheets. Her laptop, open to a monotonous document, displayed endless rows of numbers that seemed to dance before her eyes. Just as she was about to lose herself in the monotony, the door creaked open, and Patrick entered, his face alive with excitement. Maggie looked up, her eyes met his, searching for a hint of what had him so animated.

"Maggie," Patrick said, his voice filled with excitement. She looked up, her eyes widening in surprise at his unexpected visit. "Patrick, what's going on?" she asked, curiosity tingeing her voice. Patrick's eyes gleamed with anticipation as he took a deep breath, ready to deliver news that would change Maggie's life.

"Maggie," he began, his voice filled with a mixture of joy and pride, "you won't believe it. I just met with Emily Winsor, the curator of the New Voices exhibition. And guess what? Your art, your incredible talent, is going to be featured!"

Maggie's eyes widened in disbelief, her heart skipping a beat at the unexpected revelation. "What? Are you serious?" she gasped, her hands trembling with a mix of excitement and disbelief. "You shouldn't have... I mean, Emily - as far as I've gathered, has never liked me, not one little bit."

Patrick shook his head, a wide grin spreading across his face. "Not anymore! Emily was blown away by your work. She couldn't believe that the person behind these mesmerising pieces was the same woman handling the administrative tasks for Artist's Connect. You've defied all expectations, Maggie. Your art is going to be showcased for the world to see!"

Tears welled up in her eyes as the weight of Patrick's words settled in her heart. The years of toiling away at a job that didn't fulfil her, the countless hours spent honing her craft in the quiet corners of her apartment – it had all led to this moment. "I... I can't believe it," Maggie whispered, her voice filled with awe and gratitude. "Thank you, Patrick. This means everything to me."

He reached across the table, his hand covering hers in a reassuring gesture. "You deserve this, Maggie," he said, his voice unwavering. "Your talent is extraordinary, and now, the world is going to recognize it. Your life is about to change, and I couldn't be happier for you." In that simple touch and Patrick's words, Maggie felt a surge of hope and inspiration. The mundane paperwork faded into the background, replaced by the vivid colours of her artistic dreams.

She watched the door click shut behind Patrick, a contented sigh escaping her lips. There was something about his presence that always left her feeling buoyed, a warmth that lingered in the air even after he was gone. With practised ease, she sauntered into her kitchen, her sanctuary of creativity and caffeine. The aroma of freshly brewed coffee filled the room, wrapping around her like a comforting embrace. Making coffee had become a ritual, a meditative act that grounded her in the midst of life's whirlwind.

As the rich, dark liquid trickled into her favourite mug, she savoured the moment, her fingers tracing the familiar curves of the handle. With her coffee in hand, she stepped out onto her balcony, the cool breeze ruffling her hair, and the distant hum of the city providing a gentle soundtrack to her thoughts. There, waiting as always, was the stray cat, its emerald eyes fixed on her, a silent companion in her moments of solitude.

She poured a bit of milk into a saucer, setting it down on the floor. The cat approached cautiously, its whiskers twitching in anticipation. As it lapped up the milk, Maggie settled into her wicker chair, the afternoon sun casting a golden glow over her surroundings. With each sip of her coffee, she let the news of being part of the New Voices Project sink in, a bubbly concoction of calm and excitement fizzing within her.

The soft chime of her phone sliced through the quiet hum of Maggie's morning, and as she glanced down, Thomas's name bathed the screen in a warm glow. "Hello, Maggie," his voice, a symphony of gratitude and vulnerability, flowed through the line. "I just wanted to give you a call to say thanks, for, you know, giving a damn."

Maggie cradled the phone between her ear and shoulder, her fingers absently tracing circles on the coffee table. "You don't need to explain, Thomas. It's fine, really it is." She lifted her coffee mug to her lips, taking a slow sip, savoring the warmth that mirrored the newfound connection they shared.

A pause hung in the air, pregnant with the unspoken gratitude, before Thomas's voice returned, carrying a weight that demanded attention. "I've been working on some pieces around the theme of art and resilience. I think you'll connect with them."

Maggie's eyes sparkled with genuine interest. "That's a relief," she replied, the excitement in her voice bubbling to the surface. "The exhibition is just around the corner, so it's good to know that you're on top of things."

Thomas's chuckle, a rich melody through the phone, hinted at a shared camaraderie. "I even have a tidy studio these days. Clean studio, clear mind, right? Though I'll probably mess it up again soon. Old habits, you know."

Her laughter danced in harmony with his. "Well, Thomas, as long as pasta doesn't make a surprise appearance in your artwork, I think we're safe. Let's keep it reserved for your Italian escapades." Maggie's free hand mimicked the motion of brushing away an invisible strand of hair, a playful gesture underscoring the shared history between them.

Their banter set the stage for the heart of the conversation. Thomas, his voice now a canvas painted with determination, began to unravel the threads of his journey to sobriety.

"Sounds like quite the journey," she offered, her words a bridge between understanding and encouragement.

Thomas's eyes, unseen but vivid in her imagination, sparkled with a quiet resolve. "It was, and I wouldn't change a thing."

Maggie's smile widened, the physical embodiment of her genuine happiness for him. "No pasta-themed masterpieces, I promise. I'll save that for my dinner plate," Thomas teased, their laughter now a shared melody echoing through the phone.

They both shared a good-natured laugh, the absurdity of the conversation adding a sprinkle of comedy to their connection. In that moment, Maggie realised that art and friendship could be as unpredictable and delightful as a well-cooked pasta—sometimes surprising, often comforting, and always best enjoyed with good company.

As Maggie playfully bantered with Thomas, the sun cast a warm, golden glow over the whitewashed buildings beyond her balcony.

Their laughter mingled with the ambient sounds of the city below, a symphony of urban life playing in the background. The warm, golden glow of the setting sun painted the beach in hues of orange and pink, casting a magical spell over the bustling streets. The stray cat, her loyal companion, curled up beside her, its purrs harmonising with the fading daylight. From a nearby garden, the scent of blooming flowers wafted in the air, adding a touch of sweetness to the evening breeze.

Down the street, children's laughter filled the air as they played, their innocence and joy resonating with the essence of life. A street musician strummed his guitar, the melody weaving through the air like a serenade to the city. In the distance, the church bells tolled, marking the passage of time in the most harmonious way.

Amidst this vibrant tapestry of life, Maggie and Thomas continued their conversation, their voices becoming threads in the intricate fabric of the city's energy. Each word they exchanged seemed to add a stroke to the canvas of anticipation and excitement, blending seamlessly with the pulsating rhythm of the town below.

Chapter 25: Severin

The morning sun hung low, casting a warm, golden glow over the town of Rethemon, weaving a tapestry of memories for Maggie as she strolled through its narrow streets. Her time in Crete flashed before her eyes—the proposal in Santorini, her friendship with Kareryna, Rachel's confession, and the shards of her broken relationship with Alex. The past three months had sculpted her into a stronger version of herself, amidst the idyllic setting, her budding romance with Nadir added sweetness to her days.

As she meandered through the picturesque old town, vibrant graffiti adorned the walls, each mural whispering a unique tale. Her steps guided her away from the charming facades, leading her deeper into the heart of the town, where the colours of the walls faded into muted tones, and the streets bore the scars of time.

The cobblestone pathways beneath her shoes grew rougher, and the buildings transformed from quaint, well-kept structures to weathered facades, marred by years of neglect. Derelict buildings stood like silent sentinels, their broken windows and peeling paint telling tales of forgotten yesterdays. The atmosphere shifted from lively chatter to a hushed stillness, interrupted only by the occasional creak of a rusty sign swinging in the wind.

In this gritty area, where time seemed to have stood still, Studio 23 awaited. The contrast between the charm of the old town and the raw reality of this neglected neighbourhood was stark, underscoring the depth of Eva's isolation. The anticipation became almost tangible as Maggie approached the studio, the doorbell's chime cutting through the silence like a fragile thread, connecting the world outside to the secrets held within the walls of Eva's workspace.

Eva, once confident and bold, now appeared small and pale, clad in her trademark cropped sweatshirt and frayed denim shorts. Stripped of makeup, she looked remarkably young, her ombre hair framing her face like a vivid painting."Hey, how are you?" Maggie inquired, her concern etched on her face. "I'm okay," she replied, her voice soft, her eyes veiled with unease. "I have something to show you." Leading Maggie to her video installation, Eva's creation for the exhibition based on the theme of art and resilience unfolded before them. In the intimate studio space, she embarked on a profound performance art piece, captured on film.

Adorned with fragments of shattered glass, she embodied the resilience of refugees amidst the chaos of war. Each deliberate movement painted a visceral narrative—a cry for peace, a testament to the enduring human spirit. The haunting soundtrack underscored the pain of conflict and the hope for reconciliation. Eva's tears merged with her art, symbolising the collective sorrow of those affected by war. As the video reached its powerful conclusion, Maggie felt a surge of emotions—empathy, admiration, and deep appreciation for the young woman's talent.

Eager to discuss the artwork, Maggie turned to Eva, only to find her distracted, her eyes fixed on something beyond the window. "Are you okay?" Maggie asked, sensing Eva's unease. She hesitated before finally speaking, her voice laced with fear. "I'm worried that I've been found, that my fiancé Severin is in Crete. I don't feel safe." The room seemed to hold its breath, the weight of her words hanging heavily in the air. Maggie's shock was palpable as she clutched Eva's arm, her concern deepening. "How do you know?" she asked urgently.

"I was in the market the other day, you know the one in the village square," she explained, her fingers nervously twirling a strand of her ombre hair. "I felt someone watching me. I think it was him. I saw someone in the crowd with short blonde hair in a black leather jacket; it looked just like him." Maggie's mind raced, her heart pounding with fear for her friend. "Call the police!" she urged, her voice urgent. "I have," Eva said, her eyes filled with terror. "But he said if I ever left him, he would kill me. I don't know what to do."

In the soft glow of the afternoon sunlight, Maggie enveloped Eva in a comforting hug, her arms wrapped tightly around her fragile frame. "We should tell the team at the Arts Alliance," Maggie suggested, her voice laced with concern. "We need to let people know that you're in danger." Eva shook her head, her eyes clouded with uncertainty. "What if it's all in my mind?" she whispered, her voice trembling. "I can't be sure, but you know, it's a feeling that I have. I can almost smell him."

"Okay," she replied gently, her tone understanding. "I won't tell anyone yet. But if anything happens, or you feel uneasy or scared, just call me. Promise?" Eva walked away from the window, her steps heavy with the weight of worry. She settled onto a small wooden chair, the green and yellow hues of her hair illuminated by the sunlight streaming in. A sigh escaped her lips. "You can run away from your past, you know, but it always has a way of catching up with you. I thought this was my place of safety, my second chance - but now I'm not so sure." As Maggie closed the door behind her, a heavy cloud of worry settled into the corners of her heart, an unwelcome guest overstaying its welcome. The air inside Eva's studio held echoes of fear and uncertainty, momentarily paralysing Maggie in a web of indecision.

Fingers tracing a familiar path to her phone, Maggie dialled Nadir's number with a trembling hand. "Nadir, it's Eva. She's in trouble," she conveyed, her words laden with genuine concern. Nadir's voice, a comforting lifeline through the device, responded, "What happened? Is she okay?" "No, that's the problem," Maggie replied, frustration colouring her tone. "She thinks her abusive ex-fiancé, Severin, has tracked her down here in Crete. She's scared out of her mind, and she suspects he's been watching her."

There was a weighty pause on the line, and then Nadir's sympathetic voice cut through the silence. "That's terrible. What can we do?" Nadir's reassuring words, a calming presence, echoed through the receiver. "Take a deep breath, Maggie. You're doing your best by being there for her. I think you should call the police and tell them everything about the man Eva thinks she saw. Give them as accurate a description as you can." "Thanks, Nadir. I really needed to hear that. I just want to keep her safe," Maggie responded, her voice now more composed, strengthened by Nadir's steady support.

"Where are you?" Maggie inquired, her tone a blend of agreement and eagerness. "I'm at the Venetian Harbour." "Alright," Maggie replied, "meet you there in ten minutes. Your company is exactly what I need."Leaving Eva's studio, Maggie navigated through the graffiti-clad walls that gradually yielded to the charm of cobblestone streets. The air transformed, carrying the scent of salt and distant melodies, leading her towards the allure of the seafront. Approaching the harbour, the warm Mediterranean breeze tousled Maggie's hair. Nadir, seated at the familiar cafe table where serendipity had first brought them together, looked up with a welcoming smile. "Hey," he greeted, rising gracefully, "how about a walk along the beach?"

As they strolled, their conversation weaved seamlessly between Eva's predicament and plans for the upcoming exhibition. Yet, beneath the surface of creativity, a poignant sadness lingered—an unspoken acknowledgment of Kateryna's mysterious disappearance. The absent note in their shared melody left Maggie haunted by unanswered questions.As Maggie dipped her feet into the cool, clear waters of the

Aegean, her mind couldn't help but wander to Kateryna's uncertain fate. Did she manage to defy the odds and survive? Just a few days prior, Maggie had reached out to her on Go Fit, the very platform where their friendship had once blossomed. Opening the app, she discovered a stark message: "This User Can no Longer be Located."

The words struck her with a mix of grief, acceptance, and profound loss. Teary-eyed, Maggie read the message, feeling the weight of a friendship that had thrived in the digital realm. Beside her, Nadir sensed her turmoil, wrapping her in a comforting embrace as they stood on the beach, the rhythmic waves echoing the ebb and flow of emotions.

"I hoped for so long that she was still with us, still alive," Maggie confessed, her voice catching in her throat. Nadir held her tighter, offering silent solace to her wounded soul. Together, they gazed at the vast expanse of sea and sky, where a solitary seagull flew into the distance. "She's free now," Nadir murmured, his fingers gently running through Maggie's hair. In those words, there was a poignant acknowledgment of life's complexities—the delicate dance between hope and letting go. Maggie exhaled, releasing a sigh carrying the weight of years of anticipation and uncertainty.

"I'll always remember her," she whispered, the sea breeze carrying her words into the vast openness. In that moment, as the sun dipped toward the horizon, Nadir, turning to her with a tender gaze, spoke volumes without words. With the sun dancing in his eyes, he leaned in and kissed Maggie gently. It was a silent promise, an unspoken commitment to the future they were building together.

The kiss, filled with the warmth of the Mediterranean sun, held the essence of shared dreams and newfound hope. As they separated, Maggie looked into Nadir's eyes, finding a mutual understanding that transcended the concerns of the moment. Embraced by the gentle sea breeze, they continued their walk along the sunlit shoreline, fingers entwined. The air carried a sense of possibility, a tangible belief that they could overcome any challenges ahead as long as they faced them together.

In that stolen moment beneath the daytime sky, Maggie marvelled at the twists and turns life had taken. The worries that had burdened her earlier had transformed into a quiet optimism. She welcomed the unexpected love that had bloomed amidst the everyday tapestry of existence. As they walked, the promise of the future unfolded before them, like a canvas painted with the hues of hope.

The soft click of the door echoed in Maggie's apartment as she stepped inside, the memory of the walk on the beach with Nadir still vivid in her mind. The warmth of the night lingered, wrapping around her like a comforting embrace. With a contented sigh, she kicked off her sandals, the grains of sand from the beach falling onto her welcome mat.

Puttering around her apartment, she hummed a tune, the residual joy from the evening still coursing through her veins. The soft glow of fairy lights adorned the room, casting a warm ambiance. Maggie moved to the kitchen, fixing a simple but satisfying late-night snack—crackers, cheese, and a bunch of grapes. The clink of the knife against the cutting board accompanied her quiet thoughts.

Her eyes wandered to the corner of the room, where an easel stood with a canvas adorned in strokes of colour. The finishing touches for the exhibition tomorrow night beckoned, and Maggie felt a surge of excitement at the prospect of her work being showcased. She dipped her brush into vibrant hues, carefully adding the final details that would bring the canvas to life.

As Maggie delicately brushed the final strokes of her artistic creation, a profound sense of achievement settled within her. The anticipation of unveiling her masterpiece to the world sparked a joyous excitement that twirled in her chest. The room, with its lingering scent of paint and the gentle hum of the refrigerator, transformed into a haven of creative fulfilment.

By the time the clock struck 11:30, weariness seeped into her bones. She tenderly rinsed her paintbrushes in the sink, watching the acrylic remnants swirl away, and placed them carefully to dry. With a contented smile, she surveyed her living space, now adorned with the tangible fruits of her labour.

Shutting the door to her living room, Maggie made her way to her bedroom. The soft carpet underfoot provided a comforting contrast to the cool kitchen tiles. Changing into comfortable pyjamas, she cast a final glance at the canvas in the corner before slipping into bed. A profound sense of satisfaction enveloped her as she nestled under the covers, dreams tinged with echoes of creativity and anticipation guiding her into sleep.

Chapter 26: Framed Ambitions

Maggie awoke to the gentle morning glow, casting a warm embrace through her curtains. Today, the crescendo of three months' dedication and passion awaited her. Excitement pirouetted in her chest, delicate as butterflies, and anticipation hung in the air like a tangible, sweet fragrance.

In her snug apartment, Maggie slipped into her flip flops and a vibrant yellow silk kimono, cocooned by the aroma of freshly brewed coffee. As she prepared a quick cup, the rich scent intertwined seamlessly with the promise of the day. Glancing at the clock—11:30 a.m.—she felt the morning slipping through her fingers.

Cradling the warmth of her coffee, Maggie moved to her bedroom, standing before the mirror. Her long, dark hair cascaded like a waterfall, and as she brushed it, her gaze fell upon the picture of George Michael by her bedside. A gentle smile curved her lips. "Thanks, George. For everything," she whispered, half expecting the picture to wink back at her in agreement.

Stepping into the vibrant sunlight, she picked up the canvas she had completed the night before. With the city awakening around her, Maggie felt her heart harmonising with the pulsating energy of the streets. The Mode Gallery, a sleek masterpiece of contemporary design, extended its invitation. The journey into the heart of Rethymnon was a dance of eager anticipation and nervous excitement as she ventured to the gallery to apply the final strokes to the art exhibition.

The Mode Gallery materialised, its exterior a testimony to modern aesthetics. A zen garden adorned the entrance—a tranquil haven with neatly arranged stones and a koi pond shimmering in the morning light. The serenity of the garden served as a gentle prelude to the artistic haven within.

Inhaling the heady mix of anticipation and fresh paint, she glided into the gallery, where the air hummed with the soft melody of conversations. Achilleus, the gallery owner, greeted her with his customary cheer, "Hello, Maggie, ready for the big show tonight?"

"Oh, absolutely," she quipped, a mischievous smile playing on her lips. "It's going to be positively fabulous." Emily and Demetris had orchestrated an impressive turnout from their Greek contacts, and Patrick had sprinkled his magic on London and New York connections. Maggie was banking on a decent turnout, secretly hoping for the appearance of an art critic of substantial influence. After all, a bit of publicity never hurt an artist, and a few art sales would be the cherry on top.

The pristine white walls of the gallery created a captivating backdrop for the diverse array of artworks that formed the heart of the exhibition. Atticus's masterpieces, adorned with rich and vibrant hues, skillfully portrayed the resilience and courageous beauty of displaced individuals. Each stroke of the brush seemed to breathe life into the canvas, capturing the essence of the human spirit facing adversity with grace.

In striking contrast, Nadir's poignant images took center stage, offering a powerful narrative of refugees from Syria, Iraq, Afghanistan, and Ukraine. Through the lens of Nadir's camera, their stories unfolded with raw authenticity, inviting viewers to confront the harsh realities of displacement. The images, both haunting and compelling, spoke volumes about the strength found within those who endure and the universal connection that binds humanity.

Amidst this visual dialogue, the room's focal point was a trio of monumental sculptures by Thomas, each a testament to the enduring power of art and resilience. Crafted from an array of recycled materials, the sculptures stood as powerful symbols of transformation and strength. As viewers engaged with these intricate creations, they couldn't help but be drawn into a narrative that celebrated the beauty born from the discarded, echoing the theme of resilience that threaded through the entire exhibition.

On the opposing wall, bathed in the soft glow of sunlight, hung three of Maggie's paintings, strategically arranged in a row next to a window. Seizing a conveniently placed ladder in the centre of the room, she elevated herself to add the final painting to the collection of four that would grace the show. As she delicately adjusted the placement, a sense of enchantment enveloped her, the surreal reality of her long-cherished dream unfolding before her like a spellbinding tapestry.

In that singular moment, it was as if a cleansing breeze had swept through, washing away the pains of her past. Rachel's betrayal, the shards of her relationship with Alex, and the years she felt she had squandered—all of it faded into insignificance. It was as though Maggie was finally stepping into the woman she had always been meant to be, and the sensation was nothing short of exhilarating. Life's twists and turns had led her to this transformative juncture, and in the midst of hanging those paintings, she revelled in the profound joy of becoming her true, vibrant self.

Adjacent to the main viewing room, a small black screening space awaited Eva's performance art. However, it remained bare. The work scheduled for delivery the day before had simply not arrived, leaving a noticeable gap in the carefully orchestrated exhibition. The anticipation of a perfect evening hung in the air, just like the art that awaited its moment to shine.

Maggie's phone emitted a gentle buzz, cutting through the lively atmosphere of the exhibition morning like a welcome melody. Retrieving it with a deft motion, she was met with Nadir's voice, as cheerful as ever. "Hey Maggie, how's everything going this morning?"

"The exhibition is just... wow, and the space is like a dream—thanks a bunch for helping me find it. But, Nadir, Eva and her work are like, nowhere to be found, and I'm kind of freaking out," Maggie shared, her tone genuinely concerned.

"We absolutely need to find her," Nadir declared urgently. "I'll be at the gallery in 10 minutes."

True to his word, Nadir showed up right on time. They squeezed into his car and zoomed towards the outskirts of town, heading for Studio 24, Eva's haven of creativity.

As they approached, the studio door was slightly ajar, giving them a sneak peek into a world of artsy chaos. Canvases decked the walls like this incredible tapestry, video tapes were scattered around like avant-garde confetti, and props were just strewn everywhere. But, hang on, there was a major missing piece — no sign of Eva. The puzzle started to come together when Maggie's gaze fell upon a table, draped with a large tablecloth. There, in the corner, was Eva—huddled, frightened, seemingly ensnared in her own artistic sanctuary.

"Please, don't, just leave me alone. Please don't hurt me," Eva pleaded, her eyes wide with fear.

Maggie, this soothing presence, hurried to Eva's side. "Eva, it's just me. Nadir and I are here to help," she reassured, her voice a gentle anchor in the storm of Eva's distress. Leaning in, she started to unravel the threads of their recent efforts, the tendrils of hope woven into the chaos.

"We spoke to the police," Maggie began, her eyes locking onto Eva's, seeking a lifeline in the connection they shared. "We investigated the man in the village market—a tourist, nothing more. He bore a mere resemblance to Severan, nothing more than a haunting echo from your past."

Eva, visibly shaken, clutched onto Maggie's words as if they were fragile lifelines. The tumult of emotions played across her face, a battlefield where relief grappled with lingering fear. She grappled to reconcile the tangible world around her with the haunting specters of her past, the weight of her history in the cult casting a distorted reality.

"Severan is not here, Eva. He's not in this studio, and he's not in this town," Maggie continued, her voice a steady reassurance. "What you're feeling right now is the residue of a past that no longer holds power over you. You've broken free, and we're here to stand with you."

Eva's eyes, wide with fear, reflected the struggle within. The web of paranoia and fear, woven by years of trauma, clung stubbornly to her, threatening to pull her back into the shadows.

"You're safe now, Eva," Maggie affirmed, reaching out to gently touch her shoulder. "The man in the market wasn't Severan. He's a specter, a ghost of the past that we've confronted and dispelled. Let the light in, and let us help you move beyond this darkness."

As the weight of Maggie's words settled in the air, a palpable tension held the room. Eva, caught between the echoes of her past and the solace of the present, faced a pivotal moment of reckoning.

Nadir and Maggie, this dynamic duo, worked together to soothe Eva's frayed nerves. Their words, this kind of gentle melody, coaxed her from her hidden alcove, recognizing the profound psychological scars Severan had etched onto her soul.

"We're here for you, Eva," Nadir reassured, his smile a balm.

With Eva gradually calming, Maggie guided her to her apartment. She insisted on a break before the grand exhibition. Eva hesitated but eventually succumbed to the genuine concern mirrored in Maggie's eyes.

At 4 pm, Nadir dropped Maggie and Eva at Maggie's apartment, a snug retreat beside the Agean Breeze hotel. Eva, still trembling from the morning's ordeal, sought comfort in Maggie's familiar surroundings.

Once inside, Maggie enveloped Eva in a warm blanket, a gesture to ward off the lingering fear. "You're safe here, Eva. Take a moment to breathe," Maggie urged, guiding her to the sofa.

In the kitchen, Maggie instinctively reached for the universal remedy believed to mend any wound—an aromatic cup of tea. Returning with the steaming mug, Maggie handed it to Eva. "Here," she said gently. "Sip on this; it'll make you feel better."

Eva accepted the mug with shaky hands, the warmth seeping into her fingers as the soothing aroma filled the room. Nervously sipping the tea, she felt a semblance of calm returning.

"I have something for you," Maggie continued, her eyes softening. She removed a delicate eye-shaped pendant from around her neck. "This is the Mati. Put simply, it protects you against evil. In Greece, the Mati pendant actually dates all the way back to the 6th Century B.C in ancient times."

She extended the pendant toward Eva, who hesitated, admiring its intricate design but attempting to decline the generous gift. "I can't possibly take it," Eva protested.

Maggie smiled, urging her to accept, "Please do. I don't need it anymore, but it will help you feel safe."

Reluctantly, Eva took the Mati pendant into her hands, feeling the weight of both the piece and Maggie's intention. "It's beautiful," she admitted, her voice a whisper.

"You deserve to feel safe, Eva," Maggie affirmed, her gaze conveying a shared understanding of the strength it takes to overcome fear. "Wear it, and let it be a reminder that you're surrounded by protection and friendship."

As Eva clutched the pendant, a symbolic shield against the shadows of her past, she felt a glimmer of hope. In Maggie's cozy apartment, with the warmth of tea and the Mati's protective magic, the two women found solace in a bond that transcended art and the challenges they'd both faced.

While Eva sought solace in much-needed rest, back at the gallery, Nadir discreetly set up Eva's video, a silent tribute to the artist who had faced her demons and emerged triumphant. The flickering images on the screen captured the essence of her journey—her struggles, her resilience, and the unyielding spirit that fueled her art.

A few hours later, Maggie gently roused Eva from her peaceful slumber. "Feeling better?" she inquired, concern evident in her eyes.

"Yes, I feel like myself again - thanks for being there for me," Eva replied, a genuine gratitude lacing her words.

"This is your night to shine," Maggie declared, a supportive smile playing on her lips. She moved to her closet, swinging the door open with a flourish. "I don't know if any of these are your style—or even your size—but you are welcome to borrow anything."

Maggie, with her flair for fashion, gracefully slipped into a show-stopping red vintage dress that seemed to transcend eras. Completing the look with sky-high black stilettos, she radiated confidence and elegance. Meanwhile, Eva opted for a more casual yet charming ensemble, choosing a Mona Lisa T-shirt and blowing bubbles with her bubblegum.

"I've always loved that," Maggie remarked, her eyes lighting up. "It looks great on you."

Together, dressed in their unique styles, they left the apartment, ready to face the grandeur of the exhibition. As they approached the gallery, the anticipation in the air was palpable. The room was transformed into a bustling scene, with chic waiters gracefully navigating the crowd, trays of delectable canapés in hand, and champagne flowing freely. Elegant floral displays adorned the space in shades of white, creating an atmosphere of sophistication and celebration.

Amidst the lively chatter and clinking glasses, Maggie's eyes caught sight of Nadir engaged in conversation with Emily Winsor and Demitris Pappadópoulos. The trio seemed deep in discussion, their expressions animated. As Maggie and Eva made their way through the crowd, the buzz of excitement heightened.

Nadir, turning to greet them, wore a smile that mirrored the joyous energy of the evening. "Maggie, Eva! You both look absolutely stunning," he exclaimed, his enthusiasm contagious.

Maggie beamed, acknowledging the compliment. "Thank you, Nadir. It's all Eva's magic tonight."

Eva, still adjusting to the vibrant atmosphere, blushed at the praise but couldn't help but share in the infectious excitement.

The atmosphere in the gallery crackled with anticipation as the artists made their entrance. First through the door was Thomas, once grappling with the clutches of alcoholism, now standing tall and dapper in black jeans, a waistcoat, and a riotously colorful scarf that seemed to defy the conventional restraint of the art world. His presence exuded a renewed confidence, a testament to his triumph over personal demons.

Shortly after, Atticus ambled in, arm in arm with Patrick, the easy camaraderie between them evident. Atticus, the free spirit of the group, sported an ensemble that effortlessly blended bohemian chic with an understated elegance. Their arrival signaled the convergence of diverse artistic spirits, each with a unique story waiting to unfold.

As the room filled, not only with the buzz of excited chatter but with the heavy weight of significance, Maggie couldn't help but marvel at the eclectic mix of attendees. Important art critics, discerning buyers, and creative minds from Athens and Crete mingled in a harmonious dance, their energy pulsating through the air.

In the midst of the vibrant crowd, a figure stood out—Wayne Darcy, the influential critic from New York, whose mere presence added a layer of prestige to the evening. Patrick, playing the role of introducer extraordinaire, gestured towards Wayne with a flourish.

"Well done, sweetie," Patrick chimed in, wiping away a tear. "We did it," Maggie said, turning to raise a glass to her fellow artists. She smiled at Thomas, who lifted a glass of orange juice and winked at her. Atticus tipped his red fedora, and Eva beamed from ear to ear, buoyed by the fantastic response to her performance art video.

"Let me introduce you to Wayne Darcy," Patrick announced with a touch of theatrical flair. "Wayne works for the New York Metropolitan Museum of Art, among other things. Oh, and he's an art critic for The New Yorker."

Maggie, momentarily taken aback by the gravity of Wayne's credentials, composed herself and extended a hand. "Pleased to meet you," she greeted, her nerves simmering beneath a veneer of composure. As she shook Wayne's hand, she couldn't help but notice his distinguished appearance—a mane of salt-and-pepper hair, neatly combed, framed a face marked by sharp, discerning eyes behind stylish glasses. His attire, a tailored suit blending sophistication with a touch of modern flair, spoke of his multifaceted role in the art world. A subtle yet genuine smile played on his lips, adding a welcoming warmth to his refined demeanor. With an aura of quiet authority, Wayne embodied both substance and style in the bustling art scene.

"Miss Maggie Miller, I see you are the artist responsible for these extraordinary pieces," Wayne remarked, his gaze sweeping towards four of her paintings displayed beside the window.

She nodded, a twinge of impostor syndrome gnawing at her confidence. "Yes, that's my work."

The conversation flowed, a delicate dance between acknowledgment and vulnerability. Wayne, the seasoned critic, navigated the intricacies of Maggie's creations with a keen eye, unraveling the layers of her artistic expression. As the room hummed with intellectual discourse and admiration, Maggie grappled with the shadows of self-doubt, questioning her place among these luminaries of the art world. Yet, in the midst of her internal struggle, the collective energy of the exhibition surged forward, a testament to the power of creativity and the resilience of those who dared to bare their souls on canvas.

Maggie reached out for a glass of Champagne but - in the crowd she spotted a familiar face. For a moment, she felt a pang of sympathy, but reality crashed back—a cold wave of betrayal and pain. "What are you doing here, Alex?" she demanded.

His eyes mirrored a mix of determination and remorse, revealing the weight of the words he was about to utter. "I had to see you, Maggie. There's something I need to say."

Facing him with unyielding resolve, Maggie's words hung thick in the still night air. "What could you possibly say to me?" she demanded, her eyes a tumultuous blend of determination and exasperation. " That I'm proud of you and everything you've achieved."

"Too little,too late alex. The relationship is over. And this time, there are no second chances, no do-overs, and certainly no wedding. I've found someone else, and," hesitating, a subtle quiver in her voice, "I'm in love with him, " she said, looking over at Nadir who presumed she was talking to patron of the gallery.

Crestfallen, Alex demanded, "Who? Who is he?" looking utterly shocked.

"It doesn't matter," she replied, her gaze unwavering. "What matters is that you realise you have to change, you have to move on with your life. I'm stronger now. I don't want or need that in my life."

Alex took a tentative step toward her, seeking a last connection. But Maggie held out her hand, creating a clear physical boundary. "So this really is goodbye," he said, a mix of resignation and sorrow in his eyes.

"Yes," she replied, a deep breath punctuating her response. "And you can take this back," she added, handing him the vintage engagement ring. The ring, once a symbol of false promises, now gleamed with the light of her liberation from his manipulative clutches.

"Alright," he murmured, delicately taking the ring from her hand. "I just wanted to check if there was any lingering chance for us to, you know, turn the page, make things brighter," he said, his eyes carrying a hint of sorrow.

"It's too late," Maggie responded, weariness etched across her face as she rubbed her eyes. "That's fine," he conceded, a sense of resignation coloring his words. "So I suppose this is farewell... I've arranged a flight later today, but I wanted to give it one more shot."

"Goodbye, Alex," she said, offering a fleeting smile. As he turned to leave, their gaze held for a moment, silently acknowledging what was and what could never be again. He walked away, and as the door closed behind him, Maggie's heart sank with the weight of finality. The room felt emptier, the air heavier, carrying the echoes of a chapter closing. She stood there, watching the space he had occupied, a mix of relief and sorrow washing over her. Finally, she turned back toward Nadir and Patrick, ready to face the new chapter that awaited her.

In the dim-lit gallery, Emily Winsor kooking chic in a fitted white dress, approached the microphone, her voice slicing through the anticipatory hush of the room:

"Ladies and Gentlemen, a warm welcome to the breathtaking 'New Voices' exhibition, a celebration of 'Art and Resilience.' Tonight, we embark on a journey into a realm where creativity takes center stage, resilience guides the way, and the extraordinary works of five remarkable artists will leave you in awe. But before we delve into this artistic feast, allow me to introduce the brilliant orchestrator of this extravaganza, the one and only Maggie Millar."

"Not only has Maggie wowed us with her art, but she's also donned the hat of an incredible organiser. She's the maestro who somehow herded these artistic cats into a harmonious event. Bravo, Maggie! The enigma of your organisational wizardry is a marvel in itself," exclaimed Emily, breaking her usual reserve and surprising everyone with an unusually friendly tone. "Come up to the stage, Maggie. Share a few words."

Maggie hesitated, shaking her head reluctantly, but the encouraging nudges from Nadir propelled her forward. "Go on," he urged, his eyes reflecting unwavering support. "You deserve this. Get up there."

In the soft, muted glow of the art gallery, Maggie, still grappling with the weight of her recent encounter with Alex, faced the expectant audience. Her gaze sought solace in Nadir, a steady presence amidst the anticipating crowd. "Thank you all for being here tonight. It's, um, truly an honor to stand before you," she began, her words carrying a subtle hesitancy that mirrored the depth of her emotions.

The theme of the evening, 'Art and Resilience,' held a profoundly personal significance for Maggie, with roots that ran deep. "This evening is more than just an artistic gathering for me. It's a tribute to my dear friend, Kateryna, whom I lost during the tragic days of the Kiev bombing," she said, her voice trembling with emotion. "Kateryna's spirit, her unwavering strength, served as the inspiration behind this collection—but more importantly, she taught me the profound value of life."

"I'm not a wordsmith or anything," she continued with humility, "Just an artist, standing alongside my peers gathered here—Atticus, Nadir, Eva, Thomas—we are united in purpose tonight."

With a reassuring glance at Nadir, a pillar of support, Maggie underscored the significance of the exhibited pieces. "These artworks transcend the realm of mere aesthetics. They are stories, echoes of countless journeys. Each brushstroke, every nuanced shade, is a testament to the resilience of the human spirit."

A visible tremor touched Maggie's voice as she spoke of Kateryna. "In this room, Kateryna's story lives on." Tears lingered in her eyes, a poignant reflection of the silent heroine who would have been deeply moved by this moment. The room responded, raising glasses in a collective salute to Kateryna—a silent hero whose tale deserved to be shared.

"And beyond these gallery walls," Maggie urged, her words resonating with the warmth of shared experiences, "let us recognize the power of our own voices. May this night serve as a poignant reminder that silence is no longer an option."

"May this evening inspire you not only to appreciate art but to recognize the power within each of you."

In the poignant stillness of the gallery, Maggie's words lingered, carrying a weight that transcended the immediate moment. "Discovering your voice goes beyond mere expression; it's about finding the resonance within, the common thread that binds us all. It's an invitation to acknowledge the strength embedded in our collective narratives, weaving a tapestry that transcends borders and backgrounds."

She urged each person in the room to embrace their unique perspective, acknowledging that within their stories lay the potential to spark change. "Your voice is the most potent brushstroke on the canvas of the world. It's the melody that harmonizes with the chorus of countless others, creating a symphony of change."

With a fervent plea, Maggie's voice carried a rallying cry that resonated beyond the gallery's walls. "So, let this not just be a night of admiration but a catalyst for action. In the shadows of these artworks and the tales they tell, find the inspiration to make a difference. Your voice, however small it may seem, has the power to echo through time, shaping a world that desperately needs your unique melody. Let's make that difference together."

The room hung in a pregnant pause, absorbing the weight of Maggie's words. A collective silence, a moment suspended in time, gripped the audience as they digested the emotional resonance of her speech.

In the midst of this profound stillness, Nadir's eyes shone with a pride that transcended words. He stepped forward, breaking the quietude with a slow, deliberate clap. The applause rippled through the room, starting as a gentle murmur and swelling into a thunderous ovation.

As the crowd expressed their admiration, Nadir approached Maggie with a warm, appreciative smile. He enveloped her in a tender embrace, his arms a cocoon of support around her. It was a gesture that spoke volumes—acknowledging not just the significance of the evening but also the strength it took for Maggie to stand there and share her truth.

The applause continued, a symphony of approval that resonated in the gallery's walls. Emily Winsor beamed from the stage, her eyes sparkling with a newfound warmth. She had anticipated an art exhibition, but what unfolded was a soul-stirring narrative that transcended the canvas.

Maggie, encircled by Nadir's comforting arms, allowed herself a moment of vulnerability. She felt the collective energy of the room, a powerful affirmation of shared resilience and the potential for change. The audience, captivated by her authenticity, continued to shower her with applause.

And as the echoes of admiration reverberated, Nadir whispered words of encouragement in Maggie's ear. "You did it, Maggie. Your voice reached them—all of them. This is just the beginning." The sincerity in his tone was a balm to Maggie's soul, soothing the residual ache from the encounter with Alex.

"Congratulations, sweetheart," Patrick interjected, wiping away a tear of pride. "We did it," Maggie declared, turning to raise a glass in a toast to her fellow artists. And in that moment, she knew that they were not just artists. They were warriors of the soul, battling their inner demons with every stroke of the brush, every chisel of the sculptor's tool, and every word penned on the canvas of life.She exchanged a warm smile with Thomas, who held up a glass of orange juice and playfully winked at her. Atticus tipped his red fedora in acknowledgment, and Eva, buoyed by the fantastic response to her performance art video, beamed from ear to ear. "I can't believe it," she whispered into her ear. "They like me, they actually like me."

Just at that moment, Wayne Darcy stepped in. " Can I have a moment? " he asked," Wayne began, his words laced with subtle admiration, "you've got this extraordinary talent that's been hiding away all these years. Where on earth have you been, darling? The depth and brilliance of your

creations have turned quite a few heads tonight—mine included."
Maggie, eyes wide with a mix of surprise and gratitude, met Wayne's gaze. "Well, thank you," she replied, genuine appreciation colouring her voice.

Wayne continued with an air of enthusiasm, "I'm all about nurturing fresh talent, and your art, my dear, is nothing short of extraordinary. That's why I'm here with a little proposition—a scholarship right in the heart of New York. A haven for artists, a door to international recognition. Take my card; we can chat after tonight to go over the nitty-gritty details."

Maggie, still stunned by the unexpected offer, accepted the card. But when she looked down at it, a jolt of surprise shot through her. In a beautiful script, the name Wayne Darcy, Art Curator, took centre stage, but just below it was the most peculiar logo—a pale pink circle with a spiralling eternity symbol at the centre. It triggered a memory, something she'd seen before. What was it? Suddenly, it hit her—the symbol was identical to the ring the mysterious jeweller had gifted her when she first arrived in Crete. She recalled him mentioning that it symbolised the interconnectedness of all things, emphasising that Maggie was part of a grander tapestry, holding the power to shape her destiny.

The offer hung in the air, heavy with promise, as she found herself at the crossroads of her destiny. The unseen masterpiece of her life, once marred by self-doubt and past failures, now unfolded with the vibrant hues of newfound confidence and unshakable purpose.

Feeling the weight of Wayne's words, Maggie was overcome with emotion. "I... I don't know what to say," she admitted, her eyes reflecting a mix of gratitude and disbelief.

Wayne grinned, sincerity and belief in her potential radiating from his expression. "Say yes, Maggie. This scholarship isn't just about backing your art; it's about giving your voice a stage on the international art scene. Your talent deserves the spotlight."

Patrick, who had been discreetly observing from a distance, approached with a knowing smile. "Maggie, sometimes destiny knocks softly. Embrace this opportunity; let your art transcend boundaries." Overwhelmed by the unexpected turn of events, Maggie nodded slowly. "Yes, Wayne. Yes, I accept. Thank you for believing in me." Wayne extended his hand in a gesture of partnership. "The pleasure is mine, Maggie. I'm looking forward to watching your artistic journey unfold in the heart of the art world."

And just like that, Maggie's world changed forever.

Chapter 28: A Tapestry of Stars

As the night unfurled its final threads of enchantment, guests bid their adieus, leaving behind a select few who lingered in the embrace of dwindling festivities, cocooning the atmosphere in intimacy. Among the remnants of the soirée were Thomas and Eva, seemingly drawn together by an invisible force. "Those two are wrapped up in a cozy cocoon," Patrick quipped, eliciting a knowing smile from Maggie as she observed the magnetic connection weaving its spell.

In the soft glow of dimming lights, red dots danced upon Maggie's canvases, a surreal revelation that left her pleasantly astounded. Atticus, to her disbelief, had captured the gaze of a prestigious Athens art gallery. Simultaneously, Thomas had orchestrated the sale of one of his paintings, while Wayne Darcy bestowed high praise upon Eva's artistic creations.

Brimming with the vivacity of life, the allure of possibilities, and the lingering effervescence of champagne, Maggie delicately liberated her feet from the clutches of painful black stilettos. With newfound freedom, she glided toward the Zen garden nestled discreetly at the gallery's rear. In a voice as soft as the rustling leaves, she whispered an inviting entreaty to Nadir, beckoning him to share in the tranquility awaiting them.

Within the enchanting confines of the Zen garden, Maggie's senses were heightened by the heady fragrance of blooming blossoms and the tender caress of the breeze. "Join me," she whispered to Nadir, her voice a delicate melody inviting him to partake in the serenity surrounding them.

As they strolled into the garden, the soothing crunch of gravel beneath their feet provided a soothing backdrop to their conversation, creating a cocoon of intimacy amidst the lingering fragrance of flowers. "These stilettos are pure torture," Maggie confessed with a soft laugh, casting a glance at her glamorous yet tormenting footwear. "Surviving the entire evening in these is nothing short of a miracle."

Nadir chuckled in response, his eyes crinkling at the corners. "You looked absolutely stunning, but comfort might have taken a backseat."

Leaning against the edge of a stone fountain, Maggie's relief was palpable as she shed her stilettos one by one. She flexed her toes, savoring the newfound freedom. "A small sacrifice for art and celebration, but my feet will thank me. There's nothing like the liberation after a night in these torture devices."

Ever the gentleman, Nadir couldn't suppress a smile. "I've heard art demands sacrifices, but sore feet might be pushing it."

Their laughter echoed in the tranquil garden, the moon casting its gentle glow upon their exchange. As Maggie massaged her feet, the sky stretched in a canvas of clarity, adorned with stars that twinkled like a myriad of diamonds. However, it was the moon that stole the spotlight, a celestial masterpiece hanging majestically overhead.

"Have you ever seen a more beautiful moon?" Maggie inquired, her eyes mirroring the moon's luminosity. "It's colossal, a radiant orb that glows like a giant, shiny penny."

Beneath the moonlit heavens in the serene Zen garden of Crete, Maggie and Nadir stood intertwined, the celestial glow casting a spell on their hearts. As they shared a tender kiss, the beauty of the moment enveloped them, yet a silent tension lingered in the air.

"So, you know, I've been offered this scholarship in New York," Maggie confessed, her eyes fixed on the vast expanse above. "I want to go, but I don't want to lose you. You're my second chance at love, at a new life, at happiness."

Nadir gently took her hand in his, his touch a comforting anchor in the sea of uncertainty. "Not everyone gets an opportunity for a second chance, dear Maggie," he murmured, his fingers tracing a delicate path through her hair. "Follow your dearm of becoming an artist -you are someone with a voice - who touches hearts. That's your real chance at happiness and fulfillment"

A cascade of conflicting emotions painted Maggie's tear-streaked face—a symphony of happiness for the possibilities awaiting her in the bustling city and the poignant ache of leaving behind the man who had illuminated her life with love and sacrifice.

His voice, a soft yet resolute melody, broke the silence that hung heavy between them. "I'll be waiting for you," Nadir declared, his words carrying the weight of shared dreams. "I will always wait for you, dear Maggie but you have to follow your heart."

In that moment, beneath the moon's tender glow, Maggie felt the power of love and the bittersweet dance of choices. Their kiss lingered in the air, a promise that transcended the boundaries of time and space, as the universe bore witness to a love that dared to reach for the stars.

Chapter 28: Moondust memories

Three months had whispered by since Maggie first cast her eyes upon the vibrant blue-shuttered windows of her cozy apartment in the heart of Crete. As she meticulously packed the remnants of laughter, heartache, and profound discoveries, the room seemed to resonate with both the echoes of joy and the poignant resonance of a farewell yet to unfold. Beneath her gentle touch, the cat, now an inseparable companion, purred softly, oblivious to the looming void that would accompany Maggie's imminent departure.

With a lingering concern for her feline friend's welfare, Maggie whispered a silent promise as her fingers traced the fur. "Who will take care of you once I'm gone?" The question lingered in the air like a delicate sigh, an unspoken vow to a faithful companion.

With the taxi's imminent arrival in just an hour, Maggie meandered towards the beach, the azure Aegean stretching out like an endless canvas of memories. The rhythmic lapping of the waves provided a melancholic serenade—a poignant harmony that underscored the bittersweet farewell etched in the sea breeze.

As grains of sand crunched beneath her feet, Maggie reflected on the choices that had propelled her to this pivotal moment—the love kindled, the dreams awaiting their pursuit. In her hands, she cradled a small bag of trinkets, each one a tangible relic of her sojourn in Crete. The rose quartz ring from the jeweler, once a mysterious token, now symbolized newfound freedom. An old brochure from the Palace of Knossos served as a poignant reminder of her awe at the beauty of Aphrodite's statue and Pangotis's sagacious teachings that perfection is but an illusion.

With cerulean waves tenderly kissing the beach, Maggie found herself in contemplation. In her hands, she delicately cradled the Medal of St. Nicholas—a cool metal conduit to the miracles of second chances. The rhythmic cadence of the sea echoed promises of renewal, a whispered affirmation that her journey held the potential for beautiful rebirth.

Beside the medal lay a dried purple Anemone, its petals frozen in time— an intimate keepsake infused with the wisdom of Iris, a woman whose presence had fluttered through Maggie's life like a gentle breeze. Iris, with her belief in life as a garden, imparted lessons entwined with the changing seasons.

Gazing at the delicate flower, Maggie remembered Iris's words—a shared belief that life unfolded in seasonal chapters. From the innocence of spring, where discovery bloomed with exuberance, to the warmth of summer, embracing the fullness of self. Change, like the shifting hues of autumn, signaled growth and transformation. Letting go, symbolized by the gentle fall of petals, became a necessary part of the journey. Resilience, the icy winter frost, tested the roots of the soul, paving the way for jubilant celebration as life unfurled once more.

As the Mediterranean breeze carried the scent of salt and adventure, Maggie marveled at the depth of wisdom encapsulated in these simple keepsakes. The beach, where the sea painted its masterpiece, became a backdrop for Maggie's reflections on the seasons of her life. The trinkets in her hands, bathed in the soft glow of the setting sun, were not mere mementos—they were vessels of profound insight, reminders that, like the ebb and flow of the tide, her life was a continuous dance with the ever-changing rhythms of existence.

Maggie's gaze lingered on those cherished trinkets, her fingertips delicately tracing the contours of memories woven into each item—an intimate anthology of her journey. Overwhelmed, emotions surged, a blend of joy stirred by the imminent opportunities awaiting her in New

York collided with the poignant ache of leaving Nadir, the man who had etched his presence onto her heart.

Echoing in her mind were Katreyna's wise words, "Be like the willow and bend with the wind." Those syllables had become a mantra, a gentle reminder to adapt and find strength in flexibility.

With the vast ocean stretching before her, a canvas of limitless possibilities, Maggie's heart bore the bittersweet weight of separation from Nadir. Yet, within that ache, a newfound sense of purpose surged—an undercurrent of determination that rippled through her being like a quiet tide.

A soft buzz interrupted the contemplative moment, her phone vibrating with the news that her taxi had arrived. The time had come to bid adieu to the enchanting town of Rethymnon. As she gathered her belongings and prepared to step into the awaiting vehicle, Maggie carried with her the echoes of a town that had become a chapter in her story—a place where love, wisdom, and the relentless pursuit of dreams had intersected on the sands of time.

Chapter 28: New York State of Mind

As Maggie stepped off the plane at JFK, a whirlwind of emotions swirled within her like the vibrant strokes on an artist's palette. New York City, with its towering skyscrapers and bustling streets, welcomed her with the promise of a new beginning. The scent of possibilities hung in the air, mingling with the unmistakable aroma of street vendors' pretzels.

Her heart raced as she hailed a yellow cab, marveling at the cityscape unfolding before her—a landscape of dreams waiting to be explored. This was her moment, her chance to turn the ordinary into extraordinary, just like the artists she admired.

The cab weaved through the labyrinth of Manhattan, and as she stared out the window, thoughts of Nadir flooded her mind. Crete felt like a distant dream, a chapter she had left behind. Clutching the small sketch he gave her—a representation of the winding streets of Rethemon—she was reminded of the love she carried across the Atlantic.

Arriving at her new apartment in Brooklyn, Maggie couldn't contain her excitement. The city lights shimmered outside her window, a kaleidoscope of inspiration. Unpacking her art supplies, she set up her easel by the window and took a long deep breath. She couldn't quite believe that it had happened—that she was finally here.

Stepping into the cool night air, the city lights twinkling above, Maggie knew that this was not just an end but a beginning. The opportunity she had been given had painted her world in hues of triumph. As she walked into the future, she carried with her the memories of the friends she had lost, the love that had sustained her, and the dreams that had led her to this very moment.

Finding herself in the heart of Times Square—a pulsating nexus of energy that encapsulated the essence of the city—Maggie's silhouette, a confident figure against the neon-lit backdrop, resonated with a newfound sense of freedom, as if the city itself welcomed her with open arms.

With George Michael's "Freedom" serenading her steps through the rhythm of her earphones, Maggie embraced the synchronicity of the moment. The music seemed to weave a melody of liberation, each note echoing the triumph over past pain and heartbreak.

She glanced up at the stars, the same stars that shone over Crete, where Nadir waited. A promise lingered in the air, a promise to reunite when the time was right. With a heart full of gratitude and dreams that stretched as far as the city skyline, she disappeared into the New York night, the echoes of her journey lingering, whispering that sometimes, the most beautiful stories are written when life hands you a blank canvas and a second chance to paint your dreams.

Printed in Great Britain
by Amazon